My Magda

Mary Richard

WestBow Press books may be ordered through booksellers or by contacting:

WestBow Press
A Division of Thomas Nelson
1663 Liberty Drive
Bloomington, IN 47403
www.westbowpress.com
1-(866) 928-1240

ISBN: 978-1-4908-0430-9 (sc)
ISBN: 978-1-4908-0431-6 (hc)
ISBN: 978-1-4908-0429-3 (e)

Library of Congress Control Number: 2013914438

Printed in the United States of America.

WestBow Press rev. date: 09/19/2013

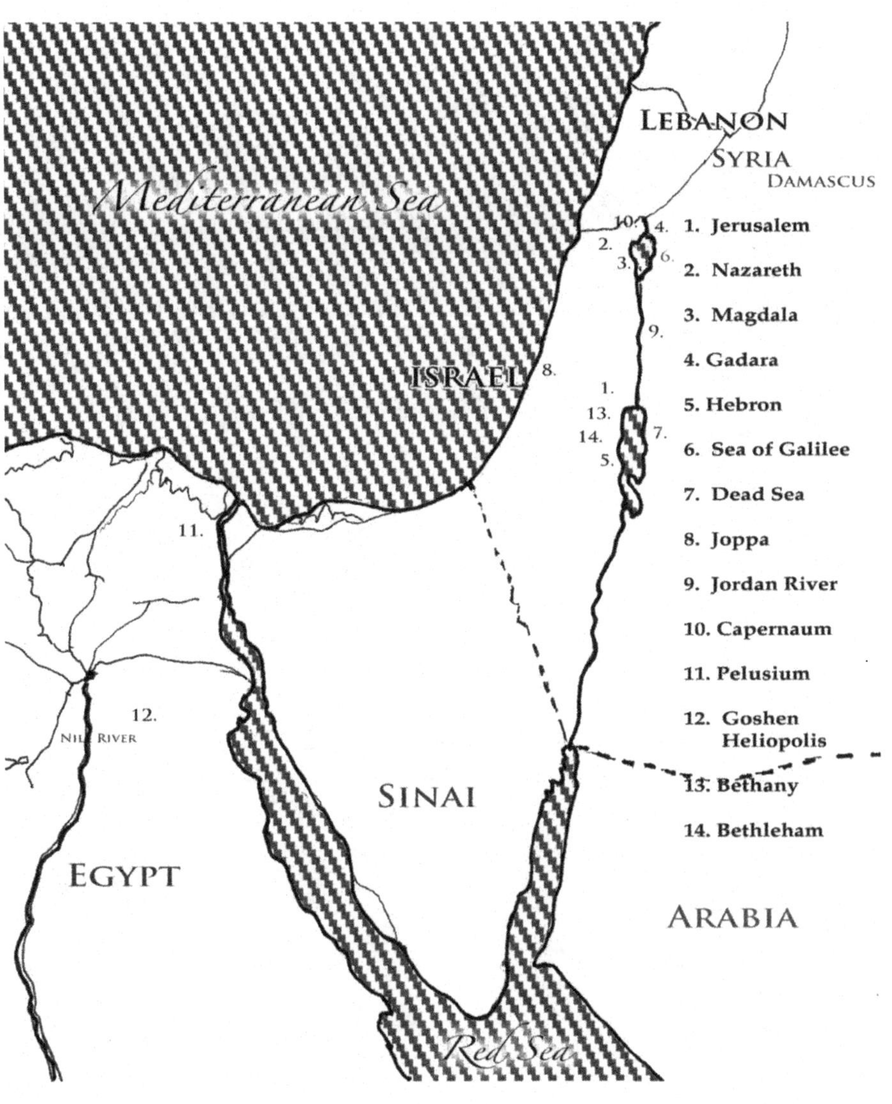
LEBANON
SYRIA
DAMASCUS
Mediterranean Sea
ISRAEL
SINAI
EGYPT
ARABIA
Red Sea
NILE RIVER
1. Jerusalem
2. Nazareth
3. Magdala
4. Gadara
5. Hebron
6. Sea of Galilee
7. Dead Sea
8. Joppa
9. Jordan River
10. Capernaum
11. Pelusium
12. Goshen Heliopolis
13. Bethany
14. Bethleham

Acknowledgments

Now I know why I suffered through ten years of hard labor at M—— S——: I was meant to meet Cindy Lacey, whose impressive intellect is balanced by equal amounts of brilliance on both sides of her brain. She gave up many Saturdays to endure reading My Magda aloud as we vetted every word, every paragraph, every fact and every fantasy. Thank you, Cindy.

Dr. Charles Steilen came along at a time when I was just beginning to write – starting and stopping - My Magda. It was the story of his struggles to earn a PhD that inspired me to resume writing and stay on task 'til I wrote that final word, "Amen." Thank you, Carlos.

A wonderful friend and early reader, Beth Cooksey, suggested I include the stoning of the prostitute episode...and that made, well, a lot of difference. Thanks Beth, I love you to death.

I owe so much to Sam and Barbara Palaio, who gave me a career in music (forty-plus years of research/people-watching from the piano bench), and so much more. I love you both, but you may have to collect your reward in heaven.

Thank you, King James. Your incomparable version of the Bible supplied all the quotes at the beginning of each chapter and the sprinkling of others throughout the story.

Thank you, Google and Wikipedia, whose little engines of knowledge sang to me, "I think I can, I think I can."

And so I did…I am thankful for that mysterious thing that comes from within to help us make it through the long night – in this case, four years of writing and research.

Be still and know that I am God.

Introduction

One of my favorite pastimes is asking questions—poking holes in balloons of delusion and ignorance.

When as a young girl I questioned my mother, who taught Sunday school for thirty years, about Mary and the virgin birth she replied, "Well, Mary might very well . . ." Her answer planted the seed that grew into a story about Mary and Jesus originally entitled, *Journey to Judea.*

That story kept growing, as did I, and eventually evolved into *My Magda*, a novel about Jesus and two women in his life—Mary, his mother, and Mary Magdalene, his companion and confidante. Despite their being prominent figures in the New Testament, there is very little known about these women. Nor were any of their writings included in the New Testament, an intentional omission (I suspect) so blatantly wrong it was partly my impetus for writing *My Magda*.

Actually, there *was* at least one gospel written by a woman. A manuscript from the 5th century AD discovered in Upper Egypt in 1896 (now known as the Berlin Codex) contained an incomplete *Gospel According to Mary*. Why has it not been included in any subsequent publication of the Bible? Why indeed? The obvious answer is the *Church*. But I found a *veiled* answer in the Middle East.

In 1980, after spending three weeks in Saudi Arabia, my eyes were opened to the plight of women in countries where they are little more than chattels. Women had no voice during biblical times, nor do they today. Most Saudi and Afghan women, and women in far too many other Middle Eastern, Asian and African countries, wear burqas, seeing only a slice of the world through the slit in their head coverings. They are completely submissive to their husbands, fathers or brothers. The more I learned about this oppressive culture, the more incredulous I became.

And then I questioned the Bible. I read it three times from cover to cover and, try as I might to suspend my bad habit of thinking logically, my reaction to most of it was, "Really?"

Old Testament questions: Was the world really created in six days? Noah and the Ark? (Why did he include cockroaches?) Burning bushes? Red Sea partings? Becalmed lions? Jonah and the whale (that's a whopper)?

New Testament questions: Did Mary, a virgin, give birth to the Son of God? Did Jesus turn water into wine? Heal the blind? Raise the dead? Rise from the dead? Revelations . . . Dear John! Was Mary Magdalene a prostitute or was she Jesus' beloved companion?

My answer . . . *My Magda*.

Ultimately, my curiosity about the Virgin Mary was supplanted by a fascination with Mary Magdalene, a far more interesting character in my opinion. Contrary to the relentless denigration of Magdalene, I do not believe she was a prostitute, but rather a liberated woman. Today she would be the prime minister of Israel/Palestine . . . IsRPals—an appropriate name for a united country where everyone would pray to one God—the God of Love. The Palestinians would not be called *terrorists,* they would be called *neighbor. Can't we all just get along?*

My Magda is a fictionalized version of the historical events covered by Matthew, Mark, Luke and John, although scholars disagree about the veracity of their gospels. Thus, my gospel will be right at home in the panoply of the dubious: Matthew, Mark, Luke, John and Mary Richard.

My Magda, the Gospel according to Mary Richard, is the work of one author, but the journey of two different people—two very different people. As I researched, wrote and re-wrote *My Magda*, I found myself changing, shifting, being still—just what God wants all of us to do: *Be still and know that I am God.*

My Magda is written in four parts: the first three written by Mary Richard *before enlightenment,* The fourth written by Mary Richard *after enlightenment.* As I neared completion of the book, I realized that I had become gentler, more loving, forgiving others as well as myself, and most important—*joyful.* I hope that the reader will have a similar experience.

My Magda—a story of how Jesus came to be born of the Virgin Mary, died of Pontius Pilate, and loved and was loved by Mary Magdalene.

Author's Notes

A FREQUENT CRITICISM OF *MY Magda* is that its campy dialogue is too contemporary to work in a biblical historical novel. The *unenlightened* Mary Richard can be blamed for that. The book began as a spoof. As I became more serious about what was unfolding, I tried to couch it in the King's (James) English. But I couldn't imagine Magda conversing in such florid or turgid speech. It was a matter of expediency. I couldn't find a voice for Magda other than that of the woman who created her – Mary Richard.

During the editing process, I lapsed into a *comma coma*. To paraphrase Oscar Wilde, I spent the morning putting commas in and the afternoon taking them out. Finally, I played it by ear: if it *sounded* like it needed a pause, I put in a comma (or sometimes a semicolon); otherwise, not so much.

My inner critic tells me that my scholarship is incomplete, that I need to dig deeper to be sure my facts are correct. That same voice tells me that my writing is amateurish, that I should take some writing courses. Another frightful nag tells me to make it less factual, less biblical, to spice it up a little to keep the reader turning the pages. As

Magda would say, "Throw in an amusing story from time to time to keep your audience interested." So I did.

But my mirror says, "This is good enough." At age 71, I want to see my opus published during my lifetime. I want to be a legend in my own mind. There came a point when I had to "wrap it up," as naughty Magda would say. "Amen," as the enlightened Magda would say.

To quote the scholar Walter Till, who translated the manuscript discovered in Egypt, "In the course of the twelve years during which I have labored over the texts, I often made repeated changes here and there, and that will probably continue to be the case. But at some point a man must find the courage to let the manuscript leave one's hand, even if one is convinced that there is much that is still imperfect. That is unavoidable with all human endeavors."

This is good enough.

Final note: Israel vs. Palestine: Since the Biblical authors refer to the Middle Eastern country which is portrayed in my book as 'Israel,' I am doing so as well. No disrespect or challenge is intended toward those who prefer to call it Palestine, the name it was given by the Romans in 135 AD.

BC yielded to AD with little more than the whimper of an infant child. About the time that unheralded event took place, two girls named Mary chanced to meet in the village of Nazareth, a small town in the Galilean province of northern Israel. They were just thirteen years old, on the cusp of puberty, when the earth's crust shifted beneath their feet and started them down divergent paths that eventually joined again in extraordinary events that changed history.

History did not treat Mary Magdalene kindly—she was labeled a repentant prostitute. She was neither. She was beautiful, brilliant, and wealthy. If she was repentant she certainly concealed it well—she was always smiling, unfailingly optimistic, and though often wrong, never in doubt.

Her best friends were Mary and Jesus.

Prologue

MARY MAGDALENE TIP-TOED DOWN THE long hallway and peeped into the room where her mother, Rachel, was in labor, giving birth to her first son. Rachel started screaming when she saw her troublesome daughter. "Go away! Get away from here!"

Magda turned and ran, mumbling to herself as her footsteps echoed down the hallway. *Did I cause something to go wrong by being where I wasn't supposed to be? Did mother see me and that's why she started to scream*? Either way, she was in trouble . . . again.

She had been strictly forbidden from visiting the birthing room, but she had done just that as soon as her nursemaid had turned her back.

"Magda, go outside to the kitchen garden and gather some lavender and rosemary," Heli had said, looking sternly at the ever-curious Magda, who had promised to obey. "If you're a good girl, we'll make some incense this afternoon. Just stay away from the birthing room."

Ordinarily, Magda would have jumped at a chance to go into the herb garden, which was usually off-limits to her. But as much as she loved gathering the aromatic greenery, today she had something more important on her mind.

Mary Magdalene—always called Magda—at just twelve years old was precocious, strong-willed, and not above telling a fib if she was on a mission.

And she was on a mission: she wanted to know where babies come from. The minute Heli had gone back to the kitchen Magda had headed to the back of the house where her mother and several women were involved in the mysterious woman's work of *birthing*.

Magda was shocked by what she saw when she dared to peek around the door. Her mother was completely nude, her stomach and breasts enormous, and she was sitting on a strange u-shaped stool. The midwife was squatting in front of her, trying to manipulate the baby, who was determined to enter the world feet-first. Beads of sweat dropped from Rachel's forehead as she endured the agony of the mid-wife's hands inside her, trying to turn the baby. The image of her mother's suffering would never completely fade from her mind.

She was so repulsed by this curious business of childbirth that she decided at that moment she would never have children. Why would a woman want to have a child if giving birth to it was so painful it would cause her to howl like a dying cow?

Magda ran up the stairs and into her room, but she was unable to escape the awful wailing that went on for hours, gradually turning into pitiful mewling. Magda put her hands over her ears to block out the sounds of her mother's suffering. Suddenly, the sounds stopped. The abrupt silence was almost more frightening than the screaming.

Where's Heli? Magda wondered. Why had no one come to tell her anything? She hadn't even been called to come down to supper. Finally she dozed off, sleeping and waking all night. She perspired in her bed until the linens were a sodden mess that clung to her like wet ghosts wrapping themselves about her.

"Magda, wake up." Magda opened one eye. Heli was leaning over her. She kissed her on the cheek and said, "Your father wants to talk to you. Martha is already there, so you need to get up right now and go downstairs."

"Heli, why are you whispering? Where's my breakfast? Why didn't you bring me anything to eat last night? What does abba want to talk about?" Magda always squeezed two or three questions into one breath while she had someone's attention.

Heli shook her head and put her arms around her. "Come on, my little lamb. Your father will explain everything."

Uh-oh. Heli never called her 'my little lamb' unless something bad had happened. Magda jumped up, threw the damp sheets on the floor and immediately crawled back into her bed, murmuring, "No bad news for me today."

Yesterday's visit to the birthing room was upsetting enough; no one needed to tell her something had gone terribly wrong. In typical Magda-playing-ostrich-style, she wriggled beneath her blanket, scrunching down to cover her head. As she lay there, unable to sleep, unbidden memories from her childhood did a dance through her head . . . memories of a mother who had never loved her.

Part One

"There was a little girl, who had a little curl,
Right in the middle of her forehead.

When she was good, she was very good indeed,
But when she was bad she was horrid."

Henry Wadsworth Longfellow
1807-1882

Chapter One

"I was glad when they said unto me, let us go into the house of the Lord. Our feet shall stand within thy gates, O Jerusalem."

Psalms 122:1-2

Three years earlier . . .

When Magda's father, Benjamin, announced that they were going to Jerusalem for the Passover holiday, she was so excited she astonished her older sister, Martha, by giving her a hug. Even her mother, who seldom smiled, had seemed in a better mood in the days leading up to their journey.

On the day of their departure, Heli held nine-year-old Magda close and begged her to be on her best behavior. "Magda, please listen to your mother and father and don't do anything to upset them. I won't be there to help you out if you get into trouble, so just try to behave yourself. And remember who you are."

Magda pulled back and looked up at her nursemaid. “Heli, don’t be silly, I’m going to be a perfect angel. Anyhow, what do you mean ‘remember who you are’? You always say that and I have no idea what you’re talking about. But I promise to be on my best behavior.”

Unfortunately, that promise was forgotten soon after they joined the caravan. There were just too many exciting things to see and people to meet. She kept disappearing from their group to meet the other young people in the long column of men, women, children, horses, donkeys, and camels that stretched as far as the eye could see.

The tinkling of bells tied onto the camels’ legs echoed in her ears long after she lay down to sleep each night. In later years, each time she heard the sound of pealing bells she was reminded of that fateful trip to Jerusalem. Those beckoning sounds always plucked some primal strings deep within her, reminding her of the time when she felt the first stirrings of desire in her innocent body.

Her father warned her several times not to stray from their group, but she continued to run ahead to examine something or speak to someone who caught her eye. She always waited for the others to catch up and she couldn’t see the harm in it. But Benjamin severely reprimanded her every time she wandered out of his sight.

Well, I guess I’ll have to wait for the right time to go exploring, she thought. And the right time came when the caravan stopped for the night outside the city of Dothan, which had a central market place that all the young people were hoping to visit. Magda used all of her bargaining powers to talk her father into letting her go with the other young people.

“Abba, they are going to be chaperoned by some of the parents. Come meet them and you will see that I’ll be in good company.”

After talking with the other parents, her father relented. But he gave her a stern lecture about Samaritans. “This part of Israel is Samaritan country and Dothan will be crawling with them. I’m warning you—stay away from them. They hate us almost as much as we hate them. Stay with the group!”

There were two wells in Dothan, one of which was named 'Joseph's Pit.' According to the scriptures, that well was where Joseph's brothers held him captive before selling him to some Ishmaelites who were traveling south to Egypt. The spot had become a popular tourist attraction and a rest stop for the weary traveler. The town was full of Samaritans.

Magda got her first glimpse of a Samaritan man that day. She was disappointed to see that, far from being an ogre, the man was just like most of the men of her acquaintance: big, hairy, and a bit fragrant for her sensitive nose.

Her excitement about the excursion was short-lived. She had thought that the trip to Dothan would be brief, but they had been walking for a long time and the town was still not in sight. She grew bored and started looking around for someone interesting to talk to. One of the older boys in the group had been looking at her all afternoon. Every time she looked over at him, he was looking at her. One time when their eyes met he winked at her. Magda wasn't sure what that meant, but he was very handsome and she decided to wink back at him. Immediately, he walked over and began to whisper to her.

"Do you want to see something much more exciting than the two wells?" he asked.

"Well," she smiled, drawing out the word, "I'm supposed to stay with the group. If it's somewhere nearby, I suppose I could sneak away for a minute."

The boy smiled and squeezed her hand briefly. "We're almost there. When we get to the square, watch where I go and follow me." A short time later the group stopped and the chaperones asked for directions to the wells. While they were distracted the boy stole away from the group.

Magda followed him, curious to see where he was going. He turned into an alleyway between two buildings, Magda close on his heels. He grabbed her hand and pulled her down beside him. Before she could get back on her feet, he pulled his tunic up and showed her a part of his body that was like nothing she had ever seen. She knew that he was showing her his male organ. Horrified, she jumped up and ran away.

But she was mostly disappointed in herself for letting the boy play such a trick on her.

When she got back to the square, she couldn't find the others. "Why did I leave the group? Why did that boy think I'd want to see his private parts? I'm going to be in so much trouble," she muttered to herself. She was beginning to think that the group had left without her when she saw a man who looked like one of the chaperones. She ran up to him and said, "Where did everybody go?" She didn't realize her mistake until the man looked at her incredulously, not believing that a young Jewish girl would dare to speak to a Samaritan man. He silently pointed to a group of young people and four adults across the square.

Realizing her mistake, she started to run across the square to rejoin the group. But she slowed down to a cautious walk when she saw the chaperones' faces and heard them warning the other boys and girls, "She is a brazen little thing and is headed for trouble. You'd best stay away from her." Obviously, they knew that she had gone into the alley with a boy; worse, they had seen her talking to a Samaritan man.

When her parents heard about the incident, they forbade her to leave their group again. Her father didn't take his eyes off her from that moment on.

The journey to Jerusalem had become monotonous. Long days were filled with hard, uphill walking, inhaling dust, and smelling the animals and the unwashed people that made up so much of the caravan. Her mother and Martha rode in a carriage nearer the front of the column, but Magda didn't want to be anywhere near to that boring pair.

She had thought they were going to travel the easier route, the *Via Maris,* along the coastal plains of the Mediterranean. She had looked forward to wading in the shallows of the Great Sea. Much as she loved living on the Sea of Galilee, she longed to see the *big* sea that stretched for thousands of miles to countries she had heard about from her father.

But Benjamin, impatient in all things, had changed his mind at the last minute. He had decided to travel the shorter route that winds south for almost one hundred miles through the rocky highlands. She began to regret that she had been included in the trip. She was homesick for Heli and for the familiar sights and sounds of Magdala.

She was surprised at the way the others in the group treated her after the trip to Dothan. The young people stared at her but looked away, embarrassed, if she caught their eye. *I don't understand why everyone's making such a big fuss about that little incident with the boy and the Samaritan man in Dothan. No harm was done. I'll just have to be more careful about picking my friends. Surely, there is a young person in this caravan that doesn't act as old as Martha.*

She asked her father to let her go up and talk with the group near the head of the caravan. But he exploded and said, "No! You're staying right here with me."

Her incessant complaints and requests that she be allowed to walk with the other young people so irritated her father that he finally tethered her to his belt and forced her to walk with him. He gave her a choice: "You can ride in the carriage with your mother and Martha or walk beside me." She chose to walk a little behind him.

And it was in this tandem fashion that they finally came to Ramah, where she got her first sight of the magical land a few miles in the distance. Jerusalem! Jerusalem! At last Magda knew why they had traveled all this long distance. At first glimpse of the temple's golden pinnacles, Magda made a vow that someday she would have a great house near this magical city.

The next morning they purchased a lamb for their sacrifice and made their way to the temple on Mount Zion. After entering through the public gate, they checked the animal and headed to the mikveh for the ritual cleansing and purifying. Magda couldn't see the point in all the bathing and cleansing when the temple was foul and a bit putrid with so many travel-worn pilgrims and sacrificial animals in its midst.

She was happy when they retrieved the lamb, which she insisted on carrying as they made their way to the Huldah Gates. She had taken one look at the little animal and decided to adopt it, naming it 'Tamar' after one of her older friends in Magdala.

Not wanting her to become attached to the animal, her father said to her, "Magda, give me the lamb. It's time to offer it as our sacrifice."

"Sacrifice? Abba, what are you talking about?" Magda thought that a sacrifice involved something insignificant like a pigeon or a dove, not a cuddly baby lamb. "I love this little lamb. Surely you're not going to take her away from me. Please don't do that! Go buy something else from one of the vendors in the Court of the Gentiles."

"I am not going to argue with you about this, Magda. Give me the lamb! You should have known that we were purchasing it to offer as a sacrifice, not as a pet for you. When we get back to Magdala, I'll buy you another one."

"I don't want another one, I want this one." She turned and ran off with the lamb tucked snugly under her arm.

"Magda, stop!" Benjamin took off after her, but he was no match for his fleet-footed daughter and couldn't begin to catch her. She was all the way to the top of the huge staircase—three stories up—when she collapsed, crying hysterically.

When her father finally caught up with her, he grabbed her by the arm and shook her like a rag doll. Usually restrained, he had never laid a hand on her and she shrieked in disbelief at his unaccustomed roughness.

When her mother arrived, out of breath from climbing so fast with Martha in tow and furious at Magda for running away, she struck her so hard Magda lost her breath. Even Martha, who seldom took her side in anything, shed a few tears for Magda, whose cheek bore her mother's palm print.

After that incident it seemed pointless to remain in Jerusalem, no one in the mood to be surrounded by crowds of celebrating pilgrims. The next morning they began the trip back home, a grinding trek of silence and resentment all the way home to Magdala.

Chapter Two

When I was a child, I spake as a child, I understood as a child, I thought as a child . . .

1 Cor. 13:11

MAGDALA WAS A GREAT PLACE to visit but not a great place to live unless you were one of the fortunate few who lived in nearby Arbela, the affluent neighborhood on the summit of Mount Arbel. Far removed from the malodorous fisheries, it was close enough to provide a magnificent view of the Sea of Galilee.

The carriage was nearing the turn into the valley road when Magda jumped out, too impatient to go with the others the long way around. She took the shortcut across the foothills, a steep path not for the halt. But Magda ran up the winding path like the wind, her tunic pulled up around her knees, her feet barely touching the ground.

She usually tried to catch a glimpse of the strange people who dwelled in the caves that honeycombed the hillside, but today she barely glanced in their direction. She made a beeline for the House of Benjamin, which sprawled at the top of Mount Arbel.

Excited about seeing Heli, she ran into the house and headed toward the kitchen. "Heli, I was trying my best to behave but still I got into so much trouble with abba and mother."

When Heli heard what had happened at the temple, she shook her head and gathered Magda into her arms. With her head against Heli's breast, Magda soon forgot about the latest trouble with her mother.

Just before going to bed, Magda went to say goodnight to Heli, who was finishing up in the kitchen. "Heli, will you rock me and sing "Looking Through the Lace?"

"Well, I'm not sure I can remember all the words. You might have to help me out a little." She took hold of Magda's hand and they walked toward the back of the house to the servants' quarters.

Magda loved going into Heli's room. It was furnished simply but smelled like a country garden. Bouquets of fresh flowers, sachets of potpourri and special candles Heli made from the herbs she grew always transported Magda into a fragrant fantasyland.

In the corner of the sitting room was the ancient rocking chair that the servant Abe had carved before his hands became too crippled to whittle. He had died several years before, his legacy the many things he had lovingly carved for his beloved Heli.

Heli sat down in the rocker and patted her lap. Magda was tall for her age, all legs and arms, her angular limbs and knobby knees like those of a beautiful big marionette—a marionette who wasn't too big to be comforted.

She laid her head back and closed her eyes as Heli sang the ancient lullaby:

Bye-o-bye, my little baby
Angels' kisses on your face
Through the nighttime watching o'er you
Looking through the clouds of lace.

Magdala was filled with abundant gold and much that glittered that wasn't gold. Located on the western shore of the Sea of Galilee, it was primarily a fishing village, but a logical site for Benjamin's boat-building business, which contributed hugely to the House of Benjamin profits. The two parallel enterprises attracted people who sought the good life in the prosperous town. Men especially loved visiting there because of the unique attractions that earned its reputation, 'depraved.'

Benjamin owned the largest fish processing operation in all of Israel. He salted, dried, and shipped fish all over Israel and to other countries as far away as Rome. Although the business had been in his family for many generations and had been passed down to him when his father died, his expansions and courage to make changes had paid off handsomely. His workers went out in the boats he manufactured and caught fish that they brought back to be processed in his fisheries.

When men spoke of Benjamin, they said, "He's richer than Croesus but works like a slave . . . and expects the same out of his workers." Magda loved hearing that description of her father. Everyone is impressed by great wealth. But they are even more impressed when a man is self-made. Benjamin had made a vast fortune with the modest one he inherited.

After his marriage to Rachel, he had encouraged her to remodel the House of Benjamin, trying unsuccessfully to make her happy. In the new house, Martha and Magda had their own rooms. The enlarged master wing was bigger than most people's houses. Rachel had designed it so that the children were upstairs on one wing, she and Benjamin downstairs on the opposite—a distancing maneuver that was a testament to Rachel's relationship with her daughters.

The servants occupied the rooms off the back portico and everyone lived in comfort; everyone but Magda. She was never comfortable in 'Rachel's Palace.' Nothing was good enough for the pretty but unbeautiful Rachel, but Benjamin never stopped trying to please her; he loved her that much—at first.

Magda learned to feed her hunger for Rachel's love in inventive ways. By the time she was ten years old she began to explore Magdala and all its perverse delights. A water baby, she knew every inch of the rocky coastline and often begged to go out in the boats with the fishermen who worked for her father.

But Benjamin's answer was always the same and always delivered with exasperation. "Magda, fishing is man's work, dangerous and certainly no place for a young lady. When will you learn your place? You always want to be somewhere you have no business being!"

The multi-leveled House of Benjamin had no secrets from Magda, the explorer. There was a back staircase, which had been so well concealed during the remodeling that no one but Benjamin, who had forgotten about it, and Magda, who had discovered it, was aware of it.

Late one night, after everyone else was asleep, she crept along the maze of hallways to the back of the house. She slid open the hidden panel, climbed the secret stairs and emerged onto the roof through the trapdoor. She propped it open for her return since it could not be lifted from the roof side.

She slipped down the side stairs and ran through the back garden, pausing a moment to pick one of her mother's prized peonies. She broke it off down to the ground to disguise her bad deed. She knew Rachel probably counted every blossom and would know she had taken one; but it was worth the risk just to bury her nose in the fragrance of its petals. Concealing the flower in her cloak, she hurried down the footpath and crossed the shore road to watch the fishermen getting ready to go out for the night's fishing. Two young men were just climbing into their boat and Magda ran up and asked to go with them. The two brothers, Simon and Andrew, were astonished that this young girl had approached them. They knew she was the boss's daughter and that they would get into trouble for even daring to look at her.

"Please let me go out in your boat with you tonight. I won't be any trouble," Magda said. In truth, Magda was *never no* trouble. "I just want to see what it's like being out at sea. It's not fair that girls aren't allowed to become fishermen . . . well fisherwomen . . . no wait . . . fisherpeople."

Simon and Andrew looked on in confusion while Magda went through her word game nonsense. Finally settling on 'fisherpersons,' she continued, "I think I can do it as well as you. I've been practicing casting some of the torn nets in the shallows, and I'm getting pretty good at tossing them out in a perfect circle. So may I go? Let's toss a coin. Heads I win, tails you lose."

Simon and Andrew stood for a moment wringing their hands, trying to decide what to do about this girl who could spell big trouble for them, regardless of which end of Caesar turned up. But when Magda made up her mind to do something, she was relentless. Finally, the young men, who were no match for her, gave in and helped her climb into the boat. They exchanged a look of resignation, knowing they had been outwitted by Magda, who never took no for an answer.

When they were far out to sea, she threw off the blanket that they had covered her with and jumped up. She couldn't wait to show off her skills. "Now then, hand me a net and let me show you how good I am," she said. The two brothers were shocked at how skilled she was at something that took them a long time to learn. Her first cast went out onto the sea in a perfect circle. She gloated, "I told you I could do it."

She was hooked. It was the most fun she had ever had. She loved being one of the boys, laughing and joking and feeling like she belonged. Night after night, she fished with the two brothers, enjoying contentment like she had never known—far out to sea and far away from the House of Benjamin.

While she was secretly thrilled that she had been accepted into the boys' club that usually barred girls from fishing, there was a limit to her interest in the enterprise. She drew the line at handling the smelly, slimy swimmers with her own delicate hands. Simon and Andrew had a permanent *eau de mer* that had seeped into their skin and clothing that no amount of scrubbing could remove.

After a few weeks, Martha became curious about where Magda went every night. One evening after everyone had gone to bed, she heard Magda's door open and decided to follow her. She lost sight of her as Magda raced down the footpath, but she had a good idea where Magda was going. By the time Martha crossed the shore road, Magda was standing on the dock, talking with two older boys. When she saw her climb into the battered fishing boat, she ran to tell Benjamin.

Martha never missed a chance to get her younger sister into trouble. And this was too good an opportunity to pass up, even though it meant another trip back up the steep hillside. Martha was out of breath and panting when she knocked on her parents' bedroom door.

Benjamin answered grumpily, "Who is it? Do you know what time it is?"

"Abba, it's me, Martha. You've got to come with me right away. Magda is about to go out in a boat with two of your fishermen."

Benjamin grabbed his cloak and headed out the door. He ignored Rachel when she asked him what the trouble was. He had enough trouble on his hands without getting his wife stirred up. He took Martha's hand and they ran out of the house, heading for the footpath. But Martha was too tired to move at Benjamin's pace.

"Abba, you go on ahead. I can't keep up with you."

Leaving Martha behind, Benjamin tore down the path and crossed the road. He arrived just in time to stop Magda before she set out to sea. He ran up and grabbed her. "Where do you think you're going, Magda? What in the name of God are you up to now? This time you've gone too far."

Then he turned to the two brothers, grabbing each one by an arm and turning them about to face him. "What have you been doing with *my* daughter out in *my* boat while you were supposed to be in *my* employ?" he demanded.

"Magda, you go back to the house with Martha. You boys come with me."

Simon and Andrew were dismissed from their jobs, and their families were made to leave the area in disgrace. It didn't matter that all three, Magda the most vehement, insisted that they had done nothing wrong; Magda just wanted to go out with them at night to catch fish. In her mind there was nothing wrong with that; in her world it was disgraceful behavior.

Benjamin had had about enough. He was tired of trying to be the peacemaker in the family and was tempted to send Magda away to live with his sister Orpah, who had no children. But he decided to make one last attempt to pull her into line. He hired a tutor for her and Martha, thinking that maybe a daily dose of education would help to satisfy some of her boundless curiosity.

But Magda quickly learned everything the tutor had to teach and soon she was teaching him. The tutor was completely awed by her, and Benjamin, recognizing that Magda had become the tutor's teacher, dismissed him.

Magda felt guilty that so many men she came into contact with were eventually punished because of her. *Oh well, this too shall pass,* she thought.

Then her father hired Alexandre, a brilliant Greek scholar, and finally Magda had met her match. Alexandre recognized Magda's extraordinary intelligence right away and suggested he be allowed to devote all of his time to her so that they would not be stymied by Martha, who was interested only in learning how to run the house.

Magda was insatiable. She wanted to study everything: literature, history, mathematics, chemistry, even astronomy, hoping to learn more about the stars and the moon that so fascinated her. She far exceeded Alexandre's expectations. He was saddened that such a superior intelligence was wasted on Magda, who had had the misfortune of being born into a society that viewed women as second-class citizens. But he had underestimated Magda, who never let anything or anyone hold her back.

Her lessons with Alexandre made her more curious than ever and she continued her visits to the seamier side of Magdala. She knew every shopkeeper, every street vendor, every beggar, and a few women no proper girl would speak to. Magda was curious about everything and everybody, never judged anyone—figuring they just did the best they could—and was fascinated by anything that was beyond her ken. Her curious mind often got her into trouble.

She wanted to know everyone's story, particularly that of the market vendors. When they saw her coming, they passed a warning down the line to the other shopkeepers, "Watch out! Here comes that little green-eyed monster."

She would pepper them with questions: "How do you decide how to price your wares? Where do you buy them? How much do you pay for them? How much profit do you make?" That question was usually the end of the conversation. No one was willing to share such personal, often damning, information—fodder for the tax collector—with a nosy young girl. But later on, when she became a successful businesswoman, she used the information she culled from these conversations to great advantage.

She was born with sensibilities that bypassed innocence—she was never young, she would never be old. A smart young girl, she grew into a brilliant woman with the gift of wisdom, contrary to King Solomon's assertion that he had never found one single woman to have any wisdom. But he never met Mary Magdalene.

On the wrong side of borderline nosy, by the time she was twelve years old, Magda had seen and learned things that many adults didn't know. One of her favorite entertainments, other than studying the evening skies, was to spy on the women who were seasoned veterans of the world's oldest profession. Her mordant sense of humor and worldliness—she would laugh at things that mortified others—were informed by the ground level education classes of her nighttime explorations. And rather than being sickened or horrified by the cavorting of those copulating adults, she found it humorous and strangely titillating.

One night she invited Martha to sit with her on the roof, hoping to interest her mostly indifferent sister in some of the subjects that so enthralled her: the moon and the stars, the oceans and the seas, the birds and the bees. But she knew she would have to be careful how she broached the latter subject lest Martha be scarred for life.

She was not about to reveal her secret back stairs to Martha so they went up the outside stairs to the roof. As she led her older sister to her favorite spot and sat down beside her, Martha said suspiciously, "So this is where you spend your time. What do you do up here by yourself every night?"

Magda put her hand on her sister's arm and said, "Martha, how can you ask? Look around you!" Magda pointed at the full moon, which held the place of honor in a cloudless sky. "Nature paints a different picture in the heavens every night. Don't you think the moon and all those stars and planets are the most fascinating things you've ever seen? And tonight is really special: Venus and Jupiter are perfectly aligned with the moon."

Martha rolled her eyes. "Hmmph! I don't see what you find so special about the moon and all those little lights—for all we know they're just fireflies. And anyway, who cares about things that are so far away you can't see them in person?"

"Martha, what are you saying? Abba has been to Spain many times and it's much farther away than the moon." She gave Martha a sideways glance to see her reaction.

Martha snapped her head around and looked at Magda to see if she might be playing a trick on her, but clearly she was confused. "Magda, for a smart person you can say some of the dumbest things. Or are you just trying to confuse me? Anyway, I know that the moon is much farther away than Spain."

"Martha, that's absurd. Can you see Spain?" Magda raised her eyebrows in mock seriousness.

Martha screwed up her mouth and squinted her eyes, deep in thought. But she couldn't come up with anything other than her old standby, "Don't ask."

Magda sighed and said, "All right, Martha, maybe something a little more down to earth will be less confusing. Let's walk into town. I want to show you something really breath-taking." Martha was doubtful but followed along dutifully, hoping for another chance to get Magda into trouble.

As they walked along the shore road, Magda spoke to everyone they encountered along the way, calling them by name and bantering with the men like she was one of them. Martha was appalled. *How does Magda know all these people? Magda may be my sister but she is the strangest person I've ever known.* She stopped and got in Magda's face. "Where are you taking me? You might not care a fig about your own reputation, but don't even think about including me in your crazy life."

"Come on, Martha," Magda said, grabbing her hand and walking faster than ever. "Do you always have to be such a stick in the mud? Don't you want to see what grown-ups do in bed at night?"

Martha looked at Magda with suspicion but she followed her all the way into a part of Magdala where no decent woman, much less a young girl, would dare to go. Just before they came to the docks, they turned into a dark alley and Magda quietly pushed open a door that had a lifetime of grime on it.

Martha was appalled. "Magda, aren't you even going to knock on the door? What if someone thinks we are intruders?"

"Sshh, Martha, we *are* intruders. At Tamar's house if you don't have any money you're an intruder."

Then Magda put her fingers to her lips and whispered, "Don't make a sound now. I'm going to pull back the curtain just enough for us to see what's going on."

Martha took one look and started screaming. The only thing visible was a man's busy buttocks and two pairs of hairy legs. But they could clearly hear Tamar shouting, "Yes!" Obviously, she was enjoying her profession to the fullest.

Martha ran out the door and didn't stop until she got to the footpath. Winded and panting, she sat down to rest for a minute. She was crying and mumbling incoherently when Magda caught up with her.

Magda was disgusted. They had missed the whole show. "Martha, you ruined everything. Tamar will probably be so angry she won't ever let me come back again, even during the day. Don't you have any curiosity about where babies come from?"

Fortunately, Martha was too embarrassed to tell Benjamin or Rachel what she and Magda had done, and Magda was spared punishment for her latest escapade.

Martha's failure to tell on her didn't make Magda any more charitable toward her prim and proper sister. *Old biddy,* Magda thought. *She was born innocent—and boring—and she'll die innocent—old and boring.*

Chapter Three

And when her days to be delivered were fulfilled, behold there were twins in her womb. And the first came out red, all over like an hairy garment; and they called his name Esau.

Gen. 25:24-25

One balmy evening after everyone else was asleep, Magda crept up the back stairs to the roof and sat down to study the constellations in the sky, all of which she could identify. The full moon with its chiaroscuro face and thousands of stars were putting on a breathtaking light display.

Magda wondered, *What's up there? Are there people living on the moon and the other planets looking down at the earth wondering if there is anyone down here?*

Once upon a rooftime, she wrote an ode to her favorite mystery in the sky:

The Moon and I

As the moon and I were exchanging glances of a clear evening one early April, a few northern-bound clouds came traveling by, reminding me of a flock of birds winging their way in an uncanny order not understood by mere, desultory man.

And as I sat on my turf of earth viewing this constant veiling and unveiling of the moon's demure face, I imagined that which I saw to be a reflection of my own changing face . . . infinitely sad (though with a strange, calm acceptance that loneliness is fate's special gift to its chosen few), knowing that there would never be more than a fleeting companion for me—a craggy, unknowable, shining creature of the sky

I guess I was meant to make my journey in flight like those drifting, ephemeral clouds—ever moving, seemingly transparent, yet defying inspection by disappearing at the probing touch of one who would try to know me, thus trap me, making me lie down in the dearth of the earth, and no more—The Moon and I.

The moon dimmed and the stars faded, and when she could no longer keep her eyes open, she tiptoed back to the corner of the roof. The hatch was closed. *I must have forgotten to prop it open. I'll have to go down the outside stairs and sneak in the house through the back porch.*

Crossing the rear portico, she crept down the central hallway where she heard her parents' angry voices coming from their bedroom. Magda had a bad feeling they were arguing about her; they usually were. She slipped down the hall to listen outside their door.

"You don't even pretend to love her," Magda heard her father say. *What was this about?*

Before Rachel could reply, Benjamin continued his sad defense of his younger daughter. "How can you in good conscience make such a difference between Magda and Martha? You are going to warp my daughter."

"Well, I know that it was my idea for this child to be born," Rachel said, "but she is so trying that I stay upset all of the time. Even you must admit that she is a troublemaker. And I know she can't help it, but her hair gets redder every day. Even so, I do the best I can. At least I let her live here."

Magda turned away and hurried up the stairs to her room, not wanting to hear any more. What did mother mean, 'I let her live here'?

She had always sensed that something was wrong between herself and her mother. Martha called her by the familiar *ima,* but Magda from her earliest days was told to call her 'mother.' Rachel rarely said her name, occasionally yelling "Magda!" when she was angry with her.

Rachel constantly criticized her. "Why do you have to be different? You act like you think you're better than the rest of us, but you're not, you're just different."

But this was something new, something ugly and twisted, far worse than just her mother's disapproval.

Mother hates me.

But Magda didn't spend too much time worrying about it. Her mother's hurtful words were dismissed as quickly as it took her to think of a solution to the problem.

It must be my red hair and green eyes, she thought. Everyone else in the family had dark hair and eyes. *Oh well, there is nothing I can do about my eyes, but my hair I can fix.* She knew that certain women in town dyed their hair black to cover the gray that was bad for their business. She would visit Tamar and ask her for the formula.

But Tamar didn't greet her with her usual friendliness. "Magda, was that you spying on me the other night? When you screamed, you scared my friend and I so bad we fell off the bed and landed on the floor. Can you imagine how embarrassing that was? Thanks to you I have lost one of my best customers—weird, but loyal."

"Scared my friend and *me,* and *badly.*" Magda couldn't resist correcting Tamar's grammar, which suffered from a dangerous little bit of learning. She often used the word *I* instead of *me* because she thought it sounded classy.

"No, Tamar, it wasn't I. You know that I would never do anything as silly as scream at what goes on behind the red curtain. That's the agreement between you and *me*, and I have always honored it," Magda fibbed.

Tamar was clearly annoyed. "Well, whoever it was—I, you, or me—tell them to stay away from my door. Now, Miss Know-It-All, how can I help you at this ungodly hour of the day?" Noon was hardly an ungodly hour, but Tamar slept until late in the day because she worked at night entertaining her customers.

Magda told her that she needed help dyeing her hair black, but Tamar was reluctant. "Magda, why would you want to do anything to your hair? The color is unique. Everybody has dark hair, but you're different, you have magnificent red hair."

"Yes, don't remind me . . . that's the problem: I'm the only one in my family with red hair. It makes me too different. I want to make it darker. Help me, please?"

"Oy. But when you're not happy with the results, don't come crying to me."

Decaying leeches and vinegar left to ferment in the sun for days was about the last thing Magda wanted to put on her hair. The smell alone was breathtaking. But according to Tamar that was the magic formula. And she ought to know. Her hair was so black it looked like she had fallen head-first into the Dead Sea, sometimes known as Lake Asphaltites, because it had pieces of tar floating in it the size of headless bulls.

She had gone on a scavenger hunt through Heli's herbs and magic potions. Finding vinegar was easy, it was a household staple, but where would she find leeches? Did Heli have such vile, smelly things in her storehouse? Leeches were nowhere to be found.

But she had an idea that the gardener might know where to find them. She went out to the vegetable garden to ask him.

He scratched the back of his head and squinted at her. "Leeches live in water and only come out at night. The pond at the back of the garden is full of them. But why on earth would you want to come within ten feet of a leech? The last thing you want is for a leech to latch onto you and suck your blood away."

The gardener feigned surprise but the truth was Magda was always up to some harebrained scheme that usually landed her in trouble . . . as well as the person she had persuaded to help her.

He mumbled, "Here we go again."

Magda sized up the man, whose skin was furrowed with dirt from too much time spent digging in the earth and too many years baking in the sun. She answered as blithely as the innocent girl she appeared to be. "I am doing a science project that my tutor has assigned to me. I'll meet you here tomorrow morning after you dig them from the pond tonight."

But the results were a disaster. Almost half of her hair was lost in the experiment. She suspected that she must look like a skunk, and she was certain she smelled like one.

There was nothing to do but borrow a veil from Heli, the long black one that she wore to the synagogue. She would figure out later what to tell everyone about her sudden urge to cover her head. She was still too young for the wearing of the veil, but no one would be surprised that she had decided to bend another rule.

She slipped out of the house, took the footpath down the steep cliff and hurried into the part of Magdala where she wasn't supposed to go. She knew it was too early to visit Tamar, but this was an emergency. She had to get advice on what to do about her hair.

Magda knocked persistently until Tamar finally opened the door to her tiny house. "Who is it? Magda? Surprise, surprise! Why are you hiding behind that veil? What time is it?"

"I'm sorry, Tamar, it is rather early, but this is an emergency. I've made a mess of my hair and I need your help."

Tamar groaned. She stood blocking the door for a moment, looking tiredly at Magda. She finally opened the door and Magda went in, removing the veil and revealing the ruins of her once lovely red hair.

"Ewww, you do have an emergency," Tamar muttered. "Obviously, you forgot to coat your hair with olive oil before you applied the vinegar and leech mixture."

Then she advised her to try a mixture of herbs, lemon juice and jojoba oil that would remove the black dye and help restore some life to her sickly hair.

The next morning Magda arose before dawn and crept through the sleeping house.

Quietly closing the kitchen door behind her, she slipped through the side gate and entered the herb garden. Only Heli and Rachel were allowed in the kitchen garden and Magda knew she would pay dearly if she were caught trespassing in it. Although the herb garden was strictly off-limits to the children—even Martha was banned from it—it was one of her favorite spots. Heli had taught her the names of every plant and had explained how each one flavored the dish it was cooked in.

But Magda was more interested in the medicinal and aromatic magic hidden in the feathery greenery; she planned to become a healer and a perfumer when she grew up.

Using Heli's sharp knife, Magda quickly cut samples of each plant she needed, trying to gather only a small amount that would not be missed, wishful thinking since Rachel would notice if a dust mite were missing.

She hurried back to her room and began to finely chop the herbs, mixing them into the lemon juice and oil she had borrowed from the storeroom.

Surprisingly, the advice Tamar had given Magda had worked somewhat—surprising since the instructions were not followed to the letter. The black dye was gone and her hair seemed to have regained some of its healthy luster. But nothing but Mother Nature, who didn't mind taking her time, was going to replace the hair that had fallen out during the dyeing process.

Now came the tricky part. She had to thoroughly wash her body so Rachel would not pick up on the smells that would spell big trouble for her. Rachel, suspicious by nature, had a nose like a bloodhound and it was nearly impossible to fool her when someone trespassed in her herb garden.

Magda removed her shift and began to soap her face, neck and hands with the sandalwood soap Heli made in big batches for the household. Then she moved down to her breasts, which were budding like the herbs she had just gathered, a sign of her coming womanhood that she had begun to dread.

Magda knew that when a girl's breasts began to swell she would soon experience her first blood. Most young girls looked forward to these events, which meant her parents would begin to think about finding a suitable husband for her. But Magda thought that men were too demanding, easily-provoked, and expected unquestioning obedience from their wives. She had already decided to tell only Heli when her bleeding began so she could help her conceal it. She wanted nothing to do with marriage or motherhood.

Checking her hands and arms and even her armpits for lingering tell-tale scents, she was satisfied that she had washed away all the incriminating evidence. She dressed hurriedly and went down for the morning meal, concealing Heli's knife in the folds of her robe.

Rachel was brushing Martha's hair and barely looked up when Magda walked into the room. She quickly passed behind them heading toward the kitchen.

Rachel whirled around and began to sniff the air like a dog tracking prey. "Magda, come back here. Your feet have grass stains on them and I can smell mint and rosemary,"

"Oh no," Magda mumbled under her breath, flinging her head back and cursing her carelessness. She had forgotten to wash her feet, and now her mother would know where she had been. And worse, she had dropped the knife when her mother yelled at her.

"What were you doing with that knife? Never mind, I probably don't want to know, and don't bother to pick it up. Heli will get it. Go to your room and gather the herbs you have cut from my garden. Heli will come up to collect them so she can at least use them for making her ointments. As for you, you will stay in your room until I decide you can come out. Go!"

Much later a chastened but not rehabilitated Magda was allowed to come out of her room—two days older but not much wiser. She thought, *Next time I need some herbs I'll ask Heli; she's always willing to help me.* "After all, I am her apprentice," she said, full of self-importance.

But in reality, Heli was slowly becoming Magda's accomplice. Heli often said, "You may be the redheaded step-child of the family, but you're Heli's angel!"

With each painful memory, Magda had sunk a little lower in her bed until she was balled up in a knot. *When I turn thirteen next month,* she moaned, *my childhood will be over, and so far I have mostly unhappy memories.*

Her father's booming voice brought her back to the present. "Magda, get out of bed and come down here . . . now!" Magda knew that he was going to tell her that her mother was dead. She feared that there was other bad news as well. Whatever it was, she knew it was going to be doubly bad news for her.

Magda took her time about going down the stairs, one miserable step at a time, dreading what she was about to hear. She walked into the room where her father was pacing back and forth in front of Martha and Heli. She couldn't believe her ears when he finally got to the point after several false starts. He cleared his throat and began to explain that Rachel had died giving birth to Lazarus.

Well at least Martha will be happy. She'll finally have a little brother to mother, Magda thought gloomily, as she sat looking out the window, wishing she could fly through it.

Her father was close to tears as he continued with the bad news. "Magda, your mother's dying wish was that you should move to Nazareth to live with your aunt. Orpah is alone now that Uncle Seth has died. She has always loved you; she has said numerous times she wished you were her daughter. Well, your mother remembered that wish on her death bed. She said that she thought you would be better off with someone to keep a close eye on you, and that a small town with a more wholesome atmosphere than Magdala would be a better environment for you."

Oh God, not Nazareth, Magda thought. *I thought my childhood was over, but I was wrong—my life is over.* She began to protest, but Benjamin cut her off. "Hear me out, Magda. You are not going alone. Heli and her sons are going with you. They're just like family to you, so you won't feel like you're among strangers. And Orpah *is* your aunt, although I know you haven't spent much time with her.

"But this was not just your mother's idea. We had talked about this many times in the past. You know that you have brought this on yourself by your nightly visits into the worst parts of Magdala. You're just out of control. And now that your mother is not here to exert her strict discipline on you, you might easily go off the deep end."

Even though Heli was going with her, she felt abandoned, that no one wanted her. She climbed into her father's lap and begged him not to send her away. "Abba, I promise I'll behave. Please let me stay here with you and Martha and my baby brother."

She didn't want to be separated from her family. And she didn't want to live in Nazareth. The one time she had visited Aunt Orpah there she had vowed 'never again.' Anything that took her away from her beloved Sea of Galilee would be a prison sentence.

Her father kept talking, ignoring her objections. "You won't be cut off from Martha, Lazarus and me. Nazareth is not that far from Magdala. We will visit you at Orpah's and you can visit us from time to time in Magdala."

Magda pleaded, "Abba, how can you do this to me at the worst time in my life? First I lose my mother and now you are sending me away and I will lose you and the rest of my family. Do you think I'll be better off living away from my family at a time when I need you most?"

But nothing she said could change her father's mind. He had been at his wit's end trying to control the head-strong Magda, and he feared that she was headed for problems even his money couldn't solve if he didn't get her away from Magdala. The likely solution was for her to live with his sister Orpah in Nazareth.

At least that was Benjamin's story . . . and he stuck to it for most of his life.

Part Two

Be still and know that I am God.

Psalms 46:10

Learn to be silent. Let your quiet mind listen and absorb.

Pythagoras (580 BC-500 BC)

Chapter Four

And the angel said unto her, Fear not, Mary: for thou hast found favour with God. And behold, thou shalt conceive in thy womb, and bring forth a son, and shalt call his name JESUS.

Luke 1:30-31

MARY LAY ON HER PALLET and listened to a sound that didn't belong to the night. Someone was in the room with her. She lay still straining to hear the noise, which was moving closer to her. She sat up and peered into the darkness, trying to see where the noise was coming from.

She wasn't sleeping so she couldn't be dreaming. She could hear a rustling in the curtain that divided her small space from the rest of the room she shared with her family. She had already said her prayers and was in that twilight just before sleep, not thinking, her mind as calm as a still, wintry pond.

Suddenly, a shadowy creature in a white robe grabbed her arm. Wide awake now, curiously, she was not afraid. Her visitor delivered an incredible message.

Mary was just thirteen years old and had never seen a ghost; but she didn't think that this was a ghost. It had too much energy and was too life-like. And it could talk.

"Fear not, Mary. I am the angel Gabriel and I have wonderful news for you." Then he told her that she would give birth to the Christ Child, the Messiah. She was to name the child 'Jesus.'

Worried that her parents might hear her, she whispered, "But how can that be, since I have known not a man?"

Gabriel assured her that very soon she would be overcome by the Holy Spirit and that her womb, without being opened, would be filled with a child who would be the Messiah the prophets had foretold would be born to a virgin.

"Behold the handmaiden of the Lord. Be it unto me according to your word," Mary said, bowing her head reverently as the angel told her what she must do to accomplish God's will.

She was to make haste to journey *alone* to Judea to visit her cousin Elisabeth, who was almost six months with child. Although she was to follow the caravan route, a dangerous uphill distance of nearly one hundred miles, Gabriel assured her that the Holy Spirit would be with her to guide and protect her. And then he vanished.

Sitting very still on her pallet she waited for the angel to reappear and tell her it was all a mistake. When he didn't come, she got up and walked over to the curtain, pulling it aside to see if the angel was still there. He was gone.

Was that just a dream? she wondered, returning to her bed, knowing sleep would not come. As she pulled back the soft blanket she saw a spot of blood on the pallet. Her first thought was that her arm must be bleeding, but there was not even a handprint, much less a wound. Then she felt the sticky wetness between her legs.

I must have started my bleeding, Mary thought. She lay back down and pulled the covers up to her ears, thinking about everything the angel had told her. She finally decided, *He's got the wrong girl.*

But she was not the wrong girl. God never makes mistakes. Even the timing of the angel's visit was part of God's mysterious works. Gabriel had imparted his message and instructions to Mary at the most opportune time: in the still, quiet time just before sleep when Mary's mind was at its most suggestive state . . . *Be still and know that I am God.*

She lay awake for a while and listened to the comforting breathing of her mother and father, the funny little noises of her baby brother, lost in his own dream, the snorting of the animals in the lean-to just outside. *Why me?* she pondered. *I am just a young girl from a poor family. I live in the little town of Nazareth, just a lowly village that most people have never heard of. Why wouldn't God choose a noble woman from a wealthy family to be the mother of the Messiah? Why me?*

But her greater worry concerned her fiance', Joseph. How was he going to react when he discovered she was going to have a baby . . . someone else's baby? What man, particularly one as reverent and straight-laced as Joseph, would believe that an angel had visited her and told her she would conceive while still a virgin?

As she pondered the happy events of the past several months since she had met and become betrothed to Joseph, she wondered if all of her dreams of being married and having a family were just the fantasies of a young girl.

Six Months earlier . . .

Joseph and his brother Aaron, both carpenters, were returning home early one evening from Sepphoris, which Herod was re-building following its destruction by the Romans. They were tired and thirsty after walking over an hour back to Nazareth, and they stopped for water at the village spring.

Joseph stopped in his tracks, thunder-struck, staring at a young girl who was filling her pitcher at the well. He had never seen anyone even in his dreams as beautiful as this winsome girl. She wore neither bangles nor rings yet her simple elegance took his breath away.

Aaron said to him, "Joseph, what is it? You look like you have seen a ghost."

"You are wrong, Aaron," Joseph said, pulling his brother close to him and lowering his voice. "I am not seeing an apparition from the past; I am looking at my future. I am going to marry that young girl, the beauty there by the well."

Aaron laughed. "Well, I bet she'll be surprised to hear that. When were you thinking of letting her in on the secret?"

In an uncharacteristic burst of bravado, Joseph went over to Mary, introduced himself and offered to help her carry her water, his thirst replaced by a man's hunger.

Mary was taken aback, not knowing whether to be offended or flattered by the older man's inappropriate attention. But the look on his face left no question as to the honor of his intentions.

"Oh thank you, sir," Mary replied, "but I'd best hurry back to my mother, who will be expecting me to arrive the same way I left her—alone!"

But as she hurried off, she looked back, smiled at Joseph and whispered, "My name is Mary, daughter of Joachim."

At that moment he fell madly in love.

Mary walked back home quickly, careful not to spill a drop of water from the heavy jug balanced on her shoulder. As she walked she wondered just how much of her meeting with the tall stranger at the well she should reveal to her mother. On the one hand, she knew her parents were starting to think about finding a suitable husband for her; on the other hand, she wondered if the man's comments to her would be regarded as improper, making him unsuitable as a husband for her. She hoped not. He was quite a bit older than she and not exactly handsome, but there was something about him, perhaps his earnestness, that made him exciting to Mary. And she felt a little thrill when she recalled the way he had looked at her.

Mary, a few weeks away from her thirteenth birthday, held the promise of great beauty. Her mother, Anne, often wondered by what magic Mary, who had been born to ordinary parents, was blessed with such extraordinary looks. Her long neck was classic Nefertiti, although as far as Anne knew there were no Egyptians among their ancestors.

With limpid dark eyes and hair and skin the color of dark amber, she turned heads wherever she went. But none of this affected Mary's demeanor. She was modest and kind and seemingly unaware that her looks were anything special.

"Ima," Mary called out as she opened the door to their small house and walked out to the courtyard, "I met someone at the well today, somebody special." And she told her about Joseph, fibbing a little bit, saying a mutual friend had introduced them.

Her mother put aside her spinning and eyed her daughter. Anne, a woman of deep wisdom, suspected that the *mutual friend* was an invention. But she was careful not to spoil Mary's excitement. "Well, that's exciting news, Mary. But now we'll just have to wait and see if he contacts your father. In the meantime it will be just our little secret. Your father would be offended if he knew that Joseph spoke so familiarly to you. But we're going to expect the best and start sewing some suitable garments for you. If he does visit we will need to prepare for the ketubah."

Mary was just returning from the well the next morning when she heard someone calling her name. "Mary, slow down, it's me, Joseph. I've brought my father to talk with your father." Joseph and an older man were just a few steps behind her.

Mary was only momentarily troubled that he had been following her. She was thrilled that he hadn't kept her waiting and wondering when he would call on her father. Too shy to speak, she looked down at the ground.

"Mary, you're looking well today. I hope I didn't startle you. You remember meeting me at the well yesterday, don't you? This is my father, Jacob, and we have come to speak with your father."

After brief introductions and a minimum of small talk, Jacob got down to business. He wasted little time in coming to the point: Joseph wanted to marry Mary. But Joachim had reservations about Joseph. He had moved with his family to Nazareth just a few years before, having left Sepphoris after the Romans destroyed it. He didn't know any of the Nazarenes very well and didn't feel comfortable asking his neighbors about Joseph and his lineage. He suggested that they wait a while before finalizing the betrothal, saying he wanted to become better acquainted with Joseph before making such an important decision for his older daughter.

But those were meaningless words, a delaying tactic that he thought would improve his side of the negotiations. It wouldn't be wise to act too eager. He knew Mary liked Joseph and he didn't plan to stand in the way of her happiness.

Mary and Joseph's parents met again just a week later. When Joachim learned that Joseph was descended from David's line, the decision was made. Joseph and Mary would be permitted to marry.

Aaron was betrothed to a girl from a prominent family who lived in Capernaum, and their wedding ceremony was just a few weeks away. As Galileans, Aaron and Rebekah's families were not overly concerned with the Jewish tradition that the wedding should take place at the groom's home. If the bride's home was more suitable for the ceremony than the groom's, then the rules were relaxed. In the case of Aaron's wedding, there was never any question about it: they would be married under the chuppah in the grand home of Rebekah's family. Thus, the groom and his guests were traveling to Capernaum.

Joseph agreed with Jacob that the morning of Aaron's wedding would be the perfect time for his and Mary's betrothal ceremony; thus, he invited Mary and her parents to accompany them to Capernaum.

On the morning of the wedding Mary walked behind Anne and Joachim to Joseph's house. Anne was not herself. She kept fidgeting and glancing back at Mary with a worried look on her face.

"Ima, why are you so nervous?" Mary asked.

"I'm not nervous, Mary," Anne fibbed, "I'm just excited. It's not every day we get to travel in a carriage to a big wedding in a place like Capernaum." Actually, Anne was a little worried that Mary was going to be upset when she learned that her own betrothal (engagement) ceremony was planned for that morning. She was on edge, wondering if Mary was going to be unhappy when she learned the truth. But the men had decided to surprise Mary with the ketubah, and that was the end of the matter. Women rarely questioned their husbands' decisions.

Mary walked into Joseph's house and immediately suspected something: it was decorated for a party. The table was filled with platters piled high with food and there were wine cups at every place setting. It was clear that Jacob had intended this to be a special occasion. An air of anticipation brightened the smudgy corners of the room like an emerging butterfly, alighting on everyone in its happy flight.

Mary was seated across from Joseph and they had eyes and ears only for each other. Usually shy and subdued, Mary was clearly excited and her happiness bloomed in her cheeks.

Anne was relieved that her daughter seemed to be so fond of Joseph, but a dozen doubts nibbled at her as the hour for the ketubah loomed ever closer: *Did Joseph ever smile? How old was he? Why were the men in such a hurry to marry off her beloved Mary?* But she kept these thoughts in her heart.

After the meal, the women and children moved to another room, leaving Joachim, Jacob and Joseph to negotiate the marriage contract. After very little discussion—when neither party to a contract has much with which to barter there is little to negotiate—they agreed on the terms for the dowry and the brideprice Joseph would pay for Mary.

To finalize the agreement, Mary was called back into the room and presented the contract for her acceptance, an act that would seal her betrothal to Joseph.

Mary was stunned. *Now I know why ima was acting so strangely. They have decided to use this occasion for the ketubah. Everyone knew about it but me, although it is MY life.* She didn't have time to think about her feelings. She hadn't been given a chance to decide whether she wanted to marry Joseph; the decision had been made for her.

The wine was poured and everyone raised their cups to drink a toast. But Mary hesitated, holding the cup in her shaking hands, not eager to raise it to her lips. She realized that once she drank the wine she would legally and formally be promised to Joseph, that the terms of the engagement were accepted by all and the marriage would follow sometime in the near future.

So in that eternity between the cup and the lip, Mary thought on all these things: *What happened to the plan that the families were going to get to know each other? Joseph is a good man and will be kind to me, but am I ready to commit to a lifetime with a much older man who can be rather stern and is not much given to smiling? Why not wait to sign the ketubah after I achieve my womanhood? And how old will I be when we finally consummate the marriage? Will I still feel the same? Is this just excitement or is it possible that I really love Joseph? Or will I grow to love this man whom I hardly know?*

But she realized that these little frissons of hesitation were just last-minute nerves and she raised her cup along with everyone else.

One small swallow for Mary, one giant leap for mankind.

Chapter Five

And thou, Capernaum, which art exalted unto heaven, shalt be brought down to hell: for if the mighty works, which have been done in thee, had been done in Sodom, it would have remained until this day. But I say unto you, that it shall be more tolerable for the land of Sodom in the day of judgment than for thee.

Matthew 11:23-24

THIS WAS A DAY UNLIKE anything Mary had ever imagined. She had left her humble home in Nazareth a mere child and would return a few steps away from being a woman. Although her marriage would not be consummated until seven months after her blood began, her budding breasts, which the tunic Anne had sewn for her did little to disguise, promised a brief sojourn to womanhood.

This was her first visit to Capernaum and she was captivated by the sights of this bustling center of government and commerce. Situated on the northwest corner of the Sea of Galilee, Capernaum was an enchanting combination of all the delights that make for a perfect place to visit but, to Mary's mind, not especially a good place to live.

Ironically, her first son, Jesus, lived there much of his life. He was to declare it, 'exalted unto heaven, but condemned to hell.'

Mary thought that living amidst this kind of hustle and bustle might become monotonous, even tedious after a while. She knew that she preferred the simple pleasures of a small town, a refuge from the complications of city life. She never wanted to live anywhere but Nazareth.

But there was nothing monotonous about Capernaum today. The hurrying to and fro of the citizens and merchants of that seaside metropolis engrossed her as she tried to take in everything around her. The women were dressed in stylish, colorful tunics belted with ornate embroidered sashes that Mary imagined carried the earth in gold coins.

There were the unmistakable smells and noises—grunts, bleats, neighs and brays—of camels, goats, horses and donkeys, their excreta and urine creating a noisome wake. This noxious bouquet floated above the filthy water rilling through the gutters, making a fetid soup of the humid air that lay above the town like a heavy blanket. Mary wrinkled her nose and thought, *Capernaum smells to high heaven.*

Merchants haggled loudly with customers who clung to their money belts even as they were bested in the deal. Boats flying the colorful banners from many Galilean fisheries undulated on the waves that broke against the barnacled harbor; wineshops lured the imbiber; food stands the hungry, brothels the lusty, while the synagogue absolved the penitent who had emerged from the former just hours before.

Capernaum was exalted unto heaven and debauched unto hell.

As they clip-clopped along the shore road, Mary wished they could stop the carriage and tarry for a while among the various shopkeepers, who called out to them as they passed: "Figs, olives, melons, pomegranates, grapes, barley cakes; fine linen scarves, embroidered tunics, leather belts; spikenard, frankincense, myrrh, perfumes and incense; golden earrings, bracelets, nose rings."

Nose rings? Mary cringed. Men used nose rings to control their oxen, to pull them along where they didn't want to go. Mary wondered why any woman would think wearing a ring through her nose like an ox was attractive. Regardless of whether it was fashionable, why suggest to the world that you could be led around by the nose?

"Oh well, no time to stop, no money to shop," Mary dismissed her musings.

But her curiosity about sophisticated treasures was not as much a desire to possess as it was to see and touch and feel. She would be happy just to hold some of these treasures in her hands for a moment.

As the groom and his guests rolled through Capernaum, well-wishers lined the limestone streets, jostling each other for a better view. As soon as they caught sight of the carriage torches they cheered the occupants, whom they imagined to be near royalty—the news had spread that a direct descendant of King David was marrying one of their very own—and they shouted, heralding the ancient message: "The bridegroom is coming, the bridegroom is coming."

Mary allowed Joseph to hold her hand, but her eyes, indeed all of her senses, were riveted on the sights and smells and sounds as they pulled into the courtyard of the bride's home. Never had she seen such wealth. *This is a palace. Why are Rebekah's parents allowing her to marry a poor man like Aaron?*

The wedding feast lasted far into the night with toast after toast to the giddy bride and groom, who finally broke away from the crowd just before dawn to disappear into the connubial tent for seven blissful days and nights.

Mary, who was usually early-to-bed, managed to stay wide awake all night for this not-to-be-missed event. She didn't delude herself that her own wedding would be anything approaching this level of extravagance. In her parent's household, spare no expense was whittled down to nothing to spare, but it would not be lacking in meaning. *Excess is so obscene,* Mary thought, unconsciously echoing her mother's oft-repeated sentiment.

Another event that day was just as important to Mary's life as her engagement to Joseph: she finally got to meet the beautiful girl she had seen so many times at the village well—Mary Magdalene.

Nazareth had only one source of water, a natural spring that was a gathering spot for the women whose task it was to provide the family's water each day. Naturally, the women who met there each morning and evening loved to visit and gossip with their friends and neighbors.

On several occasions lately Mary had seen a young girl and her servant at the well who were obviously newcomers to Nazareth. The girl, who was about Mary's age, was astonishingly beautiful, different from anyone Mary had ever seen. Fiery red hair and piercing green eyes gave her an exotic look, and Mary couldn't help staring at her, wishing she would at least glance her way. But mostly the girl seemed to resent being at the well, and was noisily blaming her servant.

One morning Mary arrived very early when there were just a few other women there with their water pitchers. The pretty girl was there and once again she was loudly complaining to her servant.

Mary smiled as she remembered that scene, perfectly recalling Magda's voice, which rang with an accent far different from that of the typical Galilean. "Heli," she said, "why didn't you bring one of your sons to help you with this chore? What am I, my servant's helper?"

To her credit, the servant did not blink an eye. "Mind your manners, Queen Magdalene! Your father wants you to learn to take responsibility. Helping me draw and carry the water is a good lesson for you. If nothing else, maybe it will teach you a little humility—something you need a lot of!"

"And does my father think that by carrying water I will lose my demons and become a quiet young maiden in the process?" Her smile belied her tone of voice. She loved Heli and would do anything for her. Well, anything but physical labor.

Mary stood in awe watching this little scene between a rich young girl and her servant, who obviously loved her young mistress very much but was not intimidated by her imperious manner.

Mary's family was very poor and had no servants. The women in her family just accepted that the chore of collecting water and carrying it back home was their job. That someone was rich enough to afford a servant to do the work was unimaginable to Mary.

Now here was this same girl sitting at the bride's table, making no secret of the fact that she wanted no part in the festivities.

When Joseph led Mary to the head table to introduce her to his new sister-in-law, Rebekah, she saw her chance to learn the name of the mysterious girl she had secretly watched so many times at the well.

She whispered to Joseph, "Ask Rebekah for the name of the girl sitting at the end of the table."

Rebekah looked up in amazement, not believing that anyone who didn't live under a rock did not know the infamous Mary Magdalene. ". . . but everyone calls her Magda because she hates being called Mary," Rebekah said.

Finally, the object of their conversation turned and noticed Mary staring at her. And she *was* staring in awe, she later confessed, at Magda's flaming red hair, elaborate purple silk gown, and undisguised air of boredom.

Timidly, Mary approached Magda, who looked at her warily, giving her what Mary would come to call her green-eyed monster look. Magda raised an eyebrow and exclaimed, "It's you, the girl from the well in Nazareth. Why do you always stare at me like I flew down from the moon?" But to herself she thought, *Maybe she's smarter than she looks.*

Before Mary could think of an answer, Magda threw down her napkin, jumped up from the table and came forward to meet her, laughing to soften her offensive remark. Magda always delivered her brash remarks with a tempering dose of laughter, which dulled the point of even the most cutting barb. Or so she thought.

Mary answered softly, "Because you are the loveliest girl I have ever seen." *And surely the most outrageous person on earth* was left unsaid.

Magda's laughter softened into a smile. She grabbed Mary's hand, pulling her away from the others and over to the dessert table. "I am so glad to have an excuse to get away from that boring group at the bridegroom's table. The bride is my cousin but that is the only way we are related. She's a few dates short of a fruitcake. I was dying to make my escape so you are giving me a way out."

Squinting a bit, her head cocked to the side, she looked Mary up and down critically. Apparently liking what she saw, she remarked, "Well, aren't you looking lovely tonight! But you need someone to help you make the most of your looks. I have a feeling there is a glamorous creature inside you just waiting for someone to bring her to the surface. For one thing, you are much too modest, and I have always thought that modesty like humility is way overrated. That's a lovely tunic, but it needs a proper tailoring to enhance your feminine curves. By the way, what's your name?"

Without waiting for an answer, she continued in this staccato style, "I have recently come to live with my Aunt Orpah in Nazareth and I don't know a soul in the entire dreadful town. How would you like to come visit me when we get back? Orpah lives practically at the top of Mount Kedumim, and it is a sight to behold. I call it 'Orpah's Corpus' because it reminds me of a mausoleum. It is *bo*-ring without someone my age to talk to."

She took a bite of a fig cake and chewed for a moment, deep in thought. "When you get back home, ask your parents if you can come up and we'll work on your hair and your eyes and, well . . . everything. You'll become more glamorous and maybe some of your sweetness will rub off on me . . . just not enough to hurt, I hope. What did you say your name is?"

In spite of the fact that Mary was patient and kind while Magda was brash and spoiled, each felt an immediate bond. And there at that wedding feast in Capernaum began a friendship that would last a lifetime despite their being so different . . . despite the gap widened in later years by the divergent paths taken by a virgin and a reputed prostitute.

Chapter Six

How beautiful upon the mountains are the feet of him that bringeth good tidings . . .

Isaiah 52:7

Magda's Aunt Orpah had used her inheritance to create a mountaintop aerie more unusual than any other dwelling in Nazareth. Its design was the artistry and building wizardry of the famous Greek architect, Hieronymus.

Never one to shy away from gilding the lily, Orpah wanted a colossus of all things Greek: Ionic thoses and Doric theses festooned with Corinthian friezes, all built to Olympic proportions. It was Orpah's overblown style that led Magda to observe, "All the money in the world can't buy good taste."

Orpah had requested that her bedroom be located at the highest point of the property, a dictate that inspired Hieronymus to design an obelisk whose stingy proportions held just Orpah and her immense bed. From that dizzying height, the mansion undulated down, overlooking a magnificent garden a few levels below.

At last Mary was going to visit Magda. She took the familiar road that curved up the mountain beyond the spring. She knew her climb would be a few hundred feet, but she was too excited about seeing Orpah's Corpus to mind the hike.

As she walked she thought about all the changes that Joseph had brought to her life: her first visit to Capernaum, being a guest at a wedding in a mansion—the biggest house she had ever seen—and meeting Mary Magdalene. And now she was going to see Orpah's Corpus, which sounded even bigger and more interesting than Rebekah's house in Capernaum, if Magda hadn't exaggerated—something Mary suspected Magda might do on occasion.

The road gradually curved left and narrowed into a path lined with towering cedar trees. Mary began to think she had taken a wrong turn when suddenly there it was, looming before her—Orpah's Corpus. Her jaw dropped. She was awed by the sight of the mammoth structure, which climbed the hillside in cantilevered levels surmounted by a towering pinnacle.

Well, Magda hadn't exaggerated, Mary thought. *This is the biggest, most extraordinary house I have ever seen.* She paused for a moment to catch her breath and take in the spectacle. Then she saw Magda sitting outside on a stone bench watching her.

"Welcome to Orpah's Corpus, Mary. I'm glad you finally made it. I hope you asked your parents to let you stay overnight. It's too exhausting a trip, coming up the mountain and then going back down in the same day if you're not used to it; although I used to run up and down the footpath on Mount Arbel in Magdala once or twice every day." Magda realized she was babbling too much about herself when she should be making her guest feel welcome. She went up to Mary and gave her a brief hug.

"I didn't find it all that tiring, really," Mary said, returning the hug. "I guess I'm used to climbing hills wherever I go around Nazareth."

The woman Mary had seen with Magda at the well opened the front door and said, "Orpah wants you to come in to lunch now, Magda.

Introduce me to your friend, and for heaven's sake, offer her a cup of water. I'm sure she is thirsty after making the climb up here."

Magda grabbed Mary's hand and led her over to Heli. "Mary, this is Heli. Heli, Mary. Heli's my favorite person in the world, even if she does cluck over me like a mother hen. By all means, help yourself to a cup of water from the well over there." She swept her hand in the direction of the well, but Heli, exasperated, went over and drew a cupful for Mary.

Mary was surprised at the closeness between Magda and Heli. Regardless of how trying Magda was at times, Heli never lost patience with her. A tall, elegant woman, the years had not taken much of a toll on her looks. It was obvious she had been a handsome young woman.

Heli hugged Mary and said, "Mary, at last I get to meet you. You are all Magda has talked about since Rebekah's wedding . . . and believe me, that is unusual." *She usually talks only about herself* was implied.

After lunch Magda took Mary to the garden and played tour guide, displaying her knowledge of Israel's geography:

"This garden is several hundred feet above Nazareth," Magda said. "To the north you can see the towns of Zebulun and Naphtali, and that's Mount Hermon in Lebanon towering above them."

Then she turned and pointed east, "Sixteen miles to the east is my beloved Sea of Galilee—it's clear today so you can almost see the 'House of Benjamin' on the Cliffs of Arbel; twenty miles to the west, the coast of Tyre on the Mediterranean Sea; and south, nothing exciting 'til you reach Jerusalem, which you can't actually see, but you know it's there."

"Jerusalem!" Mary exclaimed. "I love Jerusalem. My parents used to take us to the temple during the holy days, but we stopped going after my little brother was born. Ima said it was too tiring, but I think the real reason is that there wasn't enough money.

"Most of us Nazarenes actually prefer to observe the holidays at the synagogue in our peaceful little town. I certainly prefer it, blasphemous as that sounds, because Jerusalem is too crowded and noisy for a proper religious observance. But I'd like to go there to explore the city. Have you ever been? Silly question, I'm sure you have, but I would love it if we could go together sometime."

Magda looked momentarily sad. "Yes, I've been there many times. I love Jerusalem and I am going to build a great house near there one day. We used to go every year, but I have mostly bad memories from those trips. I stopped going after I moved to Nazareth. My mother was very religious and always insisted we go to the temple for all the important holidays. But after her death my father seemed to lose interest in almost everything, especially religion. His faith was always a little shaky, and after mother died he seemed to be angry at God. So he stopped insisting we make the trip. Anyway, my first trip to Jerusalem is one of my worst memories. But that's a story for another time."

Mary could hardly believe her ears: Magda's father was angry at God? That was so blasphemous she was almost afraid to listen to such talk. Mary's unquestioning faith gave her a reverence that would be the cause of many a disagreement between the two friends over the years. But the friendship survived them.

As different as they were, they quickly found common ground . . . they *needed* each other. Magda cared not that Mary was poor and that her cloak and tunic were tattered and mended in many places. She saw her inner perfection. She didn't care that Mary was a small-town innocent while she was, to use Mary's words, 'Miss *Mag*nificent.' Mary, though quiet, had something within, a steely resolve that was soothing to Magda, who was flighty and slightly manipulative, often using others until she was bored with them.

Mary's unshakable serenity helped to calm Magda when she was possessed by one of her demons. Although they lived in two different worlds, they spent every possible moment together. Mary would visit Magda at the mansion on the mountain and occasionally they would go to Magdala to visit Magda's family.

The two girls had been friends for several months when Magda confided to Mary that her mother had died giving birth to her younger brother, Lazarus; that her father had sent her to live in Nazareth, thinking she would be better off in a small town. She said he mistakenly thought that Orpah would be a stricter disciplinarian—the all-seeing eye of maternal love—to Magda, whose nocturnal forays into the wicked city of Magdala were so worrisome to him.

"Ha," Magda snorted in derision. "Orpah couldn't discipline a gnat, much less a wildcat like me. Does she look like she has an ounce of *self*-discipline?"

While it was true that Orpah, a pretty but morbidly obese woman, loved food and wine a little *in extremis*, Mary thought that Magda was being a bit mean-spirited towards this sweet woman who obviously adored Magda and treated her like the daughter she never had.

When Mary suggested she was being a bit ungrateful towards her generous aunt, Magda just laughed and said, "Oh, she doesn't mind, she's used to it." She paused for a moment and said, "She has an enormous sense of self-girth." She burst out laughing at her play on words, an exercise she had elevated practically to an art form.

But she laughed alone.

In their more serious moments, Mary learned that Magda had a sweetness about her that was a pleasant surprise to anyone who was patient enough to mine for that hidden gold. And poems should have been written about her smile. It was like the moon in all its phases: stingy little crescent smiles just to assure the other person that she was still awake; half-moon smiles when she was somewhat interested and willing to let a little of her light shine; and full moon smiles that could light up a room when she was delighted—usually by a naughty or amusing story.

If someone shared a secret with her, she just listened with that certain smile, nodding and 'um hmmming' with an uncanny knowledge of life that should have been far beyond the understanding of a young girl.

Mary soon changed her mind about Magda: she wasn't spoiled . . . she had been *born* with a hauteur that was off-putting to most people. And her red hair and fair skin did not serve her well in a land of dark and darker. But Magda, smiling away any possible barriers, needed Mary and reached out to her. And Mary needed the sparkle, and maybe a little of the naughtiness, that Magda brought to her life.

Mary's mother and father were loving parents, but they were so worn down by hard work and the struggle to provide for their family that there really wasn't much time for fun. When they weren't working, they were practically dead on their feet from exhaustion. Mary knew she was loved, but she felt a great vacuum in her life and a longing to be carefree and gay—Magda brought all of that to her mundane existence.

But Anne worried that Mary was overly obsessed with Magda. She was a good judge of character, and her concern that Magda might just be using Mary because she needed a captive audience—and Mary *was* captivated—wasn't too far off the mark.

In the beginning, Magda had befriended Mary because she needed a friend in Nazareth, and she couldn't resist Mary's unwavering adulation. But little by little, the tables turned a bit and the admiration became mutual. Magda began to feel a kinship with Mary she had never felt with her older sister, Martha.

Mary and Magda had their differences, luckily none of them small, so they didn't spoil their time carping at one another. The big differences they handled by avoiding the issues whenever possible.

Mary was an animal lover. She couldn't bear to see any of God's creatures suffer abuse, regardless of how lowly or vile. One morning when they were together in Orpah's garden a cockroach darted out across the stone floor. Mary picked up a palm branch and was going to sweep it safely back outside the garden walls. Magda jumped to her feet and smashed it beneath her sandal before Mary could rescue it.

They had their first falling out over that incident. Magda told Mary she needed to toughen up. Mary retorted that Magda needed to love all of God's creatures, a concept that Mary's first son tried to instill in Magda later on with no more success than Mary had had.

"I do love them, I just love them from afar," Magda fibbed. "I don't go cockroach hunting, but if they dare to cross my path, they do so at their peril."

There were some things they were never going to agree on and wisely they tried to avoid those subjects.

But they benefited from their many disparities and the friendship grew in spite of them. Mary's sweetness and genuine affection helped to end the loneliness Magda had always felt, trapped between a critical, unloving mother and a mostly absent father who was remote when present.

The material things Magda brought to Mary's life were just a happy by-product of a friendship that grew into a life-long relationship cemented by the mutual joy of childhood and the sorrows they would experience together later in life.

Mary came to love Orpah's quirky mansion on the mountain where she spent many carefree hours with Magda, sharing her dreams and young girl secrets. And it was there in the lower garden where Mary revealed to Magda the earth-shattering news that would change both of their lives.

Chapter Seven

And behold, thy cousin Elisabeth, she hath also conceived a son in her old age; and this is the sixth month with her, who was called barren.

Luke 1:36

MARY HAD BEEN CRYING OFF and on ever since the angel's visit. Her mother had tried to comfort her. "Mary, your tears are just a normal part of what a woman experiences when she has her monthly bleeding. It is just life mourning for another lost opportunity to replenish itself."

But Anne knew only a small part of the story. "Normal! There is nothing normal going on in my life! I am still a virgin and yet I am going to give birth to a child—the Son of God!" But those words Mary mumbled to herself, out of Anne's hearing. Her life was about to be turned upside down. All she could think about were the things that the angel Gabriel had said would happen to her. *Why me?* she wondered again.

She decided to confide in Magda, who would know what to do about her problem. At least, it would help just to share her story with someone who was never shocked by anything, regardless of how unbelievable it was.

Nonetheless, Magda was about to get the shock of her life.

Finally reaching the last twist in the winding path that led to Orpah's mansion, Mary walked across the courtyard and lifted the gargoyle door knocker on the massive front door. Out of breath from climbing the mountain so rapidly, her face red and blotchy, she was hardly able to speak when Heli opened the door.

Noting Mary's distress, Heli quickly handed her a cup of water from the pitcher she kept by the front door. It was not unusual for the older visitors who walked up the mountain to arrive a little out of breath, but the younger people, particularly Mary, seldom showed any ill effects at all. She wondered if Mary were ill.

"Good morning, Mary. Come in and have some breakfast," Heli said, smiling and touching her back, guiding her to the verandah at the back of the house. The walk down that long central hallway never failed to astonish Mary, and today, in spite of her distress, was no exception. There were paintings covering every surface of the limestone walls: grotesque scenes of bloody battles, rapes, pedophilia, bestiality, all so vividly real that she could hardly bear to look; but something about the graphic violence drew her in, in spite of herself.

Mary was happy to see that Magda was already up and dressed, eating her breakfast. Naturally, Mary was invited to help herself from the morning meal Heli had laid out—a bountiful array of fish, cheese, yogurt, honey, bread and fruit the likes of which her family never enjoyed. In her humble house they had perhaps a small hunk of cheese, a crust of bread with honey and a small cup of goat's milk before heading out to begin their day.

But Mary was too upset to eat. "Magda, hurry and finish your breakfast. I have something incredible to tell you. And, Magda, please hear me out before you start hounding me with a thousand questions."

"Mary, what's come over you?" Magda asked. "You're covered in a rash. You look like you've caught a healthy dose of the Egyptian plague. Heli will give you something to take care of that."

Magda squinted and gave Mary the green-eyed stare. "Have you and Joseph had a quarrel? I'll finish my breakfast in the garden," she whispered, looking over at Orpah, whose second favorite food group was gossip.

Mary and Magda made their way out of the house and walked down the hill toward the lower garden. They followed the path alongside a waterfall that splashed down to a fish pond in Orpah's prized flower garden. And what a garden it was!

There were flowers tumbling in riotous reds and pinks and corals and lemony yellows—like a living colorful tapestry over every surface of the surrounding garden walls. A tiny bird bath fashioned into a rainbow mosaic played a watery serenade in the garden's center.

Nearby olive, fig and pomegranate trees shared their fragrance under the shade of ancient towering palms, whose leafy branches rose and fell in the rhythm of the breeze. The sun, which surely blazed more brightly in Nazareth than anywhere else in the world, was shining through in the spaces between the foliage to add its dappled light to the morning.

The garden was one of Mary's favorite places, but she was hardly aware of it today as she haltingly told Magda of the visit from the angel Gabriel a few days before.

"Magda, something unbelievable is going to happen," she whispered tearfully. "I am going to have a baby." Unable to look into Magda's eyes, she mumbled this astounding news while staring at the ground, plucking at a loose thread in the sleeve of her tunic.

Magda stared at Mary in disbelief. She was stunned into silence. It was not like Mary to joke about something this serious, but what else could it be?

Magda was chewing a handful of grapes and she nearly choked. "Why, you little Jezebel. Imagine all this time I thought you were such an innocent."

Mary kept her eyes on the ground and shook her head. Why did Magda become cynical regardless of how hurtful it might be? She knew that Magda felt a deep concern for those she loved, but she often masked it with sarcasm.

Softening a bit, Magda said, "Oh, Mary, you? That can't be true. You haven't even started your woman's bleeding."

"But I have, Magda. Right after Gabriel appeared with the news that I was going to give birth to a child, I noticed my bleeding had begun."

"Gabriel? Mary, who are you talking about? Who is Gabriel?"

"Magda, it's not what you think! Gabriel is an angel, a messenger from God, and he appeared to me a few nights ago after I had gone to bed. I was not dreaming. I am going to give birth to the Messiah, as foretold by the prophets that a virgin would give birth to the Son of God. I am to name him 'Jesus.'"

Magda jumped up and started picking flowers, breathing in their fragrance. Her usual reaction to anything unpleasant was to distance herself from the ogre called bad news. Finally, she turned around to Mary.

"Mary, you're talking nonsense! You've been listening to those nutty old men who sit outside the synagogue preaching fire and brimstone. How are you going to have a baby? A woman gets pregnant when she has lain with a man. You're still a virgin. You *are* still a virgin, aren't you?

"Well, even if it is true that you and Joseph got a little carried away, you'll just have to move up your wedding date. I'm sure he would marry you tomorrow if you asked him."

Mary was disappointed that Magda didn't or wouldn't understand what she was telling her. Magda was one of the smartest people she knew but she could be mulishly bullheaded at times. But this was worse than any other time. She needed a friend, not an adversary.

"Magda, sit down and listen for a moment. Just let me tell my story before you turn it into the 'Trials of Tamar,' as you would say. Joseph has nothing to do with this. And I don't have any answers other than this message from God that the angel delivered to me. He says that I am going to have a baby, although yes, I am still a virgin. And if he says I am going to have a baby, then I believe it. And that baby is going to be the Messiah—the Son of God."

Without waiting for an answer, Mary rushed on, "Anyway, Magda, I have to make a journey and I need to ask a big favor of you. I need to borrow one of Orpah's donkeys for a few months to go to Hebron. You know my cousin Elisabeth is going to have a baby—her first—although she is past 50! Well, the fact that Gabriel was aware of that convinced me he was truly a messenger from God. He told me that it was part of God's plan that I leave immediately to spend a few months with Elisabeth and Zachariah."

Magda got in Mary's face. "Mary, I feel like I am talking to a stranger. You can*not* go anywhere as far away as Hebron. That is beyond Jerusalem! It will take you a week to get there, and if you travel the road through Samaria you won't ever get there because it is the road to nowhere. My father calls it the 'Road to Hell.' Even grown men fear to travel that route!"

Magda knew that she was upsetting Mary, but she needed to bring her to her senses! "Can I really be having this conversation with my gentle, level-headed friend who wouldn't hurt a fly? Have you lost your virginity and your senses as well—maybe not in that order?"

The look on Mary's face melted Magda's heart. She offered Mary the small nosegay she had made and put her arm around her. "Listen to me very closely now. If you are determined to make this foolish trip you need to toughen up. Roman soldiers and the other bad men you're likely to meet along the way are not going to be swept away with a palm branch.

"Why don't you take Orpah's servant, Tigabu, with you? He has family in Jerusalem and I'm sure he'd love to go with you! He would make a great body guard and you would be safe—he is a eunuch."

Mary folded her arms across her chest. "No, Magda! I have to make this trip alone. So answer me, yes or no? May I borrow one of your donkeys? I am *going* to visit Elisabeth, with or without your blessing *or* one of your donkeys. This is not my will, but God's. Yes or no?"

Magda knew this was one argument she was not going to win. "All right, Mary, I'll help you, or I should say I'll help you commit suicide."

She turned and started up the path, but stopped and whirled around. "But tell me this, why do you have to go alone? Abraham, Joseph and Moses! All right, Mary, which donkey do you want? Donkey Yotie or Yanni? Remember Yanni, your favorite, is gentle but slow and dumb as a billy goat; however Yotie, while faster and stronger, is harder to handle. Which one, Mary? Yotie or Yanni?"

"Yotie," she answered—a decision that would change her life.

Chapter Eight

And Mary arose in those days, and went into the hill country with haste, into a city of Juda.

Luke 1:39

Midnight. Her prayers would have to wait. She would pray all the way. Mary looked around the large room that was her family's home. Although the six of them—her parents, sister, two brothers and Mary—shared just one room, her mother had made heavy curtains to divide the area into four niches, which gave everyone a little privacy.

As the older daughter, Mary had a corner of the room to herself, her brother in the opposite one. Her parents shared their larger space with her younger sister and baby brother, who had not yet been weaned from his mother's breast. Theirs was a humble but happy family that subsisted on little other than abundant love.

Mary knew that soon after she married Joseph she would start her own family. But in her heart, she wasn't ready for such a big step; especially that of having a baby fathered by someone who wasn't her husband.

She had never been away from her family for more than a day or two and she knew that she would miss them. But she wouldn't think about that. She grabbed the bundle of food and clothing she had packed the night before and, pausing to gaze on the faces of her parents and siblings one last time (wondering if she would ever see them again), she slipped out the door.

A little way down the road, Magda was waiting for her with Yotie, who was pawing at the ground and being his usual difficult self. She pressed into Mary's hand a pouch containing several coins to use for emergencies and to purchase a space with a traveling group. (Magda had finally persuaded her to wait for two weeks to meet up with a caravan traveling south.) She kissed her on the cheek and shook her head in disbelief as Mary mounted the difficult donkey. This was the first time Mary had ever seen Magda with tears in her eyes.

Mary wavered a bit at the thought of her mother and father's reaction when they learned she was gone; but without a backward glance, and before she could lose her nerve, she nudged Yotie in the side and took off in the direction of the caravan road.

As she made her way through the quiet streets of Nazareth she looked up into a velvety black sky that was punctuated with thousands of fiery angel eyes looking down at her. She was glad that the night was clear with a harvest moon hanging in the sky—like a glowing red pomegranate smiling down on her—and she viewed its presence and the countless stars lighting her way a good omen.

Although the Sea of Galilee was several miles to the east, tonight as always, through the silence she imagined that she could hear its gentle waves whispering to her in their looping susurration, 'Shh, shh, all is well. Shh, shh, go with God.'

Winter was closing in but fortunately the mild weather persisted. A gift from God, the cold weather she dreaded was holding off.

This would be a perfect time to head to the Galilee to wade in the shallows and search for sea shells with Magda, *not* to be traveling alone on a stubborn donkey for many lonely days on a dangerous journey into the Judean hills far south of Nazareth.

Thinking about the wonderful times she had shared with Magda wading in the Galilee nearly caused her to lose heart for this journey. She was too young for this kind of adventure. *I just want to be me—Mary, a carefree young girl—not an instrument in God's plans for mankind,* she thought as she swallowed a rising bitterness.

For a moment she regretted not choosing gentle Yanni to accompany her. Yanni loved to swish his long tail, which ended in a tangled, tasseled switch, back and forth, back and forth, like he was keeping time to music only he could hear.

But she and Yotie had become a little friendlier and she tried to concentrate only on good things as she approached the toll station where she was to meet up with the caravan. She was happy that some of the travelers were women, but they were Egyptian women and they looked at her head covering and veil with contempt.

Egyptian women were more liberated than Israelite women. They enjoyed an equal status with men and viewed the Israelite custom of classifying women as second-class citizens a blight on the female half of the species. They had equal rights in inheritance that they used to acquire wealth, and that enabled them to hold political office. A few women even ruled as pharaohs, the last and most notable one being Cleopatra, actually a Macedonian of the Ptolemy dynasty, whose rule ended in 30 BC.

Mary ignored the women's resentment and took her place near the back of the caravan where she hoped she would be largely ignored. As it happened, she got her wish.

As the sun painted the eastern sky in pink savannas, her ride on the donkey Yotie took her farther and farther away from her identity as Mary, daughter of Anne and Joachim. She felt herself changing, 'toughening up,' as Magda had suggested. And she began to feel that inner woman emerging, pushing upward and outward from the chrysalis of her youthful innocence, mile after mile, hour after hour.

She felt a guilty pleasure in recalling Magda's appraisal of her. "Mary, you are very special. You're a pretty girl, but not half as lovely as you are going to be when you reach womanhood! You should see how your eyes sparkle when you're happy and how they flash like black ice when I annoy you. And I know it embarrasses you when I refer to your body, but you must know how wonderful your body is! I've seen you in the bath. You are lush and curvy—God's gift to men!"

God's gift indeed, Mary thought, shaking her head and trying to prepare her mind for what was happening in her life. *If what the angel Gabriel said is true, I certainly will be God's gift, not only to men, but to all mankind. From my body will come a gift that will change humankind for all eternity.*

So far, so good. She had been traveling at the back of the caravan without mishap for two days, and strangely she had been followed by a little cloud no bigger than a man's fist that she began to look upon as the hand of God. She wondered if it would disappear like a bit of fluff if she managed to grab hold of it. But it gave her comfort and helped a bit with the homesickness she felt for her family and for her beloved Nazareth.

Surely Nazareth's meadows were what David described when he wrote the 23rd Psalm, her favorite verse from the scriptures. She often repeated it when she was upset or ill at ease, which she certainly was now. She leaned down and whispered in Yotie's velvet ear the words that she loved so much:

> *"The Lord is my Shepherd; I shall not want. He maketh me to lie down in green pastures; he leadeth me beside the still waters. He restoreth my soul; He leadeth me in the paths of righteousness for his name's sake. Yea, though I walk through the valley of the shadow of death* (like now!) . . . ."

Soothed by the words of the comforting Psalm, she began to feel whole again, more secure in the knowledge that God was with her, leading her.

Long after darkness had settled over the hilly land they stopped at a caravansary in a small village near Samaria. Those who could afford it would sleep within the walls of the inn; the poorer travelers would make camp by a spring to spend the night.

Exhausted and nearly choked with dust, Mary gratefully climbed down off Yotie's back. Going a distance away from the others, she unwrapped her head, let her hair fall about her shoulders, and lay her weary body down in a woodland of wildflowers.

"Are you watching me now?" she prayed as she closed her eyes and instantly slept.

Chapter Nine

And the angel answered and said unto her, The Holy Ghost shall come upon thee, and the power of the Highest shall overshadow thee: therefore also that holy thing which shall be born of thee shall be called the Son of God.

Luke 1:35

MARY AWOKE WITH THE SUN shining in her eyes and thunder pounding in her ears. Hundreds of horses were galloping toward her. *Foolish girl,* she chastised herself for letting precious time go by while she lay slumbering. She was dismayed to find that the caravan had traveled on without her, taking her money and leaving her to fend for herself.

But there was no time for remorse, there was an earthquake of noise coming ever closer, and Yotie was braying and trying to break free from the olive tree where she had tethered him. Roman soldiers, too many to count, were riding toward her.

From a distance, the band of soldiers looked like the Coming of Yahweh. Mary thought, *Is this the end of the world, or just the end of me?*

She tried to pull Yotie deeper into the woodlands to hide behind an outcropping of rocks, but the stubborn donkey was protesting, braying loudly and refusing to move. She lifted her head and prayed, "Lord, please help me. If the soldiers find me, all will be lost!"

Finally she was able to coax Yotie far away from the road and into a thick stand of trees, where she made him lie down on his side. By now, the soldiers were galloping by, seemingly unaware of her presence.

Just as she began to feel safe, one of the soldiers doubled back and left the road to check on the noise he had heard. Yotie's ears perked up and, scenting the other animal, rose to his feet and started to bellow again. Mary burrowed down and tried to make her body disappear in the long grass.

But the soldier had already seen her, and he rode over to where she lay cowering. "What is this?" he asked, as he rode up beside her and lifted her veil with his sword. "What are you doing here? Are you lost? Where are your companions?"

Mary, too frightened to do anything but try to hide, pulled the veil back around her and covered her face. Wrapping her entire head in the long hijab, she turned away from him and refused to look at him. If she couldn't see him, he couldn't see her, she reasoned dumbly.

The soldier, a Roman centurion, climbed down from his horse, pulled the veil off her face and said, "State your business." He looked around to see if there were others. Seeing only the lone donkey, he said, "What kind of woman are you, out here by yourself on this road hiding behind your veil? Are you hoping to entice some of my men?"

Too terrified to speak, she simply shook her head—she was shaking all over—not sure what he meant by his probing questions.

Centurion Cornelius had been on the road away from his wife and family for several weeks as he and his battalion patrolled this crime-filled road. Second only to the caravan route between Damascus and Egypt as an important trade artery, the road was being terrorized by roving bands of criminals who preyed on travelers and merchants along the way. Cornelius had been ordered to handle the problem.

The great Roman army had better things to do than deal with such petty matters, and Cornelius was not happy that he had been commanded to get rid of the problem. "Just take care of it," his superior officer had ordered.

Cornelius had muttered, "Why not order me to make all the flies in the world go away? They're not as plentiful and don't multiply as quickly."

In that sour early morning mood he gazed hungrily at Mary as she lay cowering on the ground with her hair falling loosely about her shoulders. She was very beautiful and he felt a stirring in his loins that was hard to ignore. Try as he might to ignore her and leave he was weakening in his resolve to remain faithful to his wife. Mistaking her for a Samaritan woman and her solitary presence for the behavior of a harlot, he pushed her to the ground. He pulled her garments up over her hips, separated her legs with his knee as he unbound his girdle, raised his short tunic and fell upon her.

She tried to move the panting man off her body, but he was oblivious to her repeated cries, "Please sir, do not harm me, I am a virgin."

She finally stopped resisting, just going limp and leaving it in God's hands rather than wrestling with this giant who had fallen upon her so hungrily. She turned her head aside and gazed at the thousands of wildflowers that filled the woodland. How was it possible that these buttercups were blooming happily in the morning sun as though nothing were amiss?

She repeated the words from the 91st Psalm that were never far from her lips: *"For he shall give his angels charge over thee to keep thee in all thy ways."*

Where were those angels now? Where was Gabriel? Who was watching over her and protecting her? Where was God? Gradually a stillness came over her as she softly mouthed the words of her own that she always added at the end of the Psalm: "The Lord is with me; the Lord is helping me; the Lord will show me the way; the Lord will watch over me. Lord, are you watching me now?"

Calmer now, Mary held her breath waiting to feel excruciating pain; but she felt only a brief pressure and a slight discomfort that ended as quickly as it began. The soldier cried out and collapsed upon her. Was he ill? Was the worst over? Was that all there was to it?

She opened her eyes just wide enough to see that the soldier had rolled away from her and was sitting with his head in his hands. Apparently, he had finally realized that she was an innocent young girl. Being the tender-hearted girl that she was, she felt compassion for the suffering man.

Cornelius *was* suffering. He couldn't believe what he had done. How could he have missed that which was so obvious? This was no harlot, no fallen woman he had just violated. He should have realized that with her appeals to him to have mercy on her, not to rob her of her virginity . . . those appeals that had fallen on ears made deaf by the lust-driven blood pounding in them. It was unforgivable that he had failed to distinguish between Mary's pleas in the Aramaic language of the Galilean Jews rather than in the Samaritans' Hebrew.

I guess I heard what I wanted to hear, he chastised himself. "Lust is blind *and* deaf," he muttered. "And it can turn the finest man into a monster when it raises its ugly head."

"Calm down, don't be so quick to condemn yourself," a voice from within took the other side of the debate. "I don't think you robbed this girl of her virginity, O child of Onan."

Indeed, he had barely penetrated her—a feat made nearly impossible by her unyielding loins—before spilling his seed onto the ground beneath her.

Cornelius looked over at Mary, finally seeing her through other than lust-filled eyes. Wincing, he noticed how young she was. And upon hearing her prayers and noticing the small blood stain on her undergarment, the debate was lost.

"God forgive me. I have forced myself on an innocent young girl."

He walked over and kneeled beside her. He began to apologize profusely—anything to undo the horrible thing he had done. But the damage was done: he had raped a young girl and taken away her virginity . . . or had he?

He didn't think he had actually broken through that sacred cleft between her legs, and there was only a small spot of blood. Maybe she was just bruised and shaken. But she was lying so still he began to worry that she was suffering from shock.

Cornelius was the father of two daughters, and he was filled with self-loathing when he realized that she was only a couple of years older than his daughter Antonia.

Well, he couldn't exactly un-do the deed. But he could try to make amends. Although he was a Roman soldier, a centurion of the Italian band no less, he was a thoughtful man who feared God, as did his wife and daughters. He regularly gave alms to the poor and was friendly with his Jewish neighbors. He was drawn to their worship of the one true God and had even contributed generously to the building of the synagogue in Capernaum. Everyone in Capernaum admired and respected Cornelius the centurion.

But now he was ashamed and disgusted that he had allowed his passions to rule him in such a savage manner. He prayed that the good deeds he had done in his life would wipe out this very evil one.

Cornelius thought to himself bitterly, *Maybe if I live as long as Methuselah I can do enough good deeds to undo this very bad one.*

Mary watched Cornelius, thinking she should just get up and go while he was battling his conscience. But she was unable to move; it was as if she had been planted in the ground. She asked God why he had allowed this monstrous thing to happen to her. What about the virgin birth? Had all of that been just a dream after all?

Where was God, who the angel said would protect her? Now she doubted herself, wondering if this was Satan at work in her life, destroying all her hopes and dreams of being an obedient daughter, a good wife, a loving mother. Had she changed the direction of her life, getting off the track and wandering down a path of no return that would be the ruination of her? Mary feared she had been abandoned. Where was God? Was he watching her now?

She lay on the ground wondering what she should do. She was a little dazed by this terrifying experience. As her heartbeat thundered on, she heard a comforting voice from the heavens, an angel singing,

> *"Hail, thou that art highly favoured, the Lord is with thee: blessed art thou among women." And then the angel said, "Fear not, Mary, for thou hast found favour with God. And behold, thou shalt conceive in thy womb and bring forth a son, and shalt call his name Jesus. He shall be very great and shall be called the Son of the Highest. The Holy Ghost shall come upon thee, and the power of the Highest shall overshadow thee: therefore also that holy thing which shall be born of thee shall be called the Son of God."*

With that assurance ringing in her ears, Mary sat up, began to collect herself and straighten her garments, all the while murmuring her response: "Let it be, let it be."

Puzzled over her strange murmurings and even more puzzled why a young girl like this would be traveling alone, Cornelius offered to take Mary the rest of the way to her destination. *Where in the world was this young girl going alone?*

Determined to protect her from further harm, he pulled her up behind him on his horse. After tethering the hapless and stubborn Yotie to a lead, they set off at a gallop heading south.

After a few miles, Mary looked back at Yotie, who was struggling to keep up with the galloping horse. "Serves you right, donkey Yotie. You'll just have to resign yourself to paying the consequences for your loud braying that got us into this trouble."

Then she remembered herself and laughed at her private joke. *Listen to yourself, Mary; Magda would be proud of you . . . you're getting tougher.*

Calmer now, Mary began to feel less fearful. Lifting her head, hoping that God was somewhere out there listening, she whispered, "Are you watching me now?" Then she noticed the little cloud that had been following her from the start. It was still there, hovering above her, looking like it was close enough to touch—a tiny guardian angel. And slowly she began to trust this unusual man who was taking her to Hebron. A Roman soldier with a conscience! One who feared God! Feeling much more comfortable with him, she began to answer his questions. She told him a little about herself and her disappointing experience when the caravan had left her to continue alone. She revealed only that she was going to Hebron to be with her cousin, who was going to have a baby, not mentioning the angel's promise that she herself was going to give birth to a child—the Son of God.

He never understood her explanation for traveling without a chaperone and he made her promise that she would not return to Nazareth alone. Just beyond Bethlehem, he stopped and helped her climb onto Yotie's back so she could travel the last few miles of her journey alone.

Before riding off, he said to her, "Mary, I will never forget you. And in time, I hope you will find a way to forgive me—Centurion Cornelius of Capernaum."

Those words echoed in her head as she rode the last few miles to Hebron. Alone once again, reality set in and she began to relive the horror of her encounter with the man.

She thought bitterly, *I can't imagine there will ever come a day when I will forgive the man who raped me and robbed me of my virginity . . . or did he?*

Chapter Ten

But the angel said unto him, "Fear not, Zachariah: for thy prayer is heard; and thy wife Elisabeth shall bear thee a son, and thou shalt call his name John."

Luke 1:13

MARY WAS RIDING YOTIE THROUGH the narrow streets of Halhul, looking for the turn-off to Hebron. A short distance beyond the town, she found the Old Mamre Road. Just as Elisabeth had said, there was Abraham's Oak, and she knew she was almost there. She nudged Yotie in the side and continued down the ancient road.

She had gone just a short distance when she heard someone calling her name, and there was her cousin standing by a Judas gate, arms outstretched, welcoming her. Elisabeth gathered her into her arms and then burst forth in a loud voice of praise, speaking formally as she and Zachariah did on a holy occasion:

"Blessed art Thou among women and blessed is the fruit of thy womb. And whence is this to me that the Mother

> *of my Lord should come to me? For behold as soon as the voice of thy salutation sounded in my ears, the infant in my womb leaped for joy; and blessed art Thou, that has believed, because those things shall be accomplished that were spoken to Thee by the Lord."*

Mary responded with words that came not from her but *through* her.

> *"Oh, how I praise the Lord. How I rejoice in God my Savior! For he took notice of his lowly servant girl, and now generation after generation forever shall call me blest of God."*

Mary was astonished that Elisabeth was walking around with the lithe steps of a twenty-year-old, hardly slowed down despite being nearly fifty-five years old and heavy with child.

Elisabeth was great company. A seasoned midwife, she had seen things in her many years of delivering babies that gave her a wealth of funny stories, which she told Mary with surprising irreverence and a bawdy wit. ("Don't tell Zachariah I said that!")

She got very serious when she told Mary the story of Gabriel's appearance to Zachariah.

Zachariah was going about his temple duties, as it was his week to perform the incense offering. Suddenly an angel appeared to him. Zachariah laughed when the angel told him that Elisabeth would conceive and bear a child. "We are too old to become parents," Zachariah said. "Do you have a sign to verify the truth of this prophecy?"

"I am Gabriel, sent from God. I do not need a sign. You will be punished for questioning God." Immediately, Zachariah was struck dumb and would not be able to speak again until the child was circumcised and formally named 'John,' later known as 'the Baptist.'

Mary listened in amazement. She knew none of Elisabeth or Zachariah's ancestors was named John, yet that was what they were naming their child, just as the angel had said. She closed her eyes, recalling Gabriel's message. *"So it is true. This is getting stranger by the moment . . . but I believe it is God's will. Let it be,"* Mary whispered.

As one week faded into another and Mary's menstrual blood did not reappear, she knew that she had to confide in Elisabeth.

"Elisabeth, you greeted me when I first arrived as though you knew I was carrying the Christ Child; and now I have reason to believe you were right. But are you absolutely sure?"

Elisabeth answered by taking her hand and leading her into a private room at the back of the house where she examined expectant mothers. Although she herself had never had a child, she had helped bring many babies into the world. She often boasted, "I may not have any children of my own, but I've helped bring more than my share into the world."

As Mary climbed onto the linen-draped table, Elisabeth laid out a few implements. Mary's eyes widened and her mouth fell open as she eyed what looked like instruments of torture.

"Just relax, Mary. I have been taking care of expectant mothers since long before you were born and I've yet to lose a patient to a simple examination. Just pull your legs up, put your feet on the bricks, and relax!"

Much to Mary's relief, Elisabeth quickly completed her examination, not using any of the instruments after all. She stood for a moment, chewing on her lower lip and frowning. Then she said, "Mary, never have I seen such an amazing thing. No doubt you are with child, yet you are still a virgin. Just as the prophets foretold, a virgin—you—will give birth to a child conceived by the Holy Ghost."

Mary was relieved that she was still a virgin, but her eyes filled with tears as she thought about the future—would Joseph and her family abandon her? She told Elisabeth all that had happened to her, beginning with the angel Gabriel's visit. When she had finished her incredible story, Elisabeth said, "So it seems that the prophecy is to be fulfilled, not with Joseph's seed, but with that of the Roman centurion, the lusty Cornelius."

Mary frowned and said, "But how will that be a fulfillment of the prophecy that a child of the House of David will be born?" It never occurred to her that the prophecy might be fulfilled through her mother's lineage of the House of David. And she agonized with the doubt that so many women have faced since the beginning of time—What child is this?

Elisabeth, with the wisdom of her gathering years, eased Mary's guilt and fears by assuring her that all of these events, regardless of how impossible they seemed on the surface, were according to God's will—the God who works in mysterious ways. "For with God, nothing shall be impossible," Elisabeth quoted the angel Gabriel.

The next three months were some of the happiest days of Mary's life. She was almost disappointed when she received a message from Joseph saying he was on his way to take her back to Nazareth. She was relieved that he had responded so quickly to her request that he come to Hebron, but she dreaded the moment when she would have to explain her pregnancy, hoping he wouldn't think her the worst kind of fallen woman.

Chapter Eleven

But while he thought on these things, behold, the angel of the Lord appeared unto him in a dream, saying, "Joseph, thou son of David, fear not to take unto thee Mary thy wife: for that which is conceived in her is of the Holy Ghost."

Matt. 1:20

JOSEPH WAS PUZZLED WHEN MARY disappeared. She had said that she and Magda were going to Magdala to visit Magda's family, but she had been gone for several weeks with no word. Her parents were as much in the dark as he, mystified over Mary's uncharacteristic behavior. And worse, they had heard that Magda had been seen a few times in Nazareth—without Mary.

Joseph was a patient man and he felt fortunate to be betrothed to a beautiful young girl like Mary, but he was beginning to wonder if he had made an unwise choice. And worse, he wondered if Mary had changed her mind. He knew he wasn't a very exciting man and he certainly wasn't going to win a prize for his looks, but he was descended from the royal line of David. He thought that Mary had always been a little impressed with his illustrious ancestry, although her mother, Anne, was also descended from that line—a distinction without merit since the descendant was a female. *Royal line indeed*, he thought scornfully. *What good is royalty without riches?*

But he had thought that Mary saw beyond all of that to his inner character. He was extremely pious, loved God and tried very hard to keep all of the commandments. He remained celibate although all of his friends laughed at him for being so pure, and often urged him to come with them to sample the delights of Magdala's many prostitutes.

Why would he be foolish enough to lie down with a harlot for a few minutes' purchased pleasure when he was betrothed to a marvelous girl like Mary? Since the first day he had seen her he had had eyes and desire for no one but his beloved Mary.

And now Joseph wondered if all of these hopes and dreams had been just a fantasy. For almost a year he had thought of nothing but Mary and their future together. But now everything was in doubt—everything but his feelings, they were as strong as ever.

"That's what I get for trying to be a good man. No good man remains unpunished, he just remains unwedded," he said to himself; then he added, ". . . and unbedded."

He tried to occupy himself in his carpentry shop, building tables and chairs and small household items for his customers. But mainly he was building a modest house to live in after he and Mary exchanged their wedding vows under the chuppah. Was all this effort for naught? Should he just put all of these plans on hold for the time being?

He didn't have to worry very long. Just after he visited Mary's parents an angel appeared to him in a dream saying that Mary was with her cousin Elisabeth in Hebron, where the Lord had instructed her to go. And the angel told Joseph to travel to Judea to escort Mary back to Nazareth. So despite his misgivings, he set out immediately for the southern highlands.

Joseph's doubts were swept away in a wave of love when he saw Mary. She glowed with happiness, the few pounds she had gained only added to her beauty; and the questions he had wanted to ask seemed unimportant now. He was too happy to see her to harbor any doubts. And she looked happy to see him as well. *She does still love me,* Joseph thought. Nothing else mattered.

Mary was happy to see Joseph but not looking forward to the conversation they were going to have. Dreading the questions he must have and the explanation he deserved, she searched her mind for the right words. They had ridden just a few miles away from Hebron when Mary began to explain.

"Joseph, there is so much I need to tell you that I hardly know where to begin. But after I have explained myself and told you all that has happened to me, I will understand if you want to break off our engagement."

Joseph reached for Mary's hand, held it close to his cheek, and reassured her, "Do not be concerned, Mary. The angel who visited you also appeared to me in a dream and told me that you are going to give birth to the Christ Child; that I should not hesitate to take you as my wife because you are still a virgin. Yes, it's a little hard to believe, but I'm convinced that it is all part of God's plan for us. You need not explain and I would rather not know."

So Mary kept all of these things in her heart, telling no one but Elisabeth and Magda the amazing story of her encounter with the centurion Cornelius. Naturally, she wavered just a bit in the face of all these events that were churning around her, tossing her around like a kite in a windstorm, a mere child with a history worthy of someone who had lived a few lifetimes.

But slowly she came to accept in her heart that the Holy Ghost had come upon her, that Cornelius was just an instrument in God's plan and that she, a virgin, was going to give birth to the Christ Child.

After a tearful reunion with her relieved but bewildered family, Mary was bombarded with questions that she answered vaguely. "God told me to go to Hebron for a few months to be with Cousin Elisabeth." Joachim looked at her incredulously and was tempted to punish her. But then he looked at Joseph, who stood protectively by her side, and he remembered that Mary was no longer subject to him.

The next morning, just as the sun was showing a ribbon of pink in the east, Mary started the hike up the mountain to visit Magda. As she walked through the familiar streets of home, she thanked God for letting her get back safely to her beloved Nazareth.

Just beyond the village spring, she turned onto the road that would eventually narrow into the mountain path to Orpah's Corpus. Orpah had planted Lebanon cedar trees along each side of the last hundred yards of the path. They held onto their spikey needles year-round and provided shelter in the winter and shade in the summer to those who climbed the mountain to visit her. But the recent February rains made for a slippery climb for Mary, now four months with child.

I wonder what Magda will say when she sees my swelling stomach and I tell her what happened. Although she was sure Magda would get that squint-eyed look and interrupt her with endless questions, Mary knew she could count on Magda to support her. Magda was the least judgmental person she had ever known. All these thoughts swirled round in her head as she struggled up the steep mountain path.

Her extra weight slowed her down and she was practically out of breath when she lifted the heavy knocker to the front door.

The door was flung open. "Mary!" Magda exclaimed and grabbed her in a bear hug. Then Heli enveloped both of them in her arms and they cried until they started laughing. As soon as Heli went off toward the kitchen, Mary began to talk. Magda sat listening, quiet for once, only her flashing eyes responding to the incredible story.

Then Magda spoke with more sincerity than Mary had ever heard in her voice. "Mary, I thought I knew you better than any other person, so forgive me for doubting this fantasy tale and wondering if you are deceiving yourself as well as your trusted friend. But this is all you need to know: I am with you. I don't care what has happened or whose child you are carrying. My love for you is unconditional and we will get through this together. I plan to be your best friend forever as well as your son's. I can't wait to meet him and see what a Messiah looks like!"

Chapter Twelve

There be three things which are too wonderful for me, yea, four which I know not: The way of an eagle in the air; the way of a serpent upon a rock; the way of a ship in the midst of the sea; and the way of a man with a maid.

Proverbs 30:18-19

AARON WAS A *BA'AL TEKIYAH.* He had blown the shofar when Rebekah walked down the aisle during their wedding ceremony, and Mary and Joseph asked him to blow it for their wedding as well.

Orpah had generously offered them the use of the lower garden for the wedding ceremony and, blessed by an early spring, it was abloom with colorful flowers. Magda and Heli had seen to every detail, determined that Mary's wedding would be an example of elegant simplicity.

The first blasts sounded and Mary began to walk down the flower-strewn steps to join Joseph under the canopy where he stood with the rabbi from the synagogue in Nazareth. Anne had sewn a beautiful wedding gown for Mary right after she and Joseph signed the ketubah, but she had had to let out the seams a few inches to accommodate Mary's swelling hips and stomach.

Anne puzzled, *I wonder what happened in Hebron*? But she kept these musings to herself.

Mary was regal, her glowing smile belying her disquiet as she acknowledged her neighbors, friends and family, who stood in her honor as she walked past them. As she repeated the ancient vows that would bind her to Joseph, no one would have guessed that she was somewhat anxious about the next seven days and nights she would spend in seclusion with her new husband. *I wonder how Joseph is going to react when I tell him that I must remain a virgin until after the birth of my child,* she worried.

Joachim blessed Mary with the ritual seven blessings and Joseph stepped forward with a small gold ring. "Behold, you are made holy for me according to the religion of Moses and of Israel."

Then Joseph proclaimed a blessing over a cup of wine that he and Mary drank, and crushed the cup under his foot, a reminder that into each life some rain must fall.

Hours later, Jacob proposed a toast to the couple, which was followed with toast after toast by several of the guests. Finally, Joseph took Mary by the hand and led her into the chuppah, where they would spend the next seven days in seclusion. The wedding guests began to make their way up the garden path to the mansion to begin the evening's feasting and drinking.

Several of Joseph's groomsmen loitered in earshot of the tent, waiting to hear the bride's yelps and cries of pain when the marriage was consummated. But after nearly an hour of near silence, they looked at each other quizzically and wandered up the garden path in search of food and wine. They drank a silent toast to the happy couple, leaving many to wonder why the usual congratulatory speech was omitted.

Inside the tent, Joseph hurriedly untied the curtains, which Anne had doubled-lined to provide privacy for the newlyweds. Mary sat down heavily on the pallet and began to speak. "Joseph," she said softly, "there is something I need to tell you that you're probably not going to like."

As the last curtain panel pooled onto the floor, Joseph turned to her and said, "Mary, I already know what you're going to say because the angel who told me that I shouldn't hesitate to take you as my wife also told me that you must remain a virgin until your child is born. So just lie down beside me and relax, my beautiful wife. You must trust me that we can enjoy intimacy and still protect your virginity."

Chapter Thirteen

And so it was that, while they were there, the days were accomplished that she should be delivered.

Luke 2:6

FOLLOWING MARY'S MARRIAGE TO JOSEPH, her relationship with Magda began to suffer a bit, mostly because Magda wasn't the kind of woman Joseph wanted his wife to have for a friend. And Magda did admit to having a few quirks that might be viewed as wickedness by those who thought women should be subservient to men. Joseph thought her lifestyle and her refusal to keep her thoughts to herself symptoms of an evil nature.

Joseph was devout and believed that Mary shared his religious views; that they would set perfect examples for their future children by strictly adhering to the ancient laws. He saw Magda as a deterrent to that plan. He thought she was irreverent and drank too much wine.

But she argued she was practicing the wisdom of Solomon: "Eat, drink, and be merry; enjoy the fruits of your labor." Much as she disagreed with most of Solomon's philosophy, she admitted he did have a few good ideas—that being one of them. "Especially if the fruits are fermented," she added.

Magda thought Joseph was a bore and a bit dim-witted, but she was careful not to criticize him to keep the peace with Mary, her treasured friend, whom she feared she was slowly losing.

During one of their disagreements—a frequent occurrence now that Mary and Joseph were married—Mary warned her, "Magda, one of these days your sharp tongue is going to get you into trouble."

Seemingly unperturbed but inwardly annoyed, Magda replied, "Perhaps, but then my sharp tongue will get me out of it." *Or abba's money will get me out of it,* she added silently.

Magda never stayed angry with Mary for very long when they had one of their quarrels, and she quickly extended the olive branch to her friend. "Mary, I'm sure you have heard that Caesar has ordered a census and that you and Joseph will have to travel to Bethlehem to register. With your delivery time approaching, you don't want to take a chance on finding lodging. Why don't I ask my Uncle Obadiah if you can stay with him while you're there? His wife died recently and he's all alone in his big house. I am sure that you and Joseph would be welcome to stay with him."

But Joseph wouldn't hear of it; he wanted nothing to do with Magda or her relatives. He and Mary would manage without her help.

In accordance with the many prophecies that the Son of God would be born in the City of David, Mary started making plans to travel with Joseph to Bethlehem. "We can probably stay with my Uncle Samuel if his sons and daughters aren't there," Joseph said. "But surely, even if they have no room, we can find a room in the inn."

Mary was exhausted just thinking about it: another difficult trip of many days into the southern highlands. In spite of her dreadful experience when she had visited Elisabeth, once again they were traveling with a caravan; although this time they were not traveling the dangerous Roman Road and she had a man to protect her.

But after just one day, Mary began to have misgivings about making the tiring trip; and worse than the fatigue, she was cramping and worried that the baby might come early, even before they arrived in Bethlehem.

All of her life she had tried to do God's will. How had she been transformed seemingly overnight into a young woman who constantly had to face life-threatening perils, riding endless miles on a donkey for long days along dusty roads, worried about giving birth to a child with no one to help her? And Joseph was no help . . . birthing was woman's work and men were banned from this blessed but gory event. And just as well. Most men were not comfortable discussing the murky world of birthing and babies, and were repulsed by the sight of blood not drawn in battle.

When they finally arrived in Bethlehem, Mary was too exhausted and in too much pain to dismount the donkey. She waited outside while Joseph went into his uncle's house to ask if he had room for them. She sat watching the weary travelers pass looking discouraged and wandering aimlessly. Their grim faces told her that she and Joseph were not going to find a place to stay.

Joseph came out of the house looking dejected. "Mary, there is no room for us in my uncle's house, or in the inn, or anywhere else in this town. Uncle Nathan says we should just stay in the stable with his animals because he doubts that we will find anything else, even in a nearby town.

At this point Mary was beyond caring where they stayed. She knew she couldn't delay another minute; her baby was on the way and she had to find a place for her child to be born—even a stable.

"Joseph," Mary said, close to panicking, "Let's just go to the stable . . . now! And ask your aunt if she knows a midwife who can help me. My baby is coming. Hurry!"

She walked painfully into the stable, and immediately her nostrils were assaulted with the noisome smells of barnyard animals. She was saddened that the Son of God would be born in a lean-to that was hardly more than a pigsty.

Joseph's aunt and two other women ran into the stable. They found Mary lying on her side on the dirt floor holding on to her stomach and moaning. They began to massage her back and stomach with aloe and balsam oil and to murmur encouragingly into her ear. "Don't worry now, sweet Mary. Every new mother thinks that her baby is at the door when it is still hours away. Help will be here in plenty of time to welcome your little one into the world."

Their comments were meant to reassure her but she began to worry even more when they said, "The midwife is tending to another birth, but her assistant, Gomer, is coming." The women didn't seem to feel any sense of urgency. One of them was actually whistling as she began to sweep and clean; another one was lazily tethering the animals off to one side, clearing the area where the birthing would take place.

Mary was grateful for their efforts but she was not concerned with anything but getting help with her baby's birth. "I hate to keep on about this," she said to the whistler, "but do you have any idea when the assistant will be here?"

"Don't you worry about Gomer. She is dependable as the day is long and is nearly as capable as old Hannah, the mid-wife. She lives close by and will be here in two shakes of a lamb's tail."

Mary hoped that was true; her pains had become fairly intense and she had a feeling something was not quite right—there was a sharp pain in her lower groin that worried her. The pressure in her lower back was worsening and she began to worry that there was a serious problem. But she chastised herself, remembering what her mother had said: "You need to prepare mentally for what's to come. The birth of a woman's first child is very painful. After all, you're trying to push a watermelon through a grape skin."

She slept for a moment, but she was startled awake by Joseph shouting from his post just outside the stable door, "Good news, Mary, help is here." Seconds later, a dwarfish-looking person came through the door and rushed to Mary's side. A no-nonsense kind of woman, she got right to work, feeling Mary's stomach with practiced hands and listening for the baby's heartbeat. She nodded encouragingly at Mary, kneeled down and began to probe between her legs.

Mary was alarmed when, after a few moments, Gomer rose with a worried look on her face. "Hmmph! We'll have to wait for old Hannah to handle this one. I'm not skilled with the knife yet." She told one of the women to get word to the midwife to come quickly, that she was up against a wall and didn't know how to proceed.

Mary couldn't believe her ears . . . *knife*? She had never actually attended a birthing, but she had heard her mother discussing it with her friends. Never had they mentioned using a knife. Maybe Gomer meant that the cutting of the umbilical cord would require a knife, but didn't it always? Wasn't that normal? She was dripping perspiration now, worry beads of sweat standing out on her forehead.

As the time dragged by, she dozed off and on. This ordeal had started during the morning and now it was late in the afternoon. She was exhausted from the pain, the lack of sleep, and nauseated from the smell of the animals whose musty space she had invaded. Why had she relented and accompanied Joseph to Bethlehem, law or no law? She wanted her mother, she wanted Elisabeth, she even wanted Magda!

She wished she could go to sleep and wake up with it all over. But Gomer insisted that she move into the squatting position, where she was held up by one woman on each side and another one behind her.

The support of the women did little to relieve the stress brought on by squatting for so long, and the worst was yet to come. The bricks they placed under her feet were wrapped in soft cloths, but she felt as if she were crouching over hot coals. Her knees were aching from the strain of being in such an unnatural position for so long. And worse, the women were getting tired now and growing impatient with her cries at each contraction. So she bit her tongue and repeated her mantra with each pain, "Lord, are you watching me now? Lord, are you watching me now?"

No wonder men don't have babies. They would never have the patience or the stamina to handle such a painful ordeal. Where is Joseph? I hope he didn't make a detour into the synagogue to pray, she thought with mounting frustration toward her feckless husband, who had left to fetch the midwife almost an hour ago.

When the women told Joseph that there was a problem with the birth, they sent him to find the village mid-wife, who lived just outside the city. After making several wrong turns, he finally located the woman, who was just returning from delivering another baby. But she refused to go with him until he paid her. Reluctantly, Joseph counted out her fee from his dwindling funds and, his money belt much lighter, motioned to the midwife to follow him.

On the way back to town, he explained that his wife was having their first child and that she seemed to think there was a problem.

The mid-wife laughed and said, "Oh, that's what all new mothers think—that there's a problem. They have a hard time believing that all of that pain is just a normal part of childbirth."

When the stable came into view, he began to run and shout, "Mary, the mid-wife is here."

But when the midwife heard the whispered concerns of the other women in the stable, the look on her face made Mary wonder what she had been told about her condition. *Was her baby all right? Was she going to be cut with a knife? Was she going to die?*

Hannah, a wizened old woman with skin like a withered prune, hurriedly washed her hands, nudged Gomer aside and knelt to take a look.

Mary's eyes widened as she took in Hannah's blood-spattered clothing. She knew that the woman had come directly from delivering another baby, but was all that blood and gore normal? And it certainly wasn't her own blood and gore, which sickened her.

After briefly feeling Mary's stomach and kneeling down to take a look, Hannah rose, removing her soiled garments as she walked over to confer with Gomer. She tied on a clean linen shift, which brought great comfort to Mary, who wanted her child to have every possible advantage to enter the world a healthy baby. *'Every advantage' is a pretty silly notion for someone who is giving birth in a pigsty*, she grimaced, wondering what Magda would say about her predicament.

Hannah knelt in front of Mary and began to examine her more thoroughly, probing with her fingers to find the baby's head. But after a moment, she stood and said, "Well, I've seen a lot of strange things in my time, but this is a first . . . a real mystery. Young lady, you are about to give birth, but you are still a virgin.

"Gomer, you were right," Hannah said. "This delivery is going to be a bit out of the ordinary. I'll have to make a small excision. Her pregnancy isn't just a mystery, it is a miracle."

"Well, I'm glad you know I wasn't exaggerating," Gomer replied, relieved that she hadn't been wrong about the problem.

The women helped Mary lie down, which was such a relief it brought tears to her eyes. Hannah told Gomer to prepare a solution of wine mixed with a generous measure of myrrh for Mary to drink; and she applied a salve to the area to deaden the feeling somewhat. Gratefully, Mary drank the mixture and gradually drifted off into a light sleep. Satisfied that her patient was mildly sedated, Hannah instructed the women to hold Mary firmly in place.

The procedure Hannah was about to perform would require a steady hand and an immobile patient to prevent damage to the mother or the child. Hannah took a deep breath and began to cut away the membrane that was blocking the opening to the birth canal. Rare as this surgery was—the timing was most unusual—Hannah was an experienced midwife and she finished the simple task with a few deft strokes.

But most of the women, even Gomer, had to look away as Hannah wielded her sharp knife. Although Mary did not cry out, her eyes rolled back in her head and her moaning brought some of the women to tears.

Hannah allowed Mary to rest after the painful surgery, but soon they lifted her into the birthing position again. Hannah instructed her to push with all of her strength each time she felt a contraction and to breathe deeply in between. "Push and breathe, push and breathe," she was repeating in a sing-song.

But Mary was pushing and praying, "Lord, are you watching me now? Lord, are you watching me now?"

Just when she thought she would die if the pain got any worse, Hannah told her to stop pushing. "Just let your body go limp and breathe deeply," she instructed. Seconds later, Mary began to feel a stinging sensation that began in her groin and spread throughout her body.

Hannah assured her, "You're doing fine. There's the head. And now the shoulders . . . and . . . Glory Hallelujah! You have a beautiful big baby boy." Moments later Mary heard the most joyful sound she had ever heard: Jesus whimpered.

She closed her eyes and said, "Thank you, Lord."

Gomer tied off the umbilical cord and cut it with a sharp knife; she cleansed the baby with salt and oil and laid him on Mary's breast. Jesus opened his mouth, fastened onto her nipple and immediately started suckling.

So it was there among the animals in a stable that Mary brought forth her first born son, the Christ Child. From the moment she had felt the small flutterings of life inside her body, she had begun to love her child. But nothing had prepared her for the emotions she felt as this tiny creature cleaved to her breast, so totally innocent and helpless, so dependent on her.

When Jesus was filled, he nodded off to sleep on Mary's breast. The midwife said to her, "Now you need to sleep as well to regain your strength. Your work has just begun." She took the baby Jesus from her and, to ensure that his limbs would grow straight, wrapped his arms and legs tight against him in swaddling clothes. Then she laid Jesus in the straw-filled manger.

Mary was not accustomed to the ease and luxury that some of her acquaintances expected, Magda being one of them, but she was saddened now that she had not provided more fitting surroundings for the birth of the Son of God.

Word spread quickly around Bethlehem and into the surrounding hills where shepherds were tending to their sheep that a special boy child—always a cause for celebration that a boy *and not a girl!*—had been born. The Mosaic law concerning female births required twice as long for purification than it did for a male birth. When Magda learned of the law, she said, "Cleanliness is next to Godliness. For a woman, cleanliness is next to impossible."

When Jesus was eight days old, Joseph and Mary took him to the temple for the Bris—the covenant between Abraham and God who commanded that 'every man child shall be circumcised on the eighth day following his birth.'

Joseph declared that the child's name was JESUS.

Chapter Fourteen

And when they were departed, behold, the angel of the Lord appeareth to Joseph in a dream, saying, "Arise, and take the young child and his mother, and flee into Egypt, and be thou there until I bring thee word: for Herod will seek the young child to destroy him."

Matt. 2:13

JOSEPH AWOKE FROM A DISTURBING dream and knew that he and Mary and Jesus were in danger. "Mary, we must pack all of our belongings and leave Bethlehem this very night," he whispered.

Mary looked bewildered. She wondered what had come over Joseph so suddenly. Everything had been all right when they had gone to bed, but now, just a few hours later, he was grim-faced and saying they were in danger.

"Joseph, what has happened to make you say such a thing? And where are we going?" Mary asked, pulling Jesus out of his crib and holding him close to her.

"I have had another visit from our guardian angel. He came to me in a dream and warned me to take you and Jesus to Egypt. King Herod has heard that the Christ Child—our son!—has been born, and he has decreed that all male children in the vicinity of Bethlehem under the age of two be slain. Herod is a mad man and he fears that his throne is threatened by the birth of a Messiah who could eventually become King of the Jews. Jesus is the very child he means to kill."

Egypt is not that far away from Israel as the crow flies. But they were not flying and 250 miles is a grueling distance on foot. Their journey was especially difficult because they were traveling with an infant. There were desolate spots along the Gaza Road and food was often scarce. Mary worried that her milk would not be plentiful enough if she didn't get more to eat. Often they had to purchase food from the people along the way as they traveled the road south to Egypt. She wondered if she would ever be able to return to Nazareth with her husband and child and just live the ordinary life she longed for.

When they approached the land of the Philistines, they walked only at night. Mary was comforted when she saw that the little cloud was following them. As always, she felt the hand of God guiding her.

Their destination was Heliopolis near the Nile River. When the exhausted family finally arrived, they were welcomed by a large enclave of Jewish people who had fled Israel to escape Herod's murderous decree. Mary was relieved to see a couple of the women from Hebron that Elisabeth had introduced her to. Relieved to see a few familiar faces Mary thought, *Maybe this won't be so bad after all.*

The sun was just coming up over the Galilee, spreading fingers of pink and gold over the water, when Magda jumped out of bed and dressed, wanting to catch her father before he left to check on the incoming fishing boats. She ran upstairs to the look-out he had built on the roof to view his fishery and factory in the distance. He was sitting at his desk, working on some plans for a new fishery a few miles down the coast. Benjamin had heard that Herod was nosing around in Maoziyah, and there was talk that he was planning to build a city there. Benjamin had been thinking about opening another fishing operation in the area for some time. After hearing the rumor about Herod's plans, he made the decision to go ahead with the expansion to get ahead of the others that would have the same idea.

Magda walked up behind Benjamin and kissed him on top of his head. A handsome man with silvery flowing hair, he was vain about his looks and was very proud that he had kept his thick mane of hair well into his later years.

Magda perched on the desk beside him. "Abba, Mary has had her baby—a boy—and I want to see them before they leave for Egypt. Will you go with me to Bethlehem?"

"They're going to Egypt?" Benjamin asked. "I guess they're leaving Judea to escape Herod's order to kill all the newborn male babies. Surely Mary and Joseph know that they are welcome to stay in the House of Benjamin, which would provide a safe haven for them. Herod wouldn't dare darken my door with his thugs. I know too many of his embarrassing secrets," he laughed grimly. "I know where all the bodies are buried—wives, sons and daughters—and that's the short list.

"Even Augustus Caesar supposedly said, 'I'd rather be Herod's pig than his son.'" (Herod had had three of his sons murdered but was too pious to eat pork.) "But I guess Joseph wouldn't consent to anything as sensible as staying here because he doesn't want to be obligated to you. One day his foolish pride will be the undoing of him."

"Well, that's not the worst of it," Magda said. "He even allowed his son to be born in a stable rather than accept the hospitality of Uncle Obadiah; they were welcome to stay with him while they were in Bethlehem. But Joseph refused my offer lest I gain some sort of imagined advantage over him. I wish Mary had never laid eyes on that old dullard."

Benjamin walked over to the railing and looked down toward the seashore. His fishing boats were just coming in and he smiled as the fishermen emptied their nets of the hundreds of fish they had caught. It had been a good night—the fish were biting and not many would be thrown back today—and the men would be celebrating after they were paid their generous wages.

When Benjamin had taken over running the fisheries, the first thing he had done was to pay the men bonuses when they exceeded their quotas. It was a brilliant move: the House of Benjamin consistently outranked its competitors.

Benjamin often boasted, "Other firms watch the bottom line; the House of Benjamin watches out for the bottoms of the men responsible for the bottom line. Happy employees make for happy, prosperous employers."

He turned back around to Magda, looking pleased. "Now where were we?"

"We were on our way to Bethlehem. But mostly we were talking about Mary's dolt of a husband, Joseph."

"A dolt and worse—a religious fanatic," Benjamin said. "I must admit I was a bit surprised when I met him for the first time. Considering his royal lineage, you would have expected a little sharper stick than Joseph. I think Mary's father just sold her out to the first man that came along. I guess Joachim was impressed by Joseph's illustrious heritage. But when you consider that a couple of his ancestors were David, a musician, warmonger and adulterer; and the wealthy Solomon, a poet and a misogynist—although he had 700 wives and 300 concubines—what's there to be impressed about unless the brideprice was generous? And I know for a fact that it was hardly more than a pittance; far less than the customary fifty shekels."

Magda was surprised. Her father was never very generous in his praise of his fellow man, but to criticize the legendary David and his famous son Solomon was a little extreme even for Benjamin.

Oh well, she thought, *what do I care about Joseph and his illustrious ancestors? The only thing I care about is seeing Mary and her baby.*

"So now that we've got that settled, can we leave first thing tomorrow?" she asked.

Magda was not easy to refuse. When she wanted something, she didn't give up until she got it. And after Benjamin had sent her to live with Orpah in Nazareth, his guilt usually overcame his objections to most requests she made. Actually, he had planned to visit his attorney in Jerusalem and then go on to Joppa to check out a fishery that was for sale; so he could take care of that business during the trip to Bethlehem.

They set off the next morning, traveling in one of the carriages that the House of Benjamin kept for long journeys. Benjamin never traveled far without his two body guards, so there were four of them traveling that rocky road into the southern highlands. With one guard riding the lead horse and the other in the rear, Magda and Benjamin felt fairly safe from the perils of the road.

After spending two days in Jerusalem, they traveled a few miles farther south to Bethlehem. But when they arrived, they learned that Mary and Joseph had already left for Egypt.

Before she could start on him, Benjamin said, "Magda, now we're talking about a journey of a few hundred miles. I didn't agree to travel to another continent." But he finally gave in after Magda convinced him she was going to Egypt with or without him.

"Magda, one of these days when I'm dead and gone—this trip might well kill me—you're going to wish you had taken it a little easier on your old abba."

"Nonsense, Benjamin." (She used his first name when she was trying to level the playing field, but who had the advantage here?) "What has happened to your sense of adventure? Besides, you've always wanted to see the pyramids and the Great Sphinx; you can do that while you're there."

So the foursome headed to Joppa on the coast of the Mediterranean, where Benjamin inspected the fishery that was for sale. Magda was content to wade in the shallows and hunt for sea shells while Benjamin took care of business. But after two days, she started to ask him when they could leave for Egypt. Rather than listen to her complaints that she was bored, he quickly wrapped up his business and booked passage on a boat sailing to Pelusium on the Nile Delta—the Gateway to Egypt.

As they sailed southwest out of Joppa, Magda quipped, "Now leaving Israel. Oy vey."

Benjamin replied, "Oy vey indeed. Every time I leave Israel it saddens me, particularly if I am going to Egypt. I am always afraid old Pharaoh will take a liking to me and won't let me leave when I'm ready to go back home."

The trip to Egypt with her father was to become one of her favorite memories, and she was glad he had agreed to go with her. When he got away from his businesses for a few days, he became a completely different person—a witty, adventuresome man who was excellent company.

Even Benjamin seemed to get a little excited when they pulled up to the dock in Pelusium and learned that Goshen/Heliopolis was just a few miles away. This was the area that Joseph had told his relatives in Bethlehem they planned to settle in.

The mid-day Egyptian sun was scorching hot and they hired a carriage with a brightly striped awning to travel the remaining distance in comfort. Reclining on the colorful cushions, Magda warbled, "Just call me Cleopatra: 'All strange and terrible events are welcome, but comfort we despise.'"

But Benjamin was tiring and not in the mood for Magda's theatrics. "Listen, Cleopatra, if we don't find them in the land of Goshen, we are turning around and heading back home. This trip has turned into an odyssey."

In Goshen Benjamin asked some Egyptian men for directions to the Jewish community. The men were sitting outside in the shade discussing the day's events. They stared in awe at the carriage, at Magda's red hair, and then at the rest of her. Now they really would have something to talk about.

Following the men's directions, they traveled the road toward the river. They had gone just a short distance when they saw a young woman walking down the road, carrying a baby in her right arm, balancing a water jug on her left shoulder.

Some things never change, Magda thought as she bounded from the carriage and nearly knocked Mary to the ground with a bear hug.

Benjamin helped Mary into the carriage and they drove the half mile to Mary and Joseph's house, Jesus sitting on Magda's lap.

Magda was relieved that Joseph was out of the house working. Shortly after arriving in Heliopolis, he had hired on as an apprentice with an Egyptian builder who was impressed by Joseph's talent for woodworking and construction. That was no surprise . . . Joseph was meticulous in all things.

As they climbed out of the carriage in front of a small house, Mary pointed toward the river and said, "The famous pyramids are just a short distance beyond the far side of the river. If you're interested, you should visit them while you're here. It's only about thirty kilometers to Giza, where the largest one is. You can board a ferry to cross the Nile and walk the remaining distance. But of course, if you don't want to walk you can hire a litter."

Benjamin said, "Well, I plan to start back to Israel tomorrow, so maybe I'll make a detour west to Giza before heading back. Do they allow you to go inside?"

Jesus was cranky and Mary reached over to put his thumb in his mouth. "Yes, there are visitor entrances. We haven't visited because Joseph thinks it would be sacrilegious to disturb the burial place of King Khufu and his queen. But those who have visited say it is a bit eerie with guards posted throughout the narrow passageways. And it's a good thing they're there; vandals are forever trying to find a way to steal the many treasures buried there for the king and queen to use in the afterlife. You would think that Joseph, being a builder, would be curious about its construction. They say it is in such perfect alignment that not even a needle can be inserted between the joints of those huge limestone blocks."

"In that case, I am definitely going there before I head back to . . . ," Benjamin nearly said, 'civilization,' but caught himself in time to say, "Israel."

But Magda called him on it later. "Abba, the Egyptians are more civilized than the Israelites in many respects—most notably, in their treatment of women. And to whom did the Israelites have to go begging during the great famine of Jacob's era? True, I'm forgetting that Jacob's son Joseph, my favorite character from the scriptures, was responsible for Egypt's stockpiling grain during the pre-famine years. But did you know that many famous Roman and Greek physicians attended the medical school in Alexandria? I'm surprised to discover that you have a touch of xenophobia, world traveler that you are."

"Well, I guess you don't want me to come back to escort you back home, aywa Cleopatra?"

After lunch Mary began to tell Magda and Benjamin about Jesus' birth in Bethlehem and the *bris* ceremony when they named him Jesus.

"Jesus?" Benjamin asked, surprised. "Why did you name him Jesus?"

Mary just smiled and said the name came to her in a dream. Benjamin rolled his eyes and looked over at Magda, who simply shrugged. *Women,* he thought and abruptly rose to leave, saying he would see Magda in a couple of months.

Magda was relieved when she was finally alone with Mary so they could talk freely. As the afternoon shadows lengthened, she said, "Mary, is there a chance you have any wine in the house? You know I want to drink a toast to your son, the Messiah."

Mary looked nervously toward the door. "Well, I guess one glass wouldn't hurt. Joseph keeps some on hand for special occasions. And what could be more special than my best friend meeting my firstborn son?"

"My sentiments exactly! Let me hold Jesus while you play hostess. You don't think he'll have an accident, do you?" Magda said, holding Jesus aloft.

"No, Magda, Jesus doesn't have accidents; his offerings are by divine design. But in your honor he is thoroughly wrapped in clean swaddling so you'll probably never know when it happens. Ordinarily, he is uncovered back there and I've learned to read the signs when he's about to go. So I usually catch him before he makes a mess."

Magda wrinkled her nose and thought to herself, *Ah, Motherhood!*

When Mary returned with a bottle of wine and two cups, Magda said, "Mary, 'divine design'? That was funny! That's quite a change from the Miss Mary all sweetness and light that I first met in Nazareth about a hundred years ago."

Mary laughed. "Magda, after what I have been through during the past two years—well, all right, it does seem more like a hundred—it was either develop a sense of humor or die. You can laugh or cry, so I chose to laugh.

"What about you, Magda? How's Orpah? How's Heli? How's your love life?"

Magda dandled Jesus on her knee and chortled, "Big as ever, great, and not so great, in that order."

The afternoon raced by as the two friends sat talking, catching up on all they had missed; filling in the blanks of the past several months.

But when Mary started to describe the details of Jesus' birth, Magda put her palm up. "Stop right there, enough!" Magda didn't want to hear anything that would bring back memories of Lazarus' birth. It didn't take much to bring back the sounds of her mother's screaming.

As Mary talked she put Jesus to her breast to hush his hungry cries, a rite of motherhood that was almost too intimate for Magda to watch. She knew she was witnessing one of the most poignant moments a woman experiences in life; and the beauty of Jesus cleaving to Mary's breast brought tears to her eyes. *I'll probably never know the satisfaction of such an act of love*, she thought wistfully.

When Joseph arrived, it was like someone had pulled a cloud over the sun. Magda had sat talking with Mary for hours, perfectly content when it was just the two of them. But when Joseph walked in, suddenly she became aware of the crudeness of her surroundings. Mary and Joseph's home was but a step above a hovel.

Joseph acknowledged Magda's presence with barely concealed resentment. He said a quick hello before abruptly disappearing into the back of the house. *Oh no*, Magda thought, *I can't spend even one night here with Joseph treating me like that. I'll just check into the inn where abba is staying.*

When Mary saw Magda eyeing their small house and its crude furnishings, she whispered, "Joseph keeps saying there is no point in wasting money on this place because we are not going to remain in Egypt very long. But I do wonder just how long it will be until it's safe to return to Israel. At any rate, when we do go back I want to live in Nazareth."

Magda raised an eyebrow and said, "Mary, why Nazareth? I'm surprised you don't want to move to Sepphoris, where your grandparents live. It's a wonderful city—so much more to do there than in boring Nazareth. After Magdala it's my favorite city in Galilee, particularly now that Herod is planning to move his capital from there to Maoziyah. Sepphoris will be a much more pleasant place after he leaves."

"Magda, my parents moved away from Sepphoris after Herod ruined it. I refuse to live anywhere named after Herod—*Autocratis.* He should have named it *Despot.*"

"Mary, you have developed quite a wicked sense of humor since moving to Egypt. I'm surprised to find that you have a little Gypsy in your soul. I find it very appealing, but I have a feeling your friends back in Nazareth won't especially like it."

Mary laughed, nodding in agreement. "Well, I find that the longer I stay away from Nazareth and my family the more I feel myself changing, *toughening up,* as you put it. But I love Nazareth as much as you love Magdala. It's my favorite place on earth. How about you, Magda? Where do you spend most of your time these days?"

Magda took the sleeping Jesus back into her arms and walked outside into the tiny courtyard to get some fresh air. When Joseph was around, she found it difficult to breathe.

"When I'm in Galilee, I divide my time between Magdala and Nazareth. Lately, I spend as much time as possible with Heli and Orpah. Orpah and I have grown close recently in spite of my resentment toward her when I first moved to Nazareth. And I spend a lot more time with abba nowadays. We are finally on good terms, although I'll probably always have some resentment toward him for sending me away after my mother died.

"But when you and Joseph return to Nazareth, I am going to be like the fourth member of your family. Whether Joseph likes it or not, I'm going to be Jesus' second mother . . . well, make that big sister."

Chapter Fifteen

And Jesus increased in wisdom and stature, and in favour with God and man.

Luke 2:52

MAGDA WAS SHOPPING IN THE market place in Nazareth when she heard a familiar voice. Anne was buying incense at a nearby stall. Magda went over to ask her about Mary. "Magda, what a pleasant surprise . . . are you just visiting Nazareth?" Anne asked.

Magda, impatient to get past the small talk to ask about Mary and Jesus, flipped her hand back and forth, and asked, "When are Mary and Joseph returning from Egypt?"

"You didn't know? They moved back a few months ago. You won't believe how big Jesus is. They are staying with us temporarily while Joseph adds on to their house. You know he built a small house for them before they married, but they have outgrown it because they have another son, James. And we're all excited because Mary is expecting another child any day now. We are hoping for a girl this time."

Magda was a little hurt that Mary had not got in touch with her when she returned to Nazareth. But her momentary disappointment at Mary's omission turned to excitement at the prospect of seeing her and Jesus. She knew Mary still loved her, and she knew that Mary was not herself. She was Joseph's wife, a union that shackled her to judgments that didn't reflect her own values, but those of the religious zealot she had married.

Magda asked Anne if she could accompany her back to the house. Her shopping forgotten, Magda took Anne's arm and they started walking hurriedly to the same house Mary had grown up in, now bursting at the seams with grown-ups and children.

It was as if no time had passed, as if nothing had changed between the two friends. Mary greeted Magda joyfully, laughing and crying, hugging and kissing her. "Magda, I have missed you so much. I even missed the fights." They embraced again, ending it only when Magda pulled back to take a long look at her friend.

"Mary, Anne said you're expecting another baby. From the looks of you, we had better call the midwife. Have you got a cradle in there too?"

Mary jabbed her old friend playfully and replied, "That's what it feels like . . . a cradle *and* the kitchen table. I guess I'm going to have another big baby. Jesus and James weighed over eight pounds each at birth. Did you see them outside?"

"Umm, maybe," Magda said. "I saw a couple of boys, but they looked too big to be Jesus and his younger brother."

"No, they are my sons; they're pretty big for their age. Let's go out and say hello."

James was playing leapfrog with some of the other boys, but Jesus was alone, sitting under a big oak tree reading from the Tanakh. Magda sat down beside him and took his hand in hers.

"Jesus, I am your mother's best friend, Mary Magdalene."

"Oh, I know who you are, but ima calls you Magda."

"Yes, that's what my best friends call me. So please call me Magda because you and I are going to be best friends."

And from that day forward that's what they were . . . and eventually more than friends . . . and more than lovers.

Mary sat down beside Magda and began to talk animatedly about their years in Egypt. And Magda, holding Jesus' hand, was content to listen.

"As you know, shortly after we arrived in Heliopolis Joseph found work as a carpenter. Our plans to return to Israel kept getting pushed back because of one thing and another. Then after we learned James was on the way, we decided to stay down south until he was older before making the trip back. I learned my lesson about traveling with an infant when we went to Egypt with Jesus. Once was enough. Then after Joseph and his employer built a bigger house for us, life got a little easier. And Joseph was happy to remain in Egypt because we were close to the Nile and he learned to swim.

"As you know, Joseph never does anything halfway; in no time he became a strong swimmer, going to the river every day to cool off after working long hours in the carpentry shop. When Jesus was old enough, he started taking him as well, hoping he would join the other boys his age who took great delight in racing and ducking each other as they played in the water. Did you know that the waters of the Nile flow north?"

Magda let her jaw drop in amazement. "No, Mary, I did not know that. I guess I need to bone up on exciting river facts." But Magda laughed as she said it and Mary laughed along with her, thinking, *Some things never change.*

"Anyway, before long Jesus was diving and swimming fearlessly, venturing out so far Joseph was often afraid he wouldn't be able to make his way back through the strong currents, which were a challenge even to him."

Mary seemed to enjoy just being able to converse with an adult, and she was more talkative than Magda ever remembered her being. It was like she was starved for a little companionship that didn't involve mothering or being a wife. *She has probably never had a conversation with Joseph except to say, 'Yes, dear; no, dear,'* Magda thought, uncharitably.

"Magda, you remarked on my lighter sense of humor the first time you visited us in Egypt. That's the happy effect of living far away from home. It's as though you're invisible. I felt a bit like I was on an extended holiday and I sort of took a more relaxed attitude toward everything. But I'm glad to be back at home. And happily, I brought my sense of humor with me, much to Joseph's chagrin. Sometimes I think the merrier I am, no pun intended, the more morose he is."

Mary looked wistful for a moment but quickly changed the subject and started to talk about her children. Mostly she talked about Jesus, who had attended an Egyptian school and had excelled in all subjects. "Egyptian boys from wealthy families attend school as early as four years old. We were able to enroll Jesus because Joseph had done some carpentry work for one of the instructors, who was impressed with Jesus' precocity.

"When Jesus began to talk, he spoke in complete sentences—a confusing jumble of Aramaic, Hebrew and Egyptian words. So he was eager to attend school and show off his talent for languages. I'll never forget the first day he went to school. When he came home that afternoon, I heard him running down the road, yelling 'ima, ima.' I rushed outside, thinking something terrible had happened until I saw the big smile on his face. Even before he went into the house, he said, 'Ima, I can read.' He sat down under a tree and read aloud to me, racing through the pages until he had finished the entire book.

"There were several Greek children in the school, and soon he was speaking Greek fluently. He has a good ear for languages. But mainly he is interested in his fellow man and hungry to learn the lessons from the Tanakh, which he began to study on his own even before he began to be tutored by the rabbis. He is well on his way to completely memorizing it," Mary said proudly.

Jesus had sat quietly, listening to his mother brag about him. He looked up from his book and said, "Well, somebody in this family has to do it."

Mary told Magda that the seriously-devout Joseph was a poor scholar and rarely spent any time studying the scriptures.

Magda had been enjoying her visit so much she had lost track of time. But Mary, knowing how Joseph felt about Magda, reminded her that he would soon be returning home. When he came walking up a short while later, Mary's light mood turned somber.

Magda said she had overstayed her welcome, but when she stood up to leave she made a vow, looking intently at Jesus. "I am sad that I have missed out on all of the fun of watching Jesus grow into this fine young man. But I am going to make up for every minute I've missed by never letting another day go by without seeing him."

And although Joseph wasn't thrilled at her constant presence she didn't let that discourage her. She was a daily visitor to their house, often bringing expensive gifts to the boys. She never failed to include Jesus' brothers, which pleased everyone but Joseph.

The Joseph versus Magda drama continued.

Chapter Sixteen

Be still and know that I am God.

Psalms 46:10

Mary and Joseph were taking their family to Jerusalem to celebrate Passover. As they entered the city and approached the temple, Jesus lagged behind, taking in all the amazing sights—so many diverse people, so much wealth, so many cripples and beggars sitting outside the temple gates.

Joseph was tired after the long trip and called out for Jesus to catch up with them. "Jesus, stay with us, we have business to take care of. You can see the sights later."

He gave Jesus some money and told him to go to the Court of the Gentiles to buy a pigeon and a dove for their sacrificial offerings. When Jesus finally returned hours later, he was empty-handed—no money and no animals.

Joseph was very upset with him and demanded an explanation. "You left with my money, you were gone for hours, and you returned empty-handed. And now you cannot understand why I am angry. Jesus, where did you go and what were you doing?"

Jesus was surprised that Joseph would question him. "Abba, did you not see the men outside the temple gates who were begging for alms? I gave the money to a few of them because they are crippled and cannot work. They were hungry; and I am sure God would rather we feed the hungry than waste food on sacrifices."

Over the years Joseph had become increasingly frustrated with his oldest son. He tried to talk with Mary about it. "Mary, Jesus is barely twelve years old, but it is obvious that he has little regard for us as parents. It's as though he is answering to a higher authority. I find it insulting."

But Mary took Jesus' side. "Joseph," Mary said wearily, "I have accepted that Jesus is an exceptional child. And yes, even though he is still a child, he has already outgrown our parental yoke. You would be happier if you accepted that fact, as I have."

Mary was tired of Joseph's complaints about Jesus. Even though she could understand that he was worried about Jesus' increasing distance from them, it seemed that he talked of little else. It was wearing on Mary and was driving a wedge between them.

Although Jesus worked alongside Joseph learning carpentry skills, clearly his heart and soul were elsewhere. Rather than build furniture, he wanted to build a happier, more serene human being. Joseph dismissed those lofty aspirations as the fantasies of a dreamer.

Mary and Joseph saw hardly anything of Jesus during that Passover week. He spent nearly all of his waking hours in the temple. He was so consumed by his desire to learn everything possible from the scribes and the elders that he had no interest in anything else.

So Joseph went to the temple to tell him that they were leaving the next day. "Jesus, we are leaving before sunrise tomorrow to head back to Nazareth. Be sure you join the caravan and return with us," Joseph warned Jesus.

Jesus looked up at Joseph, annoyed that his father had come to find him. "I plan to visit the temple first thing in the morning," he said. "I have a few more questions for the scribes. I'll be in the last group to head out." He turned back to his studies and Joseph could sense that he had already forgotten the conversation.

When Mary and Joseph began the trip back to Nazareth, Mary was anxious because Jesus was not in their group. "Mary," Joseph said, "now you're the one who is worried. Remember your own advice: don't fret about Jesus because he has outgrown our parental yoke. Anyhow, Jesus assured me that he would return with us; I'm sure he is in the last group, as he said he would be."

So Mary relaxed, thinking that he was with his friends farther down the line. But two days later when they asked about him, no one had seen him.

Mary said, "Joseph, we must double back. What if he left the temple too late to join the caravan and was forced to travel alone? He might be attacked by robbers."

Joseph replied, "Where has that dreamer disappeared to now?" He was not happy that they had to retrace their steps, and he didn't try to hide his annoyance. He grumbled and complained all the way back.

When they arrived in Jerusalem, they knew just where to go. They found him where they had left him—still in the temple. He was sitting with the elders, asking questions as he read from Leviticus. He was surprised that Mary and Joseph were worried about him. "Again, you were worried about me, searching for me. Did you not know that I must be about my Father's business?"

Jesus' words infuriated Joseph. Never before had he so blatantly dismissed Joseph as his father. Although neither he nor Mary had ever discussed the subject with him, Jesus just accepted the fact that he was the 'Son of God.' Joseph didn't speak a word to Jesus all the way back to Nazareth.

This was just another sign that the angel's promise was true—that Jesus was the promised Messiah. Jesus was no ordinary boy and it was clear that he was responding to a higher authority than that of Mary or Joseph's.

As Jesus matured, he became aware of the strength of his prayers and his touch. He began to look forward to the day when his miraculous powers would be used to heal the sick and the lame. Early one morning as he sat with Magda in the lower garden, he offered to work on her demons.

"Magda, I think you're actually fond of your demons. But I suspect they cause you more harm than you're willing to admit. Let's get rid of them."

"Oh no, Jesus, maybe later," Magda said. "It's too beautiful today for such serious work. And that will require a lot of serious work.

"Besides," Magda added, trailing her fingers through the water in the bird bath, "who's to say what I might be without my devils? They just may be keeping an even naughtier Magda at bay. You know what they say, 'Better the devil you know.'"

The closer Magda grew to Jesus the more distant she became from his mother—not Magda's choice. She knew Joseph didn't approve of his son's relationship with her, and even Mary was a bit jealous. Unmindful of anyone's disapproval, they were inseparable. She was part big sister, *all* confidante, and his biggest fan as he began to prepare for his ministry that she would be a big part of.

Jesus used Magda as an audience as he practiced his sermons on her. And inevitably, she would ask him about stories in the scriptures, peppering him with questions about the many things that troubled her: How could a loving God inflict such suffering on his children, destroying them with fire and floods, hunger and sickness? How did Noah find enough room in the ark for every kind of animal? Where did he find the food to feed all of them? And why did he include cockroaches?

Why did he encourage all the killing—even of children and babies—the torture, and the havoc wreaked on everyone along and in the way as his chosen people made their way from Egypt to the land flowing with milk and honey that God had promised Abraham and his ancestors—God-ordained practitioners of smash and (land) grab?

When God destroyed Sodom and Gomorrah, why did he spare Lot, one of the few inhabitants he judged to be righteous? When a 'pride' of perverts insisted that two visitors to Lot's house come out so they could rape them, Lot offered his two virgin daughters in their place.

> *Behold now, I have two daughters which have not known man; let me, I pray you, bring them out unto you, and do ye to them as is good in your eyes; only unto these men do nothing; for therefore came they under the shadow of my roof.*
>
> Genesis 19:8

Lot was a righteous man?

Why would a loving God cause a Godly man like Job to lose most of his family, all of his animals, his servants, and to suffer boils and other painful infirmities to win a point in a debate with Satan? Why did he bless David, who sent the soldier, Uriah the Hittite, to his death on the front line so he could steal his wife, Bathsheba? That union produced a son—Solomon—who was also anointed king and became the wisest, richest man in Israel's history.

Solomon authored several books in the scriptures that were rife with his contempt for women—women *without a shred of wisdom.*

> *"I applied mine heart to know and to search, and to seek out wisdom . . . Behold, this have I found, saith the preacher, counting one by one, to find out the account . . . but I find not: one man among a thousand have I found; but a woman among all those have I not found."*
>
> Ecclesiastes 7:25-28

Jesus answered all of her questions with his own provocative questions: why question a force so mysterious that it could create a giant tree from a tiny mustard seed; or fashion a human being from two seeds that joined together in an act fueled by a desire more powerful than any other? Why question the God who created the universe and everything in it that worked together magically to put the sun in the sky for day and the moon in the sky for night?

"Why question the God who works in mysterious ways not understood by mere mortal man?" Jesus asked.

Magda pinched his cheek and said, "Why do you always answer a question with a question?"

"Because I'm Jewish?" he asked.

He stressed that she should strive for the peace that passes understanding; that she should nurture the faith that would enrich her life; that believing was an end in itself. He told her to study a child at play; that children believe what makes them happiest. Then he told her a story:

"A little boy in school was drawing a picture. The rabbi asked him what he was drawing and he replied, 'God.' The rabbi said, 'But no one knows what God looks like.' The boy replied, 'Well, they will when I finish drawing this picture.'

"You must become more accepting—like a little child. Just believe in believing, Magda."

It was during these spirited debates with this skeptical woman whose inquisitive mind made her a formidable opponent that Jesus began to use the parable as a teaching method.

Jesus' message was simple: "The kingdom of God is within you. Stop looking. Stop seeking. Be silent. Look within. Sit quietly in a place where the only noise is the whisper of the wind; there you will find what you are seeking—the rapture within—the kingdom of God."

But a poor Nazarene who was born in a stable and preached 'love your enemies' was no one's idea of a true Messiah. Everyone was waiting for a God-like warrior, a sword-wielding giant who would energize the Jewish people to overthrow the Roman occupation and release them from the chokehold by which Caesar and his government dominated them.

Chapter Seventeen

And the Lord said unto Moses: Take unto thee sweet spices, stacte, and onycha, and galbanum; these sweet spices with pure frankincense, of each shall there be a like weight. And thou shalt make it a perfume, a confection after the art of the apothecary, tempered together, pure and holy: and thou shalt beat some of it very small, and put of it before the testimony in the tabernacle of the congregation . . . it shall be unto you most holy.

Exodus 30:34-37

MAGDA'S EYES GLAZED OVER WHEN Jesus tried to engage her in deep philosophical discussions; she was a doer, not a thinker. She would put him off saying, "I would rather be a doer who doesn't dream than a dreamer who doesn't do."

Jesus answered, "Everything, even God's creations, started with a dream."

Magda was a doer. As an apothecary and a perfumer, she had become a successful importer of exotic ointments, oils, and spices from the countries east of the Red Sea. She was a wizard at combining herbs and ointments into medicines that could heal the suffering of the sick and injured and calm the torments of the mentally tortured.

Frankincense, aloe, myrrh, spikenard—these were just a few of the ingredients in the infusions that she bottled and sold to merchants, doctors, apothecaries and even to wealthy individuals who had heard of the amazing results of her medicines and ointments. She was convinced of the healing, restorative powers of the herbs and aromatic resins she sold, particularly that of frankincense, her best-selling import. Frankincense was worth more than its weight in gold and was one of the most valuable commodities in the world.

Used to awaken higher consciousness and to enhance spirituality, meditation, and mental perception, her imports were used by doctors and other healers who practiced the discipline of treating ailments with herbal remedies. The ancient recipe for making incense that God inscribed onto sacred tablets and gave to Moses was handed down by word of mouth from generation to generation of perfumers in Magda's family . . . finally to Heli, who never took it more seriously than a hobby. But Magda, who supplied all the incense used by the temple in Jerusalem, developed the hobby into a thriving business that made her a very wealthy woman in her own right.

Because she often extolled the virtues of frankincense as an aphrodisiac, explaining the many ways it could be used to heighten the senses during lovemaking, many believed that she was a prostitute; except those who knew how wealthy she was. Those people merely believed she was a fallen woman. Those who knew her best knew she didn't care what anyone thought.

Chapter Eighteen

And he saith unto them, Follow me, and I will make you fishers of men.

Matt. 4:19

Early one morning while walking by the Sea of Galilee in Capernaum, Jesus met two brothers who were just coming to shore after a night of fishing. Jesus asked about their catch, but they said, "Fish weren't biting tonight." Their nets were practically empty.

Jesus said, "Go back out and try it again." He told them to let down their nets on the right side of the boat. A few hours later they returned with nets that were overflowing with fish.

Then Jesus said to them, "Follow me and I will make you fishers of men." Without hesitation, the two brothers left their boat by the shore and followed him.

When he told Magda that he had made friends with two fishermen in Capernaum named Simon and Andrew, she became very excited and started dancing around with him in a circle. "Oh Jesus, please take me to them at once. I know these two brothers. They used to live in Magdala and I met them when I was just a young girl. They must have moved to Capernaum when my father fired them for taking me fishing."

Jesus looked at Magda blankly, thinking, *I can't wait to hear that story*. He took hold of her hand and they walked up the hill to Simon's house. Magda said, "Go in and tell them an old friend wants to see them. Don't tell them my name, I want to surprise them."

When Andrew and Simon saw their old fishing buddy, they started whooping and hollering for joy. They spent the next several hours celebrating the reunion with the girl who had got them fired.

Andrew said, "Magda, we thought we would never see you again. This is a great day!" Even Jesus joined in the revelry, moved by the mutual joy of these three long-lost friends who had found each other again.

"Magda!" Simon said in disbelief, hugging her and sobbing with happiness. "We thought you had moved to the moon."

"Close," she said. "Nazareth."

"It's a small world," Andrew exclaimed. "We wondered where you had gone. We heard a rumor that you were living in Nazareth although we couldn't picture our friend Magda living in such a place . . . how did that happen?"

Not willing to dampen the celebration, Magda said, "It's a long story, my friends. I'll just say that you two are not the only ones who were run out of Magdala."

Several days later Jesus and Magda were sitting in Orpah's garden watching a magnificent sunset. Magda had been toying with an idea ever since her reunion with Simon and Andrew, and she thought Jesus would be interested in it.

"Jesus, I've been thinking," Magda said, her business hat on. "We need to draw up a plan for your ministry. You need to choose several good men to be your assistants—disciples, as you call them.

"Of course, Simon and Andrew and their fishermen friends will be honored to serve, but I urge you to recruit Benjamin's advisor Matthew as well. He is a published historian as well as a whiz with numbers; he will make an excellent financial manager. Now if we just had some finances to manage. Maybe abba will match my contribution.

Eventually, Jesus chose twelve men to be his apostles. They were:

Simon, later called Peter
Andrew
James, son of Zebedee
John, son of Zebedee
Philip
Bartholomew called Nathanael
Matthew
Thomas
James son of Alphaeus
Simon the Zealot
Judas Iscariot

At first the men were uncomfortable around Matthew because his was the most hated of all professions—tax collector; but they quickly understood. Matthew was a plain-spoken, honest and brilliant man. He quickly became one of the favorites among the disciples.

But Jesus' choice of Nathanael from Cana was a tougher sell. They didn't understand his sarcastic sense of humor and often found him abrasive.

Jesus explained his choice. "Nathanael is a true Israelite in whom there is no guile. He says what he means and means what he says. He can be a bit caustic at times, but I enjoy his humor and brilliant wit. Besides, he's a good foil to Magda."

But Simon didn't understand Nathanael and couldn't dismiss what he had said when told Jesus of Nazareth was the Son of God—the promised Messiah. In Jesus' presence Nathanael said, "Can anything good come out of Nazareth?"

Jesus said, "Well *me*, but that's not where I'm coming from now."

Nathanael was accepted as one of the disciples.

Magda wasn't as successful at recruiting women to join the ministry, but the ones who were willing were very special: Mary, wife of Cleophas, Salome, Joanna, and Tabitha, a wealthy woman nearly as beautiful as Magda.

Most of the disciples were from in and around Capernaum, where Jesus made his home after being snubbed by his fellow Nazarenes. Simon and Andrew invited Jesus to share their home—a modest dwelling slightly redolent of fish located in a vibrant area just a short walk from Lake Galilee.

And it was there in Capernaum that Jesus began to minister to the troubled, the sick, to exorcise unclean spirits from the afflicted, to restore sight to the blind, to cure the lame and even revive the dead.

Jesus' first message to his disciples and his followers was: "Be still and know that I am God."

A few of the disciples questioned Jesus about his method of preaching. "Why do you always use the parable in your sermons?"

He answered them, "Unto you it is given to know the mystery of the kingdom of God; but unto them that are without, all these things are done in parables: that seeing they may see, and not perceive; and hearing they may hear, and not understand."

Simon looked at him blankly and thought, *I guess I haven't yet received the mystery of the kingdom of God because I haven't the foggiest idea what he is talking about.* That sort of confusion would be Simon's biggest challenge as Jesus' right hand man: to gain an understanding to match his fervor.

Chapter Nineteen

This beginning of miracles did Jesus in Cana of Galilee, and manifested forth his glory; and his disciples believed on him.

John 2:11

MARY AND JESUS WERE GOING to a wedding in Cana. Mary's niece Abigail was getting married, and it was to be a huge affair with all their friends and family invited. Abigail, who had heard that Jesus had become a much sought-after rabbi, was eager for him to attend because she wanted to impress her friends with her famous cousin. She sent a special invitation to Mary, urging her to bring Jesus *and guest.* Even though there was no money to buy a gift, Mary accepted the invitation, hoping that Jesus would go with her.

Jesus, almost thirty years old and busy preparing for his ministry, was aware that he spent very little time with his mother. Since Joseph was working in Sepphoris and was unable to attend, Jesus consented to escort Mary to the wedding.

Mary was overcome with feelings of love and pride that this beautiful man with an ever-widening circle of followers was walking hand in hand with her as they made the nine-mile trip north to Cana. Naturally, she wanted to show him off to her relatives, who did little to disguise their feelings of superiority to their poor relatives who lived in the backwater of Nazareth. Although Abigail warmly welcomed them to her wedding, she was obviously appalled by Mary's humble, homespun garments; even more embarrassing was Jesus' *guests*—three of his disciples who looked like they should be slaving away in the kitchen.

Mary saw her chance to put them all in their place when the head steward announced with embarrassment that they had run out of wine. She asked someone to find Jesus and bring him to her.

"Jesus, they have run out of wine, can you help?"

Jesus looked at her sadly, momentarily disappointed that his mother was eager to impress their shallow kinsmen. Not unkindly, he said to her, "Woman, what has that to do with me? My time has not yet come."

Undeterred, Mary said, "Jesus, there is no time like the present—and this will be a great present! Please, will you do this for me?"

There were six stone pots sitting nearby. Jesus said to the servants, "Fill the pots with water."

The servants looked at each other in amusement and one of them dared to reply, "It is not water they want; the guests want wine."

"Do whatever he tells you to do," Mary said with unusual sharpness.

Jesus raised the first jug himself and took it to the cistern where he filled it with water. Then the solemn-faced servants, who were inwardly smirking, filled their jugs and soon there were six water pots filled to the brim.

Jesus said to one of the servants, "Draw out a cupful and present it to the head steward."

The steward raised the cup to his lips and took a small swallow. Then he took a much larger swallow, swirling it around in his mouth with his eyes closed. *Unless my palate deceives me, this is the best wine I have ever tasted*, he thought.

He raised his cup high and called for everyone to be served the *water* that Jesus had changed into wine, loudly proclaiming, "Drink a toast to the bridegroom, for he has saved the very best wine for last."

By changing water into wine, Jesus had performed his first miracle, an incident viewed by most as a pretty nifty party trick that made him a sought-after guest. But Jesus preferred the raw honesty of those with sin-sick souls to those who partied to forget their sins.

Chapter Twenty

He hath showed thee, O man, what is good; and what doth the LORD require of thee, but to do justly, and to love mercy, and to walk humbly with thy God?

Micah 6:8

NEWS OF JOHN THE BAPTIST and his ministry was spreading throughout Jerusalem, beyond Jordan and into the Judean wilderness. People often asked John if he was the Messiah, but he always answered, "I baptize with water unto repentance, but there is one coming after me who is mightier than I. He will baptize you with the Holy Spirit and with fire." John asked his former apostles, James and John—now Jesus' disciples—to tell Jesus that he wanted to meet with him.

Jesus was excited when James and John gave him the message. He said to Magda, "My cousin John has sent a message that he wants to meet with me. He has been preaching the Word of God and I want him to baptize me.

"And Magda, this is your personal decision, as I do not want to influence you, but would you like for him to baptize you as well?"

Magda was emphatic. "No, thank you. You know how I feel about rituals. I just don't understand them. All that dunking into dirty water to be cleansed? Does that make sense? It's a moronic oxymoron. The Jordan River is muddy and disgusting.

"And while I'm on the subject of nonsensical rituals, the sacrificing of animals? I am not even much of an animal lover, but I think that it is beyond cruel and such a waste. Tell me one time you have ever seen God swoop down and scoop up the dead animal to feast on it to show that he appreciated the sacrifice. I bet he thinks it as big a waste as I. Rules and regulations about what is clean and unclean, and what you can and cannot eat—what's all that got to do with what's in your heart?

"I agree with Micah:

> *'Wherewithal shall I come before the Lord, and bow myself before the high God? Shall I come before him with burnt offerings, with calves of a year old? Will the Lord be pleased with thousands of rams, or with ten thousands of rivers of oil? Shall I give my firstborn for my transgression, the fruit of my body for the sin of my soul? He hath shewed thee, O man, what is good; and what doth the Lord require of thee, but to do justly, and to love mercy, and to walk humbly with thy God?'"*

"Well, Magda, my humble friend, I appreciate the sermon but I suspect there is something else going on here." Jesus waited patiently, knowing the other shoe would drop in a moment.

"Well, the thing is I don't look good with wet hair, and I am very careful about where I wash it," she admitted, always willing to move the subject from personal matters to personal appearance. "All those unwashed penitents befouling the waters of the Jordan . . . I don't think so, my love. But I'll go with you, how's that for a compromise?"

Jesus laughed and shook his head. "Magda, remind me never to fence with you where the weapon of choice is a sword." One could never win a battle of wits with Magda, so why even bother?

Early the next morning, Magda and Jesus and James and John headed across the Jordan River to Bethany-Beyond-Jordan, looking for John. According to a man he had recently baptized, he was just a mile or two downstream. "Just a word of warning, 'The Baptist'—that's what most people around here call him—might look a little strange to you. He doesn't care much for conventional clothing, or conventional *anything* for that matter. He was practically raised by the desert nomads, so you might think him a little weird."

They weren't overly surprised when they found John in a Bedouin camp, oddly arrayed in camel's hair with a leather girdle, eating a sumptuous meal of locusts and honey. Even Jesus looked taken aback at this shaggy man who was his close kin. He knew that John preferred living in the desert away from society, but nothing had prepared him for this hirsute creature who seemed more animal than man.

John looked up from his meal and shouted in a loud voice, "Look! It's the Lamb of God, who takes away the sin of the world. This is the one about whom I have said, 'After me comes a man who is greater than I am because he existed before me. I am the voice of him that crieth in the wilderness: make straight in the desert a highway for our God.' Although he does not recognize me, I know who he is because I have been expecting him for some time; and I am convinced by that aura of holiness that surrounds him. Besides, he looks just like my cousin Mary."

"This is a little raw for my tastes," Magda whispered to Jesus. One look at John and Magda had seen enough. "I'm going back to Bethany—to civilization—for a late lunch and a glass of wine; have a locust for me, Jesus."

Although locusts were a staple of the Jewish diet, Magda had never tasted one and didn't want to be around those who did. Dead locusts smelled like rotting garbage and Magda insisted those who ate them had garbage breath.

Almost relieved that Magda wouldn't be present for the serious conversation he planned to have with his cousin, Jesus sat down with John, although he declined to share in his meal. After hours of discussion, during which John surprised Jesus with his sharp intellect and a philosophy that echoed Jesus' message, he asked John to baptize him.

But John was reluctant. "I am not worthy to baptize you. I am not even worthy to fasten the thongs of your sandals."

But Jesus insisted and finally John relented. The two of them went down to the river and waded in. John held Jesus in his arms and dipped him beneath the surface of the water.

As soon as Jesus emerged, a dove flew down and alit on his right shoulder. Then a mysterious voice from above said, "This is my beloved Son in whom I am well pleased."

Later, as Jesus and Magda shared a meal with some of the disciples, they discussed how special John had made the baptism. Magda asked them to repeat what had happened. "You mean a talking bird flew down and landed on your shoulder?" she asked, playing dumb.

"Not exactly, Magda," Jesus explained. "The bird didn't talk; a voice came down from heaven saying, 'This is my beloved Son in whom I am well pleased.'"

Amidst all this light-hearted banter, Judas spoiled the moment by complaining, "Jesus, I know John is your cousin, but I seriously doubt whether he is the man of God he claims to be. If cleanliness is next to Godliness, then John is about as ungodly as a man can get. And you allowed him to baptize you in that animal clothing he was wearing. All that camel hair floating on the water didn't leave much to the imagination about his private parts! I wouldn't let him touch me with a ten-foot pole."

Magda looked contemptuously at Judas and said, "Speaking of private parts, Judas, from what I hear, you don't exactly have a ten-foot pole."

But Jesus, who was rarely angry, wheeled around to him, "What did you go out into the desert to see? A reed swayed by the wind? A man dressed in fine clothes? No, men who dress in fine clothes are in kings' palaces."

He waved Judas off when he started to interrupt, "Then *what* were you expecting to see? A prophet? Yes, a prophet and more. I tell you, John is the one about whom it is written, 'I will send my messenger ahead of you, who will prepare your way for you.'

"I tell you the truth: among those born of women there has not risen anyone greater than John the Baptist."

While Magda was glad that Jesus had spoken harshly to Judas—he was her least favorite of the disciples—the resentment on his face was unsettling.

Later that evening Jesus made light of the moment, insisting that Magda was overreacting. "You know how Judas is; he likes to pump himself up by putting others down. He may be a bit annoying, but he's harmless."

Worriedly, Magda thought, *I hope Jesus is right about that. But just in case he's not, I'm going to keep my eye on him. Judas is a troublemaker with a terminal case of greed.*

Chapter Twenty-One

Then saith Jesus unto him, "Get thee hence, Satan: for it is written, 'Thou shalt worship the Lord thy God, and him only shalt thou serve.'"

Matt. 4-10

JESUS WAS GOING TO SPEND the next forty days and nights fasting and resisting the temptations put before him by Satan. Magda failed to see the point of the sabbatical.

"Jesus," she argued, "you are contradicting yourself. Why pray, 'lead us not into temptation,' and then deliberately put yourself in harm's way, flirting with Satan with this so-called sabbatical?"

They had a fairly heated discussion about it. Magda, a little vexed at Jesus for ignoring her point—Magda was not a gracious loser—decided to visit Magdala while Jesus was away. She would use the time to visit with her family while Jesus tested himself against Satan's power.

Thoroughly miffed, Magda packed a bag and walked down to the water's edge to await the ferry. *I have stayed away from my family too long and Jesus and I could use a little break,* she consoled herself as she paced back and forth on the water-logged boards of the ancient dock, impatient to get away from Capernaum.

As soon as the boat was fastened to the moorings of the Magdala dock, she jumped down and started walking at her usual breakneck pace toward the cliffs. She crossed the shore road and took the shortcut up the footpath, which was lined with daffodils that covered the grassy area like a carpet of nodding yellow heads. Heli and the gardener had planted the daffodils every fall for many years and there were thousands of them waving together to announce the coming spring.

Pausing to gather a few flowers for her room, Magda ran the rest of the way to the house, arriving at the top of the cliff a little winded. *I must be getting old,* she thought. As she walked past the flower garden and then the herb garden, she resisted the urge to spend some time gathering the early blooming flowers and herbs to add to her bouquet. Even though Rachel had been dead for many years, Magda still felt a little guilty when she went into the herb garden.

She opened the gate and walked through the back portico. This was a surprise visit and she wanted to sneak up on everyone. Quietly opening the back door, which always squeaked a little, she tip-toed into the dining room, where she knew the family would be. They were just sitting down to the noonday meal when she poked her head through the door.

"Yoohoo, am I too early?"

Martha didn't like surprises; anything that disrupted her carefully laid plans was unwelcome. She complained, "You might have let someone know you were coming; I didn't expect to have another mouth to feed."

"Yes, fine, thank you, and good to see you too, Martha," Magda trilled, slipping off her scarf and wrapping it around the bust of Homer. She went over and kissed Lazarus on the cheek.

"Magda, you're back from the dead." Lazarus always said the same thing to her, regardless of whether he had seen her five minutes or five months before.

She had been there just two days when Martha knocked on her bedroom door late one night and said, "Magda, you need to get dressed and come downstairs right away."

Oh no, this doesn't sound good, Magda thought. *The last time someone told me to get dressed and come downstairs was when mother died and I was sent to Nazareth. What stale hell is this?*

Zachary was waiting for her, pacing the floor and looking like the angel of death. As soon as Magda saw his face, she knew that he must have come to deliver bad news about Heli.

"Magda, ima is seriously ill. Orpah sent me to get you because the doctor doesn't think she will last the night."

Oh God, no. Not Heli, please don't take my Heli from me.

Magda went numb but started giving orders in full take-charge mode: "Martha, I am leaving in ten minutes. Please ask Oli to bring a couple of his fastest horses around to the front."

"But Magda," Martha protested, "don't you think Zachary deserves to eat a good meal and get a good night's sleep before returning to Nazareth?"

Magda was in no mood to argue with Martha about eating and sleeping—right up there with dusting and mopping as Martha's favorite pastimes.

Magda just shook her head and repeated, "As I said, I am leaving in . . . now nine minutes; have Oli bring around the horses and hitch them up to Zach's carriage, Martha; just do it! That is, please."

Magda packed a few of her things in a small bag and ran down to the waiting carriage. As she settled onto one of the seats in the back, she thought about how remiss she had been toward Heli and Orpah in the past several months. But much as she loved them, she had such unpleasant memories of Nazareth she could hardly bring herself to visit them. Following Jesus' harrowing experience in the synagogue when he was ridiculed and nearly killed by his neighbors, they avoided going there.

She recalled the Sabbath day early in Jesus' ministry when he had persuaded her to go with him and his parents to the synagogue in Nazareth. The rabbi, recognizing Jesus as one of their own who was destined for greatness, asked him to read some passages from Isaiah.

Jesus walked to the pulpit and began to read from Isaiah 61:1:

> *The Spirit of the Lord God is upon me, because the Lord hath anointed me to preach good tidings to the meek; he hath sent me to bind up the brokenhearted, to proclaim liberty to the captives, and the opening of the prison to them that are bound."*

The people sat in awe of his eloquent reading and authoritative delivery. They insisted he address the congregation with some of his own remarks.

Solemnly, Jesus proclaimed, "This day is this scripture fulfilled in your ears."

The people sat for a few moments without moving; they were shocked as the enormity of Jesus' words settled in: was he declaring himself to be the promised Messiah? That was blasphemy!

One of the elders stood up and said, "Why, this fellow is the son of Mary and Joseph, the carpenter, sitting there on the third row. I know his brothers and sisters, all just ordinary folk. If he's the Messiah, then I am the Queen of Sheba."

Alarm bells started going off in Magda's head. She knew the Nazarene men were a rough bunch and that Jesus was in trouble. She grabbed his hand and whispered fiercely, "Time to go." But as they ran out a side door and headed toward the mountain road to Orpah's, an angry mob followed them, shouting at Jesus and threatening to kill him. Magda felt terror unlike any she had ever known.

Even though Magda and Jesus were younger, faster and had a head start, she feared that they would eventually be overrun without a little divine intervention. Just as she began to realize that the men were gaining on them, she heard the sound of hoof beats coming down the path in their direction. It was Nathanial and he was in a horse-drawn cart. Magda ran toward him, waving her arms in the air and yelling at him to stop.

"Magda!" Nathanial said as he reined in the horse and gentled it to a stop. "Is everything all right?"

"It is now," she answered. "Help us get into the cart and cover us up. Jesus and I are being chased by some old men from the synagogue."

Since it was Magda, Nathanial was not overly surprised. He didn't waste time asking questions. He helped her and Jesus climb into the cart and covered them with some empty feed sacks. Seconds later they heard shouting in the distance from the angry crowd of men. But Nathanial, a big man wielding a whip, urged the horse into a gallop and drove right through the group of men, who looked back suspiciously as the cart disappeared around the curve.

Disappointed in his fellow Nazarenes, Jesus decided to move to Capernaum. After his bad experience, he rarely visited Nazareth even though both he and Magda had family there. Since Nazareth was not on Jesus' itinerary, Magda seldom visited there either.

The swaying of the carriage brought her out of her reverie as Zachary drove the horses at great speed down the mountainside and made the sharp turn onto the valley road. The fifteen miles to Nazareth was covered quickly, but the last stretch was maddeningly slow as the tired horses struggled up the steep mountain road. It was nearly midnight when they arrived. Magda jumped out of the carriage and ran directly to the back of the house to Heli's room.

The door was closed and there was a wreath of lily of the valley hanging on it. Magda braced herself against the wall, holding back tears that she refused to shed until she could grieve privately. Nathanial opened the door and silently motioned for Zachary and Magda to come in. Orpah was standing beside Heli's bed, crying and twisting a square of linen in her hands.

Magda stood beside Orpah for a moment, eyes closed, breathing in the fragrance of Heli—a potpourri of herbs and flowers that perfumed the room even in the presence of death.

The usual stoic Zachary collapsed beside his mother, crying unashamedly for the woman who had given all to love and all her love to him and Nathanial, as well as to Magda.

Orpah, always a bit intimidated by Magda, searched for the right words. "Magda, I am so sorry. I loved Heli too, you know. She tried so hard to hold on 'til you got here, but she was just too sick. At least she didn't suffer long."

Magda thought sourly, *Why do people always say that? The way they talk about it you would think they had died and come back to tell others what a lovely experience it was.*

Orpah continued her unctuous murmurings, "It just seemed like she was well one day and deathly ill the next. I noticed she had lost weight and looked a little pale, but I really thought she was just sad, missing you. You know Heli loved you like a daughter."

Magda couldn't listen to any more. She bent down to kiss Heli's forehead, now as cool as marble. She knelt beside Zachary and Nathanial who began to cry, great racking sobs that released a lifetime of tears.

Magda was devastated, much more so than when Rachel died, but she was too numb to cry. And her grief was worse because of her enormous guilt. She hadn't felt such pain since her father had sent her to live in Nazareth. How could she have neglected Heli so much in the past few months? Heli was the one person in her life who had nurtured her and loved her regardless of how unlovable she had been much of the time. And what had Magda ever given her in return? A lot of trouble and very little gratitude.

A few days later Magda left the mansion on the mountain wishing she never had to return. With Heli gone and Mary practically a stranger these days, there was nothing left for her in Nazareth except Orpah, who refused to move to Magdala to live in the House of Benjamin.

Why do all the people I love the most always leave me? she wondered miserably.

Chapter Twenty-Two

Then when lust has conceived, it bringeth forth sin; and sin, when it is finished, bringeth forth death.

James 1:15

FOLLOWING HELI'S DEATH, MAGDA BECAME completely obsessed with Jesus and their relationship. Although it bothered her that she was several years older than he, Jesus seemed unconcerned about the difference. Magda finally concluded that their ages were not an issue with him because he regarded her as a mere friend—a beloved friend—but nothing more. That realization was hurtful, but what choice did she have? Her cup was not exactly full, but she would settle for half-full, telling herself, "With Jesus in my life, my cup is running over."

He was his mother's son in his physical perfection. Everything about him was elegant: a straight, neat nose, small ears close to his head, beautiful limbs, long graceful hands and feet that Magda loved to bathe and massage with her ointments. Magda would stare at him until he looked away, uncomfortable. "Magda, why do you always stare at me?"

She would take his head in her hands, pull it toward her until they were nose to nose and say, "Because you don't have eyes—you have mesmerize."

He was not oblivious to her feelings, but he would merely give her a hug when he sensed her hunger, whispering to her in his calm, deep voice, "Magda, my love for you is pure and sacred. I would never jeopardize our friendship by indulging in the temporary physical pleasures we might find together. We might spoil what we have and damage the relationship. Then what would I do if I suddenly found myself without you?"

She would answer under her breath, "What I'd like to know is what you would do *with* me." But in her saner moments, she knew he was right. Nonetheless, where Jesus was concerned, her moments of being rational were rare.

If Magda knew the truth she would know that my feelings are just as strong as hers, just different, Jesus thought, worried that Magda's needs would eventually overpower her restraint.

During his forty days of fasting, he had proved that he could resist hunger for food and lust for power, and could even thirst for righteousness' sake; but he knew that the biggest challenge would be to resist Magda's desire for more than friendship.

He prayed for the strength and courage to resist all the earthly pleasures that life offered to mortal man. And although there were times when he felt the need to pray with increased fervor for God to direct his paths, through the strength that God provided he held steadfast, as immortals are wont to do.

Magda was a good conversationalist and Jesus a good listener. She had a turn of phrase that he admired. She suggested that he put a bit of humor in his sermons from time to time. "Inject just a little levity sometimes. Most people's attention spans are short. You stand a better chance of holding their interest if you throw in an amusing story from time to time."

"Well, Magda," he replied, "I'm open to your suggestions; what story do you suggest I tell? The funniest stories I know are about you."

"No, no, keep me out of it. All right, maybe funny isn't what you need, but something a little thought-provoking. Here's one of my favorites:"

Long ago, during the reign of the Kings in Israel, there lived a great prophet named Elijah, who was a miracle worker, healer, rainmaker and cult leader. Knowing his time on earth was nearing its end, Elijah chose a young man named Elisha as his apprentice and groomed him to take over his prophetic duties when the time came. To denote his separation to the prophetic office, Elisha completely shaved his head, a cleansing requirement of lepers mandated by the law of Moses, and therefore usually interpreted as a mark of shame.

One afternoon when Elijah and Elisha were on their way to Gilgal, a chariot suddenly appeared with horses of fire, separating the two of them. Elijah went up in a whirlwind to heaven, leaving Elisha to carry on the prophesying business by himself. Elijah was gone but he had left his mantle behind; it had dropped to the ground as he whirled away. When Elisha saw it, he ripped off his own clothes, tore them into pieces and donned Elijah's mantle. Then he returned to the Jordan and did just as his master had done: he took off the mantle and struck the water with it. Immediately, the waters parted and Elisha walked over on dry ground. Wearing Elijah's magic mantle, Elisha journeyed to Bethel. As he neared the city, a group of children ran up behind him and started to mock him, saying, "Go up, thou bald head; go up, thou bald head."

Elisha was tired of hearing comments about his bald head and he turned around, looked at the children, and cursed them in the name of the Lord. Immediately, two she bears ran out of the woods and tore all forty-two children from limb to limb.

Jesus sat looking at Magda intently, frowning at her obvious enjoyment of such a macabre story. "Magda, surely you don't think that kind of violence has any place in my sermons. My message is one of love and forgiveness, not killing and mayhem."

"Exactly, but it got your attention."

Chapter Twenty-Three

But when Herod's birthday was kept, the daughter of Herodias danced before them, and pleased Herod. Whereupon he promised with an oath to give her whatsoever she would ask. And she, being before instructed of her mother, said, "Give me here John Baptist's head in a charger."

Matt. 14:6-8

All Israel was abuzz with the news that Herod Antipas, the governor of Galilee, had married Herodias, the wife of his brother Philip. It was not clear whether she was divorced from Philip, but it was certain that she was the daughter of Herod's half-brother, Aristobulus.

Nearly everyone had heard of Herod's wicked behavior; but for such gossip to reach the ears of John the Baptist, purposefully far removed from society, it had to have traveled all the way to John's lifelong friends—the Bedouin, who viewed as unwelcome any news from outside their close-knit society.

John had been told of Herod's shameful behavior by one of his recent converts to warn him that there was nothing beneath Herod, the message being, *Take care, stay away from there.*

John wasted no time in his fiery condemnation of Herod. His friend's words of warning were a waste of breath. John immediately traveled to Herod's Castle to rebuke him.

Even before he could be announced, John roared into Herod's presence, shouting, "You adulterous worm of wickedness, do you not realize that you will burn in Hell for all eternity for indulging your animal lusts?"

Herod, unaccustomed to such an upbraiding from anyone, was so stunned he was momentarily lost for a response. He sat fidgeting and thinking, *He is just ranting like a prophet and trying to scare me with this threat of damnation.*

Herodias and some of the guests were looking at him expectantly, wondering when he was going to order his soldiers to silence this raving lunatic. But Herod wavered, secretly afraid that John was Elijah or Elisha with their direct line of communication to God, so he spared John's life and had him imprisoned instead.

In spite of John's denunciation, Herod was curious about the fiery, singular man. He brooded about the out-spoken man of God, worried that his followers were going to stage a rebellion. One night he went in secret to talk to him in the Machaerus prison. He ordered the jailer to unshackle John from the hooks in the walls and be brought out to him. Herod spent the rest of the evening questioning John and asking him if he truly thought God was going to punish him for his sins.

John answered him with a quote from the book of Numbers: "Your hour is at hand. Repent! But if you will not do so, behold you have sinned against the Lord." John stood and pointed his finger at Herod, shouting, "Be sure your sins will find you out!"

Herod reacted like a frightened dog. He ordered the jailer to have John flogged and to shackle both his arms and his legs with chains. "Let him eat his food off the floor like an animal," Herod ordered. He regretted visiting John and wished he had not asked him questions about the hereafter. Conversations with John always made him think too deeply, which left him feeling guilty.

Meanwhile, Herodias was seething that this desert animal would dare to criticize her behavior. She began plotting to have him killed. *And I know just the person to help me with that project,* Herodias thought as she walked down the hall of the palace to find her beautiful, exotic-looking daughter.

"Salome, you must dance before the king today to give him a special birthday gift. I want you to drive him to distraction with your body, which you must allow him to see in all its glory, one veil at a time until your beauty is completely uncovered."

Salome began her dance, covered by many multi-colored veils. But as the tempo of the music increased, she began to shed them, dropping them one-by-one to the floor, much to her step-father's delight.

As she reached the finale, she began jumping higher and higher until she collapsed in front of him, completely nude, her last scarf thrown at his feet.

Herod was so greatly pleased (and so busy trying to hide his arousal) he offered her a present of her choosing—anything she wanted, including half his kingdom. Herodias hurriedly collected the discarded scarves and covered her daughter's glistening body, whispering in her ear, "Now ask for your reward."

Salome bowed before Herod and announced her wishes for all to hear. "I have decided to ask for a very special gift, my Lord: bring me John Baptist's head on a platter."

Herod looked around with dismay. He was reluctant to murder John—what if he was indeed a prophet? But he could hardly renege on his offer in front of people who were looking on expectantly. So Salome got her wish: John's head was delivered on a charger to Herod in front of his visitors, who were thrilled—a nude dancer and a severed head all in the same afternoon.

Jesus was greatly upset when he learned of John's murder. He had found John to be a highly spiritual man, and after John baptized him they had become good friends. He was one of the most righteous men who ever lived. He never touched wine or strong spirits and lived as an ascetic in the wilderness of Judea. A man of courage, he never shrank from what he considered his God-given duty—to rebuke all sinners, paupers as well as kings (he even called the Pharisees and the Sadducees a 'brood of vipers')—as he prepared the way for 'someone whose sandals I am not worthy to carry'—Jesus.

Jesus said to Magda, "I want to grieve John's death properly, and the only way to do that is in his beloved desert. Will you go with me to Bethabara?"

Magda twirled a ringlet of her hair around her finger for a moment, stalling until she could think of a better plan. *I hate the desert; all that sand and nothing to do. I wish we could just cross over to a remote spot on the eastern shore of the Galilee and pretend we're in the desert . . . Jesus could sit in the sand and grieve with his back to the sea and I could wade in the water and hunt for sea shells.* But she knew better than to suggest such an absurd plan, so they crossed over Jordan to the desert where John had preached for so many years. Desert or not, she was with Jesus. She was content.

While Jesus was greatly sorrowed at the senseless murder of such a good man as John, he was equally saddened for Israel, which suffered under the tyrannical Romans, who exerted their power over the people with an iron fist. Jesus' tears were for John and for Jerusalem, and indeed for all of Israel.

Magda consoled him, "You know that the pure in spirit will always be persecuted, even murdered, for their courage to speak out against evil. John's denunciations of everyone, especially someone of Herod's power, were a death sentence of his own making.

"And lately I am very concerned about your safety as well. Don't even think about leaving me behind in the future; as the number of your enemies multiplies, someone with my connections and means to buy you out of trouble needs to be at your side at all times."

She took a deep breath and paused before continuing, letting her innermost thoughts tumble forth before she could lose her nerve.

"In fact, Jesus, I need to confess something that has been weighing on me heavily: my physical needs have become such an obsession that I am having a problem being around you as just your friend. I want to have a physically intimate relationship with you, and I suspect you feel the same."

Jesus was silent for so long Magda wondered if he was simply going to ignore her. But if she had looked into his eyes she would have seen that he had heard, and that he was clearly upset that she had given voice to those needs. He sat in deep thought before answering her, knowing that his words would be hurtful and perhaps deal a fatal blow to their relationship.

Finally he spoke, lovingly but firmly. "Magda, you know that as the Son of man I am committed to leading souls to God. I must lead by example. My physical needs must take a backseat to the mission.

"I am aware that you need a complete relationship with a man—one that satisfies your physical needs. But I am not that man. It would be unfair for me to give you any false hope that our relationship can be anything but that of loving friends. I love you more than any earthly being, even more than my mother, father and siblings, but I love you as a friend, not as a lover. Your failure to accept that will be the ruination of our relationship."

Magda slowly sank down into the sand, insulted and deeply hurt. She had built a fantasy world where she and Jesus would live happily ever after as friends and lovers, if not as husband and wife. Now her dreams had been struck down with one blow. Once again, she had been wounded by someone whose love she had sought in vain. Jesus had become as much of a disappointment to her as Rachel and Benjamin, whose love, while dangling above her like a carrot on a stick, was always just out of reach. *Perhaps I seek out those whose love I can never have; maybe that's my way of staying free.*

She had never allowed herself to think about the reality that Jesus had just painted for her with brutal honesty. As the Son of God, he must remain celibate and pure; he must avoid the kind of woman Solomon described in Ecclesiastes: "*I find more bitter than death the woman who is a snare, whose heart is a trap and whose hands are chains.*"

Magda did not even say good-bye. She turned and ran, stumbling a bit, her tears making tracks in the desert sands, while that familiar refrain echoed in her ear . . . *I guess I was meant to make my journey in flight, like those drifting, ephemeral clouds—ever moving, seemingly transparent, yet defying inspection by disappearing at the probing touch of one who would try to know me, thus trap me, making me lie down in the dearth of the earth, and no more—The Moon and I.*

Part Three

"When a true genius comes into the world, you may know him by this sign: that the dunces are all in confederacy against him."

Jonathan Swift

Chapter Twenty-Four

Beware of false prophets, which come to you in sheep's clothing, but inwardly they are ravening wolves.

Matt. 7:15

MARTHA KNEW THE MINUTE MAGDA came through the door something was wrong. Her usually rosy complexion was ashen and it was obvious she had been crying. In truth, she had cried all the way back to Magdala and all the way up the footpath to the house, not caring who saw her tears.

Martha knew better than to question Magda when she was in one of her moods, so she just patted her on the shoulder; but she couldn't resist her usual greeting, "Magda, sit down and have something to eat. I have just pulled some bread from the oven."

Magda ignored Martha and ran up the stairs to her bedroom. Two days later she left, carrying several traveling bags.

Something really bad must have happened, Martha thought. She had never seen Magda in a bad mood for so long. She was worried about her younger sister, who had come and gone again without eating or drinking anything. (As usual, Magda's nighttime forays through the house were unknown to anyone but the servants, who noticed the evidence of her visits to the wine cellar.)

Following her estrangement from Jesus, she was insatiable. She began to indulge her every appetite. She was eating too little and drinking too much, sleeping fitfully and sharing her bed with too many men, some whose names she couldn't remember the morning after.

Magda was in too much pain to stay in one place for very long. By constantly moving from place to place, from lover to lover, Magda eased the longing she felt for Jesus. But he visited her in her dreams as the lover he would never be. Those dreams turned into nightmares so real she would wake up with tears on her face.

Slowly she began her descent back into madness, into an abyss far worse than her childhood foolishness. Whereas her childish missteps were mischievous escapades that could be laughed away, no one was laughing anymore, especially not Magda.

While she neglected her body, her family and friends, she became more attentive to her perfume and incense business. Her wealth increased, but her spiritual health was at an all-time low. Her life became one of manic business travels to Arabia, India, and Egypt; and for pleasure to Italia and her favorite—the Greek Isles.

The lusty Greek men would roll out the red carpet for her when she arrived. Gregarious and rowdy, they were captivated by her beauty, but they enjoyed her company even more. She was unlike any woman they had ever met—she could out-drink and out-party all of them.

As she traveled, rarely declining an invitation from a would-be lover to visit some far-flung spot, her infamy grew. Soon the gossip among her new acquaintances spread to her friends in Israel, some who were loyal, others who turned their backs on her saying, "Magda has finally gone off the deep end."

When news of Magda's behavior made its way to Nazareth, Joseph said to Mary, "I hate to say I told you so, but I always knew that Magda had a wicked streak a mile wide that even Jesus couldn't conquer. For all her pious mewling after him, it was just a matter of time until she reverted to her evil ways. A leopard doesn't change its spots."

More and more troubled by Joseph's judgmental attitude, Mary thought, *Look who's calling whom a leopard . . . the only difference is Joseph's spots, colored by his religious fervor, seem to get larger and darker the more pious he becomes. But I wonder if his sins are actually worse than Magda's since she is kinder, her heart is purer and she is never judgmental.*

Augustine was the favorite son of a wealthy Greek ship-builder whose main residence was in Athens. But his island home on Crete was a favorite haunt of the spoiled young man whose parties in the seaside mansion were legendary. Augustine's father favored him above his other children because, while the others resembled their mother, a dark Egyptian woman who had not aged well and had long ago lost the affections of her husband, Augustine was the very image of his father—in appearance. There the resemblance ended. His father had sacrificed and worked hard to provide a lasting legacy for his children, especially for Augustine. But his hopes that his troubled son would mature into a man of character were fading as he struggled to deal with his son's loathsome behavior and the complaints of his abusive treatment of his inferiors—especially women.

Augustine had never been refused anything as a child, and he had exchanged the yolk of childhood indulgence for the cloak of a grown man's greed. He denied himself nothing, nor did he attempt to curb his appetite for sexual cruelty with his many partners. His deviant habits were discreetly indulged on the remote island far away from the reproachful eye of his father. The risk of reprisals from the Cretan officials, particularly proconsul Prilus, whose money belt was lined with Augustine's hush money, was mitigated by his generous bribes. But even Prilus was often disgusted by the complaints from some of the guests about the injuries suffered during an Augustine party.

During a weekend on the island of Cyprus, he met a wealthy Israelite woman whose beauty surpassed any woman's he had ever known. She was clever, witty, naughty and different from all his previous lovers. He had never bedded a redhead, and his pulse raced at the stories he had heard of their fiery temperaments.

At the moment that redhead was sailing to Crete to spend a week with him.

In the midst of a fierce storm, Magda's boat approached the Fair Havens' dock, which was barely visible through the rain and the fog. She couldn't shake the gloomy feeling that the trip was doomed to end badly. Despite the storm, she stood on deck at the railing of the boat and scanned the dock for Augustine, hoping he would recognize her. The rain had flattened her hair and soaked her garments, but her appearance was the least of her concerns.

She felt a bit unsettled as she looked into the heaving waters and worried. *What is the matter with me? I'm on my way to meet a handsome rich man and we are going to spend a glorious week together; any minute now I'll be happy.*

Instead of looking forward to seeing the new man in her life, all she could think about was Jesus and the look on his face when she had run off, following his rejection of her. Time was not healing the empty feeling she had had since that awful day when she had left him standing by the sea; and distance was not helping with the pain of missing him. She had handled her misery by pushing it down into that abyss called 'Oh well, this too shall pass.' She tried to cure her blues by thinking about the lusty Greek man she was sailing to meet.

As a precaution, Magda never stayed at anyone's personal residence. But for Augustine she had made an exception. He was handsome, worldly and rich—almost as wealthy as she—and she thought at last she had found someone with whom she could have a lasting relationship. She thought the feelings were mutual.

She was mistaken.

Augustine was waiting for her as the boat pulled alongside the dock. As he reached down and helped her out of the boat, his hand brushed against her breast. A little warning voice whispered to her, "Your new friend is not a gentleman, far from it. Get back on the boat and leave now."

She should have listened to that little voice.

"Welcome to Fair Havens, pretty lady," Augustine said, enveloping her in a hug and kissing her with more force than affection.

He took hold of her arm and led her to his carriage. Not much of a conversationalist, he spoke little during the ride to his seaside villa. But he held her hand in his sweaty one and sat close to her, a little too close for comfort.

She moved away from him a bit and reminisced about her relationship with Jesus. Apparently, what she was looking for didn't exist. Well, it did exist, but there was only one problem: Jesus was saving his virginity . . . for what? She realized she had closed her eyes and was shaking her head. Augustine was looking at her with a slight frown on his face as he pulled her closer to him.

Little alarms started ringing loudly in her ears and she thought, *He's not getting off to a very good start with me. He's no different from the rest of my long-lost lovers who don't realize that the way to a woman's heart is through affection.*

Her visit to Fair Havens was to be the low point of her life. She had finally hit bottom.

Magda became aware of voices close to her ear. "Is she breathing?" Two ragged beggars with carrion breath were kneeling beside her where she lay on a crumbling pier. They were trying to decide if they should bother to get help for her.

Little by little it came back to her what had happened, although she didn't remember anything after she had passed out in Augustine's room. She knew she must have been dumped unconscious, like so much refuse, on this rat-infested wharf. She had to make these men understand that she was alive and needed a doctor.

"Help me," she begged in a voice that sounded like it was coming from the bottom of a well. "Please take me to a doctor. I can pay." Then she lost consciousness again.

Hours later she opened her eyes to see a man bending over her. She was totally nude, her only adornment the woven Kabbalah bracelet that she always wore. She was lying on a table beneath a blanket. Someone she hoped was a doctor was examining her. He was looking at her with a kindness that didn't conceal his curiosity about how a woman of her class could be found in such low circumstances.

He said to his assistant, "Bring over a cup of wine, our patient is waking up."

Then he touched her arm gently and said, "I am Luke, a physician. A couple of beggars brought you to my doorstep in the wee hours of the morning. Although you were completely unclothed, they swore they hadn't harmed you. They said that they had found you lying unconscious on the dock. But it's obvious someone has done you grievous harm."

Her body was so brutalized it hurt even to speak. She said, "I am Mary Magdalene of the House of Benjamin in Israel. I will be happy to pay you if you will allow me to remain here until I am able to travel."

Luke held her hand and said, "I am familiar with The House of Benjamin. But who did this to you? You were viciously beaten, even bitten, and sodomized. The Cretans do not tolerate such attacks on their citizens or their visitors. I'll report this to the authorities and make sure your attacker is punished to the fullest extent of the law."

Magda shook her head and said, "I do not want to prosecute, which will only delay my departure. I am even more concerned that this madman might come back to kill me. I just want to get well enough to go home to Magdala."

Luke looked at her thoughtfully and turned to his assistant. "You may go now," Luke said to him.

When they were alone, he said, "You can speak freely now."

"Well, first things first, please call me Magda." She debated how much she should reveal, but decided to trust the doctor.

Magda began haltingly, but soon the words spilled out of her. "His name is Augustine, but beyond that I'm ashamed to say I don't know a lot about him. I was visiting him at his villa by the sea and during a wild party he attacked me."

The doctor snorted. "Augustine! I want you to tell me exactly what happened. Don't leave out anything. If I am to help you I need to know all of the facts."

Bit by bit Magda began to tell the story, trusting the doctor would hear her out before forming any opinions. It was painful to relive what had happened . . . painful but cathartic.

"Soon after I arrived at Fair Havens, Augustine hosted a feast in my honor with enough food and wine to feed all the Cretans, the most important of whom were guests at the celebration. There were dancers—a few mere children—who wore very little other than grotesque masks that I assume were intended to conceal their identities. Their dancing became more lewd and suggestive, the music louder and faster, the crowd more frenzied as the night wore on. I tried to join in, but it's impossible to have a good time when you're a stranger at a party for the insane.

"The finale was much too debased for my tastes. I like a good time but have not fallen so low that I enjoy the kind of depravity that is obviously common Augustine party fare.

"Augustine was dancing with a young girl who appeared to be drugged. I took advantage of that opportunity to slip out into the night air to clear my head somewhat. I was drunker than I had ever been, and I began to feel dizzy as I staggered back to my room."

Magda paused for a moment before continuing with her sordid story. She had never been very open with anyone – even Mary or Jesus – about her secret life, but somehow talking with a stranger was different. She took a deep breath, which hurt everywhere, and went on with her story.

"Regardless of how it must sound to you, I am not evil incarnate. I do believe in a loving God. But most of the time I put off worrying about Him until it's time to ask for His help. This was one of those times. I fell to my knees and prayed, 'Lord, if you're out there somewhere, please help me.'

"I was not so far gone that I failed to notice someone in the shadows who seemed to be following me. As I quickened my pace, so did my stalker. Soon I was running, by now very much alarmed that the person behind me seemed intent on doing me harm. I was being pursued by the most subtle and violent of all predators—Augustine.

"My feet became entangled in my cloak and I fell onto the stone walkway. I was dazed but alert enough to feel terror. Augustine was instantly upon me, dragging me to the end of the colonnade and into his private quarters, which were foggy with opium fumes. He threw me onto his bed and kissed me roughly, his pointed tongue like a dagger in my throat.

"He began to abuse me, violently pulling my hair and beating me until the world went dark.

"The rest you know."

Dr. Luke was quiet for a moment, his eyes revealing his disgust. Finally he said, "Augustine is a disgrace to Greece; I cannot believe you got mixed up with him.

"I'm sorry that you suffered such ill treatment at the hands of someone on this peaceful island that I love so much. But I'm not surprised to learn that your attacker was Augustine; he is a savage! That's why they call him 'Doggie Augie.' This is not the first time I have heard complaints about him. The problem is getting someone to listen to me. I have reported complaints about him many times in the past to no avail. Apparently, he has bought off some of the officials. But there are other ways of handling the problem. A word to the right person is all that is needed. Now that I have heard the story first hand from a credible victim, I intend to see that he is taken care of."

Magda nodded drowsily and was asleep before he walked away.

The next morning she awoke to find Luke back at her side. "You're looking much better today. Since you seem to be interested in going back to Israel as soon as possible, may I offer my services as a chaperone? Actually, my main residence and medical practice are in Jerusalem, and I had planned to return next week. I've been in Crete meeting with an old friend named Nicodemus, a native of Crete who lives in Jerusalem now. I invited him to visit me here where we could freely discuss some unsettling things that are happening in the city."

Magda perked up at the mention of unusual things happening in Jerusalem. "Dr. Luke, would you mind telling me more explicitly what's going on in Jerusalem? Do they by any chance concern a man named Jesus?"

He hesitated a moment, but he felt that Magda, if she was an acquaintance of Jesus, deserved to hear the truth about the dangers he was facing.

"Well, Magda, as a matter of fact there is a lot of unrest in Jerusalem, and Jesus is right in the middle of it. He has ruffled the feathers of some pretty important people with his claims to be the Messiah. Despite the incredible miracles he has performed—healing the blind and the lame and even raising the dead—the elders and the scribes think that he is an imposter and a rabble rouser. While the number of his followers has grown impressively, the number of his enemies, mostly powerful men, is growing as well."

By now the doctor had her full attention. "The Sanhedrin, of which my friend Nico is a member, fear that Jesus is a threat to Israel's peaceful coexistence with the Romans, and they are gathering damning evidence, mostly false, to have him arrested and possibly even sentenced to death.

"While we are not convinced that Jesus is the Messiah he claims to be, Nico and I certainly do not agree that he should be prosecuted as a criminal. As you know, he is innocent of their charges and has done many wonderful things. We are determined to convince many more like-minded people to join in opposing the Sanhedrin—not a thing to be undertaken lightly—and we seem to be gaining ground."

Magda was sickened by Luke's revelations and she felt that familiar tug of guilt for running off and leaving Jesus alone to face his problems. She knew that Jesus had created some enemies by declaring himself to be the Son of God, but she had no idea that some of those enemies were members of the powerful Sanhedrin. All of the resistance to him must have escalated while she was away.

"Dr. Luke, please forgive my asking you to change your schedule, but I need to get back to Israel right away. Is it possible for us to leave earlier than next week? And can you send someone to collect my things? I can't travel in a nightgown."

Luke frowned, worried about Magda's acquaintances and the problems she might bring into his life. "Your clothes have already been collected, but I'm not sure you are ready to travel. Let's have a look and see how your healing is progressing."

He helped her turn over and began to examine her buttocks, fearful that some of the deeper bite marks might have become infected. But she was young and healthy and healing nicely.

"Well, everything looks much better. None of your wounds is infected, but it's going to be pretty painful for you to sit down for a while. Your buttocks are bruised and swollen and they're going to be very tender for a few weeks."

He was a little concerned that their conversation about Jesus had sparked her sudden urgency to return to Israel. She needed to rest and heal, but he knew that she had more important things on her mind—namely Jesus.

And he was right. She could endure pain now that she had an urgent need to get back—she needed to reconcile with Jesus right away and nothing was going to slow her down. She needed him and now he needed her as well, more than ever.

"Dr. Luke, I have a high threshold for pain. In two days I'll be ready to go. So can we plan to leave the day after tomorrow?" she asked.

For the next two days, Magda recuperated in Dr. Luke's second bedroom, which reminded her of her childhood room in Magdala with its view of the sea. Like the House of Benjamin, Luke's house was perched high on a cliff overlooking the water. It was balm to her wounded soul and made her homesick for her family. How long had she been away? The months were a blur.

Just as she had lain in her bed reliving her troubled childhood after her mother died, now she lay in bed on this beautiful Greek Isle and relived the madness of her life since she had left Jesus by the sea.

She closed her eyes and thought about the decadent life she had led since she had run away. It hadn't even seemed right at the time. How many men had she opened her body to, only to leave them the next day hungrier than ever? How many miles had she run trying to lose the dark shadow that had finally caught up with her? She tried to blot out everything, to clear her mind and her conscience.

"This time you've gone too far, Magda," her father's oft-repeated admonition came back to haunt her.

I want to go home, she thought. "Home," she said out loud. Then an idea began to take shape. She made a promise to herself: *I am going to find a place near Jerusalem and build a great house . . . my own home.*

Magda had been back in Magdala for just two days when she asked Benjamin to come to her room. "Abba, I need your help with a matter that concerns Jesus. Doctor Luke told me that the Sanhedrin are building a case against him, accumulating mostly false evidence, and I fear that they are going to have him arrested on these trumped up charges.

"If I remember correctly, your attorney, Joseph of Arimathea, is a member of the Sanhedrin. Will you please ask him what his colleagues are planning to do and find out when they plan to arrest Jesus? Abba, promise me you'll talk to Joseph right away and ask him to intervene on Jesus' behalf. You know that he and Mary are my dearest friends and I couldn't bear it if he were harmed, particularly since he is innocent of any wrongdoing."

Benjamin stood silently, his brow furrowed, studying his younger daughter. "I'll talk to Joseph when I'm in Jerusalem next week, Magda. And now, as much as I hate to bring up such an unpleasant subject while you are recovering from your injuries, I want to talk with you about your behavior over the past several months.

"You know I have never paid attention to idle gossip or have cared much for other peoples' opinions of me, but when it comes to what people say about my children, that's different. People are talking about you, saying terrible things. By chance, I overheard a conversation two men were having about you in a wineshop.

"You remember Constantine, who used to be my partner in the boat building company. Since he sold out his half of the business to me, he spends his idle time gossiping and imbibing a bit of the grape with some of his cronies.

"Although he was embarrassed when I told him I had overheard him discussing you, he was candid when I asked him to tell me what he was talking about. Seems as though he has a good friend, a wealthy and powerful Greek from Athens named Aristotle, who told him quite a tale about an incident in Crete you were involved in. Obviously, your injuries are the result of that incident, not the carriage accident you invented."

Childishly, Magda put her hands over her ears. *Oh God, will it never end? I can't believe Dr. Luke told anybody what happened to me, especially Ari the Greek. Doesn't that violate the Hippocratic Oath?* Then she realized that Ari must be the man Dr. Luke had said would fix the Augustine problem.

Magda knew that the best thing, the *only* thing to do was to be honest with Benjamin. She needed to get rid of her habit of telling 'little white lies' that rolled off her tongue like pomegranate seeds.

"Abba, I must confess that I fibbed about falling out of the carriage. I just wanted to spare myself the embarrassment of admitting to you what really happened." And she told him how Augustine had lured her to Crete and attacked her in a mad frenzy.

Benjamin's face went from red to purple as she told him the story. He started pacing the room, his hands clenched, vowing to bring down a world of misery on Augustine. But Magda begged him not to get involved.

"Abba, please let Dr. Luke take care of it with Ari and the Cretan authorities, as he has promised to do. If Luke confided in Ari, I'm sure he asked him to talk to the right people to ensure that Augustine is taken care of. Luke says that if anyone ever needs a favor from the higher ups or the Greek underground, Ari is the man to ask. Maybe the Cretan police won't handle it, but I'm quite sure Ari will."

Calmer now, Benjamin sat down beside her and took hold of her hand. "Well, that makes me feel a little better about the immediate problem, but to get back to what I'm most upset about, is this going to wake you up to how dangerous your behavior is? You need to stop the madness; next time you might not be so lucky."

She knew he was right, and she knew who would help her stop the madness.

Chapter Twenty-Five

He that is without sin among you, let him first cast a stone at her.

John 8:7

MAGDA WAS ON HER WAY to Jerusalem. She had learned that Jesus had been teaching in the temple for the past several weeks and she was eager to find him and beg his forgiveness for deserting him.

She was traveling with her father's bodyguards in a closed carriage, unwilling to show her face. Her bruises had yellowed from the ugly purple of recent weeks, but her healing was far from complete. She hoped by the time they arrived in Jerusalem, she would be ready to face Jesus.

They were taking the route along the west banks of the Sea of Galilee and the Jordan River because she wanted to bathe in the warm springs of Tiberias. The Romans had installed a large set of baths on the site, and the waters were considered to be healing.

As she soaked her wounded body in the mineral waters, she asked God to help her. "Lord, am I evil? I don't want to be. Please help me. Please forgive me for always disappointing you and myself and the people who love me. I want to become the Magda I know I can be. But I can't do it without your help. Please help me when I don't even help myself."

The warm waters soothed her and seemed to whisper to her, "This is the refreshing."

The Jordan River flows out of the Sea of Galilee and narrows into a winding, watery snake as it crawls south on its muddy belly into the Dead Sea. Magda was thankful that they would bypass the infamous Machaerus Prison, where John had been beheaded. She averted her eyes, not even willing to glimpse the distant hilltop where Herod's fortress overlooked the Dead Sea.

She breathed a sigh of relief when they turned toward the west and followed the Jericho Road that rose into the foothills of the Mount of Olives. Remembering happier times when John had baptized Jesus in the Jordan, Magda looked for the inn near Bethany where they had stayed for a couple of days on that special occasion. As they came around a big bend in the road, there it was, just as she had remembered it, nestled in a shady grove of fig, olive and almond trees.

She decided to spend a few days in the inn while her face and body healed completely. She knew Jesus would see beyond the bruising to the person within; but after all, she was a woman, and she wanted to look her best when she saw him again after so many months.

On the third day, she rose earlier than usual, determined to explore the surrounding countryside until she found what she was looking for. She turned off the road into a dirt path and suddenly came into a clearing where the morning sun had painted acres of wildflowers in pink and gold. She heard the sound of falling water and followed her ears to a high waterfall. The water had split a massive cliff in half before cascading down into a stream that flowed across the back of the property.

This is everything I have dreamed of and more, she thought as she walked the land, mentally sketching the boundaries that she would encircle with a stone wall. A rambling stone cottage began to take shape in her mind. *I will build a livable sculpture right in the middle of this wild garden.*

Visualizing the house in her mind, she pictured an herb garden beside the kitchen door. "Heli's Herb Garden," she said aloud. "Heli," she said again. And suddenly she was sobbing, releasing tears she hadn't been able to shed since Heli's death. It seemed that everything that had happened since, all equally tragic, had been pushed back until she could hold it in no more. She began to unravel with misery and grief.

"Oh, Heli," she cried again. And then again. All of the sorrow she had held inside—not properly mourning the loss of Heli; not giving into the sadness of her abrupt parting with Jesus; barely acknowledging the traumatic experience with Augustine—erupted now in a tidal wave of pain so wrenching that she lay down in the damp grass and wept until she was empty and exhausted. Finally, she slept.

The cooing of a mourning dove awakened her. Her first thought was, *It is too pretty a day to waste on regretting things I cannot change; but while I can't do anything about Heli, I can certainly fix the problem with Jesus. But first things first: my long-awaited home near Jerusalem—"Malama."*

She walked down to the pond, sat down on one of the boulders, and began to visualize the house she would build. Martha, Lazarus, Zachary, and Nathanial would each have a bedroom—after all, it was going to be their house, too. But just as important, the house would be a haven for Jesus: a place he would be welcome to visit, or maybe even live if she could convince him he would be safe—from her.

She was planning her future with Jesus as if there were no question they would be together again. But she had to be healed enough to face him.

She went back to her room in the inn and pulled her mirror out of her bag. She held her breath and shut her eyes before looking in the ornate silver mirror—a memento from Rachel. Opening one eye at a time, she peered at her reflection. She was back. Almost. The skin was pulled a little tighter than usual over her cheekbones, but she was healing nicely and glowing again.

Time to face Jesus. On to Jerusalem.

She pulled a veil about her head, covering her face loosely, and walked out of the inn, headed to the temple. But soon she realized she wasn't up to walking even a short distance. For the first time in her life she would have to hire a litter.

Just before the litter reached the Beautiful Gate to the city, she gave the panting bearers a break, which she also needed to reflect on what she would say to Jesus when she saw him.

When they arrived at the temple, she started to climb out of the litter. Not completely steady on her feet, she stumbled and fell gracelessly into the street. The long veil came off her head and her garments flew up, revealing her legs and ankles, which were marred by bruises and bite marks. Unmasked and exposed, she faced a rabble of men, who were gawking at the litter and its spilled passenger.

The crowd consisted of about twenty men—a few Pharisees and Sadducees, but mostly idle-looking men—who were listening to the man who was preaching in the middle of the circle.

One of the men was a fisherman from Magdala, whom Benjamin had fired. He recognized Magda and began to shout, "Harlot, prostitute, evil woman, what are you doing here? You don't belong here, this is a holy place. Go back to your drunken orgies. Men, let's give her some encouragement to leave."

An inventive liar, he started telling everyone who would listen—the Pharisees were always willing to listen to a description of a fallen woman—that he had witnessed some of her evil deeds with his own eyes. Then he picked up a stone, urging the others to do the same.

Magda was humiliated. She tried to disappear, covering her face and head with the veil, but the men surrounded her, taunting her and pulling at her garments. "This time your father's money can't buy you out of trouble," yelled the disgruntled fisherman. "Now you're going to answer for your wicked behavior."

Magda wasn't truly back; if she had been herself, she would never have been caught in such a compromising situation. This was a diminished Magda, her confidence in tatters.

One of the Pharisees drew back his arm to throw a stone. But someone grabbed his upper arm from behind and held it in a death grip. It was Jesus.

"What is the trouble here?" he asked as he moved in front of Magda, who lay in the street, veiled and not moving.

Another one of the men stepped up and shouted, "This woman is the bride of the devil; she is a harlot and an adulterer, a disgrace to all women. She deserves to die for her sins against the laws of Moses."

Jesus, like John the Baptist, had been very vocal in condemning the self-righteous piety of the Pharisees. They believed that a man could enter the Lord's kingdom only if he had proven his devotion by obeying every one of the hundreds of religious laws that had accumulated over the centuries. The majority of Pharisees were educated men who knew just enough to be dangerous. It was their extreme piety rather than their spirituality that set them apart from others; and they often went to great lengths to demonstrate that piety.

Magda lay curled in a ball, her head and body completely covered lest Jesus discover her identity. He began to ask her questions, but she remained silent, fearing he might recognize her voice.

One by one, the other men had picked up rocks to participate in the stoning, but Jesus remained standing protectively in front of her. Then he kneeled and began to write in the dust.

The meaning of his writings was not lost on the Pharisees, who had cited the law from Deuteronomy in condemning Magda. Jesus wrote the part of the law they had omitted: '. . . only one who has never committed the accused's sin can cast a stone.'

Then he rose from the ground and addressed the crowd, "He who is without sin, let him cast the first stone." Although a few men left, a few diehards remained, grumbling and calling the other men cowards.

Jesus remained in front of Magda, kneeling to write in the dust again, shouting even louder than before, "He who is without sin, let him cast the first stone." One by one the men left until there was just Jesus, who knelt beside Magda.

"Woman, where are your accusers now? No man remained to accuse you."

Magda shook her head, unwilling to speak or to show her face.

He placed his hand on her head. "Neither do I condemn you; go and sin no more," he said.

"Rabboni," Magda cried hysterically.

"Magda," Jesus cried as he sank to the ground beside her. He pulled her veil aside, held her face in his hands and stared into her eyes. Then he gathered her into his arms and pulled her close.

When he finally pulled her to her feet, he realized she was in no shape to walk. He called to Simon and Andrew, who had stood off to the side while Jesus and Magda had their reunion, "Peter, summon a litter for Magda, she is unwell."

Several hours later Magda opened her eyes. Jesus was sitting in a chair by her bed, holding her hand and looking at her.

Magda sat up and took in her surroundings. Then she got that look. "Jesus, there are two things I am puzzled about: since when is Simon called Peter?"

She was back.

"Since I named him that after telling him that he is the rock upon which my church will be built."

Magda rolled her eyes but didn't comment. Then she said, "All right, second question: how did you know I was staying here?"

A bit sheepishly Jesus said, "I have sort of been keeping tabs on you, Magda. Benjamin's bodyguards came through Jerusalem on their way back to Magdala. I just happened to run into them and they told me where you were staying. And yes, I had an idea you were the woman in the street that the Pharisees were going to stone."

Magda didn't know whether to laugh or cry, but she decided she had shed enough tears for a while. "Jesus, can I come back home? Can we go back to where we were before my demons took me away? Can I just come back without making a fuss about it, knowing I don't have to explain anything? It's too painful."

Jesus answered by kissing her on both cheeks. "You're back, that's all that matters."

Magda was too emotional to answer. They sat quietly for a moment until Jesus said, "Magda, let's see now, where were we, a few lifetimes ago, before we were so rudely interrupted?"

"I remember exactly where we were. We had just returned from the desert and had crossed the Galilee to Bethsaida. Then after a few days in Capernaum, we were going to Gadara . . . back across the Galilee . . . and then . . ."

Chapter Twenty-Six

So the devils besought him, saying, If thou cast us out, suffer us to go away into the herd of swine.

Matt. 8:31

You take my life,
When you do take the means whereby I live.

Shakespeare, "The Merchant of Venice"

MAGDA WAS ONCE AGAIN AT Jesus' side, and the ministry continued. First stop, Gadara. As they pulled onto the eastern shore of the Galilee, they asked some men for directions to the region of the Gadarenes. "Just follow your nose, snort, snort . . . you can't miss it," the men said, looking in amusement at the group and shaking their heads. *Why in the world would a bunch of swine-hating Jews be going to Gadara, the pig capital of the world?*

The directions were good, and by following their noses, they found the town without a problem. As they headed down a road that ended in a high cliff overlooking the Galilee, they came upon a farm with as many as 2000 pigs that were noisily feeding from enormous troughs. Obviously, this was Gentile country. A herd of pigs that large should have indicated to Jesus and his disciples that pig farming was the mainstay of the Gadarene economy and therefore off-limits to any religious rites that might result in their harm.

Suddenly a demon-possessed man ran up. He fell down before Jesus, crying out in a loud voice, "What have I to do with you, Jesus, thou Son of God? Please do not torment me."

Jesus replied, "What is my business? It is dealing with troubled human beings like you. What is your name?"

"Well, I don't exactly recall. Just call me Legion, that's what most of the good citizens of this town call me." He was so called because of the many demons that possessed him, some sad, some mean, and all so crazy that one never knew what he might do next. He was so strong in his manic energy he broke the chains that the townsmen used in an attempt to keep him from running naked through the streets of the city and terrorizing its residents.

Jesus reached out his hand to the man, who reared back in terror. But Jesus stood patiently, waiting for him to take hold of his hand. Sobbing and trembling, a becalmed Legion reached out to Jesus, who commanded the demons to leave the man's body. Immediately, the demons entered into the herd of swine that, bedeviled, hurtled down the cliff, all two thousand falling into the sea.

When the herdsmen saw what had happened, they hurried to find the pig farmer to tell him what Jesus had done. The farmer was furious. The pigs were his only resource and now he was left without an income.

As the pig farmer, Ham, and his herdsmen approached, Magda took him aside and asked him to calculate the amount of the damages. "I will cover your losses, but you are to tell no one who paid you, and you must promise to give safe passage to our group so we can leave the area without reprisals from you and your neighbors."

Ham kept his word and no one was harmed, but that didn't keep the angry mob from following Jesus and his followers as they left the town.

Raising their fists they shouted, "Leave Gadara and never show your faces in this town again. You are lucky to escape with your lives."

Magda grabbed Jesus' hand and pulled him along, walking in equal amounts of anger and anxiety, back to their boat. Legion ran alongside them, now clothed and in his right mind. He grabbed hold of Jesus' robe and said, "Let me join you. I am a believer and a walking testament to your healing powers."

But Jesus sent him away, saying, "Return to your own house, and show what great things God has done for you."

Magda was upset with Jesus over the pig incident. But she had learned her lesson and she was gentle as she chastised him.

"Jesus, what were you thinking . . . that pigs can fly? Maybe those pigs were nothing to you but swine—vile and unclean—but they were the farmer's livelihood. You must stop short of hurting innocent people in your miraculous healings. It is dangerous for you and harmful to your ministry."

Jesus pulled her down beside him in the middle of the boat and put his arm around her. "Magda, as you well know, sometimes a huge result begs a huge example. Everything that happens is God's will.

"What just happened in Gadara? A farmer's pigs went for a swim. Can pigs fly? No. But pigs *can* swim; not only can they swim, they enjoy it. And that pig farmer knows it. I promise you that he and his herdsmen are downstream right this very moment rounding up a bunch of wet and much better smelling pigs—probably all 2000 of them. And tonight he will be counting the money you gave him and patting himself on the back for swindling the rich city girl out of her money, probably singing '. . . 2000 swines-a-swimming.'"

As usual, Magda had the last word. "I just hope the Gadarenes like deviled ham."

As such stories spread throughout Israel, more and more people sought Jesus, gladly receiving him and spreading the message throughout the land that Jesus was the Son of God—the promised Messiah.

But many others despised him, believing him to be a false prophet. And they added the story of the lost swine to a growing list of grievances against him: that he did more harm than good; that too many suffered in the wake of his good works for the few.

Jesus was not bothered by the complaints. He returned to Capernaum and continued his ministry, often turning down requests from his converts to become followers.

A wealthy man said, "Lord, I will follow you wherever you go."

But Jesus said to him, "Foxes have holes, and birds of the air have nests; but the Son of man hath nowhere to lay his head."

Chapter Twenty-Seven

While he yet talked to the people, behold, his mother and his brethren stood without, desiring to speak with him . . . . but he answered and said unto him that told him, "Who is my mother? And who are my brethren? And he stretched forth his hand toward his disciples, and said, Behold my mother and my brethren!"

Matt. 12:46-50

As gossip spread of Jesus' relationship with Mary Magdalene, Joseph grew more distant from his son. The elders took him aside many times in the synagogue in Nazareth and asked him to speak to Jesus about his unsavory relationship with an older woman of ill repute.

They also complained to him that Jesus was flagrantly ignoring the Jewish laws by working on the Sabbath and failing to perform the ritual of washing before eating.

Joseph was embarrassed and disappointed that Jesus was turning his back on the lessons and teachings that he and Mary had tried to instill in him. But instead of sitting down to talk with him, Joseph just distanced himself from Jesus, never going to hear him preach. And Mary felt somewhat snubbed by Jesus on the rare occasions she went. He was always too busy for anybody but Magda and his disciples. So Mary was seldom among the crowds that flocked to hear him, even when he was preaching in a nearby town.

Joseph buried his feelings and concerns in work, never turning down a job as too large or too small. He had been hired to build the framework on a structure in Sepphoris, and he took his sons, James and Joses, to help him with the challenging job. He complained to them, "I really could use another hand on this job. I may have bitten off more than I can chew, but you don't say no to Herod's project manager. It's too bad your older brother is too high and mighty to get his hands dirty."

James was surprised at his father's bitterness toward Jesus. "Abba, you should be proud of Jesus and what he has accomplished. He is known practically all over Israel, and his popularity is still growing."

"His popularity is growing? Is that a good thing, James?" Joseph asked. "At any rate, I don't want a famous son. I just want a son who acts like a son. I want Jesus to act like *my* son." He shook his head in disgust and began to climb the ladder. He was nearly to the top when he paused, grabbed his chest, and fell three stories to the ground.

Joses ran over and tried to get a response from Joseph, but he was unconscious. The boys picked up their father's lifeless body and loaded him onto their cart. They began the three-mile trip south to Nazareth, arguing all the way over who would tell Mary what had happened. Joses agreed to deliver the bad news to his mother.

He began to sob when he saw her. "Ima, abba has had an attack of some sort. He fell off a ladder, and the doctor in Sepphoris said there was nothing he could do for him. We have brought him home but we don't think you should see him. Do you think we should get word to Jesus to try to revive him?"

Mary burst into tears. "Oh no, I told Joseph that job was too much for him to take on. I was afraid something like this was going to happen, but lately he has seemed to be interested in nothing but his work.

"I think Jesus is preaching in Capernaum this week. We need to go there and ask for his help."

The three of them climbed into the cart and rushed to Magdala, Mary crying all the way. By the time they boarded the ferry boat to cross the Galilee, Mary had calmed down somewhat. But she worried about what Jesus would say when they told him of his father's accident. Would he take time away from his ministry to return to Nazareth with them?

When they arrived in Capernaum, they went directly to Peter's house, which was crowded with many people who had come to hear Jesus preach. As they made their way through the throngs of people in the courtyard, they were disappointed that there was not one familiar face in the crowd. Mary knew they had made the trip for naught.

James found Philip and asked him to give Jesus a message that his mother and brothers were there and needed to see him about an urgent matter.

But when Jesus heard the message, he said, "Who is my mother? And who are my brothers?" He stretched forth his hand to the crowd and said, "*These* are my mothers and *these* are my brothers, for whoever does the will of God, the same is my brother and my sister and my mother."

When Mary heard Jesus' words, she hung her head, stung. He was the Son of God, but he was also her son. Yet he had turned her away when she needed him. Disappointing but not surprising.

Just then Magda burst through the crowd. "Mary, what is it?"

"Joseph has fallen off a ladder and we fear he is dead. We wanted Jesus to try to revive him. But now I have changed my mind. If I am no more mother to Jesus than the women who come to hear him preach then Joseph is even less his father; after all, they haven't been that close in the past few years.

"Tell Jesus that he needn't interrupt his sermon for something as trivial as the death of his father."

Magda was in disbelief. *What has happened to that humble man from Galilee that I have known and loved all these years? Where has this hubris come from all of a sudden?*

Once again she was tempted to run off, to spend some time alone or with some anonymous stranger who never disappointed because there were no expectations.

Relationships are so difficult, she thought. *If I can't have a successful relationship with a man as perfect as Jesus, what hope is there for me? Maybe he's too perfect.*

After asking Philip to tell Jesus about his father, she left Capernaum and sailed across the Galilee to Magdala. She needed to spend some time away from Jesus and cool down a little bit. While she didn't want another hiatus of several months, neither did she want to risk being with him while she was this upset; saying things she would regret later. Better to take a little break. But eventually, she would have to ask him how he could have humiliated his own mother and brothers.

Magda was glad that she had come to see her father. He looked much frailer than the last time she had seen him. Martha said that he had been declining for the past couple of months. Worse, he was suffering from occasional dementia, often not even recognizing his own children. Magda knew that she was probably going to lose her father soon.

She went into Benjamin's room and said, "Abba, it's Magda. I'm sorry I've been away for so long. You still recognize me, don't you?"

He seemed to rally at the sound of her voice. "How could I not know my beautiful Magda? I'm so glad you've come." He lay back and closed his eyes for a moment. "I'm a sick old man and I'm not going to be very good company. Sad to say, I'm tired of being ill and I'm ready to go. But I did want to say goodbye to all my loved ones first.

"I've become a burden to my children and I never wanted that to happen. What good is life if someone has to wait on you hand and foot, feed you, bathe you, and do other things no person should have to do for a grown man?"

Magda realized how much her father had declined in her absence. He was failing fast. "Abba, do you want me to send for the rabbi to come and pray with you?"

"No, what good would that do? I've been a pretty good man and I'm sure I'll go to heaven."

"Well, abba, you *will* go to heaven if you know Jesus as your personal savior."

Benjamin frowned and looked puzzled. "Who's that?"

She laughed in spite of herself and answered, "Abba, you know Jesus. Jesus is Mary's son."

Then in a more lucid moment he commented, "Oh, Mary's son—that's who you're talking about. Now I recall. Everyone says he has become a popular teacher and a gifted healer. Hmmph! He looks more like a beggar to me. Where are his phylacteries? I've never seen him wearing them and he doesn't look like any priest I've ever seen."

"Well, abba, he's not like any priest you've ever seen. His love of God goes far deeper than the fancy tunics and tefillin worn for show by those whose spirituality is no deeper than the hairs on their skin. Jesus is real. Jesus is love. And Jesus is the love of my life.

"Abba, promise me you'll hang on until I return with him. After you pray with him, if you don't want him to prolong your life, at least you can die in peace."

Benjamin lay back, depressed by their conversation. Nobody likes to talk about death, particularly when it's one's own death. But then he started to talk of practical matters. The more he talked, the more Magda smiled. *Maybe he's not as far gone as I thought.* Benjamin's business sense was as sharp as ever.

"Magda," he said, "there's a good bit of business stuff to cover while you're here, and before I die, I have something personal to tell you; so don't wait very long before you return or it might be too late."

He spoke at length about the division of his estate. She was to contact Joseph of Arimathea, who would help her sort through the maze of financial holdings, have her sign some papers, and lastly, give her a diary that her mother had written for her.

Magda returned to her room and started packing for the trip back to Capernaum. "Oh God, just when I need him most, Jesus and I are having one of our misunderstandings. Or rather, I am having a misunderstanding. Jesus is probably not even aware that anything is wrong." Magda was mumbling to herself more and more these days as her troubles seemed to weigh her down.

Now she answered herself, "Nothing to do but go back to Capernaum and straighten out everything. I need Jesus with me more than ever now."

As soon as the ferry boat arrived in Capernaum, Magda jumped down to the dock, ran across the shore road and up the hill to Peter's house; the house was empty. She knew exactly where to look for Jesus. He had preached one of his first sermons on the mountain behind Peter's house and she knew that is where he probably would be.

There was an area near the summit with flowers growing in abundance, and Jesus was sitting in the midst of them with his back against a huge boulder.

When she got to the top of the mountain, Jesus stood and held out his arms to her. "Magda, I thought I had lost you again. You're not still angry with me, are you?"

Magda hugged him and pulled him down beside her. "Well Jesus, after the scene in Peter's house when you insulted your mother and brothers, I think you have some explaining to do. And since your favorite thing is to walk and talk, will you go to Jerusalem with me to see Benjamin's attorney if I agree to walk? On the way we can talk about why you treated your mother and brothers so disrespectfully."

"Yes, we do need to talk about many things, Magda," Jesus said. "I need to go to Jerusalem anyway; I want to go to Olivet to pray about some things in my future."

She asked, "Jesus, why do you prefer to pray in the hills, or rather, in a garden at the top of a mountain? In Nazareth you always made a beeline for the garden at Orpah's Corpus. And in Capernaum you always head for these hills. Why is that?"

Jesus didn't answer right away. He appeared to be deep in thought. But Magda was accustomed to Jesus' studied responses, seemingly to the simplest questions. While he pondered, she picked a bouquet of daisies and pulled the petals off one by one, grinning at him mischievously and singing in a *falsetto* voice, "He loves me, he loves me not."

Ignoring her silliness, he said, "Mountains are like temples, only better. I would rather sit in the mountains and think about God than sit in the temple and think about the mountains. There is so much beauty on a mountaintop you feel as though you can reach out and touch God. In nature's beauty there is truth."

Magda studied Jesus intently while he spoke. This man was so unusual, so other worldly, that it amazed her how two people as opposite as they could enjoy such a close relationship.

"Sometimes I wonder just what it is that makes us so close," Magda mused aloud. "You love the mountains, I love the shore. You love the quiet of a mountaintop, I prefer the busyness of a city. I love indulgence, you are practically an ascetic. You are celibate, I am . . . well never mind what I am. Besides, I have left all of that far behind, you should pardon the pun." She laughed raucously at her bawdy reference to her recent troubled past.

Then she became serious again. "You have come into my life and changed me so completely I hardly recognize myself these days.

"We are different in many outward ways. Yet we are drawn to each other. Whatever it is, even when I'm angry with you—like I'm supposed to be right now—I still love you. I think one of the things I love about you is that you recognize my inner goodness. Few people do."

Chapter Twenty-Eight

Joseph of Arimathaea, an honorable counselor, which also waited for the kingdom of God, came and went in . . .

Mark 15:43

MAGDA WANTED TO TRAVEL THE Via Maris, along the coastal road of the Mediterranean. Once they reached Caesarea, they headed south toward Joppa, stopping frequently to wade in the water.

It was blissful walking hand in hand with Jesus, no crowds following along, nowhere to be at any certain time, just the two of them following the shoreline of the Mediterranean.

And they talked, although Magda, unusually quiet, mostly listened. She walked contentedly beside the man she loved more than anyone in the world, especially now that her world was shrinking. Rachel was dead, Heli was dead, and her father was fading fast. After he was gone, she would have just a sickly brother, a bossy sister, an aging aunt, and Mary and Jesus—who were like family to her.

She realized she was shifting, that a change was slowly taking place within her. She was becoming more serene, more at peace with herself and her world. She was healthy, wealthy and close to being content, perhaps a little too content. *Being this happy makes me nervous. I wonder how long it will last?* Magda thought, hating her fleeting moment of gloom.

So Magda was pensive as Jesus explained why he hadn't interrupted his sermon at Peter's house in Capernaum for his mother and brothers.

"Magda, you have heard me say more than one time that being one of my followers is not for the faint of heart. Those who are called must leave their families to fend for themselves; they must let others bury their dead; they must lose their lives and the stuff life is made of. No time for goodbyes when the mission calls.

"I had just preached on that very subject to the crowd that was gathered about me so my actions had to speak even louder than my words. That said, as much as my father's death grieves me, I do not regret my handling of the matter.

"How many times have you heard me say, 'No one who puts his hand to the plough and looks back is fit for the kingdom of God'?"

Magda snorted. "Pardon the non sequitur, but how many times have you put *your* hand to the plough? Well, at least you made it to Joseph's burial, so we don't have to rehash the 'burying the dead' line."

Magda enjoyed sparring with Jesus. She understood the symbolism of his statements concerning *the hand to the plough* and *letting the dead bury the dead*, but she liked to challenge his parables with the more plain-spoken language of his typical listener. If he was going to reach the poor and uneducated—his typical audience—he needed to speak their language.

Jesus ignored Magda's needling remarks and continued his explanation. "My mother and brothers are my blood kin, true. But think about it, Magda: all the people in the world are God's children; as such they all are my mothers and fathers, brothers and sisters."

"But Jesus," Magda countered, "God chose Mary to be your earthly mother, not the other women in the world. Surely that gives her the right to expect a little favoritism from you."

Jesus nodded in agreement. "I certainly love her dearly and have tried to show her special attention all of my life. But my ministry makes it a little difficult to devote *all* of my attention to any one person, except of course to you, Magda.

"You know that my relationship with Joseph had been troubled for many years. When I started my ministry, he was ashamed of me, and on more than one occasion he asked me to stop upsetting the priests and the elders with my radical ideas. He turned his back on me and my ministry, embarrassed by the truth I preach.

"He lacked the faith to be resurrected from death. Even if I had left Capernaum and returned to Nazareth with my mother and brothers, his bitterness would have defeated my attempts to revive him. The road to eternal life is blocked by anything negative in its path.

"I grieve for my father, for the waste of his life and his untimely death. I kept hoping he would become more spiritual, but he never did and now it's too late."

Jesus stopped for a moment to watch a sandpiper dig in the wet sand. He seemed to need a moment to deal with his emotions.

Magda took hold of his hand. "But he *was* your father, Jesus. He cared for you in his own way. He provided for you and raised you. That counts for something." Then, remembering her troubled relationship with Rachel, she said, "But I guess the same thing could be said for my mother, and I certainly did not shed many tears at her death. But we're different: you're a God; me—I am a mere goddess." Jesus did not join in her laughter. No one was more serious than Jesus when he was wrestling with a weighty problem. He ignored Magda's attempt to lighten up the conversation.

The wind was whipping their hair into their faces and Jesus reached over to brush a strand out of Magda's eyes. "I'm aware of what my father did for me," Jesus said. "He was always right in the eyes of the world. But my father lost his life a long time ago. He was more interested in rules and what others thought of him than true spirituality and compassion for his fellow man. From a very young age, I think I realized that about my father, which greatly saddened me.

"Sometimes I think the only person he truly loved was my mother. Even so, I think he had a deep resentment over the circumstances of my conception and birth, to the detriment of that relationship."

"I disagree," Magda said. "I think theirs was a strong marriage. Her life without him is going to be difficult and empty. That's why it is important for you to make more time for her now that Joseph is gone. The point is, ignoring your mother when she came to tell you of your father's death, hurt *her,* not Joseph. It was *she* who needed you.

"And it was your lack of concern for her—for the living—that troubled me. That is what I am pointing out to you that you need to change."

"Well said, Magda. On those rare occasions when I am wrong, I can freely admit it," he said. But Magda didn't laugh; she knew he was serious. He didn't think he was ever wrong.

He continued, "In the future I am going to make more time for my family. I do love my mother and appreciate her support of what I am trying to accomplish, but she has to accept that I will never give her the attention that the others do. They're on a little different path and can tolerate a shorter leash than I.

"You know as well as I that mother worries about her sons and daughters if they don't check in with her every day. She has always said that she was born to be a mother, and I guess that is why she is reluctant to let us venture very far out of her sight. That's the reason she dislikes being called The Virgin Mary. She says she would rather be called Mother Mary. I just call her *woman.*"

Magda thought, *Oh, enough about everyone else, what about me?* "And what should I be called, Jesus?"

He thought for a moment. "You should be called *mine,* but I guess I'll have to be content to call you 'My Magda.'"

They walked for a while in silence. Later on, Magda would recall that day as one of her favorite times with Jesus. They spent many hours just walking without talking. Who needed conversation? She was with Jesus.

After a while Jesus said, "There is so much to be done and so little time to do it." He stopped and put his arms around her. Looking out to sea, he indulged in some rare wishful thinking. There was a ship on the horizon heading north, probably to Caesarea. From where they stood, it looked like a child's toy boat bobbing up and down over the waves. *I wonder what it would be like just to climb aboard a boat heading for some distant land with Magda, not having to worry about the horrors I will face in the future. But, Satan, get thee behind me.*

They started to walk again and he said, "When we return from this trip, I am going to devote every possible moment to the mission . . . and to you . . . ." And before Magda could finish his sentence he hastily added, ". . . and to my family, of course."

"Great," Magda said. "Since you put it like that, all is forgiven, if you'll pardon my stealing one of your lines. But I think you can afford to relax a bit; you've got plenty of time to mend those fences."

Jesus reached for her hand. "One's time on earth can be short or long, depending on the plans God has for him."

Magda looked at him sharply, remembering Luke's warning about Jesus' enemies in the Sanhedrin. But unwilling to spoil the moment, she decided to ignore it.

She changed the subject. "Well, I feel better now that we have had our talk. Somehow you always convince me that what I thought was the error of your ways was just my own shortsightedness. That said, you do know that I'm a little nearsighted, don't you? That's why I squint so much."

"I'm relieved to hear that, Magda, I always thought it had something to do with your myopia."

"Very funny, Jesus. At least I don't suffer from Presbyopia, a condition I am far too young and much too Jewish to suffer from.

"Anyway, I'm so relieved I think we ought to celebrate in Joppa tonight by having a wonderful dinner at a charming little place right on the water," Magda said with her big moon smile.

Joppa was one of Magda's favorite cities. Just a little under fifty miles west of Jerusalem, it was a small town with interesting people who escaped the big city of Jerusalem to rest and relax by the Great Sea.

Because of the sophisticated traveler it attracted, the food in its inns was gourmet, the wines sublime, and the seaside village a shopper's delight. But Magda didn't want to waste a moment of time away from Jesus, so the shops, on this occasion, didn't interest her.

By the time they arrived at the inn, the setting sun against the water had turned the late afternoon sky to blood red, which caused a shiver down Magda's spine.

After eating buttery tender fish that had been swimming in the Great Sea earlier in the day, she was relaxed and mellow. She was enjoying a carafe of wine while Jesus sipped from a single glass that he had been nursing for over an hour. Magda watched him in wonder.

"Jesus, you are so disciplined. Maybe while we're on this trip, we should work on reining in some of my bad habits."

But Jesus knew she wasn't ready. "You've waited this long, you can wait a little longer. We'll talk about it again after you finish your business with the attorney in Jerusalem. When you have a clear head, we can work on a few things. As you know, timing is everything, Magda."

"Whew," she whistled, "am I glad you didn't use your 'hand to the plough' line! But judging from the little bit abba has told me about managing the businesses of the House of Benjamin, I'm going to be so busy I won't have time for a big demon demolition project."

"You are in control of that," Jesus assured her. "You'll find the time when the time is right."

When she met Joseph, she understood why Benjamin had chosen him to handle his legal affairs. Not only was he knowledgeable of the law, he was wise and had a canny understanding of business, life and people. A tall, dignified man, he welcomed her into his office with a bow, all the while looking at her intently, taking her measure.

"Magda, I am honored to meet you after hearing about you all these years from your father. I hope you know that your father admires you more than anyone. Frankly, he favors you over your siblings, even giving you the birthright upon his death that ordinarily would belong to

Lazarus. But we all know that Lazarus has too many personal struggles to cope with such a serious responsibility.

"In time you will become the director of a huge empire with financial holdings that spread far and wide, as do your father's business interests. Although he inherited much of his wealth, he worked hard, made wise investments, and parlayed it into a massive fortune. And soon it will be your responsibility not only to retain the fortune but to make it grow. And I expect you will."

And she did . . . and then some.

Joseph rose, and Magda began to collect her things, thinking the meeting was over. But the attorney went over to a cupboard and pulled out a large scroll. He asked her to sit back down for a moment.

"Before you go, there is one unfinished piece of business. Benjamin may have mentioned the journal that your mother started keeping when she was quite young. She was always interested in history, and she recorded some of the events of your lives—both hers and your father's—beginning with the troubles between Jacob and Esau."

Magda arched an eyebrow. She had never heard anything said about Esau being her ancestor, although she supposed that all Jewish people in Israel were related to each other one way or another.

Joseph continued, "Thus, your father's last and most important bequest is this portion of your mother's diary that she left to be given to you upon both of their deaths. His exact words to me were, 'Tell Magda that the diary is a blend of my recollections as well as her mother's; they explain some things about her childhood.'"

Magda took the journal, hardly glancing at it as she tucked it into her bag. "Well, I am going to take my time before reading my mother's memoirs. I am not even going to open it until my father dies.

"My friend Jesus—I think abba talked with you recently about him and his troubles with the Sanhedrin—is the wisest man I have ever known. He knows me better than anyone, and I know he would advise me to wait until the time is right. I have never handled bad news very well; and, judging by some of my childhood recollections, I'm sure a lot of painful memories are going to resurface when I read them.

"Maybe I'll read it when I grow up," she quipped. "Until then, it's going to stay locked away in a safe place where I keep my most treasured possessions."

Joseph showed her out without letting on that her comments about Jesus were troubling. He hid his concern, but surely she knew that Jesus was in danger of being arrested in Jerusalem. He had angered several of Joseph's colleagues in the Sanhedrin, and his own attempts to change their opinions of him had failed. In fact, he was surprised at how strongly they rejected his arguments on Jesus' behalf. He feared for Magda's safety as well if she were as *close* to him as she intimated.

As she was going down the stairs, she turned and said to him, "Jesus is here in Jerusalem with me. Would you be able to join us for dinner? You strike me as the type of man who would be very interested in what he has to say."

It took just one three-hour dinner for Jesus to make a believer out of Joseph. *I can't believe that this humble fellow, who looks nothing like a Messiah—whatever one looks like—is blessed with such a wealth of wisdom and perception,* Joseph thought as he walked back to his home in the upper city.

As soon as he walked into the house, he started telling his wife, a very spiritual woman, the simple truth of Jesus' message, a message that the Sanhedrin wanted to destroy along with the man.

"Deborah," Joseph said, "Jerusalem is going to be turned upside down by the man I just had dinner with. Magda calls him *Jesus*, but you may know him by the name *Yeshua*. At any rate, he convinced me that he is the Son of God . . . me, a wizened lawyer who questions everything and believes almost nothing!

"I've had an epiphany tonight. Many people's lives will be changed by this man, who already has an impressive following. But I fear for them. The Romans will not tolerate the Jewish population's recognition of a Messiah and the uprising it could lead to. I predict there is going to be real trouble ahead."

He was not mistaken.

Chapter Twenty-Nine

For as Jonah was three days and three nights in the whale's belly; so shall the Son of man be three days and three nights in the heart of the earth.

Matt. 12:40

News that Jesus was back in Galilee had traveled like lightning through Capernaum. Within a few days, a vast crowd had gathered outside Peter's house, hoping to see the famous healer. They brought with them their lame, maimed, blind, and many who were near death. Jesus healed all of them to the amazement of those who thought he was a false prophet.

Several Sadducees and Pharisees, who had come from Jerusalem to test his powers, remained skeptical even though Jesus had performed many miracles in their presence. One of the Pharisees challenged him. "You promise a place in paradise to all who believe in you. Since you are apparently so well-connected in heaven, prove it by demonstrating some miracles in the sky."

Jesus answered them, "You Sadducees and Pharisees—scoffers and hypocrites—you claim you can read the weather by interpreting signs in the sky. When it is evening you say, 'It will be fair weather tonight, for the sky is red.' In the morning you say, 'It will be foul weather today, for the sky is red and lowering.'

"But for all your star-gazing and predictions, you cannot read the obvious signs of the times. I'll leave you with this reminder as I bid you farewell. Consider what happened to Jonah: that miracle is the only proof you need."

He left them standing there with their mouths open wide in disbelief. To a man they thought, *How dare he speak to men of our stature with such impertinence?* But each of them was looking confused, saying, "What happened to Jonah?"

Jonah, a prophet from Galilee, was ordered by the Lord to go to Nineveh to prophesy its destruction. But Jonah feared the challenge of such a divine mission, and he fled to Joppa to board a boat that was sailing to Tarshish in far-away Spain. God, greatly displeased at Jonah's cowardice, caused a great storm at sea, which Jonah admitted to the sailors was probably his punishment for failing to obey God's command. The captain ordered the crew to throw Jonah overboard. As he was flailing helplessly in the water, a whale came along and swallowed him whole.

For three days and nights Jonah languished inside the whale's great belly, praying and asking God for his forgiveness and thanking him for his mercy. Finally, God answered Jonah's prayers and caused the whale to vomit Jonah out onto dry land.

Jonah immediately headed to Nineveh, a great city of 120,000 people, and warned the citizens of its coming destruction. Jonah became one of the most effective prophets, turning the entire population of Nineveh to God.

Chapter Thirty

"For I also am a man set under authority, having under me soldiers, and I say unto one, Go, and he goeth; and to another, Come, and he cometh; and to my servant, Do this, and he doeth it." When Jesus heard these things, He marveled at him, and turned him about, and said unto the people that followed him, "I say unto you, I have not found so great faith, no, not in Israel."

Luke 7:8-10

One afternoon as Jesus walked to the synagogue in Capernaum, he was approached by a Roman centurion, who asked if he might have a word with him. "Rabbi, my chief steward is gravely ill. Daniel is not just a valued servant, he is a dear friend. He will lose his life unless you lay your hands on him and save him."

Jesus looked into the centurion's eyes and straight into his heart. "I know who you are. You are the God-fearing Cornelius. I have heard of your many acts of kindness toward the Jewish people in Capernaum, and

I know that you and your father funded the building of the synagogue. You have but to ask and your servant will leave his sickbed today. Let us go to your house."

But Cornelius felt oddly discomfited in the presence of Jesus and took a step back. He felt a curious fear of getting too close to this man with his penetrating gaze. He had the feeling Jesus could see right through him—all of his weaknesses and failings exposed.

Cornelius said, "My servant has been loyal to me, and I wish to save him. But I am humbled before you. I do not ask that you trouble yourself by coming to my house, for I am not worthy to have you under my roof. But I am a centurion, with many men under me who respond to my every command. If I say 'Come,' they come; if I say 'Go,' they go. If I tell my servant, 'Do this or do that,' it is done. And I know if you just say, 'Be healed,' my servant will be made well."

Jesus, amazed to hear these strong words spoken by a Gentile, turned the centurion about and exclaimed, "I have not heard such great faith, no, not in Israel. Amen, amen, I say that many Gentiles from the east and the west will take their places in heaven alongside Abraham, Isaac, and Jacob."

Cornelius pursed his lips and thought about what Jesus had just said. *Is he implying that he is going to convert me?*

With those thoughts swirling round in his head, he hurried back home. He walked into the house and asked, "How is Daniel?"

His wife said, "Miraculously, he took a turn for the better and got up from his bed. Apparently, he is healed."

Chapter Thirty-One

Jesus therefore again groaning in himself cometh to the grave. It was a cave, and a stone lay upon it. Jesus said, "Take ye away the stone." Martha, the sister of him that was dead, saith unto him, "Lord, by this time he stinketh; for he hath been dead four days."

John 11:38-40

THE YEARS WERE NOT KIND to Orpah, whose weight increased each year until she could hardly move about. Her love of fine food and wine was finally her undoing. One morning as she sat in the lower garden feeding the birds, she bent over to pick up a fallen blossom and never got up again.

Once again, Zachary came like an ill wind to Magda, who was with Jesus in Capernaum. "Magda, it seems that I am always the bearer of bad news. This time it's Orpah—she collapsed this morning and died."

Magda fell into Jesus' arms and sobbed, "O Jesus, one by one the people I love are leaving me."

Over the years she had grown close to Orpah, the only woman other than Heli who had ever shown her any love or affection. Her world was getting smaller and only Mary was left of the women she loved.

"Zachary," she said. "I want to take the carriage to Nazareth. Will you drive me?" She had been feeling a little queasy lately, and just the thought of taking the ferry across the Galilee through the rain made her ill. *No wonder I've been feeling so out of sorts; I'm sick of death,* she thought.

Magda was not surprised that Orpah wanted to be buried in the lower garden, but she was shocked to learn that Orpah wanted her tombstone to read, 'Orpah's Corpus.'

All those years she was aware of my rudeness, yet she never mentioned it. All those years she was such a lady, yet I never mentioned it, Magda thought sadly.

When the will was read, Magda was surprised that Orpah had left almost everything to her, with small bequests to Martha and Lazarus.

Back in Magdala, Magda sat down with her siblings to discuss their future. "It seems that none of us is likely ever to marry. For as long as I can remember, I have dreamed of building a fine house near Jerusalem—big enough for all of us, including Jesus, Zachary, and Nathanial. The last time I was in Judea, I found a wonderful piece of land in Bethany in the foothills of Olivet. It is close enough to Jerusalem for Jesus to travel back and forth in one day. But it is far enough away from the city's noise and chaos to provide a peaceful place for us to live out the rest of our lives.

Magda paused and searched for the right words. "Laz and Mar, I don't want the two of you to feel like you're living in *Magda's house*, so I propose that each of you contribute a portion to the building costs of our family home."

Lazarus said, "What's wrong with continuing to live in abba's house where we grew up? I thought you loved living by the sea, Magda. But whatever you and Martha want to do is fine with me. Can I decorate my own room?"

Martha was close to tears when she replied, "I can't imagine living anywhere but Magdala; I've lived there all of my life, and it is home. But

Laz, after abba is gone, there will be no reason for just the two of us to live in his huge house. So I say yes. Let's build a house in Bethany. Laz, you and I will spend part of the year in Bethany, and part of the year in Magdala. And yes, you can decorate your own room. I, too, have a request: I want a big kitchen."

Magda met with Hieronymus to discuss the design of the house. "Forget what you did for Orpah . . . nothing weird or pretentious. I want a spacious, comfortable home—an enchanted cottage."

The result was a quaint, rambling work of art—a story and a half built of cedar and stone from the same quarry in East Jerusalem that had supplied the stone used in the building of the temple. Magda insisted in overseeing every phase of the building—a project that took several months. She could hardly contain her tears when the building was complete. There was room for everyone and everything she loved. Special niches held her prized collection—Abe's small wooden carvings that he had whittled for Heli when she was a child.

Martha and Lazarus had rooms downstairs while Jesus and Magda's rooms were upstairs. Not an early riser, Magda preferred the room that overlooked the front courtyard, away from the morning sun. She decorated her room very simply . . . with white walls and ivory bed linens. The wide-plank cedar floors were whitewashed with her own pickling solution, and the subtle shine from the soft wood underfoot reminded Magda of moonglow. The only color came from the fresh flowers that she changed daily, and from the string of bells she strung up outside her window. Attached to a brightly colored braid, the bells would chime when the wind was up, stirring a longing within her that had yet to be satisfied.

Jesus preferred the room that looked out on the back gardens. It was the sunniest, most pleasant bedroom in the house. The moment he awoke to the cooing of the mourning dove—*Oo-wah-hooo-hoo-hoo*—he would leave his bed, dress in a simple robe, and head to the garden. And there he would spend the quiet time of early morning meditating and talking with God.

Although there were several bedrooms in the main house, Zachary and Nathanial insisted on living out back in the servants' quarters. They were born servants and they would die servants, although Magda insisted they were like family to her. If being a servant was good enough for Heli, the most wonderful woman they had ever known, it was good enough for them.

True to her original plan, Magda had planted 'Heli's Herb Garden' right outside the kitchen door. She took a lot of good-natured kidding about it from Martha and Lazarus, who would often tease her and say, "Yes, Miss Rachel." It was an unwritten rule that no one but Magda was allowed in this hallowed place.

The waterfall that Magda had fallen in love with at first sight was at the back of the property, just a short walk from the main house. After Magda worked her magic on it, the falling water meandered downward over lichen-covered rocks before spilling into a deep pond in the flower garden, reminiscent of Orpah's lower garden. Countless water lilies floated like flower-masted sailboats across the surface of the water. When Magda needed to find Jesus, she would head to the pond. And there he would be—sitting underneath an ancient weeping willow tree—pondering whatever it was he pondered all the time.

Martha was irritated with Lazarus. He was late to breakfast and she wanted to clear the table. To her knowledge, Lazarus had never missed a meal. He was stick thin but had a voracious appetite. When he was an hour overdue, she got worried and went to check on him. She knocked several times on his door, and finally pushed it open when he didn't respond. He was lying on the floor, feverish and delirious.

Martha yelled for Magda, who thundered down the stairs with her heart in her throat. *Now what*?

She examined Lazarus and found only a weak, erratic pulse. "Oh God, please not again," she moaned. "I'm not about to let Lazarus suffer the same fate as Heli and Orpah."

Martha had already sent for Dr. Luke, and the two sisters sat beside Lazarus' bed, holding hands while they waited for Nathanial to return with the doctor, their rivalry forgotten in their grief.

Luke arrived and sent the women away while he tended to Lazarus. "I know both of you look after Lazarus like he's a little boy, but give me a little privacy for my own sake. I don't want any feelings of awkwardness or embarrassment to impede my examination, which is going to be thorough."

But Luke was shocked at the deterioration in Lazarus since he had seen him a few months before. He had lost weight and his color was terrible. There was a growth in his abdomen that Luke knew was the cause of all of Lazarus' problems. Despite his efforts to revive him, after thirty minutes, he could get no response. He opened the door and just shook his head as he gave the sisters the bad news: there was nothing he could do. Lazarus was beyond a medical miracle.

Magda knew that Lazarus' difficult birth had weakened him and made him susceptible to illness. He had struggled from one sickness to another all of his life, but she was not giving up. There might not be a medical miracle to save Lazarus, but there was someone who could succeed when all else failed.

Zachary saddled his horse and left that afternoon for Bethabara. He crossed over Jordan and headed south to the desert, where he finally found Jesus surrounded by several of his disciples. He was preaching to the crowds of people who sorely missed the fiery sermons of John the Baptist.

Jesus saw Zachary approaching and motioned for him to come closer, fearing that there was bad news from Bethany. Zachary whispered urgently in his ear, "Rabbi, Magda wants you to come right away to Bethany. Lazarus is ill; he may even be dead. Dr. Luke was unable to revive him and Magda sent me to get you. She told me not to leave without you."

Jesus stood and put his arm around the big man. "Zachary, walk with me." When they had walked a few feet away from the crowd, Jesus started asking questions, mostly about Magda's frame of mind: how she was holding up? After he was convinced that he could wait a few days before leaving for Bethany, Jesus said, "Zachary, thank you for coming out to the desert to find me. But I have business here that makes it impossible for me to leave for another day or two."

He urged Zachary to have something to eat and to rest a while before returning to Bethany with a message for Magda. "Tell her that I will arrive in a few days and will handle the problem when I get there. Tell her to keep the faith. It is never too late for God's miracles."

Zachary shook his head and replied, "Well, I dread being the one who tells her that. When I left Bethany, she was pacing back and forth as upset as I have ever seen her. I think all these recent deaths are more than even Magda can handle. But if you can't leave right now, I understand. But Magda won't."

Two days later Jesus left for Bethany, although his disciples warned him that he was a 'wanted man' in nearby Jerusalem.

Philip said, "Lazarus is probably just sleeping. Every time I have ever been around him, after a while he wanders off, saying, 'I'm going to lie down and take a little nap.' Then you don't see him for a couple of days. It wouldn't surprise me if he is just taking one of his little naps."

But Jesus knew better. "Lazarus is not sleeping, he is very ill. But his sickness will not end in death. He will recover and be better than ever."

Thomas wouldn't hear of him going alone. "Let us also go so that we may die with him."

And he was not exaggerating. There was growing evidence that the Jewish officials and priests were discussing a plan to get rid of Jesus *and his disciples*. News of the Sanhedrin nightly meetings was proof that they were not just discussing business as usual. Something major was afoot.

Jesus prayed for guidance, delaying his departure for two days until he was sure that it was God's will for Lazarus to be revived. His disciples didn't understand why he hadn't left right away. He explained his reason for delaying, "It is for God's glory so that God's Son may be glorified through it."

When they were just a few miles away, Jesus sent Andrew, a swift runner, ahead to warn Magda and Martha that he would arrive shortly.

When Martha heard that Jesus was on the road to their house, she ran out to meet him, shouting at him from a distance, "Jesus, why didn't you come right away? Lazarus wouldn't have died if you had been here to save him."

Unhurriedly and silently, Jesus walked toward Martha. He grasped her hands in his and said, "Your brother will rise again."

Martha replied, "Well, I know that. He will rise again on Resurrection Day."

But Jesus said, "I am the resurrection and the life. He who believes in me, though he die, will live again. And whoever lives and believes in me shall never die. Do you believe this, Martha?"

Martha didn't want to get into a philosophical discussion with Jesus about life and death. To end the conversation she said, "Yes, Jesus, Magda has convinced me that you are the Son of God. Do you want me to run ahead and let her know that you are close by?"

"Yes, I'm sure she will be glad to know that I have finally arrived. I hope she is not too upset."

"No! Magda upset? That's an understatement if I ever heard one, but I am upset as well. After all, our beloved Lazarus is dead."

Martha ran back down the road to the house and found Magda upstairs in her room, lying on her bed, her head buried beneath her pillow.

"Magda, Jesus is coming around the bend at Simon's house," Martha whispered.

Magda jumped up and flew out of the house, pulling her tunic around her as she ran down the road to meet him. When they met in the middle of the road, she fell into his arms, weeping and tearing at her clothing. Jesus was very upset at Magda's distress and he pulled her over to the side of the road. He sat down with her, his arms around her, his lips against her hair.

Jesus wept even as he consoled Magda. "Magda, my beautiful Magda. Your tears are not in vain, I hear you, and your prayers will be answered."

After she had calmed down a bit, he said, "Take me to Lazarus. Perhaps he is not dead but sleeping."

By this time, they were outside the wall of Malama and Martha had joined them. Ever poetic, she scoffed at him, "Only sleeping? Well, he has been 'only sleeping' for four days now—in a tomb. You are too late, Jesus; by now there will undoubtedly be a terrible stench."

"Martha, Martha, my dear friend and sister, where is your faith?" Jesus gently chided her for her doubt.

Grieving, Martha turned away and ran back to the house, covering her nose and mouth with her veil, looking a little green just thinking about the shape Lazarus must be in. But Magda, used to the sweet perfume of putrefaction from dealing with lepers, and thinking only of seeing her brother alive again, grabbed Jesus' hand and led the way to the tomb.

He and Zachary rolled away the stone and Jesus walked down the stairs into the crypt, raising his eyes and praying for God's help. Feeling the power, he cried out in a loud voice, "Lazarus, come forth."

Immediately, there was a movement on the shelf where the body lay. Lazarus raised his arms above his head, slowly sat up, placing one foot and then the other on the floor. He finally rose and stretched and took a deep breath, still covered in the burial shroud. They were not afraid. This was not a ghost, this was their beloved Lazarus. They ran to embrace him.

Pulling the linen gauze from his face and kissing him, Magda was giddy with the excitement of being reunited with her brother who had died and now was alive again.

To keep the peace with Martha, before she let him enter the house, Magda insisted that Lazarus bathe with sandalwood soap; but she sent him back a second time after he emerged none too clean from the wading pool.

"Lazarus, don't make me go with you and bathe you as I used to do when you were a little boy. Go back and do a good job. Lather your body from head to toe several times with the soap and rinse thoroughly."

But when he emerged a second time, the death smell stubbornly clung to him. Convinced that soap and water weren't going to remove the sickly sweet odor, she made him sit patiently while she scraped his skin with a metal strigil. Lazarus loved the feel of Magda's soft hands on his skin and he was as docile as a child. Finally she slathered on spikenard from the alabaster jar she had broken open to anoint him.

"Ewww, Laz," Magda said when she inspected him for any lingering smell, "maybe one more application will do it." She broke the seal on another box of the costly spikenard, liberally massaging it into Lazarus' hair and working her way down to his feet.

Fully revived, bathed and perfumed, Lazarus went straight to the kitchen where Martha was preparing the evening meal, not hiding her resentment that she was working while the others sat and talked.

When Lazarus walked into the room, for the second time in her life Magda saw Martha cry. She sank to her knees and wrapped her arms around her brother's legs, sobbing, "My sweet Lazzy, I thought I had lost you forever."

Martha had been the only mother Lazarus had ever known, and they were very close. Although he was nearly thirty-five years old, Lazarus was still child-like and depended on Martha for everything.

"Mar, I'm back from the dead," he said. "Is my supper nearly ready?"

"Bite your tongue, Lazarus," Martha said, wincing at his choice of words—his favorite expression. "I am going to prepare a celebratory meal. If your sister would offer to help it would be ready a lot quicker."

Martha's elation, usually a short-lived emotion, was already evaporating. She slid the cooking pots to the side of the fire and said, "Let's go find her."

Magda and Jesus were sitting outside in front of a large gathering of friends and neighbors who were celebrating Lazarus' revival. Each one was trying to get the position of honor next to Jesus, the miracle-worker who had brought Lazarus back to life. Magda was sitting at his feet, which she had just rubbed with the spikenard that was left over from Lazarus' massage.

Martha was back to her querulous self. "Magda," she complained, "I think Jesus can do without you for a little while, and I could use your help in the kitchen."

But when Magda didn't jump up and follow her, Martha appealed to Jesus, "Master, don't you agree that Magda should help out more with the chores in this house? I do everything that is done for Lazarus, as well as all the cooking. Surely you can manage without her so we can eat before dark."

But Jesus never put eating above spiritual matters. "Martha, you are worried and upset about many things, but only one thing is needed. Magda has chosen what is better and it will not be taken away from her."

Shortly after dark, Martha called them to come in. "Supper's ready," she said sweetly, in a much improved mood, for Zachary had pitched in to help her. Magda had suspected for some time that he was sweet on Martha, who loved the special attention he showed her. But, alas, love in bloom had not improved her disposition, which Magda knew would have to change if the romance were to survive.

Lazarus was seated in the place of honor at the table. He insisted that Jesus sit to his left, to give him even more honor—seated at the right hand of Jesus, the miracle-worker who had raised him from the dead. Jesus put his arm around Lazarus and said, "Well, Lazarus, you are looking well this evening. No one would ever suspect that you had been ill."

Lazarus said, "Ill? You mean dead."

After feasting and drinking the best wines, everyone toasting Lazarus and celebrating his return to life, they insisted he make a few remarks.

"Speech, speech!" everyone cried, loudly banging their knives against their wine goblets.

Lazarus, being a man of few words, said, "What took you so long?"

Chapter Thirty-Two

There was a man of the Pharisees, named Nicodemus, a ruler of the Jews. The same came to Jesus by night, and said unto him, "Rabbi, we know that thou art a teacher come from God: for no man can do these miracles that thou doest, except God be with him." Jesus answered him and said unto him, "Verily, verily, I say unto thee, except a man be born again, he cannot see the kingdom of God."

John 3:1-3

SOME OF THE JEWISH ELDERS had secretly been coming to talk with Jesus; they couldn't believe everything his followers were saying about him . . . no one was that perfect. One night after supper as Jesus sat talking with Simon the Pharisee at his house in Bethany, a fellow Pharisee came to have a discussion with Jesus.

Nicodemus, a respected Jewish leader, bowed to Simon with the respect reserved for one Pharisee meeting another—but few were pretentious enough to observe it.

"Simon, my good man, you are looking well. I was happy to hear that you have been cured of your malady and are seeing your friends again. I'm sorry I couldn't attend your feast this evening. Are your guests still here?"

Simon, a plain-spoken man, had little patience for Nicodemus' pompousness. "Nico, you damned peacock, you can hardly call 'leprosy' a malady. That's sort of like saying you have a hangnail when you have had your foot amputated.

"But welcome, come in and have a glass of wine. Everyone is gone but Jesus. He and I were just going out to the verandah to wait for Magda to return from Jerusalem. He is going to walk her back home," Simon said, waggling his eyebrows up and down.

Nicodemus gave him a conspiratorial wink and said, "Understood, Simon, but I'll pass on the glass of wine until later. Actually, Jesus is just the man I want to see. I want to have a serious discussion with him."

Jesus walked in as Nico was saying, "As you know, several members of the Sanhedrin are upset with Jesus' claim to be the Son of God. I want to talk with him about how foolhardy those claims are."

Jesus thought, *Here we go again. All these self-important elders are coming to show me the error of my ways and the wisdom of theirs. I hope Magda will show up soon and rescue me.*

Simon left the room, wanting nothing to do with the discussion they would have. He wondered why they chose to talk at his house rather than Magda's since Jesus practically lived there now.

He poured himself a glass of wine and went out to the verandah to drink by himself. During his long bout with leprosy, he was considered unclean and had been shunned by all of his friends, especially by the Pharisees. He had grown used to spending most of his time alone and was surprised to discover that he liked it. Now that he was cured he had many visitors, mostly the curious who wanted to see how many of his body parts had fallen off. He missed his solitude.

But he didn't miss his hair. He had been forced to shave his head after being diagnosed with leprosy, and now he preferred it that way. Having a bald head was certainly simpler and cleaner than having long hair that had to be groomed with oil. ". . . Thou anointest my head with oil." *But leaveth my scalp alone,* Simon thought. Bald was better.

After they were alone, Nicodemus said to Jesus, "Rabbi, we know that you are a teacher come from God, for no man can perform the miracles you have except that God be with him. But miracles notwithstanding, your arguments are based on a false premise."

Loving a spirited debate, Nicodemus began to challenge Jesus on every subject, demanding explanations for the many statements he made in all of his sermons concerning man's path to eternal life. He was baffled by Jesus and found him to be a frustrating opponent. Rather than offering concrete proof for his arguments, he spoke as a poet and a storyteller, offering parables instead of facts to back up his premises and his promises.

Jesus said to Nicodemus, "I say, unless you are willing to be born again, you will not see the kingdom of God. The kingdom of God is within you. Know the truth and the truth will set you free."

Nicodemus made a rude noise with his mouth. "That is very poetic but it is a perfect example of the nonsense you hide behind when you can't think of a good answer. Nevertheless, I will respond to it: I thought I was born okay the first time. Are you saying I should enter into my mother's womb a second time and be born? How is that possible? I am too old. And besides, I am much too fat."

Jesus laughed and said, "How is it possible that you are an officer of Israel and yet you know not the simplest truths? Balaam's donkey was smarter than you. Do you know from whence the wind comes or where it goes? You hear it and feel it, but you cannot see it. And so it is with everyone who is born of the flesh."

Nicodemus stared in disbelief at Jesus and thought, *Who does he think he's talking to?* He had vast personal wealth, a palatial home with many slaves and servants, and was respected as an influential leader in both the civil and religious communities. A corpulent man who considered living well the best revenge for his impoverished childhood, Nicodemus enjoyed drinking fine wines and dining on rich foods. And yet, here was this man who owned practically nothing, had nowhere to lay his head, whose only title was self-appointed Messiah, telling him he was not fit to enter the kingdom of God.

Nicodemus stood up and started to walk around the room, inspecting some of the wonderful paintings and tapestries on the walls. Magda had helped Simon with the decoration of his house and it reflected her artful touch.

Thinking the debate was ended, Jesus breathed a sigh of relief even though the point might not be won. He was beginning to find these nighttime visitors a little tiresome. They were, practically to a man, derisive of any ideas that conflicted with their own, scoffing at ideals not backed up by science, or their version of it.

But Nico was just getting started. He sat back down, changing tactics. "Since we have begun this debate about man's soul and his quest for eternal life, I must point out that your arguments and your sermons are inconsistent. You *argue* that I must give up everything I have worked for; that I must give away all my possessions—does that include my wife? However, you *preach*, 'ask and it shall be given, seek and ye shall find, knock and the door will be opened.'

"Well, I have labored long and hard for what I have. Nobody has ever given me anything, and the things that I have I greatly enjoy; they are not just for show. I love beautiful things and I enjoy being surrounded by them. Does that make me evil?

"Moreover, your suggestions for how man should live are counter-intuitive. It is not in man's nature to live in deprivation. Most men work from sunup to sundown to get ahead, and you tell them that they should give away all they have struggled to acquire—all their creature comforts, if you will—or sell everything and give the money to the poor. Then the cheerful giver will be poor and will become the supplicant.

"Someone said they heard you make the following statement during a sermon: 'For I say unto you, that unto every one which hath shall be given. And from him that hath not, even what he hath shall be taken away from him.' That proves that even you have no compassion for the poor, so why should I? Do you not see that your argument is so full of holes it wouldn't even hold holy water?" Nico leaned over, slapped Jesus on the knee and roared at his joke. Nico was very funny at times, but this was not one of those times. Jesus sat unmoving, unsmiling—like the Great Sphinx.

Undiscouraged, Nicodemus pressed on. "If the flesh were not important, God would not have bothered to wrap the soul in it. If the edifice were not important, God would not have allowed, even encouraged, Solomon to build the temple to very exact specifications that he dictated right down to the curtains that separate the temple from the Holiest of Holies.

"To my mind, the body is of utmost importance, thus I eat sumptuously, drink good wines and enjoy other delights of the flesh. The edifice is important, thus my house and its furnishings are the best. It gives me great joy after a hard day's work to come home to a beautiful home filled with beautiful things. Give away my beautiful treasures? Never! By the way, remind me to ask Magda for some decorating advice for a seaside cottage I'm building in Joppa.

"But I digress. I was not always wealthy. My parents were very poor people who lived on the island of Crete and had little more than the clothes on their backs. My father labored hard all of his life and left very little when he died. But I was determined to be rich so I worked long hours, saved and invested wisely, finally accumulating enough of a nest egg to start my own building firm. Surely you realize that I built the Moriah Gate. And by the way, I own all of the houses to the east of the temple; they are inhabited by my workers. And that is just a drop in the bucket compared with my other holdings.

"Over the years I have grown wealthy. Just now am I able to relax a little and enjoy the fruits of my labors. Give it all away? Preposterous! And if everyone who had money did give it all to the poor, within no time the poor would be poor again, the rich would be rich again. The same imbalance would exist.

"Poverty is a state of mind. I've been broke but I've never been poor. And I have never resented those more successful than I, not that there are many of those anymore. Money is no longer important to me. Money is only important when you don't have it."

Jesus listened to Nicodemus with waning patience, finally interjecting, "Nicodemus, do you know the story of Job? Job lost all his possessions and suffered many bodily afflictions, a test to measure his trust in the Lord. When he refused to curse God, God gave him twice, three times what he had had before. Once his wealth was restored, Job was peaceful and happy again."

"Happy?" Nicodemus exploded. "Job lost not only his wealth, his health, his servants, and his livestock, he lost all seven of his sons and his three daughters as well. Do you think that if Job had been given any say in the matter, he would have chosen to have his sons and daughters murdered, regardless of how evil they were? What? Are you suggesting you could take all of my children, murder them, and placate me by replacing them with others? Surely you cannot be serious! Are children interchangeable? I'm sure Job was perfectly content with things just as they were before he lost everything."

Before Jesus could respond, Nicodemus jumped up and walked over to stand before him. "What about Magda and her wealth? She has more money than all of us. Is Magda exempt from this re-distribution of wealth? I can only imagine what she would say if you suggested that she sell everything and give it to the poor. I can hear her laughing all the way to the bank. Come to think of it, Magda *is* the bank. Have you ever had the nerve to suggest that Magda give away all of her riches?"

Satisfied that he had delivered the *coup de grace* in the debate, Nico sat back down, mopped his brow with the sleeve of his tunic, and took a sip of wine. It was a cool evening but he had worked up a sweat while debating with Jesus.

Jesus took advantage of Nico's pause. "Nicodemus, point taken, but allow me to point out one thing. Magda is not the one who is asking me questions about what she must do to enter the kingdom of God . . . you are. Apparently, you are troubled about the condition of your soul; Magda isn't. It is her outlook that makes her wealthy in all ways.

"You quoted me as saying, 'He who *has* will get more, whereas he who *has not* will lose even what he has.' That statement refers to one's *state of mind.* If, in your mind, you *have,* you will gain more; if, in your mind, you *have not,* your poverty will increase.

"All too often, wealthy people are too comfortable for reflection. They're oblivious to their fellow man. But people like you, Nicodemus, are a little uncomfortable with their wealth, suspicious of their good fortune; in your case, good fortune that might keep you from heaven's door. Many newly-rich people carry their wealth as a burden. Why? Maybe their wealth does nothing to enrich their self-image. Spiritually, they remain impoverished.

"It is not *money* or the possession of it that is evil, it is the *love* of money that is evil. And that is your problem, Nico. You love money more than anything, even more than the beautiful things it can buy. You love the feel of it, the look of it, the touch and smell of it. As you have grown older and richer, you have grown more miserly. Recently, I heard you tell someone in the temple that the reason you don't give alms to the poor is that it makes you physically ill to part with money.

"Job's *fear* created all of his problems. He habitually feared something was going to happen to wipe away all of his wealth and blessings. He said it best, 'The thing which I greatly feared is come upon me, and that which I was afraid of is come unto me.' His constant thoughts of failure and fear of losing what he had were his downfall.

"Pride goeth before a fall. Fear goeth before a failure. A mind filled with doubt and negativity eventually repels success. On the contrary, if you are filled with positive thoughts, you will attract success, good health and well-being—joy—the true wealth! Which category do you fit into, Nicodemus? I suspect the former. I'm not sure what is causing your heaviness of heart, but I *am* sure that you carry a great burden. Do you have a grievance against someone that you haven't settled? Do you have hatred, envy, or resentment in your heart? Are you, in your mind, a victim? Do you harbor fears of failure? Again I say 'you must be born again' . . . as free from sin and negativity as a newborn babe.

"Until you have purged every negative sentiment from your being—that *being* that is far removed from your conscious being—you will not, *cannot* enter the kingdom of God.

"Every time you catch yourself thinking negatively, substitute an affirmation of something positive. Rejoice in how lucky you are and never dwell on the rain that falls into your life. You will have good times and bad, concentrate on the good. Especially do not dwell on the failures of the past. No one is exempt from those. And do not worry about the future. Be content to live today, in this moment.

"These are the qualities Magda exudes that make her so special. She refuses to let anything get her down. When bad times come, she knows the good times are not far behind. When good times come, she knows they'll be followed but not swallowed by bad times. She doesn't fret over the sand in her sandals. She takes a moment to shake off the dust and continues on her merry way, comfortable in her own skin.

"What does she have that makes her special? *Joy.* When you are a true believer—when you have exorcised every trace of negativity from your being—you will have joy in your heart."

Simon walked into the room, looking annoyed. *They're still at it and I'm ready to go to bed.*

Jesus got up and went to the front door, hoping to see Magda. She was coming down the footpath, her basket of ointments and incense swinging from her arm, keeping time with a little tune she was humming. He grimaced at her and mouthed, *Help!*

Magda walked into the house and batted her eyelashes. "Did someone call my name? Are you two solving the world's problems? Take a break, have a glass of wine. Are you going to waste away a perfectly good evening arguing?

"Nico, what you need is a good massage to take your mind off all your troubles. Sit down and let me treat you to one of my magic foot rubs."

She reached into her basket, pulled out an alabastrum and broke the seal on it. Immediately, the room was filled with the exotic, heady aroma of the costly India nard. She dipped her fingers into the ointment and began to rub it into Nico's feet, which soothed him and practically put him to sleep.

Then she turned to Jesus and said, "And now, my love, it's your turn."

Touched by Magda's giving spirit, he stood and embraced her before she poured the oil over his head. Simon raised an eyebrow and looked away. He disapproved of Jesus' relationship with Magda, whose constant presence at Jesus' side he viewed as evil. She made Jesus happy and looked after him like a mother hen, so she certainly played an important role in his life. But one of the Pharisees' complaints against Jesus was his relationship with a reputed prostitute . . . especially since he claimed to be the Son of God.

Simon complained, "Magda, why are you wasting that costly ointment when you could sell it for at least three hundred denarii and give the money to the poor?"

Magda was hurt by Simon's insensitive remarks. After all, she had cured him of his leprosy when no one else would come near him. She looked down in disappointment and kneeled to wash Jesus' feet.

Jesus turned to Simon and said, "Allow me to share a short story with you to give you a little perspective in this matter:

"One man owed a creditor about 500 denarii and the other 50. When neither debtor could pay the man, he canceled their debts."

Jesus asked, "Which one of them will love him most?"

Simon replied, "Obviously, the one who owed him the most."

"You're absolutely right," said Jesus.

Then he went on to chastise Simon for failing to greet him with the standard custom of washing his feet or kissing his cheek. He pointed out that Magda washed his feet with her tears and anointed them with ointment each time he came into her house. This evening she had kissed his feet without ceasing, even as her tears splashed down on them.

"Simon," he continued, "I say to you her sins, which are many, are forgiven, for she has loved much. But to whom little is forgiven, the same loveth little."

Simon stared at Jesus, confused. Jesus laughed at Simon's thick-headedness. "You hypocrite, first take the log out of your own eye, and then you will see clearly to take the *speck* out of another's eye."

Jesus motioned for Magda to sit down beside him. "And to answer another question that seems to trouble you, there is a very good reason why Magda is always by my side. She is love and laughter and joyousness and forgiveness and generosity and unselfishness. Yes, her behavior might be a little off-putting to those who judge others, but *I* judge her by what's in her heart. That's what puts the sparkle in her eye and the smile on her face. Her *joy* is evidence of the light in her soul."

Nico was ashamed of Simon. His fellow Pharisee had behaved badly, speaking so disparagingly of the woman who had befriended him when he was a leper. He looked at Simon with disappointment.

To end the unpleasantness Jesus said, "So, Nicodemus, my friend, I have just felt a weight lifted from your being. Go on your way, free from every burden, filled with peace and joy."

While Nicodemus was not convinced of the truth of all that Jesus had said, he did acknowledge that the warmth spreading through him was like a healing balm. As he sauntered out of Simon's house, smiling in spite of himself, he was aware of the lightness of his step.

He was walking out to the road with Jesus and Magda when he suddenly grabbed Jesus' arm and said, "Oh Jesus, I got a little sidetracked and nearly forgot to tell you something. I came to warn you that Herod wants to have you put to death. You should leave this place and go somewhere else."

Jesus stopped in his tracks and said, "That's quite a *big something* to have escaped your mind, Nico. So you're saying I am suddenly one of Herod's enemies? Well, this is my answer: you go tell that fox that I will drive out demons and heal people today and tomorrow, and on the third day I will reach my goal."

Nico snickered and made a scary face. "Well, Jesus, that'll put the fear of God into him. I think I'll just let *you* explain that one to him. But you do realize that Herod himself is not your actual enemy. He is simply bowing to the Sanhedrin's wishes that the Romans arrest you for your many crimes."

"What crimes are they referring to?"

"What crimes?" Nico's jaw dropped and he peered at Jesus to see if he was serious. "Jesus, I'm sure you've heard all of the complaints, but the most serious is your revolutionary activity and your claim to be King of the Jews, which is what is bringing the Romans into the picture. They can successfully seek the death penalty for those charges alone. But to make matters worse, they are discussing arresting Lazarus as well. They are afraid his presence will add fuel to the fire—a Messiah cum grifter who not only fakes healing but raising the dead as well.

"I suggest you take Magda, Martha and Lazarus to Greece for a long vacation . . . no wait, on second thought, leave Martha here. You can set sail from Caesarea to Greece and stay there for a couple of years until this threat has passed. The Greek isles are the most beautiful place on earth.

"Opa!"

Chapter Thirty-Three

On the next day much people that were come to the feast, when they heard that Jesus was coming to Jerusalem took branches of palm trees, and went forth to meet him, and cried, Hosanna: Blessed is the King of Israel that cometh in the name of the Lord.

John 12:12

LATER THAT EVENING MAGDA HEARD Jesus pacing the floor in his room across the hall. She tapped on his door. "Jesus, what is troubling you?"

Jesus stopped pacing and opened the door. "Well, I do have some things on my mind. Walk outside with me, Magda."

Hand in hand, they walked out to the flower garden and sat down beneath the willow tree.

"Magda, I need to borrow a donkey, preferably one that has not yet been ridden. I am going to ride into Jerusalem. I could walk, but it is important that my entrance there be viewed as triumphant, bold and unafraid, yet humble."

Magda felt the hairs rise on the back of her neck. Another journey to Jerusalem: an event eerily similar to the one that had taken place years before when Mary had borrowed the donkey Yotie for her journey to visit Elisabeth. Mary had chosen the difficult donkey and now Jesus wanted to ride one that was not broken—another difficult donkey. Mary's journey had resulted in the *birth* of Jesus, would this one result in his *death?* Was she again going to be the unwitting accomplice in epochal events, the latter of which would shatter her life?

Magda hesitated. She closed her eyes for a moment and swallowed down the bile that had risen into her throat. Then she realized she was holding Jesus' hand in a death grip. *Another donkey, another dilemma,* she thought. She wished she could say no, but she said, "Of course you may. You have only to ask, my love."

"My Magda, I can always depend on you. I know that your love for me is going to cause you a lot of pain and heartache in the coming days. Just know that you will always be in my heart. Nothing, not even death, will part us."

Once again she felt the hairs on her neck rise. She felt as if she had looked into the face of death.

Then Jesus made another request. He asked her to have Zachary leave the colt and its mother tied to a tree just outside of Bethany.

He offered a chilling explanation. "I don't want you or anyone in your household to be perceived as part of my ministry. The next few days will be a time of great danger for anyone who is associated with me. Nico said that many of the Jewish leaders are now claiming I am guilty of treason and sedition.

"They know of the miracles I have performed: giving new legs to the lame, giving sight to the blind, even raising Lazarus from the dead. Yet they refuse to acknowledge me as the Son of God . . . that my claim to that title is blasphemy, a blasphemy that they will not allow to go unpunished. Nor will my friends and followers escape the wide net of their wrath.

"After we finished our supper tonight, I had a serious talk with my disciples. I told Peter and Andrew to collect the ass and her colt that are tethered to the big oak tree outside your stone wall. They will bring them back to me at Simon's. If anyone asks what they are doing, they are to say 'the master needs them.' They shouldn't have a problem if they act with confidence. The wicked flee when no man pursueth, but the righteous are bold as a lion."

Chapter Thirty-Four

And he went into the temple, and began to cast out them that sold therein, and them that bought; saying unto them, "It is written, 'My house is the house of prayer;' but ye have made it a 'den of thieves.'"

Luke 19:45-46

On a day that came to be called Palm Sunday, Jesus climbed onto the donkey's back and began his ride into Jerusalem. As he rode into the city, the crowds gathered on either side of the road waving palm branches, throwing their cloaks in his path, shouting "Hosanna, Hosanna. Jesus, Jesus."

They had come in great numbers to show their support for him and his message. "Blessed be the King that cometh in the name of the Lord. Peace in heaven, and glory in the highest."

Jesus was deeply moved by the show of love and support by the multitudes of people who had come out to welcome him.

But a number of men in the crowd were his enemies. These men planned for Jesus to be arrested, found guilty and given a death sentence that would cause the maximum pain and humiliation—crucifixion. However, that was a form of execution banned by the Jewish faith, and only an officer of the Roman court could hand down such a sentence. Pilate would have to agree to impose the harsh sentence.

Peter ran up to Jesus and motioned for him to lean down so they could talk. "Jesus," he exclaimed excitedly, "I believe that this huge showing of support for you is good news, very good news indeed. Surely your enemies would not dare to harass you or arrest you in the presence of all these people who obviously believe in you."

Jesus smiled down at Peter but shook his head sadly, "I'm very much afraid their celebration will soon turn to lamentations. Not my will, however, but God's be done."

Peter quickly lost some of his optimism. Some of the Pharisees who stood outside the temple shouted at Jesus. "Rebuke your disciples. Their insinuations that you are the Messiah are blasphemous, dangerously blasphemous."

Jesus was not worried by their warnings. As he rode past them, he said, "I tell you if they were silenced, the very stones would cry out."

Entering into the Gentile's Court, he was assaulted by an atmosphere that was more animal fair than a House of God. Surely even Herod the Great would be upset by this desecration of the temple, the crown jewel of his buildings. But his son Herod Antipas didn't care what was going on as long as the coffers were full.

When they entered the temple, instead of finding a place of worship, they found animal sellers hawking their wares and money changers exchanging foreign coinage for Jewish and Tyrian money. People were driving their livestock through the Court of the Gentiles, using it as a shortcut to the Mount of Olives—a veritable circus in a holy place traversed by an animal thruway.

Mayhem! Peter had never seen Jesus so angry. He created a whip from some cords and began lashing out at the merchants, overturning their tables and driving out the animal sellers with their doves, sheep and oxen, shouting all the while, "Is it not written, 'My house shall be called of all nations the house of prayer.'? But ye have made it a 'den of thieves.'"

When the high priests and scribes heard the story of Jesus' tirade, they were outraged and more determined than ever to be rid of him. "How dare he desecrate the temple with his crowd-pleasing antics!"

The disciples were meeting privately to discuss what to do about the mounting opposition to Jesus and by association to themselves. As Passover approached, the Sadducees and the Pharisees were becoming more vocal in their opposition to Jesus. Each time the Sanhedrin met, they discussed what to do about him. And each time a larger number of members added their voices to the chorus to rid Israel of the man named Jesus, who had convinced so many people he was the true Messiah.

The news of his raising Lazarus from the dead, rather than helping him, actually added to the clamor to be rid of him. In fact, it was upon hearing of this miracle that the priests decided to arrest Jesus and have him put to death for his illegal activities.

Peter, always braver in words than in action, spoke boldly, "Well, if they come within ten feet of Jesus, they'll be very sorry they ever laid eyes on him. Their tears and their blood will mingle on the blade of my sword. I will defend him with my life."

The others had a good laugh at that, and Nathanael said, "Well said, Peter the poet, but you had better ask your wife's permission to borrow her sword. You know that's what she uses to chop off the heads of her chickens."

Even his brother Andrew joined in, "Yeah, Peter, but your enemies may be fooled. Your sword isn't rusty, it's crusty—with chicken blood."

But all the jousting soon died down and they became quiet as they thought about the coming days. There was real danger ahead for all of them.

Chapter Thirty-Five

And one of them, named Caiaphas, being the high priest that same year, said unto them, "Ye know nothing at all. Nor consider that it is expedient for us, that one man should die for the people, and that the whole nation perish not."

John 11:49-50

All that is necessary for evil to triumph is for good men to do nothing.

Tolstoy

CAIAPHAS HAD PROBLEMS, SEVERAL THOUSAND problems. Jerusalem had swollen from its manageable population of 30,000 to many times that number because of the coming Passover festival. Almost 200,000 people were squeezed into the houses and inns, even camping out in the streets just to be near the temple to observe Passover. But Caiaphas knew that the real reason most of them were there was to celebrate and congregate. Any excuse for a party.

Why do people have to mob together to worship? Caiaphas puzzled scornfully. *If they truly wanted to observe a holy day, they would stay at home and worship quietly with their families. Even I, the High Priest, have never truly felt connected to a higher power in a crowd.* But those were his innermost sentiments, the ones he kept to himself, astute political animal that he was. No use ruffling the feathers of the religious birds that flocked together.

The crowds were huge and still growing. While that kind of crowd management was a headache for the temple guard, it was nothing compared to Caiaphas' problem. Many of them had come to Jerusalem hoping to see Jesus of Nazareth, the self-proclaimed Messiah who had ridden into town on a donkey several days before wreaking havoc wherever he went. Just after his arrival, he had disrupted business in the temple by flogging the merchants and moneychangers and turning them into the streets.

Actually, Caiaphas secretly agreed that such commerce had no place in the house of God; on the other hand, their presence was a convenience that increased the contributions by the pilgrims. He was all about convenience, a practical man who put expediency above all else. With the money changers on site, the worshippers had no excuse not to drop a denarius or two in the collection box. Or anyone who had arrived without a sacrificial animal could simply buy one from one of the animal vendors—a smelly, but profitable enterprise.

Everything Caiaphas had worked hard to accomplish was at stake, and he was not about to let one man with a gaggle of rag-tag followers upset what he considered to be his shining achievement—a peaceful co-existence between the Jewish population and the Romans, who ruled them with an iron hand. He was determined that nothing was going to upset that precarious balance or threaten his reputation as the consummate diplomat.

Early Thursday morning he was awakened from his sleep by the sounds of a city turned into a circus. Judging from the noise coming from every quarter of the city, none of the visitors was bothering to sleep.

"Why do religious fanatics worship with such imbecilic and decibelic fervor?" he grumbled aloud after being awaked from a sound sleep. Caiaphas often made up words as he talked to others as well as to himself.

He got up and dressed quietly lest he wake his wife, who lay beside him snoring softly. He was out the door before daybreak to consult Annas, his father-in-law, from whom he had inherited the priesthood. He would know what to do about the Jesus problem.

Annas had already heard many stories about the man Jesus who claimed to be a Messiah, but after Caiaphas spelled out all the appalling details, he was deeply troubled.

"Caiaphas, you must take action now while this trouble-maker is in the city. It's a shame that it has to happen during Passover, but we've got to stop this imposter before he causes any more problems. If what you say is true, too many religious sheep believe that Jesus is the Son of God. Isaiah must be turning over in his grave that this ragged beggar from Nazareth has convinced people that he is the promised Messiah.

"Call a special meeting of the Sanhedrin and see if we can reach an agreement on how to resolve this problem before the holy day begins. We have to be very careful to get this right because failure could be catastrophic."

Caiaphas walked the short distance back to his home in the affluent upper city, just west of the temple. In contrast to the crowded, noisy warrens of the lower city where the working people lived, here were brick-paved streets lined with ancient palms providing shade for the villas and palaces of the rich and powerful Jewish families and high-ranking Roman officials. These grand homes graced the streets of this hilly enclave like low-lying, marble clouds.

Caiaphas was humming tunelessly as he sauntered through the gate to his house. After an unusually cold winter, the weather had changed practically overnight into a cloak-shedding early spring. The warm weather felt wonderful on his arthritic body.

He patted the ivory Mezuzah and kissed his fingers as he entered the courtyard of his grandiose house—a little *too* grandiose for his tastes . . . but it was his wife's pride and joy. If it made her happy, it was a small price to pay.

Actually, he was proud of this monument to his talent and hard work. Nothing pleased him more than spending his hours of leisure feeding the exotic swimmers in his fish pond and caring for his prize orchids in the solarium. Life was good and he was determined to keep it that way.

He needed a couple of hours alone to come up with a plan for solving the Jesus problem. Removing his turban and ephod, the elaborate, colorful linen apron upon which the Hoshen rested, he handed them to his servant and said, "Malchus, go to the hall and make sure there is plenty of food and drink available for the Sanhedrin meeting tonight."

Grabbing a handful of grapes, he walked out to the solarium, where he did his best thinking. And it was in this peaceful setting where the plan was conceived to end the life of Jesus.

The solution was simple—the Romans had to be brought on board. To his credit, Caiaphas considered every alternative to put an end to the Jesus problem; but he discarded each one until he was left with one option—Jesus must be put to death . . . *by crucifixion.* They needed to make an example of him to discourage future contenders.

Later that afternoon as he walked to the meeting, passing through one of two arched passageways that spanned the valley across from the temple, he basked in the respectful attention of the passersby. A vain man, he enjoyed their curious glances, mistakenly thinking they were admiring his good looks and dignified bearing.

Actually, he was a weird-looking duck. He was short, borderline obese and suffered from a mild spinal deformity. His upper body canted left, his right shoulder much higher than his left, which gave him a curious gait. Someone watching his approach might wager that his left side would arrive before his right. It was hard not to stare at this short, stout man whose arrogant swagger loudly protested his oddity.

One of the first to arrive for the meeting, he was disappointed to discover that few of the Sanhedrin members were assembled. Apparently, the others were not as anxious as he to get this difficult business over and done with. He sent Malchus and Rufus to gather the other members, and by late afternoon, all of the members were assembled and waiting expectantly.

Any hopes he had had for a prompt decision regarding the fate of Jesus were dashed as the meeting dragged on hour after hour. Much to his chagrin, Caiaphas' request that the members vote to have Jesus put to death were met with reluctance.

Frustrated by the cowardly members that preferred discussion to action, Caiaphas mumbled to Annas, "We should just invite Jesus to this meeting. Our fellow members would talk him to death."

Caiaphas began a long rant: "This is what we're up against: here is this man, performing many so-called miracles in front of a crowd of fools who are always searching for someone to adulate. If he is not silenced permanently, everyone will eventually believe in him, and then the Romans will come and take away both our place and our nation."

He paused for effect: "Do you not realize that it is better that one man die for the people than for an entire nation to perish?"

Hiram rose to speak, his diffidence causing him to stutter worse than usual. "I'm, uh, inclined to think we should act with caution here. We sh-shouldn't be too hasty to condemn this fellow, who certainly seems to be harmless. Since he is from Nazareth, ma-maybe we should send him to Herod, who has rightful jurisdiction over Galilee."

Joseph of Arimathea said, "As an officer of the court, I cannot condone a rush to judgment. Surely the Sanhedrin are not going to condemn this man without allowing him to speak on his own behalf. Otherwise, how can we make an informed decision as to whether he is guilty or innocent, the latter of which I presume him to be?"

Caiaphas had wondered when Joseph was going to show his true colors. It was rumored that he and Nicodemus had been making secret nighttime visits to Bethany to talk with Jesus. Obviously, they had been converted, or *subverted*, as it were.

Determined to end the meeting before anyone else could voice an objection, he said, "I agree with Hiram: sending him to Herod is a good idea, but first we must take him to Pilate to follow the proper pecking order. You know how Pilate is—he never wants to take responsibility for anything, but he gets upset if we go over his head."

There was a grumbling among many of the members. Despite the fact that they hadn't voted, Caiaphas was proceeding as though they had a consensus. But there was little to be gained by continuing to discuss the matter, and to a man they abstained from making further comment.

Caiaphas said, "I sense that some of you fear that Jesus' supporters will cause trouble if we arrest their leader. But his support has dwindled. Why, just yesterday one of his faithful, Judas Iscariot, approached me and offered to give Jesus up for the right amount of money."

Caiaphas threw his cloak over his shoulders and said, "Hiram, I suggest you accompany the guards that deliver Jesus to Pilate. Remind him that Herod is in Jerusalem for Passover and should be consulted over the sentencing of one of his own. Pilate will send him to Herod so fast it will make his head spin."

Chapter Thirty-Six

And Jesus answered him, "The first of all the commandments is 'Hear, O Israel; The Lord our God is one Lord: And thou shalt love the Lord thy God with all thy heart, and with all thy mind, and with all thy strength: this is the first commandment. And the second is like, namely this, Thou shalt love thy neighbor as thyself. There is none other commandment greater than these."

Mark 12:29-31

IT WAS TIME FOR THE feast of unleavened bread, which is called Passover. Jesus said to Peter and John, "Go now and make preparations for the Passover meal that we may eat. When you enter into Jerusalem, you will meet a man near the Huldah Gates who is carrying a pitcher of water. Ask him where the guest chamber is that Mary Magdalene has reserved for her friends."

When Peter and John arrived at the Beautiful Gate, the crippled beggar who always sat in that spot asked them for alms.

Peter said, "Look at us."

Expectantly, the man looked up and held out his hand.

Peter said, "Silver and gold I do not have, but what I do have I give you. In the name of the Lord Jesus Christ, you are healed."

Peter held out his hand and the man grabbed hold of it. Then he stood up, his feet and ankles made straight in an instant. He ran around leaping and praising God. And all who saw him were amazed, for he had been crippled all of his life and now he was healed.

John was reeling from the miracle Peter had just performed. "Peter, what a wonderful thing you just did. I just hope that the people who witnessed the healing of that man heard you say it was in the name of the Lord Jesus. How many miracles will it take before the people realize that Jesus is the true Messiah?"

They walked through the Court of the Gentiles and emerged on the west side of the temple. As they neared John Mark's house, they came upon a man carrying a pitcher of water just as Jesus had described.

Peter called out to him, "Peace be upon you! We are looking for the room that has been reserved for Jesus and his disciples. Are we in the right place?"

The man bowed to them and replied, "Upon you be peace! Indeed, you are in the right place. Follow me upstairs. Everything has been made ready for your meal." He motioned for them to follow and led them to the upper room, where they would eat their Passover supper together.

As soon as the disciples came in, they started vying for the place of honor next to Jesus. They were still arguing over who was the most important when Jesus and Magda arrived. Magda was disappointed that they were having their usual, 'who is the greatest?' debate.

This is getting tiresome and I'm in no mood to put up with their bickering tonight of all nights, Magda thought. She was not her usual smiling self, and the mood in the room turned somber as the realization dawned on the disciples that this probably would be the last supper they would share with Jesus. Suddenly, the debate over who was the most important ceased to be important.

As they were sitting down at the large table, Magda on Jesus' right and John on his left, Judas came in looking guilty and avoiding Jesus' eyes, fearing that Jesus knew he had entered into a scheme to betray him.

When everyone was present, Jesus stood and began to speak. "With great anticipation I have looked forward to sharing this Passover meal with you, for I will not eat again until my fate is fulfilled in the kingdom of God."

He took a cup and gave thanks and said, "Take this cup and divide it among yourselves, for I say unto you that I will not drink of the fruit of the vine until the kingdom of God shall come."

Then he took the bread, blessed it and broke it, giving a piece to each one of them, saying, "This is my body which is given for you: this do in remembrance of me."

Usually, when the disciples sat down together for a meal, the atmosphere was convivial, everyone in good spirits and enjoying each other's company. But tonight no one seemed to have much of an appetite; they sat together almost morosely, drinking heavily, going through several pitchers of wine—this was far from a happy occasion. They were glad when Jesus stood to make his final remarks.

He lifted his cup of wine, saying, "This cup is the New Testament in my blood which is shed for you."

Jesus paused for a moment and looked around the table at the disciples gathered there. Sighing heavily, he resumed speaking. "But my heart is heavy, for there is one in our midst who has agreed to betray me for a few shekels of silver."

Magda grabbed Jesus' arm and pulled him close, whispering fiercely in his ear, "Who, Jesus? Which one has betrayed you?"

He didn't answer.

Then Judas came over, leaned down and whispered in Jesus' ear, "Is it I, Lord?" *How did Jesus know?*

Jesus answered him softly, "You have the answer."

And the others began to talk among themselves in great agitation, wondering which one was guilty. Even so, in the midst of such betrayal and treachery, soon they returned to their favorite debate – 'who is the greatest?'

Jesus tented his hands and rested his forehead on his fingers, briefly closing his eyes and grimacing.

Trying to lighten the moment, Magda said to him, "Are they still debating who's the greatest? That's easy: I am!"

Jesus didn't answer. He was not himself. Magda knew better than to push him when he went silent. Best not to jest when he was in this mood.

So she became more serious. "They may have their plans to destroy you, but I have other plans. I am going to prepare your body so that you may better handle the pain and possibly survive the injuries they are going to inflict on you. Go into the other room and remove all of your clothes. I am going to massage your body with the ointments and salves that I hope will help you to survive this ordeal."

Jesus emerged from the room wearing only a towel about his hips. He poured water into a basin and began to wash the disciples' feet, wiping them with the towel about his waist. When he came to Peter he said, "Peter, listen to me: you are in the grips of Satan's power; he will sift you like wheat. But I have prayed that you will be strengthened and overcome all temptation so that you will be able to lead the others when I am gone."

Peter said, "Lord, why are you washing my feet?" Uncomfortable, he pulled his feet under him. But Jesus stood waiting until Peter relented. He stuck his feet out, removed his sandals, and said, "Well, go ahead if you must. And while you are at it, please wash my hands and my head."

Magda burst out laughing. "Behold, Jesus, this vain man is Peter the Rock upon whom your church will be built."

When he finished washing the disciples' feet, Magda said, "Jesus, now I am going to anoint your body to prepare you for what's to come."

Wearing just the towel about his hips, Jesus lay down, stretching out full length—all six feet of him—on the table that Magda had cleared of the cups and dishes.

Magda gazed at him, thinking, *He is such a beautiful man. If God has truly made Jesus in his own image, how beautiful God must be. Jesus has treated his body like a temple, and his perfection reveals that loving care.*

She couldn't bear to think of his smooth skin being lacerated by the whips she knew the soldiers would use to flog him. *Man's inhumanity to man is something even inhumane men don't understand,* thought Magda. But she knew that there were some things that would defy understanding as long as men ruled the world.

She thought on all these things as she spent the next hour ministering the healing balms that she hoped would save Jesus' life. She picked up his right hand and held it to her cheek.

Removing the seals from the alabaster jars, and dipping her hand into the spikenard, then the frankincense, she massaged the oils into his skin, rubbing layer after layer into each finger, into each palm and the front of each hand.

She massaged the costly oils over most of Jesus' body, concentrating on his back because she knew that the metal tips on the ends of the Romans' whips would rip into that flesh as they followed him through the streets.

Only after she had used every last drop of the ointments was she satisfied that she had done a thorough job. She looked at his face and wondered if he was sleeping. His eyes were closed, his breathing even, peaceful.

The room was eerily quiet, filled with twelve disciples who normally would be talking and joking among themselves after a big meal with free-flowing wine. Magda looked around, and to a man they were all groggy. Even Peter was unusually quiet, steadily drinking wine from the pitcher he had positioned in front of his place at the table. He was practically asleep.

"Peter," she said, "you need to sober up, we have a long night ahead of us."

Magda thought, *Am I the only one here who's awake*? Then she turned back to Jesus, who hadn't stirred. She gave him a little thump on his chest. He sighed and reached out to her. She held him in a tight embrace until the lovely moment was ruined by another's evil thoughts.

"This is like watching a mating ritual," Judas Iscariot mumbled. "Magda, why are you wasting those costly oils on Jesus when you could sell them and use the money to feed the poor?"

That's a familiar refrain; Simon and Judas have been comparing notes, Magda thought.

Judas was as slippery as an eel. She had determined long ago that he often dipped into the disciples' money bag for his personal use.

She had held her tongue as long as she could. "Judas, you couldn't care less about the poor; you would just like to see the money I spent on the ointments go into the disciples' bag in case you need to *borrow* some more money from it."

Judas jumped to his feet, angrily demanding that Magda apologize for her accusation.

But Jesus said to him, "Peace. Be still. Magda is preparing me for my burial. Remember this—wherever this gospel is preached in the whole world, what Magda has done will be told in memory of her. Now Judas, you have more important things to worry about this evening. Take this sop I have dipped into the wine and go about your business."

Glaring at Magda, Judas stalked out of the room, his anger turning to sadness as he looked one last time at Jesus, whom he was about to betray. But he quickly recovered from his bout with a guilty conscience, thinking about the money he would be paid.

After Judas left, Magda said, "Jesus, go back into the room where your garments are and put on the loincloth before you get dressed." She insisted that he refuse to take it off regardless of what happened in the coming hours.

Jesus stood and motioned for everyone to gather round him and join hands. They began to sing the Hallel Psalms, Magda's soprano voice lifting above the tenors, baritones and basses of the men. Jesus had a beautiful deep voice and he sang, surprisingly well, the last verses of the hymn with great emotion:

> *Thou art my God, and I will praise thee: thou art my God,*
> *I will exalt thee.*
>
> Psalms 119:28-29

As the hymn ended, their voices blended into a glorious harmony: *O Give thanks unto the Lord; for he is good: for his mercy endureth for ever and ever.*

The final note was sustained by the others as Jesus spoke, his words rising above their voices, "A new commandment I give to you: that you love one another as I have loved you. Greater love hath no man than this . . . that he lay down his life for another."

But Nathanael, always sarcastic, commented under his breath, "I'm sure you are not commanding us to love one another as you have loved Magda."

They were used to Nathanael's sense of humor and unfiltered comments: what came into his mind came out of his mouth.

Peter followed Jesus and Magda down the stairs and out into the night. "Jesus," Peter cried, "where are you going? Why can't I go with you to protect you? You know that I will lay down my life for you."

"Oh, Peter, that is brave talk, but the truth is, you will deny even knowing me three times before the cock crows."

Peter started to protest, but Jesus put his hand on his shoulder and said, "Peace, be still, Peter. It is all part of God's plan. Let not your heart be troubled and do not be afraid. For now I return to my Father's House to prepare a place for you that where I am there you shall be also. And do not ask where I am going, for although I will leave you for a little while, during which time you will not see me, after a while you will see me again. And when I return, no more shall I speak in proverbs but will speak plainly that you will know the Father."

The Mount of Olives is a short walk east of the temple, and it was there in the Garden of Gethsemane that Jesus went to pray. He had chosen Peter, James, and John to accompany him. He stopped at the entrance to the garden and said to them, "Remain here while I go into the garden to pray. Stay alert so you can warn me if any of my enemies approach."

Actually, Jesus was also concerned that the disciples might be taken unawares while they lay sleeping. None of Jesus' followers was safe from his enemies.

Jesus walked away, looking back doubtfully one last time at his three disciples, who were anything but alert as they scouted around for a comfortable place to lie down. *So much for my three bodyguards; I should have brought someone to guard the guards,* he thought.

He walked a little deeper into the garden to his favorite place in a thick stand of olive trees . . . here, he could pray unobserved. In happier times, he would rest his back against a huge rock while he prayed and meditated. But tonight he lay down prostrate on the ground and began to pray more fervently than he ever had done. "Father, if you are willing, take this cup from me, but not my will but thine be done." He was sweating so profusely blood poured out of his pores along with perspiration.

An hour later he rose and went to find the disciples. They were all asleep!

"Get up," he shouted. "I am going back to pray again. Do not go back to sleep and allow them to take me by surprise."

But once again when he emerged from the garden, he found the men sleeping. He said sorrowfully, "Peter, again you are sleeping. Couldn't you stay awake for even one hour?"

Embarrassed, Peter reassured Jesus, "Go back into the garden, Lord. This time I will not fail you. No one will get past me."

Jesus smiled sadly and said, "Peter, watch and pray so that you will not fall into temptation. The spirit is willing, but the flesh is weak."

At that moment, Judas and a group of soldiers were crossing the Kidron Valley, nearing the entrance to the garden. "Be careful how you approach these men," he warned the soldiers. "Peter is strong and will not be taken easily. His sword is a lethal weapon that he wields with lightning speed and accuracy. Unlike Jesus, he is totally unpredictable."

But Peter, still feeling the effects of the wine, had sat down and dozed off again.

Judas and the soldiers crept past the sleeping men, careful to avoid making any noise that might announce their approach. They worried needlessly; the disciples were sleeping soundly, blissfully unaware of the danger that surrounded them.

Meanwhile, Jesus was on his knees in the garden, praying for the strength to endure the coming ordeal. Suddenly, his prayers were interrupted by loud voices; an angry mob of men was approaching. And no one had come to warn him.

Out of the darkness walked Judas, followed by the high priests and Roman soldiers; they entered the garden and surrounded Jesus.

Judas stretched out his arms to embrace him. Jesus said, "Judas, you needn't kiss me in front of this group. I will not deny my identity to these men."

Turning to the priests and the Pharisees, Jesus asked, "Whom do you seek?"

"Jesus of Nazareth," they answered.

"I am he."

When they asked him once again if he was Jesus of Nazareth, he said, "I have told you that I am he whom you are seeking. But let my disciples go on their way, they have done nothing wrong."

By this time the disciples had come into the garden and observed the group of men who were carrying weapons and lanterns and torches. Thoroughly awake now, Peter drew his sword and cut off the ear of Caiaphas' servant, Malchus.

"Peter, enough! Return your sword to its sheath! If you live by the sword, you will die by the sword," Jesus shouted, disappointed in his impetuous disciple, who had slept when he should have been awake, and struck when he should have slept.

Jesus pressed his hand to the servant's head, instantly healing him. Even so, that was not enough to convince the priests and the soldiers that they were arresting the Son of God.

Realizing that he was in danger after cutting off the servant's ear, Peter grabbed James and John. The three of them ran out of the garden, putting as much distance as possible between themselves and Jesus, who was sure to be arrested and sentenced to death. But after a few minutes John had an attack of conscience. He turned around and ran back up the hill to the garden, determined to find Jesus and show his support.

When the captain of the Jewish guard saw John, he ordered his soldiers to arrest him. "This man is one of the disciples. Take him and any of the others you can find and put them in chains to be tried along with the accused."

When the centurion saw that the guards were arresting John, he ordered them to free him. "This man is neither a coward nor a traitor; he drew no sword to resist us. According to Roman law, the accused is allowed one friend to stand with him at the judgment bar. I order you to honor that law."

"What is your name?" he asked John.

"My name is John, son of David Zebedee." He couldn't believe a Roman officer was intervening on his behalf.

"Well, John, I am Centurion Cornelius. I am ordering you to stand by the accused and remain there throughout his trials—there will probably be several—sentencing, and punishment. Go now and take your rightful place beside him."

Then the centurion talked to his second in command about Jesus' handling. "Longinus, I want you personally to escort Jesus to wherever the Jewish guards are taking him to be tried—whether it is to Annas, Caiaphas, Pilate or Herod. Stay with him, and wherever he goes, his friend John is to accompany him. Those are the prisoner's rights under Roman law, and that law is going to be followed to the letter."

John walked into the group of priests and Jewish guards as Jesus was saying, "I have been in plain view every day this week teaching in the temple, why didn't you approach me then? Why come out now with swords and staves like you are arresting a thief? Is it because you need to do your business under the cover of darkness?"

The priests answered by silently motioning to the guards to take the prisoner away. They tied his hands behind him and began to pull him along, roughly leading him out of the garden, across the ravine, taking him to Annas' palace in the upper city.

Magda had returned to Bethany to wait for Nico and Joseph. They were meeting to discuss Jesus' burial . . . *Jesus' burial,* she thought, *heinous words.*

When Nico and Joseph arrived, she hurried them into the house, saying, "There's a chance that you might have been followed here. We'll talk inside where there's no danger of anyone overhearing us."

Nico pulled out a chair for Magda, but held her arm for a moment. "I'm sorry to tell you this, Magda, but they probably have already found Jesus and arrested him. As we were coming here, we saw Judas Iscariot leading some of the priests and a group of Roman soldiers across the Kidron Brook. Apparently, that greedy scoundrel Judas has sold Jesus out. I always thought there was something shady about him, but I never thought he would stoop so low as to betray his friend, Jesus."

Magda sat down heavily, resting her head on her hand for a moment. "Oh God, that's terrible news, but not surprising. Jesus knew Judas was going to betray him. But I thought he would come to his senses before he did such a thing. Jesus trusted him enough to put him in charge of the disciples' money bag, and look what it got him: no good deed goes unpunished.

"It's hard to believe that Judas is greedy enough to sell out his friend. That just proves you never really know who your enemies are; which is almost as dangerous as not knowing who your friends are." She paused for a moment, chewing on her lip and thinking. "I guess the Sanhedrin wanted to arrest Jesus while he was in Jerusalem. Judas must have followed him when he went to Gethsemane to pray."

While she would trust Nico and Joseph with her life, she wasn't about to trust them with Jesus' life. It was that thinking that kept Magda from revealing to Joseph and Nico her plan to save Jesus' life. They would just say she was crazy anyway; and she had to admit, the chances of it succeeding were slim. But it was better than just doing nothing. It wouldn't be the first time she had been called crazy, and it wouldn't be the first time one of her crazy schemes worked, if it did.

Nico was pacing back and forth in front of the windows, watching to see if anyone had followed them. "Magda, I know that it is your desire to have Jesus' body placed in your family crypt, but Joseph and I don't think that would be wise. That is the first place they will look if they wish to steal Jesus' body."

"We think we have a better plan," Joseph said. "I own a piece of land that is an ideal spot. It has a crypt that has never been used and it's located in a garden that is in full bloom now, which makes it especially hard to find. Hardly anyone knows about it. But the best thing is that it has a secret entrance at the back that is completely hidden from view by the trees and foliage. We think we should take Jesus' body there."

Magda saw the wisdom of their plan and agreed it was far superior to hers, which she had to admit was based more on emotion than logic.

So they spent the next hour discussing how they were going to put each piece of the puzzle together to deal with the aftermath of Jesus' crucifixion. Joseph and Nico would go to Pontius Pilate and request that they be allowed to take Jesus off the cross and secretly bury him. If they could get Pilate to agree, the rest of the pieces should fall into place.

Mary had come to Judea for Passover. She was staying at Malama in the guest room, which was right above the room where Magda was talking to Nico and Joseph. She was not exactly eavesdropping, but she couldn't help but hear bits and pieces of their conversation, especially since she heard them mention Jesus' name several times. Judging from the little she could hear, there was no doubt that they were discussing Jesus' imminent arrest.

This is not good, she thought. *Something bad is happening and I fear Jesus is at the center of it. Why didn't he listen to Joseph when he tried to talk to him about how dangerous his activities were? Now Joseph is gone and I fear it is too late for anyone to save Jesus from the trouble he must be in. That's probably what Magda is discussing with her visitors. Why am I always excluded from everything that happens in my son's life? Sometimes I feel that I was no more than the vessel that brought him into the world. I'm always around for the pain, but when I need something, I'm told, "Who is my mother?"*

She made up her mind to have a frank discussion with Magda. She was not going to be excluded from whatever was going on with Jesus.

After all, how bad could it be?

Chapter Thirty-Seven

When Pilate saw that he could prevail nothing, but that rather a tumult was made, he took water and washed his hands before the multitude, saying "I am innocent of the blood of this just person: see ye to it."

Matt. 27:24

PETER AND JAMES RAN OUT of the garden and headed toward the city, Peter with his head down and looking guilty. He regretted cutting off the servant's ear. And worse, he had disappointed Jesus . . . something he would do a few more times before the day was over.

When they reached the cemetery in the Kidron Valley, they sat down behind a tombstone to rest and to see if anyone was following.

James was not happy that Peter had put the disciples in so much danger. "Peter, I can't believe you cut off the ear of the High Priest's servant right in front of everyone. Caiaphas will take it as a personal insult that you would dare to strike one of his staff—his chief steward, no less. If we weren't in trouble before, we are now."

Peter looked sheepish, but not all that concerned. "Well, if Jesus hadn't healed him then and there, I might be more worried about it. That was really something, wasn't it? One minute the ear was lying on the ground all bloody and dirty, and the next minute it was back on his head—good as new. A miracle like that performed right in front of their eyes, and still they didn't believe. Well, it might have been too dark for them to see very well; that's why I'm not too worried about them getting a good look at me."

As usual, Peter skipped on to his next thought without missing a beat. "Let's go directly to Caiaphas' palace and wait for them to take Jesus there. I'm sure that is where they will take him after Annas has finished questioning him."

They entered the city and were surprised that there were crowds of people milling about at such an early hour. There was an air of anticipation far beyond the usual Passover stir, and Peter and James were glad that they could blend in as they made their way through the city squares. Even so, several people turned to stare at them as they entered the spanned arches leading to the wealthy enclave on the west side, wondering why men in such shabby clothing were going to the elegant upper city.

The Sanhedrin Hall was ablaze with light. It was clear something important was happening. The talk among the crowd was of nothing but Jesus, who was going to be tried for claiming to be the King of the Jews and the Son of God.

Jesus had already been questioned in a brief hearing before Annas and was waiting—in chains in a basement cell—to be taken before the Sanhedrin council.

John roamed about restlessly, warming his hands by the fire in the courtyard, keeping a lookout for Peter and James. He was sure they would show up in time to watch Jesus' trial, and he was looking forward to asking them about their cowardice in the garden. His older brother, James, was shy and as restrained as any man he had ever known; his running away was a little easier to understand. But he was very disappointed in Peter, who talked such a tough game, but took flight at the first sign of trouble. Peter, always there to ignite the flame but never around to put out the fire.

As John paced, he tried to hear what the people around him were saying about the likely outcome of the trial. In his heart he knew that Jesus was doomed; he had made too many enemies.

Rahab, the doorkeeper, recognized John and walked over to him. "Your brother and his friend are outside and they want to talk with you."

Peter and James were waiting just outside the front gate. "Well, you finally made it," John said. "Did you find some liquid courage in the city?"

"John, don't be so hard on us," James said. "After all, Jesus told the soldiers to release us, that we had done nothing wrong. Of course, that was before Peter cut off the servant's ear. But when they agreed to let us go we wasted no time in getting away from that place. But we're here now! Can you get us in? We want to see what happens to Jesus."

John stared at James and sighed. *How had the sons of Zebedee become involved in this kind of madness?* But he agreed to ask Rahab if they could come in.

She shook her head and replied, "John, I can admit only one other, and he'll have to stay in the courtyard by the fire. By the way, they are about to bring Jesus up for the trial; be ready to stand with him."

James didn't hesitate to give up his place to Peter. "Peter, you go, you're Jesus' right hand man." He was relieved that he did not have to attend the trial; he was afraid someone might recognize him as one of the disciples. Peter went in with John and they stood by the fire and talked worriedly about Jesus' almost certain conviction.

Rahab looked at Peter suspiciously. She came over and asked him if he was one of Jesus' followers. He denied him . . . once.

But an angry looking man said, "You're the man who slashed my cousin's ear on Olivet. I was there and saw you do it."

"You saw someone else. I was nowhere near Olivet and I have never laid eyes on the prisoner," Peter denied him . . . twice.

By now a group of men were gathered around Peter. One of them said, "But you have that strange Galilean accent and you are wearing a fisherman's clothes; you must be one of his followers."

Peter began to curse and wave his arms around, "I just came in here to get warm. I tell you I don't even know who you're talking about." Three times.

Just then several soldiers led Jesus, bound and shackled, up from the basement. He was in bad shape, bleeding from the wounds from the many whips and stones that had pelted him during the walk across the city. He turned around and looked at Peter sorrowfully before they took him in to be tried.

Somewhere in the distance a cock crowed.

Peter burst into tears and ran out of the courtyard, realizing Jesus' prediction that he would deny him three times before the cock crowed had just come true.

They led Jesus into the chamber where Caiaphas was presiding over the council that would hear the complaints against him.

Caiaphas called the hearing to order and said to Jesus, "Are you the Son of God?"

Jesus answered, "Thou hast said; nevertheless I say to you, hereafter ye shall see the Son of man sitting on the right hand of power and coming in the clouds of heaven."

Caiaphas leaned forward in his seat and said, "That's not an answer. I repeat the question. Are you the Christ, the Son of God?"

"That is what you say," Jesus answered.

A soldier struck him in the face and said, "Do not speak disrespectfully to your superiors."

John, standing next to Jesus, jumped at the violence and moved toward the soldier with a murderous look on his face; but Jesus gave John a look that rooted him to the spot.

Caiaphas tore his robe and leaned back in his chair. "What need do we have of more witnesses? The accused has not denied his guilt. Take him to Pilate for sentencing."

Pilate was not happy that he was forced to hold court *outside* the Praetorium. The Jewish priests could not enter into the Romans' (Gentiles') court lest they be defiled and unable to partake of the Passover supper.

These Jews and their archaic laws. They make life doubly hard for themselves as well as for others, from whom they seek favors, thought Pilate as he strode out to the portico to hear the case against the man who claimed to be the Son of God and King of the Jews.

So it was a very annoyed Pilate who looked at the bleeding Jesus and asked, "Are you the King of the Jews?"

Jesus said simply, "For that cause I came into the world, that I should bear witness unto the truth."

Pilate laughed contemptuously. "What is the truth?"

Jesus refused to answer any further questions. The Romans were going to defer to the priests who were demanding that he be found guilty, so why take part in the farce?

Pilate found it hard to believe that Jesus wouldn't defend himself against the Jews' charges. "You choose not to speak to me although you must know that I have the power to order your crucifixion or to release you. Speak, man, and save yourself."

Jesus answered, "You would have no power at all except the power granted you from above. Those that delivered me to you have the greater offense."

Pilate grew bored with the man before him, who did not look capable of stirring up an entire country against Caesar. Upon learning that Jesus was from Galilee, which was Herod's jurisdiction, Pilate sent him to the tetrarch, happy to hand the problem off to someone else. He wanted nothing to do with this very bad business, particularly since his wife had dreamt that Jesus was an innocent man, unjustly accused, and had pleaded with him to let Jesus go free.

They blindfolded Jesus and paraded him through the streets of the upper city, leading him to Herod's Palace. Again, an unruly mob followed him, pelting him with rocks and insults.

When Herod saw Jesus, although he was repulsed by the blood and ripped flesh of his battered body, he was excited because he had heard so many stories about this man who could heal, restore sight, and even raise the dead.

While not really believing that the prisoner was capable of committing all the crimes he was accused of—he didn't look that sinister—Herod was hoping that Jesus would perform a miracle or two. He was shallow, easily amused and loved to be entertained. But when Jesus refused to answer any of his questions, Herod was disappointed and sent him back to Pilate.

Pilate was incredulous that the problem was once again in his court and that the onus of sentencing Jesus or releasing him was on his shoulders. It was obvious that Caiaphas was involving him in a Jewish vendetta against one of their own and he wanted nothing to do with it.

He made a half-hearted attempt to release Jesus, saying to the Jewish officials, "You have brought this man before me saying that he is subverting the people; but I have found no crime that rises to the level of a capital offense. Nor did Herod find him guilty as you charge. I will chastise him and release him since it is customary to release one prisoner during Passover."

But the people shouted, "Nay, nay, release Barabbas instead." Barabbas had been arrested along with many other criminals who were accused of murder and sedition.

And soon all the people were chanting, "Release Barabbas and crucify Jesus, crucify Jesus."

So Pilate gave in to the people's demands and sentenced Jesus to be crucified. But to demonstrate his doubt about his guilt, he took a pitcher and poured water over his hands, saying, "I wash my hands of the whole affair."

Chapter Thirty-Eight

And at the ninth hour, Jesus cried with a loud voice, saying, "Eloi, Eloi, lama sabachthani?"

Mark 15:34

When Judas learned that Jesus was going to be crucified, he returned the thirty pieces of silver to the priests. "If I had known that my actions were going to result in Jesus' death, I never would have agreed to deliver him to you. You have tricked me. You said that he would be banned from the temple and from preaching anywhere in Israel, not that he would be sentenced to death.

You have given me a death sentence as well. I cannot live with myself, knowing that my actions have led to the death of an innocent man."

The priests used the thirty pieces of silver—blood money—to purchase a burial site for foreigners called Potter's Field. Judas went into the field, later called *Akeldama* (Field of Blood), and hanged himself. He took his own life rather than live with his guilt and with the scorn of the other disciples.

After Pilate was done with Jesus' final trial, the soldiers jammed a *crown* of plaited thorns onto his head. As a mockery of him and his ragged followers, Pilate had the soldiers dress him in one of his purple robes, forgetting that its governor's seal loudly proclaimed his role in crucifying a man he believed to be innocent.

Thus arrayed, Jesus was paraded through the crowded streets for all to ridicule. "Behold, the king of the Jews," they shouted as he passed by them.

The Jewish priests argued with Pilate about the wording of the title he had instructed the soldiers to write on Jesus' cross: "JESUS OF NAZARETH THE KING OF THE JEWS." They asked him to change it to "I AM THE KING OF THE JEWS;" but Pilate, tired of the Jews and their demands, said to them, "What I have written, I have written."

The crowd followed the procession, wild with excitement over the prospect of celebrating both the Jewish holiday and the executions of Jesus and two criminals, who were condemned to die on crosses on either side of him.

Jesus was making his final walk in Jerusalem. Following a route that would come to be called the *Via Dolorosa,* he walked up the hill to Golgotha, where he would be nailed to a cross. He had been beaten, spat upon and mocked by the soldiers and even by some of the Jewish officials.

He was forced to carry the heavy crossbeam, but a kind-hearted Cyrenian, a giant named Simon, offered to carry it for him; and this unlikely entourage made their way to Skull Hill, where Jesus would hang from the cross until death came to rescue him.

Suddenly, a young man came running crazily through the crowd following the procession. When the soldiers grabbed at him, the narrow strip of loincloth he was wearing came away in their hands, and he ran completely naked through the narrow streets, adding to the afternoon's entertainment.

That mad streak probably influenced the soldiers' decision to allow Jesus to wear the cumbersome loincloth that Magda had created for him. Watching from a distance, Magda witnessed this scene, not daring to breathe as the soldiers discussed what they should do: should they remove the loincloth or leave it in place? If they removed it, they would discover the ointments, aloes and infusions she had hidden inside the old wineskin that was sewn into the folds of the linen cloth.

After consulting an officer, the soldiers finally decided to leave it in place, unwilling to remove the cloth lest they learn the unpleasant reason it was so bulky. Then they cast lots to determine who would win the beautiful robe that bore the Roman governor's seal. But before the winner could claim it, Magda walked up to the group of soldiers and demanded they give it to her. She had other plans for it.

"I have been ordered to return this robe to Pilate." Without waiting for an answer, she grabbed it and quickly disappeared into the crowd. The soldiers were mostly upset that they had been bested by a mere woman . . . a Jewish woman.

The executioners went about their duties matter-of-factly. Using spikes seven-inches long, they nailed Jesus' hands and feet to the wooden beams. Finally satisfied that he was securely fastened to the cross, they raised him high for all to see.

The crowds yelled curses at him, "Jesus, you say that you can destroy the temple and build it back in three days; save yourself and come down from the cross."

One of the priests said, "He saved others, himself he cannot save. Let Jesus, the Son of God, descend now from the cross that we may see and believe."

Jesus said, "Father, forgive them, for they know not what they do."

The criminal on the left scoffed at him, "You claim to be the Messiah? Well, if you're the Son of God, save yourself, and me and my friend here, also."

But the criminal on the right shouted across to his friend, "You don't speak for me, my friend. I believe this man is truly the Son of God."

He looked at Jesus and said, "Remember me when you come into your kingdom."

Jesus looked at him and solemnly promised, "Truly I say to you, today you will be with me in paradise."

Suddenly, the sky turned the day into night, the sun hid its face in shame, and darkness fell across the land for three hours. The crowds that had been watching the crucifixions with great curiosity started to thin out, many hurrying to get away from the site that they feared was now under a curse from God.

The more curious gathered closer to the condemned, anxious to see if this man who claimed to be the Son of God would free himself and the two criminals. There were several women standing at a distance from the cross, one of whom was Mary. She was being held up by the disciple John, who moved closer to the cross to hear what Jesus was saying. "Woman, this is your son." (Speaking of John.)

Then Jesus said, "John, this is your mother."

Mary shook her head. She didn't want another son; she wanted Jesus, her first born child. But she knew she was losing him. He was growing weaker by the minute, his head drooping ever lower onto his chest.

Jesus cried out, "I thirst." The soldiers offered him vinegary wine mixed with myrrh, which he refused.

"Eloi, Eloi, lama sabachthani?" (My Lord, my Lord, why hast thou forsaken me?)

Suddenly, there was a commotion near the foot of the cross. Someone was pushing through the crowd to get to Mary. It was Magda.

She pulled Mary away from the crowd so they could talk without being overheard. "Mary," she said, "it is time for you to send for Cornelius, the centurion. Only he can save Jesus now."

Mary looked doubtful. "Oh, Magda, do you think a Roman soldier would intervene in this? After all, the Romans ordered Jesus' crucifixion."

"Mary, you're wasting precious time. Send for Cornelius and tell him the truth! What do you have to lose? Do it now!"

At that moment, Nicodemus walked up, concerned that the two women were alone in the dangerous crowd. No one who knew Jesus was safe from this blood-thirsty group, and people were looking their way and pointing, "There is his mother and his concubine."

Magda grabbed Nicodemus' arm and said, "Nico, we need for you to find a Roman officer who might be able to help us; a centurion by the name of Cornelius!"

"Cornelius, the centurion from Capernaum? Certainly, I know him," Nicodemus said. "He's with the group of soldiers near the cross; but what do you expect him to do? After all, he is the officer in charge of these crucifixions!"

Magda shouted, "Nico, *please* . . . just go get him and bring him to us. Tell him Mary needs him—the Mary he met on the Roman Road many years ago. Just go, Nico!"

Nicodemus raised his eyebrows, wondering what crazy thing Magda was up to now. But he turned and ran up the hill toward the cross. While they waited for him to return, Magda held on to Mary, trying to give her more encouragement than she herself felt. "Mary, I have a plan that requires the cooperation of Cornelius. You must put away any feelings of embarrassment and focus on one thing only: saving Jesus."

"Magda, surely you know me better than that. I am not embarrassed; I'm afraid . . . afraid for Jesus. If anything, involving Cornelius might make it even worse for my son, *and* for you and me. I haven't seen Cornelius in over thirty years. We are not even sure if this is the same man."

About that time, Nicodemus came walking up with the centurion at his side. Magda looked at Mary, questioningly. Mary nodded. It was the right man, but the look on his face said he was not pleased at being pulled away from his duties.

"Mary, is that really you? What are you doing in this place?" Cornelius stared at her in disbelief. This woman kept popping up in the most unlikely places. How was it possible that the young girl he had encountered on the Roman Road so long ago had matured into this comely, albeit tearful, woman?

Mary stepped closer to him, hoping to see some trace of caring in his eyes. "Yes, Cornelius, it is I—the Mary you met over thirty years ago. Do you remember your promise that you would never forget me? You told me that I should call on you if I ever needed help. Well, that is my son that they are crucifying. He is innocent of any wrongdoing. You must stop them."

Cornelius was stupefied. "Mary, unfortunately, I cannot change an order from my superiors. Pilate has ordered this man's death and I cannot ignore my orders. I am not the only one in charge here."

Magda, driven mad by all the time-wasting blather, got in his face and shouted, "Cornelius, listen to me, Jesus is *your son*!"

Cornelius felt the breath go out of him. He was momentarily too astonished to respond. He looked sharply at Mary, who nodded vehemently. So it *was* true, he knew Mary wouldn't lie.

Finally, he answered, "Mary, you have kept this secret all these years—that I have a son. Why have you waited until this moment to tell me this? I could have intervened and stopped all of this before it started. I don't know if it is too late to save him now. I'm not sure he is even still alive."

Magda couldn't listen to another word. She grabbed Cornelius' arm and pulled him up the hill, whispering fiercely in his ear. He nodded that he understood and ran the rest of the way to the cross, shouting as he ran.

"Longinus, do not break the legs of the man on the middle cross!"

The soldiers had already broken the legs of the men on the other two crosses, but when Longinus heard Cornelius shouting, he stopped them from breaking Jesus' legs. It was customary to break the legs of the crucified in order to hasten their deaths, it being against Jewish law to leave a body hanging on a cross if the Sabbath or a holy day were approaching.

Cornelius approached Jesus, realizing that the son he had always wanted had been tortured to near death by the soldiers under his command.

Vivid memories of Jesus' saving his servant's life raced through his mind. And now he knew why he had felt such mixed emotions when he saw Jesus that day. Cornelius realized he had felt an immediate bond with the man who had miraculously healed his servant.

I have a son, Cornelius thought with a fleeting joy that dissolved into pain. Now it was up to him to save his life, if it was not too late. He was going to try what Mary Magdalene had suggested, but it seemed like such a far-fetched idea he doubted if it would work. The increasing darkness was on his side, and it was crucial that no one—especially Longinus—see what he was about to do.

Cornelius debated how much to trust his fellow officer. On the one hand, he was the best friend Cornelius had ever had—they were like brothers. On the other hand, the indisputable fact was that Longinus' loyalty was first and foremost to Caesar and the Roman Empire. Friend or not, Cornelius could not take the chance that Longinus would go along with a plan to save Jesus. Thus Cornelius, an unfailingly honest man, deceived his friend.

"Longinus, I'll take over here. You should check with Pilate to see if there are special arrangements for disposal of the bodies."

Cornelius was relieved when Longinus replied, "Well, coincidentally, I have just been ordered to report to Pilate. He probably wants to confirm that Jesus, the man on the middle cross, is dead. If I have your word that you will take care of that, I'll meet with Pilate and give him my assurance."

Longinus started to walk away, but turned back around and said, "Incidentally, I hear that Pilate is worried about the robe he dressed Jesus in after sentencing him. That robe bears his insignia and he wants it returned to destroy anything that could link his name with Jesus' crucifixion. He thinks by publicly washing his hands of the whole business, he will avoid taking responsibility for executing a man that he actually believes is innocent. He's worried about his place in history. Do you have any idea what happened to the robe?"

Cornelius knew that Magda had the robe and he hated lying to Longinus, so he told a half-truth. "Some of the soldiers cast lots for it and I do not know who won. The last thing I was worried about was a robe. You might ask around, but I doubt that anyone will admit to having it; that robe is a quality garment—and a great souvenir."

Longinus grimaced. *Some souvenir: the cloak of a coward.* But he kept those dangerous thoughts to himself as he mounted his horse and took off toward Pilate's palace.

Cornelius watched Longinus until he was out of sight. Confident that there was no one near enough to hear him, he said, "Jesus, I have come to help you, do you understand me?"

"Yes, Cornelius, I do. I understand everything. I have always known that you are my earthly father; I knew that even when you asked me to heal your servant in Capernaum. And now I know that your sword will pierce my side, because that is what is written."

Cornelius nodded uncertainly and said, "Well, Jesus, are you ready to do this?"

Jesus breathed deeply and replied, "Yes, Cornelius, I am ready. It is God's will."

This exchange and the emotional toll it was taking on him were so overwhelming Cornelius was afraid he would not be able to perform the challenging task before him. He certainly needed a cool head and a steady hand.

He thought of what Abraham must have felt when God told him to sacrifice his son Isaac on the altar, stilling Abraham's hand just before he plunged the knife into his son's throat. Now he was faced with a similar gut-wrenching challenge. But as Jesus continued to look down at him, a peace came over him, and he was filled with the assurance that God would guide him.

Meanwhile, the crowd was urging him on, shouting impatiently, "Break his legs, kill him, what are you waiting for?"

He looked at the crowd contemptuously. He was a centurion. An officer in service to the great Roman Empire did not take orders from fools and ghouls. He shouted to his soldiers, "Get these people out of here, move them way from this area."

The soldiers, using their whips and the threat of their swords, moved the rowdy group of people away from the crucifixion area, allowing Cornelius to act without an audience. If news of his crime against the Roman Empire became known, he would be put to death for his treachery.

From the time he was a young boy, Cornelius had had one ambition only—to become a Roman general like his father and so many of his ancestors. But he lacked the killer instinct necessary for an officer of that rank. By the time he rose to centurion he knew that he would never advance beyond that level. He accepted that because he preferred spending time with his men in the field, in the middle of the action, to the more treacherous life of a general, where the enemy was one's political opponents.

He had not earned his rank because of his illustrious ancestry. His courage on the battlefield and leadership abilities were the rungs on the ladder he had climbed. But more than any other talent, his mastery of the sword was what had earned his rank. His swiftness and accuracy made him a formidable opponent in a contest or on the battlefield.

Now he was in the contest of his life. His accuracy was a matter of life and death—of his own son.

Using his body to shield his movements from view, he pulled his sword from its scabbard and held it steady in both hands for a moment. Then, taking a deep breath, he thrust it surely and smoothly toward Jesus' side, intending to inflict only a shallow flesh wound. But Jesus seemed to swerve at the last minute, moving his body into line with the plunging sword. Cornelius tried to deflect his aim, but he felt his sword connect with Jesus' flesh with a sickening thunk. Horrified, he slowly withdrew his sword and watched while blood and clear liquid gushed forth from Jesus' body.

Jesus cried out in a loud voice, "It is finished. Father, into thy hands I commend my spirit."

Cornelius couldn't believe what had happened; he had missed his mark. He had delivered a death blow to his son!

Immediately, the earth began to shake and fissures opened up in the ground. Rocks split apart, tombs were broken open, spilling their grisly occupants. Dead bodies came back to life and started to walk about the city, howling as night swallowed up the day. Truly this was a hallowed eve.

Someone shouted, "The inner veil in the temple has split from top to bottom. We have angered Jehovah and now we'll all be punished."

The people who had been such willing spectators to the horrific spectacle, feeding some sick need for violence, now beat their breasts, tore their robes and put handfuls of dirt in their hair.

Cornelius cried out, "Surely this was a righteous man. Truly this man was the Son of God." Then he clutched his heart and thought to himself, *He is also my son. Merciful God, I have killed my own son!*

Mary and Magda, holding on to each other, cried out in disbelief, thinking that Cornelius had betrayed them, that he had not spared Jesus' life as he had promised. What kind of man murders his own son? At the end of the day, he was just a Roman soldier.

Magda anguished, *All my scheming and planning for naught. How foolish of me to trust a Roman soldier, to think that he would put his own flesh and blood before the Roman Empire. How could I have been so naïve?*

Joseph and Nicodemus asked Pilate for permission to take Jesus' body off the cross and bury him. He was all too happy to grant their request.

"Yes, take him," Pilate replied. "I have been assured by Officer Longinus that Jesus is dead. So you may remove the body. Take him and put him in a place no one will ever be able to find him. Just do it quickly before this mob starts a riot."

Cornelius shouted to his soldiers, "Lower the middle cross to the ground. Remove the spikes and take care that you do no further harm to the body. We are Romans not barbarians. At least spare his family the spectacle of a body more ravaged than it already is."

The soldiers gently laid the cross on the ground, taking care not to further mutilate Jesus' nail-torn hands and ankles.

Simon had been standing near the cross since he had carried it for Jesus, watching the gory crucifixion, sometimes turning away and refusing to look when the brutality became too much for a decent man to witness. Now he approached Joseph and Nicodemus, offering to carry Jesus' body to the burial site.

Leading the procession was Simon, carrying Jesus in his arms like a baby. He was followed by Joseph of Arimathea with Nicodemus at his side. Mary walked a few steps behind them, supported by John and Magda.

Magda was so moved by the spectacle of Jesus being carried by the giant Cyrene she cried out. Jesus' body looked shrunken. He looked like a little boy in Simon's muscular arms. She pulled the purple robe out of her bag and tenderly covered him with it. "Don't leave me, my love," she whispered to him.

Simon stooped down to enter the crypt and walked over to the shelf where the burial shrouds awaited the body. He laid Jesus down and knelt beside him for a moment. It was almost as though he had been touched by holiness.

Then Magda inspected the flesh where Cornelius' sword had pierced Jesus' side. She cleaned the clotted blood from the wound and tried to determine how bad it was. It didn't look deep enough to be fatal, but Luke would have to determine that; she was an apothecary, not a doctor.

She massaged the embalming ointments into his body, brutalized by the thongs of the whip, the nails that had pierced him and by the agony of hanging on the cross for so many hours.

While she worked she worried. *No one, not even Jesus, can survive such torture. At least they spared his face; otherwise I wouldn't even recognize him. Is he dead or alive? Did Cornelius spare his son or did he follow his orders to plunge his sword into Jesus' body?*

She sat back on her heels and brooded, pondering what else she could do. More for herself than for Jesus, she sang an ancient lullaby that Heli used to sing to her when she was little. Magda had sung it to Jesus when he was a little boy. She hoped it would awaken something in him now.

Old black sheep, she had a little lamb,
She laid him by the llama,
The birds and the butterflies picked out his eyes,
And the poor little lamb cried, 'amah, amah.'

No Response.

She whispered to him, "Jesus, can you hear me? Are you sleeping or have you left me? I thought I had saved you, that I had talked Cornelius into sparing you. But now I wonder. Where are you?"

Nothing.

While she rubbed the oils and ointments into his cool flesh, she poked and pinched and prodded and even tried tickling him, hoping he would at least twitch a little if there was any life left in him.

No Life. No life in him, so no life in her. If Jesus was dead, Magda wanted to lie down beside him and die as well.

She finished her work and walked away from the garden, heading toward Golgotha. She was going to find Cornelius. She wasn't going to rest until she asked him why he hadn't kept his promise to spare Jesus' life. She didn't care if he was a Roman soldier, she was going to get answers to her questions; and if he had betrayed her and his son, she would find a way to make him pay.

She began searching among the groups of soldiers at Golgotha, some of whom were gawking at the criminals on the remaining two crosses. The two men were taking a long time to die as they slowly asphyxiated, their chests compressed, unable to stand on the shelf after their legs were broken.

Magda looked away from the sight of the dying men, sickened by those who enjoyed another's pain and suffering. Carefully scrutinizing the face of every Roman officer she passed, she finally asked a soldier if he had seen the Centurion Cornelius.

His eyes strayed down to her breasts. Who was this woman who was brazen enough to address a Roman soldier? "What business might you have with an officer of the Roman army?" he asked.

Magda, being Magda, was not intimidated. She crossed her arms over her breasts and answered him, "I have personal business with the officer. That business is not your business, now have someone get a message to him that Mary Magdalene needs to speak with him about an urgent matter."

The soldier was so taken aback that his hand instinctively went toward his sword. But common sense took over and he told another soldier to find Cornelius. This woman might have powerful friends in high places and he decided not to ignore her lest she bring down a world of trouble on his head.

Surprisingly fast, the soldier returned with a message from Cornelius. He was in a meeting with Pilate and would meet Magda at Golgotha in one hour.

Magda, too impatient to wait and not wanting to remain at Golgotha, walked to Pilate's Palace in the upper city. She was relieved to see that Cornelius was just walking out, flanked by two members of the Sanhedrin, who were making no secret of their wishes.

"Pontius Pilate has assured us that guards will be posted at the entrance to the crypt for three days, and we expect that order to be obeyed no matter what. If given half a chance, his followers will take his body away and claim that God has lifted him into the heavens. We cannot allow that to happen. The rumor mill has already started that we have murdered an innocent man, a Godly man. We can't risk an uprising by the people. Do we have a meeting of the minds on this?"

Cornelius looked down at the two men, who were considerably older, shorter and fatter than he, and replied, "The guard will be posted as you have requested. Do not question my authority or my judgment. And never forget who is in charge here. Are we clear on that?"

Witnessing this exchange between Cornelius and the two Sanhedrin members gave Magda hope. Cornelius certainly seemed to be a man of character, someone who didn't mince words, whose word was his bond. As soon as the men had stalked off, obviously unhappy that Cornelius had dared to rebuke them, Magda walked over to him.

"Cornelius, I can't believe you just disappeared after they took Jesus' body away. Didn't you realize that I would be anxious to hear what happened? Was Jesus alive when he was taken down from the cross? I have just prepared his body for burial and could get no response from him."

Cornelius, whose patience was worn thin by the demands of too many people, wheeled around and grabbed her by the arm. "Do you think that I have nothing better to do than worry about your anxiety? I am responsible for 100 soldiers and three crucifixions—and that's only today's agenda; I'm just a little busy."

But the look on Magda's face touched him. "But I kept my word, my aim was true. Everything went according to plan right down to the last moment. It seemed like Jesus intentionally moved his body into harm's way. I aimed for the loincloth, but Jesus was a willing victim. It was obvious that he wanted my sword to pierce his side. What is the saying? 'Man plans, God laughs.' And now I may have mortally wounded my own son."

Magda heard only his last sentence. She sank to the ground, weeping and tearing her robe. She shouted at Cornelius, "You have murdered Jesus. What kind of man kills his own son? You betrayed Mary and me. You're a disgrace to the human race. But I'm sure you're a hero to the Romans."

Several soldiers were standing nearby and staring in their direction. Cornelius gently pulled Magda to her feet, trying to calm her. He whispered, "You aren't listening to me, Magda. I did not betray you. I aimed for the loincloth, but Jesus moved right into the path of my sword. I'm not certain whether he convulsed with pain or he wanted my sword to pierce his side. I got the feeling it was deliberate."

He shouted at the soldiers, "You men report to Officer Longinus at Skull Hill."

He turned back to Magda and tried to reason with her. "You and Mary waited too long to bring me in on this nightmare. Regardless of whether my sword pierced his side, Jesus was practically dead when I got to him. I am a soldier, not a miracle worker. And I have disobeyed a direct order, a military offense punishable by death. I have risked everything, even my own life, to save this man who, I am told some thirty years after the fact, is my son.

"However, the wound I inflicted may not be fatal. There was no resistance when I withdrew my sword, and there was not a great deal of blood on the blade. There is a chance he is still alive and is simply unconscious. But we must get him into the hands of a doctor. He will never survive a night in that cave. The temperature is dropping and if he doesn't get medical care and a little divine intervention we'll lose him. Start praying for a miracle."

Magda let out a deep breath. "The miracle has been found," she said, calmer now. "My friend Luke is a great physician and a man of honor and discretion. He *is* a miracle worker. However, he is not expecting to deal with a deep sword wound. We'll have to tell him when he meets us at the tomb. If Jesus is still alive, I believe he will survive.

"There is another opening to the cave that only Joseph of Arimathea knows about. He and Nicodemus have already planned to move Jesus in a cart at midnight and take him to Dr. Luke's surgery."

Cornelius was only momentarily torn as he considered his choice: allow Jesus' body to be taken from the cave and risk court martial for dereliction of duty, or prevent him from getting medical help and end any chance of his survival. Easy decision.

"Ride with me," he said, grabbing Magda's hand and pulling her up behind him on his horse. "We need to find Joseph and get a workable plan in place."

Meanwhile, Joseph and Nico were discussing what they would do if Cornelius didn't go along with their plan to move Jesus from the tomb. Surely he would not be a party to anything that meant ignoring an order from Pontius Pilate; although they were sure Pilate didn't care what they did as long as it didn't come back to haunt him.

When Magda came in followed by Cornelius, the look on her face said it all—Cornelius was with them. Their relief shone on their faces. If they had the help of the centurion, the rest was just details . . . and the grace of God.

Nicodemus took Magda aside. "Magda, for your own safety, please go back home to Bethany. Do not reveal any of these plans to anyone, even to Mary. You are the first person the Jewish officials will suspect when they discover Jesus' body is missing, so the less you know the better. You cannot reveal what you don't know."

Perhaps he didn't know that Magda always knew everything.

Chapter Thirty-Nine

And it was about the sixth hour, and there was a darkness over all the earth until the ninth hour. And the sun was darkened, and the vail of the Temple was rent in the midst.

Luke 23:44-45

THE EARTH WAS IN MOURNING. The midnight sky hid its moon and stars in the deep folds of its black cloak and a heavy fog of shame hung over the land. Joseph, Nicodemus, and Cornelius slowly drove a cart down a dirt path along the back of Joseph's property, coming to a halt at the bottom of the hill. It took all three of them to roll away the huge rock from the opening.

When Dr. Luke arrived, each man took a lantern and slowly walked down into the tomb, nervous about what they would find. Was Jesus alive? Coming to the shelf where he lay, they were surprised to find that, while his body was completely wrapped in linen strips, his head was only partially covered, his mouth and nose exposed—the artful legerdemain of Magda.

Dr. Luke uncovered Jesus' right arm and closed his fingers just below his swollen wrist, waiting for several seconds to feel the rhythmic throb of life. Feeling nothing, he looked grim and shook his head slightly. Then he laid his head on Jesus' chest and listened for a heartbeat. "Sshh! everyone, absolute quiet," he said as he shut his eyes and listened. Luke heard the sound of his own heartbeat, but there was no sound of life in Jesus' body.

When he placed two fingers under Jesus' jaw and found no pulse there, he looked as if he had lost all hope. He could not recall one instance where anyone had survived crucifixion. He had not held out much hope for Jesus' survival, especially now that he knew Cornelius' sword had pierced his side.

He looked at the others and slowly shook his head.

Nicodemus and Joseph spoke nearly in unison: "Let's not give up hope yet. We'll just proceed with the plan to load him onto the cart and take him to your office, Luke. Maybe he is just in a deep sleep."

They removed the head covering and linen strips and put them aside. Gently lifting his body—Joseph and Nicodemus by the arms, Cornelius and Luke by the legs—they carried Jesus out of the cave to the cart. They wrapped him in Pilate's beautiful, now somewhat bloody, purple cloak. With the seal of the Roman governor on it, no one would dare to inspect what it covered.

Cornelius nearly stopped breathing at what happened next: Jesus' fingers moved.

Cornelius cried out, "Look, he's alive," pointing to Jesus' hand and his moving fingers. Then he knelt for a moment in the small hope that Jesus had survived after all.

But no one else shared his illusion. And although he didn't say it, Luke doubted that the hand movement was the vigor of life but rather the rigor of death.

Cornelius took hold of Jesus' hand and said, "Jesus, squeeze my hand if you can hear me."

Nothing.

Joseph was sad for Cornelius as the smile faded from his face. "Cornelius, let's not jump to conclusions either way. Let's just wait and see if Luke can work a miracle."

Now came the tricky part: getting Jesus to Dr. Luke's practice in the inner city without arousing suspicion. If anyone was out, they would wonder what was so important that it had to be transported at this ungodly hour.

But Joseph had not accumulated his incredible wealth by being stupid. He had two of his trusted servants take over the cart, telling them that they were making a delivery of some butchered lambs for the Passover supper of some friends. The servants simply thought that Joseph was honoring the Jewish law that forbade working on Shabbat, passing along the task to his foreign servants, who were not troubled by breaking a law of someone else's religion.

As the servants rode off pulling the cart behind them, Joseph brooded. *Why worry about my servants breaking the Mosaic laws when I myself am guilty of breaking so many of Caesar's laws today? Even Jesus said, 'Render unto Caesar that which is Caesar's.'*

Nicodemus consoled Joseph. He found many of the Jewish laws a bit cumbersome—stuff of superstition. "You are doing God's work! God will bless you with even more abundance for having an abundance of common sense."

But Cornelius found all the discussion annoying. There were lives on the line with this illicit operation—Jesus' as well as his own. He would be executed if his superiors discovered the extent of his treachery against Rome and Caesar. The last thing any of them should worry about was breaking nonsensical laws made to enslave the sheep that followed them.

Part Four

"... and, lo, I am with you always, even unto the end of the world."

Matt. 28:20

Chapter Forty

And the angel answered and said unto the women, "Fear not ye: for I know that ye seek Jesus, which was crucified. He is not here: for he is risen, as he said. Come, see the place where the Lord lay."

Matt. 28:5-6

MAGDA IGNORED NICO'S SUGGESTION THAT she go home. She waited in the shadows outside the garden, pacing and watching for the cart. Finally, she heard it trundling noisily along, heading for the arched colonnade that spanned the valley to the inner city; she fell in behind it. Then her heart stopped.

There were two Roman soldiers patrolling the passageway. Magda had anticipated just such a problem and she ran up to the cart and began to yell at the servants, "Why are you taking so long to deliver these lambs to my customer? At this rate they will be mutton by the time they arrive . . . spoiled mutton."

The confused servants looked at her like she was crazy, but realized that the greater obstacle lay in dealing with the soldiers. Nobody had told them that this might be a dangerous mission.

Magda walked up to the soldiers and said in her most imperious manner, "I have papers signed by Pontius Pilate granting this cart entrance into the city. Your commanding officer, Centurion Cornelius, is going to dine with his fellow officers later today, and we are delivering butchered lambs for their meal. These orders bear the prefect's seal guaranteeing safe passage for me and my servants."

Magda knew the soldiers probably could not read the documents she pulled from her bag (actually, they were bills of lading written in Aramaic for an incense delivery). The soldiers glanced uncertainly at the papers and back again at the cart and the impressive seal of the cloak covering its cargo, wondering why butchered lambs were wrapped in the governor's cloak. But they waved them through.

The unwieldy cart resumed its lumbering journey, noisily rocking over the cobblestone streets to Luke's office in the inner city. When they finally pulled up at Luke's front gate, Magda took her first full breath since they had left the crypt. The 'lambs' that were being delivered to Luke were going to be resurrected from death. Jesus would survive if the doctor could work a miracle.

Magda walked in behind Luke's servants, who carried Jesus' body into the back room where Luke was preparing for surgery.

If Luke was surprised to see her, he made no mention of it. He was never surprised at anything Magda did. As her personal physician, he knew that she loved Jesus like a brother, like a beloved friend, and wistfully, like a lover.

She was babbling, more nervous than he had ever seen her. "Luke, give your assistants the night off, I will assist. No one must know the identity of the man on this table. Unfortunately, the wound from Cornelius' sword is deeper than just a scratch in his side. I'm afraid our patient is more seriously injured than I first thought, and . . ." Then she started to sob.

When Luke examined the wound in Jesus' side, he understood Magda's concern: it was inflamed and draining. He would have to open him up to cut away the dying flesh and thoroughly cleanse the wound. He marked the spot to make the incision and Magda, back to herself, handed him the surgical knife. When he drew the sharp blade through Jesus' flesh, blood began to flow.

Luke and Magda cried out in unison, "Thank God! Jesus is alive!" Luke's blade had struck gold—Jesus' blood.

They worked for hours, putting Jesus' battered body back together. All of his wounds were bathed in frankincense, aloe, honey and myrrh. There was hardly an inch of his body that had escaped injury. Finally, they closed him up and bandaged the deeper cuts and wounds.

Exhausted, Luke said, "Magda, there is nothing more we can do. It's all in God's hands now. Jesus will probably sleep for a couple of days." Luke paused and added gravely, "That is, *if* he survives."

Back in Bethany, Magda fidgeted and paced back and forth, knowing that this Sabbath was going to be the longest day of her life. Even in the best of times, Magda suffered through Shabbat—a day of rest to be endured by those who are happiest when they're busy. With walking and working out of the picture, there was nothing to do but fret and worry.

If Jesus survived, what kind of life would he have now that he couldn't walk about freely? Would he have to live in hiding, in fear of discovery? Would he be a cripple or an invalid? Would he be the same man she had known and loved? Would he still love her and want her by his side?

These concerns nibbled at her as she walked the floor and thought about her future—hers and Jesus'. But a few glasses of wine helped with the boredom, and her eyes were closing before dark.

The next morning, just as the sun was beginning to rise, she hurried back to the city to meet Joanna and Salome, who were going with her to Jesus' tomb. It was important to keep up the pretense of embalming the body with spices and ointments, so she carried a basket containing frankincense and myrrh.

Joanna and Salome were weeping as they walked. But Magda was too numb to cry, and she was beginning to be annoyed by her friends, whose steps got slower the closer they got to the tomb. When they entered the garden, they were surprised to see that the stone had been rolled away.

Inside the crypt sat a young man in a long white robe. Magda was shocked. Who was this person? She was momentarily at a loss; and the other women began to wail even louder and to tear their garments, fearing that they were going to be blamed for helping to spirit Jesus' body away.

Magda was almost as upset as Joanna and Salome. She was expecting the garden entrance to be blocked by a great stone. She puzzled, *I wonder who rolled away the stone to this entrance?*

"Why are you weeping?" the man asked the women.

"Because they have taken our Lord away," Salome cried.

"There is nothing to fear," he assured them. "I know that you are looking for Jesus, who was buried here. He has left his burial shroud behind, for he has risen and left the sepulchre."

Joanna and Salome started to run away, but Magda called out to them, "Wait, I want to go with you." And they ran all the way into the city, where they found Peter and the other disciples hiding out in another follower's house.

"Peter, the most amazing thing has happened," Joanna said, and she told him that Jesus' body was not in the crypt.

But Peter scoffed at the women, thinking that they were confused. Who but one of the disciples would have taken the body? And none of them knew where he was buried. Jesus couldn't possibly have walked away. No one survived crucifixion.

"Are you sure you went to the right place? You know that it is a new tomb located in a garden just north of the city," Peter said knowingly. *Why do women always allow their emotions to cloud their thinking?*

Magda folded her arms across her body. "Yes, Peter, we went to the right place. I knew exactly where it was because I followed the men who took his body there. Where were you, O Peter the Rock?" she asked.

Peter and John insisted on going with the women to see for themselves if what they had said were true. As they walked into the garden, they saw a man in a dazzling white robe standing by the entrance to the sepulchre. No one but Magda recognized him. It was Jesus. She began to cry. She was relieved to see him looking so healthy—he looked as though nothing had happened. But she was worried about him. What was he thinking, being out of bed and in the public eye this soon?

"Woman, why are you weeping? Who are you looking for?" Jesus asked, keeping his distance.

Magda pretended he was the gardener who worked on Joseph's property. "Sir, have you taken my master's body away? If so, pray tell me where he is."

But Jesus whispered to her, "My Magda."

Despite her impulse to grab him and embrace him, she restrained herself, merely saying softly, "Rabboni."

"Noli me tangere." (Touch me not.)

Fearing the bad news would reach the officials before they could report their findings, some of the palace guards that had been assigned to watch the tomb went to tell Caiaphas that Jesus' body was missing.

Caiaphas was enraged! He started yelling for Malchus to find all the Sanhedrin members and summon them to an emergency meeting. But Malchus resented being involved in this bad business that had nearly cost him his right ear. He took his time about finding the other members.

By the time all of the elders were assembled, Caiaphas was somewhat calmer, having discussed with Annas a sensible plan. After he told the members what had happened, they agreed on a story: they would pay the guards to say that while they were sleeping, the disciples had come and taken the body away. They were to stick to that story no matter what.

"Even if the governor sends for you to learn what actually happened, that is what you must say. And you have our word that we will back you up."

So the guards took the money and did as they were told, and everyone believed their story.

Later on Sunday, the disciples were in Jerusalem, hiding behind locked doors from the Roman and Jewish officials who had ordered Jesus' crucifixion.

Without knocking, someone opened the door and walked in. It was Jesus. He greeted them, "All hail. Peace be unto you."

But they didn't recognize him and no one returned the greeting. To a man they were afraid that their visitor had been sent to arrest them. Patiently, Jesus showed them his nail-scarred hands and the angry red scar on his left side where the centurion had plunged his sword.

"Be not afraid," he said.

He sat and talked with them just like old times. He urged them to return to a normal life. "Go back to Galilee and start fishing again. Soon I shall join you."

And just as suddenly and as silently as he had arrived, he was gone, leaving some of them to question what they had seen.

"I won't believe that was Jesus until I feel the places in his hands where the nails pierced his flesh, and place my fingers in the wound in his side," Thomas said. From that day forward he was called 'Doubting Thomas.'

After eight days of hiding out in Jerusalem, the disciples returned to Galilee. Peter and Andrew were looking forward to fishing again to support their families.

When they got to Peter's house in Capernaum, he grabbed his fishing gear and said to the others, "I go a fishing." The others laughed at Peter's use of the Galilean dialect, happy to be back at home among familiar sights and sounds. They grabbed their gear and followed Peter out the door and down the hill to their boat, which was tied up right where they had left it.

After fishing all night without success, they rowed back with empty nets. As they neared the shore, they saw a man standing in the shallow water. It was Jesus, but again they didn't recognize him. He didn't look like himself.

Even his voice sounded different. "Brothers, did you have any luck fishing?" He had lost his Galilean accent.

"No, the fish weren't biting tonight." The disciples raised their empty nets as proof of their lack of success.

Then Jesus said to them, "Go back out into the deep and try casting your nets on the right side of the boat; you'll find more fish than your nets can hold."

John shouted, "Peter, it is the Lord!"

Peter, who had stripped off his clothes while fishing, pulled his fisherman's coat about him and impulsively jumped into the sea, mistakenly thinking that he could touch bottom and wade to shore. But he was in over his head. Encumbered by the heavy fishing coat, he started going under. He floundered about, gasping and swallowing large amounts of sea water, not realizing that he might save himself by simply removing the coat.

Seeing his distress, Jesus swam out to rescue him. Peter was a big man, and swimming back to shore with him would have been an impossible feat for a poor swimmer. But Jesus, from his boyhood days of swimming in the Nile, had a powerful stroke and he brought Peter, minus his coat, safely to shore.

Peter lay on the sand, coughing up water and sputtering incoherently. Jesus knew that anyone who could make that much noise was in no danger of dying, so he just waited for Peter to return to normal.

Somewhat recovered, Peter began to thank Jesus for saving his life. "Jesus, you just performed another miracle—you walked on water and carried me back to shore. You saved my life!"

Unconcerned about his nakedness, he crawled over to Jesus, kissed his feet and hugged him about his ankles.

Jesus laughed joyfully. It was good to be back with his dear friends, even if a couple of them were a few sardines shy of a fish fry.

"Peter, I was not walking, I was swimming. I can't believe you never learned to swim, as much time as you spend on the water."

"Oh no," Peter said. "I can paddle around a bit on the surface, but I am deathly afraid of my head going under the water. Andrew and the others do all the diving down to the nets. But I've never seen anyone do what you just did in the water. You were moving your arms and your legs just like you were walking."

"Peter, I was swimming, which I learned to do in the waters of the Nile. What all of you do is called 'dog paddling.' The Egyptians would laugh you out of the water if you tried that in the Nile . . . if you survived."

Magda, averting her face and laughing, said, "Peter, you'd better learn to swim if you're going to fish for a living. But first you'd better put some clothes on before they name a small fish after you."

And from that day forward, the locals called Tilapia, 'St. Peter's Fish.'

Meanwhile, the others had gone back out to the deep water and lowered their nets on the right side of the boat, following Jesus' advice. In a short while, they had caught so many fish—153 by count—the nets were close to tearing. They rowed back to shore with their catch. The disciples were happy as they pulled the net onto the sand. Full nets meant full bellies . . . and contented wives.

Jesus called out to them, "Come and eat." To their amazement, he had made a fire of coals and cooked breakfast, giving a piece of bread and fried fish to everyone.

After they had eaten, the disciples went home to their beds, exhausted after a long night of fishing.

But Jesus said, "Peter, please stay with me for a while. I want to talk with you."

Peter turned around and walked, head down, back to where Jesus was sitting in the sand. Magda was looking for seashells farther down the beach and it was just the two of them. He dreaded hearing what Jesus was going to say because he knew he had let him down by denying him, not once, but three times. There was nothing he could say to redeem himself other than just to confess that he had been afraid. Would Jesus forgive him, as he taught everyone to do?

Peter sat down heavily on the sand and waited for his comeuppance. But he was surprised when Jesus asked, "Peter, who do people say I am?"

Peter replied, "Some say you are John the Baptist, others say Elijah, but most people think you are a prophet sent from God."

"Who do you say I am, Peter?"

"You are the Christ."

"Do you love me more than the others?"

Peter answered, "Yes, Lord, you know that I love you."

Then Jesus told him, "Feed my lambs."

Then he asked a second time, "Peter, do you love me?"

Again Peter answered, "Yes, Lord, you know that I love you."

Jesus replied, "Feed my sheep."

Then he asked yet again, "Peter, do you love me?"

Peter was upset that Jesus had asked him three times if he loved him. Didn't he believe him? Then it dawned on him; maybe he had asked three times because Peter had denied knowing him three times. Was this Jesus' gentle way of reminding Peter of his earlier betrayal?

Peter answered him the third time, "Lord, you know my heart, and you know that I love you!"

Jesus said, "Then feed my sheep."

"But Jesus," Peter asked, with a furtive glance at Magda, who was walking toward them, "why do you love her more than all of us?"

Jesus answered him, "Why do I love Magda more than you? When a blind man and one who sees are both together in darkness, they are no different from one another. When the light comes, then he who sees will see the light, and he who is blind will remain in darkness."

Chapter Forty-One

This is the day that the Lord has made; let us rejoice and be glad in it.

Psalms 118:24

After Jesus' resurrection, Magda had bargained with him before she agreed to travel with him from Jerusalem to Galilee to be with the disciples—a trip she was too emotionally drained to make. She had agreed to go with him if he would promise to stay just one week.

They had been in Capernaum for seven days and Magda was getting antsy; she was sick of the rain that had fallen every day since they had arrived and was worried about her father. She was depressed and the rain wasn't helping.

"Jesus, let's go home," she said. "Abba said that he had something very important to tell me, and I'm getting increasingly worried that I won't arrive in time to hear it. And of course I want to be with him in his final days."

She knew that Jesus wanted to tarry a little longer in Capernaum, but she reminded him of his promise to stay just one week.

"My Magda, you know that I lose track of time when I am with my disciples. I will keep my promise—we'll leave tomorrow."

She looked drawn and pale and he knew she was suffering from the aftermath of his crucifixion and resurrection; and worse, she was worried about her father.

She went to bed right after dinner, saying they needed to get an early start the next day. Jesus sat for a while watching her face as she slept. When Magda was asleep, she was as innocent-looking as a child. *How I love her. How I will miss her*, he thought sadly.

The next morning Magda was her old self again. "Jesus, the last time I saw abba I promised to visit him again in a few weeks. Those weeks have turned into months. I don't want to waste any more time and now is not the time to quibble over whether we should ride or walk. With this rotten weather, we can't take the ferry, so I am going to hire a carriage."

Jesus nodded in agreement. "That's just what I was going to suggest. And when we arrive, I want to pray with Benjamin to relieve him of the burden I know he carries."

Magda frowned. "Burden, what burden? He's always been like that. Abba has had his share of heartaches—losing my mother, always working too hard, and dealing with Lazarus' struggles. And then I guess I gave him more than my share of problems for too many years. But he seems all right to me. Maybe I'm just used to seeing him as he is. He certainly never was a very lighthearted man. That's just his way."

"Well, that's not *God's way.* That's not the *way* God wants us to be. If you truly believe, you have *joy.* I hope to instill that in him before it's too late."

As they were leaving the inn, they saw Benjamin's stable foreman Olibamah. Benjamin had sent him to Capernaum to buy supplies. He was returning to Magdala that morning and when he spotted Magda and Jesus, he offered to give them a ride.

But soon she discovered why she had felt an initial reluctance to accept his offer. Magda remembered the man was a chatterbox who never met a metaphor he didn't like. He seemed troubled if a prolonged silence broke out in his presence.

"Miss Magda," he began his monologue as he slapped the reins and the horses took off, "I hope you're going to find your father in better health than he has been in the past few weeks. The talk is that he is very ill. All of us employees are worried what will become of the business and our jobs now that your father is unable to work."

Magda thought, *Ahh, the truth comes out: he's not concerned about abba, but about himself!*

He paused for a moment, as if deciding how safe it was to voice his concerns to the boss' daughter, but his love of gab got the better of him. "Lazarus comes into the office every day to oversee the operations but, and maybe I shouldn't say it, things are just not the same with him at the helm, so to speak." He was quiet for a moment as they crossed over a narrow bridge.

Magda took advantage of the lull in his chatter to ask him how long it would take to get back to Magdala. She hoped to distract him from the discussion of her father, which was upsetting her. She groaned when he told her it would take over two hours.

He picked up right where he had left off. "Forget about trying to get a straight answer out of Lazarus. He's as closed-up as a clam. Sometimes he comes in and leaves without ever saying a word to anyone. I have tried to ask him about Benjamin's condition, is he better or worse, just asking if there is any change. Lazarus just gives me a look like he has no idea what I'm talking about and says, 'Abba? Don't ask.'"

That brought a smile to Magda's face. Lazarus was parroting Martha's standard reply when she was at a loss for an answer. There was never a day that Martha didn't say, "Don't ask."

Olibamah prattled on. "Actually, Lazarus seems like he's almost as ill as your father. He never stays a full day. After about four hours you can see he's as limp as a dishrag and leaves. Pardon my loose lips, Miss Magda, but the House of Benjamin is like a rudderless ship."

Chapter Forty-Two

For now we see through a glass, darkly; but then face to face; now I know in part; but then shall I know even as also I am known.

1 Cor. 13:12

Magda was relieved when they finally reached Magdala. "This is a good place to let us off, Oli. We'll just take the shortcut up the hill from here."

But she was disturbed by Oli's comments about her father's health. She and Jesus ran all the way up the footpath to the house.

Martha greeted them at the back door and one look told Magda that things were bad. "You certainly took your time about getting back here, Magda. I'll be surprised if abba lasts through the night."

Magda and Jesus went straight to Benjamin's room. She was shocked at how frail he looked. The veins in his hands were like purple worms underneath his gray skin. His fingernails were long, jagged and yellow—this in a man who had always been vain about his appearance. But the dying are beyond vanity, and Martha had not exaggerated, it was obvious Benjamin was dying. Even so, he opened his eyes when he heard her voice.

He whispered, "Magda, at last you're here. I've been so worried you were not going to make it in time for us to talk. Can we have a word in private?"

Jesus gave her hand a squeeze and left the room. "I'll be in the garden, Magda."

Benjamin took a rasping breath. "Magda, I have something to tell you that I should have told you years ago." But then he went silent and closed his eyes. He began to weep.

Regardless of how sad or how close to death he was, Magda was not about to go easy on him. "Abba, whatever it is, just say it. I'm a big girl now, I can handle it." She sat down, crossed her legs, and tapped her foot—determined to wait him out.

He turned back toward her. "It's a shame I didn't talk with you about this long before now, but the truth is I gave an oath that I wouldn't. However, I have decided that that oath is not going to follow me to my grave. I cannot die in peace unless I reveal this secret I have kept for too many years."

But then he paused and said, "Magda, I'm sorry, I cannot bring myself to say it. Go read the diary. Your mother wrote it better than I could ever tell it. Go!" He shut his eyes.

Magda was having none of it. She rose from the chair, got right in his face and said, "I want to hear it from your lips. I couldn't care less about reading Rachel's memoirs. Abba, look at me."

What he did next would become one of her fondest memories: he raised his head until their noses were practically touching, looked right into her eyes and smiled.

But the smile faded and he took a deep breath.

He finally said, "Well, Magda, the truth is, they are not Rachel's memoirs, they are Heli's. Rachel was not your mother. Heli was."

Chapter Forty-Three

He that covereth his sins shall not prosper: but whoso confesseth and forsaketh them shall have mercy.

Prov. 28:13

"What?" Magda shouted. It took a moment for Benjamin's words to sink in. There was a roaring in her ears and she felt numb all over. Her knees buckled and she sank to the floor, holding her head in her hands. When she finally could speak, she bit off her words one at a time. "All those years both you and Heli lived a lie and forced me to live it. I suppose Heli kept the secret to honor the same oath you did—an oath that was more important than my well-being."

As the truth settled in, she put her hands over her face and started to wail, "Oh God, Heli, my sweet mother, I wasn't even at her side when she died. Orpah said she kept calling my name after she got sick, and toward the end she kept repeating, 'My darling Magda, forgive me.'

"The unforgivable thing though, abba, is that you let me grieve for Rachel's love, both while she was alive and when she died. You let me mourn my *mother's* death when she wasn't even my mother. She wasn't even my friend. I mourned the death of my enemy.

"And now I will mourn your death in a different way than I would have, knowing that the man I loved and admired deceived me my whole life."

She rose and glowered at him. "You have robbed me of so much."

She turned to leave, but Benjamin clutched at her hand. "Magda, just read Heli's diary. Maybe after you have read it, you will begin to understand and will be able to forgive me. Proverbs says the road to hell is paved with good intentions. Well, it just seems like we were caught up in life, moving down the wrong roads. We let our unhappiness lead us to the wrong choices. I'm so sorry I failed you. Just remember Heli and I always loved you. Our deaths will not change that."

Magda snatched her hand out of Benjamin's and ran out of the room. She stumbled down the long back hallway and opened the door to Heli's old room. And there it was, the sweetly familiar musk of rosemary, lavender and sandalwood . . . of Heli, *her mother, Ima*—the word she had always longed to say. How odd and yet oddly comforting: her *ima* had loved her, and just knowing that helped.

"Oh Heli, my ima," she cried. "Of course, the truth was as close as the nose on my face." She had inherited her nose from Heli. It was her favorite feature, not just for its graceful shape but for the unique ability it gave her to identify and classify scents. She was what the perfumers called a 'nose.'

How did I miss what was so obvious? I am supposed to be a smart woman, and yet I was so caught up in my own selfishness, I failed to realize that Heli's love was too unfailing, too unconditional to be anything but the love of a mother for her child.

Of course, her green eyes and hated red hair were gifts from her grandmother, Maria. She had wasted so much of her life regretting the things about her that made her different, she had been blind to the things about her that said—'You are Heli's child!' At last she understood why Heli always said to her, "Remember who you are."

The moon was spreading fingers of light over the Galilee when she forced herself to look for the diary in her old room. She opened the wooden chest where she kept all the things that were precious to her: the little doll that Abe had carved for Heli; a lock of Rachel's hair; most of the poetry she had written as a young girl; some special sea shells; and other bits and pieces of memorabilia.

She took the diary and the lock of hair out of the chest and left the house, headed for her old hideaway beyond the breakwater. Raising her tunic up to her knees, she clambered over the rocks and sat down in the sand on the other side.

She had spent many childhood hours hiding among these rocks when she was in trouble with Rachel. *Well, at least I can purge that poison from my life now*, she thought.

As she walked to the water's edge, she considered removing the red Kabbalah bracelet from her left wrist, to let it drown in the sea. It had belonged to Rachel, and she wondered if anything that had been worn by such an evil person could ward off the 'evil eye,' as the bracelet was believed to do. But it had become an important part of her. When she was upset, she would count the seven knots, which were separated by chunks of gold. And the simple exercise would comfort her. She couldn't bear to destroy it. Instead, she slowly unwound the ribbon from Rachel's lock of hair. Strand by strand she let them fall into the sea to be carried out on the tide. She felt better after she watched the waves carry off a portion of her miserable childhood.

She sat down and began to read the diary—the 'Apologia'—as she would come to call it.

Chapter Forty-Four

For three things the earth is disquieted, and for four which it cannot bear . . . an handmaid that is heir to her mistress.

Prov. 30:21, 23

MAGDA, IF YOU'RE READING THIS journal that I started writing for you many years ago and later rewrote to include some of Benjamin's memoirs, both Benjamin and I are dead. I guess this diary is the last cowardly act of two people whose several mis-steps, however well-intentioned, conspired to rob you of a happy childhood. Know only this: Benjamin and I—your parents—truly loved you. And I think you knew you were loved even though you might not have been clear about the exact identity of those who loved you.

You always said when I tried to tell a story, I would go back to Adam and Eve to begin it. That's because I have always been a frustrated historian. Well, this story doesn't go back quite that far, but you do have to know a bit about our family history to understand all the actors and the warring factions of this drama.

I begin with a story of your ancestors:

Abraham, whose wife, Sarah, was barren, lay with his slave girl Hagar. That union produced a son, Ishmael. In her old age Sarah gave birth to Isaac; then she told Abraham to send Hagar and Ishmael away. But God heard Hagar's despairing cries and rescued her and her son. He promised to make a great nation out of Ishmael's descendants.

Isaac married Rebekah, who gave birth to twins, Jacob and Esau. When Jacob and Esau went their separate ways, that contentious split divided the Jewish people into the Israelites—Jacob's progeny, and the Edomites—Esau's progeny. Although later on Jacob and Esau met briefly to bury the hatchet, they didn't dig the hole deep enough. Their descendants were constantly at war with each other, fueled by a hatred that time will probably never extinguish.

After God spared Lot from the fire and brimstone of Sodom and Gomorrah, his two daughters made him drunk, lay with him on succeeding nights, and gave birth to his sons, the descendants of whom became the Moabites and the Ammonites. Eventually they joined forces with the Edomites, the Ishmaelites, and various other tribes to become a formidable force—the Arabs.

The ongoing struggle between the Arabs and the Jews no doubt will be a scourge on civilization until the end of time. No matter that the Arabs were Semites and brothers of the Jews, the bitter enmity between these peoples drew a line in the sand that one crossed at his peril.

Your grandmother, Maria, of Esau's progeny, fell in love with a descendant of Jacob and dared to cross the line. My story begins approximately at that perilous point.

Magda laid the scroll in her lap, gazing out to sea for a moment, thinking about what she had just read and what was sure to follow. She knew just bits and pieces of Heli's ancestry, which she now realized was hers as well. She dreaded reading the rest of her diary, knowing that long-buried wounds were going to be reopened.

I was just four years old when my mother, Maria, and I moved to the House of Benjamin. I had never seen such a big house—the house that would be my home for most of my life.

I did not want to leave the only home I had ever known, but ima told me that we didn't have a choice. The mistress was ill and was going to close up her house and move in with her son. That meant ima was forced to find a housekeeping position with another family.

The widow's son had found a position for ima in the House of Benjamin, a huge estate in the Arbel Cliffs overlooking Magdala on the Sea of Galilee.

I cried most of the way to our new home, which surely tried the patience of my already suffering mother. The trip was only three miles, which is not a great distance under normal circumstances, but when you're walking in the rain with an unhappy four-year-old, who is moving at a snail's pace, it is torture.

Ima finally snapped, "Heli, please stop your whining." She was cold, tired, wet and somewhat anxious about the new job. A housekeeper's job could be pleasant or miserable, depending on the disposition of the mistress.

"We are lucky to have a place to live, Heli. We could be out on the street."

But we are out on the street, I thought; and then I asked the question I had asked a dozen times in the past hour, "Are we almost there?"

Ima was not the type to look back with regret, but so much had happened to her in the past year she couldn't find a big enough corner inside her brain to hide it. My father had been killed when he and his employer were attacked by bandits on the way to Damascus; then the mistress had fallen ill—ima suspected that her illness was the result of her grief—and when she didn't recover after several months her son decided she should move in with him.

The house was being sold, leaving ima unemployed and soon-to-be homeless. Her own family had disowned her when she had married Reuben, of the tribe of Simeon—one of Jacob's sons—and had refused to accept her back into the family.

When Omar, the red haired descendant of Esau, first learned of his daughter Maria's traitorous deed, he threatened to kill her. But her mother had intervened on her behalf and begged Omar to spare her life. So he had merely disowned her.

The gene of Esau, called Edom because of his red hair, had traveled down several generations to my mother, Maria. But her red hair didn't carry much weight with Omar, a zealous man who looked upon his daughter's marriage to Reuben as a defection to the enemy camp. Ima had dishonored the family by marrying a descendant of Jacob.

"I guess I forfeited any rights of inheritance when I married Reuben," ima often said. "But at least I didn't sell it for a mess of pottage as Esau did." She didn't regret marrying Reuben, who was a wonderful man, even if it did mean that she was banned from her family. She had followed her heart and always said she would do it again.

When I was born, my parents decided to name me after Esau's first son, Eliphaz—thank God they called me 'Heli'—mistakenly thinking his granddaughter's name would soften Omar's resentment toward them. But he refused to see me, his only granddaughter. I often wondered if he would have felt any different if I had been a grand*son.*

Ima hadn't seen her mother and father in years, and as we walked along in the rain, she shed a few tears of regret, wishing she had a sympathetic shoulder to lean on.

Just a year before she had been married to a man she loved, the three of us living in comfortable quarters at the back of a big house; life was good. Then in a matter of moments everything changed.

Ima and I had been walking for almost three hours when the sun finally fought its way out from behind the clouds, and we finally caught sight of the Magdala docks. When I saw all the boats bobbing up and down in the water, I started pulling on ima's hand in excitement, begging to go down to the water to get a closer look. I had always loved seeing the boats docked in Maoziyah—now called Tiberias—and I was happy to see something reminiscent of home.

Ima knelt down and held me close. "Not today, my sweet. But I promise that the first chance we get I'll bring you back and let you look to your heart's content." Ima was relieved that I had stopped crying and was distracted from my homesickness. Maybe this was a sign of better things to come.

We stopped in the marketplace to ask for directions to the House of Benjamin. The man in the stall was selling fresh fruits and vegetables, and my mouth watered at the fragrance wafting up from the figs, grapes, pomegranates and melons.

He pointed to the hills behind us and said, "It might be a bit of a climb for the little one, but the fastest way is to follow that winding footpath to that monstrosity at the top of the hill—that's the House of Benjamin. Or you can walk a little farther up the road, take the Sepphoris Road between the cliffs, a couple of lefts and you're there. Either way you can't miss it."

He held out his hand to me and opened his fingers. There were several grapes nestled in his palm. I crammed all of them into my mouth and began to chew noisily.

Ima said to me, “What do you say, Heli?”

But my mouth was too full to talk. The man looked at ima and winked. “It’s all right. She’s a little busy right now. Anyhow, you’d best be on your way; I think the rain is threatening again.”

He began to rearrange the grapes as we walked off in the direction of the Sepphoris Road. When we turned into the road, ima looked back. The man was watching us and called out, “Good luck.”

When we came to the top of the hill, we stopped for a moment to catch our breath and to stare at the House of Benjamin. It was even bigger and more beautiful than she had expected. It was twice as big as the house in Maoziyah, and ima was apprehensive that her new employer might be difficult. Servants had a saying, ‘Bigger the house, badder the boss.’ She was hoping this time would be an exception.

As she walked into the front courtyard, holding onto me with one hand and carrying our meager possessions in the other, an elegant woman walked out of the house. When she saw ima and me, she said, “You must be the new housekeeper. Go round to the back and ask for Abe. He will show you to your room.” Without a backward glance, she walked away and climbed into a waiting carriage.

“I hope that wasn’t the mistress,” Maria said worriedly. “If so, I don’t have a good feeling about this.” She stood and puzzled over which direction to walk. The house had so many levels and courtyards and doors it wasn’t clear which was back and which was front.

When we finally found the back of the house—a long walk down a winding stone path—and met the servant who would be ima’s overseer, her hopes that this would be a good situation vanished. He was stern looking and not happy that the new housekeeper was encumbered with a bratty child. I guess I sensed that I was not welcome and I hid my face in ima's skirts, refusing even to look at the man whose weathered face looked like it would crack if he smiled.

Following behind the mostly silent old servant, we walked across the back portico under an arched ceiling of bricks laid in a herringbone pattern. Without turning around Abe said to us, "Your daughter will be allowed beyond this area only to perform her chores; otherwise, see that she doesn't go beyond this porch."

We continued down the long covered walkway to a massive, iron-clad wooden door. Abe opened it and motioned for us to enter. "This will be your living quarters."

Ima walked across the threshold and let out a small cry. It was beautiful, spotlessly clean, and spacious. There was a big bed for her and a smaller one for me, but we both knew where I would sleep.

"Put your things away and I'll give you a brief tour of the house, pointing out the areas you'll be expected to take care of. Your daughter will be expected to do menial chores as well, things that any six-year-old would have no trouble managing."

Ima didn't dare correct him. If he expected a four-year-old child to do chores, they would get done, one way or the other. I'm sure she started adding up in her head how many hours she would put in every day as she did my chores and then took care of her own.

He was ticking off her chores one by one. "You will plan the meals, do the shopping and the cooking and have the care of the kitchen garden."

Ima smiled when he said that. She was a wizard with herbs and could grow rare plants in dirt that other gardeners said was fit for nothing but weeds. "I'm going to be busier than ever, but that's good. I won't have time to think," ima mumbled, thinking out loud.

The one consolation was the beauty of the house and its furnishings. The mosaic floors were covered with priceless Persian carpets. There were frescoes, tapestries, and paintings on pale limestone walls. Quiet, good taste.

Ima, though poor, was an elegant woman who appreciated the finer things in life even if she would never own any of them. She was starting to get a better feeling about the House of Benjamin.

As they climbed the stairs to the second floor, Abe said, "Now you are going to meet Young Benjamin and his nurse. He has just finished his lessons with his tutor and will have an hour to play before his naptime."

"Poor child," ima said under her breath. "It sounds like they're raising a houseplant."

At first the boy clung to his nurse, who stood rigidly, almost on guard, as though an enemy force had invaded her domain. But even at just four years old, I knew a handsome boy when I saw one, and I ran to him and gave him a big hug. No one said a word for an uncomfortable moment.

Then Young Ben surprised everyone by giving me a big kiss. He looked like the sun had come out in his world.

Soon the house was filled with laughter as Young Ben, who was just a few years older than I, adopted me as his pet and victim of his endless pranks. For me it was love at first sight. I followed him about like a parrot on a leash, mimicking his every word and mannerism. And soon even old Abe, the head servant, was won over, becoming my adopted grandfather.

An accomplished whittler, he carved a wooden doll for me, complete with flax hair hennaed a bright red to match Maria's curly hair. I dragged the doll around with me everywhere I went and even insisted on sleeping with it. I gave it to you because I felt as though it kept me safe and brought me good luck.

The woven red bracelet that your father gave you after Rachel died belonged to his mother and is part of Jewish lore. I hope you will continue to wear it even after you learn that Rachel was not your mother. I believe that it truly works in warding off the 'evil eye.' However, its magic works only for those who are pure in heart.

For obvious reasons it didn't save Rachel from dying a painful death . . . she was evil incarnate. She wore the bracelet to ward off unfriendly stares while giving you unkind glances all of her life. Her evil nature canceled out its powers. But Magda, you are pure in heart and the bracelet will bring you good luck—something you're going to need a lot of.

Magda was glad that she hadn't thrown the bracelet into the sea after all. She sat thinking about what she had just read. *Why does Heli say I'm going to need a lot of luck?* But she refused to get bogged down in over-analyzing every word and she returned to her reading.

Abe also carved the rocking chair that lulled me and then you to sleep through many good and bad times. I hope someday you will rock your own children in it. If Abe made it, it will last forever.

Young Ben always said he loved me even more than his brothers, who were much older and called him 'Sweet Baby' because he was his mother's pet. But I was Benjamin's pet. Where Young Ben went, I went.

He even asked his mother why I wasn't allowed to eat with the family during their meals. That is where she drew the line.

"Young Ben," she said firmly, "some things are just not done because it would be unseemly. Heli is a sweet girl and we all like her, but she is our housekeeper's daughter, not a member of the family."

But in his heart I *was* family. He shared everything with me, especially his dreams and his secrets, many of which are revealed here.

When Ben became a young man, his father began to lecture him on a regular basis. "Benjamin, you have to learn where to draw the line with the servants. Now that you and Heli are no longer children, it would not be wise to continue your close friendship. You should be polite to her, but you need to keep your distance.

"Servants need to be kept in their place because if you don't control them, they will control you," his father warned him.

(Perhaps I am being a bit immodest, but what Ben's father really meant was that while I was not classically beautiful, I had a body that even he had had a few lustful thoughts about. A woman always knows these things. I guess he feared that the friendship between young Ben and me would not remain innocent much longer.)

Ben accepted his father's warning with a nod of his head, but the look on his face said otherwise: he wasn't happy being told whom he could befriend, and he had no intention of turning his back on his friend Heli. From his earliest memories I had been there. Maria and I had lived with and served the family of the House of Benjamin for as long as he could remember.

Young Ben greatly resented his father's constant interference in his personal life. He was being groomed to take over the day-to-day operations of the business and his father seemed to be taking over his entire life with his watchful eye and constant admonitions: "Keep your eye on the bottom line.

Keep a watchful eye on the help. Pick your friends with care. Be polite to the overseers but keep your distance so you will be able to discipline them if they get out of line." He was an overflowing fount of that vice called advice.

Now his father was meddling in his friendship with me. Did his father think that his feelings were just meaningless impulses to be controlled much the same as one rids himself of a bad habit? I was his best friend and nothing was going to change that or how he felt about me.

But it did change. Apparently, Ben's mother warned ima that the friendship ties between Young Ben and me had to be severed. Almost overnight our friendship ended and I was banned from the main living areas. I could no longer help to serve the family their meals in the vast dining room, and most of my chores were limited to behind-the-scenes work. I rarely ventured beyond the porch. On the rare occasions that I saw Ben, I always scurried away, eyes downcast, fearful that Maria and I would be homeless again.

So Ben did the unthinkable: he came to the servants' quarters to find me. He had practically followed ima across the back portico after she was finished with her evening duties, and he knew she was on the other side of the door when he knocked.

"Who's there?" ima asked.

"Maria, I need to speak to Heli, please."

Ima cracked the door open just enough to whisper her answers. "Young Ben, what are you doing here? If your parents learn that you came here looking for Heli it would be very bad for you, but disastrous for Heli and me. Please go before someone sees you."

And nothing he could say would change her mind. Uncharacteristically, she turned her back on him and firmly closed the door.

In time, both Ben and I accepted that our friendship was gone along with our lost childhoods. But somewhere deep inside where he buried his feelings, Benjamin's love for me lived on.

When his father retired, Ben took over running the businesses. He married a girl that his parents had chosen for him, the beautiful but moody Rachel. A few months later she conceived. As she became heavy with child, she became increasingly unhappy. Her confinement cast a heavy pall over the House of Benjamin, especially over its master. The staff whispered among themselves, "Maybe if Rachel gives birth to a boy, Ben will be happy again."

While Benjamin was never abusive to the help, he was coldly impersonal. The old timers shook their heads and said what a shame it was. Abe said, "After Maria and Heli arrived, he was the happiest little boy you ever saw. But I guess all the responsibilities of running the family businesses put a heavy burden on him."

In time, I also married and had two sons, Zachary and Nathanial. Although I moved away from the house for a brief time while I was married, I returned to take over the household duties from my aging ima after my husband, a fisherman, drowned when his boat capsized.

On the few occasions Benjamin and I caught sight of each other, I was saddened to see his joyless face. Even sadder was the chasm between us. After all these years, there was still something there, suppressed feelings that made our brief meetings awkward and painful.

In later years, in a rare moment when he opened up to me, Benjamin admitted the sad truth that, with all his material wealth, he had been emotionally impoverished. Rachel and he had had very little in common, and he poured all of his time and energy into the businesses. Benjamin told me that the reason he hadn't married me after Rachel died is that a man in his position couldn't marry a servant. I guess that would have been unseemly.

When the time came for Rachel to deliver her child, the entire house knew she was giving birth. Everyone could hear her shrieking. The women servants were not surprised that she couldn't give birth 'like a real woman'—she was what they called a 'screamer.'

Actually, her child's birth was difficult. They eventually called in a doctor to take over after the midwife failed to coax the baby out of the birth canal. The doctor told her and Benjamin it would be dangerous for her to try to have another child.

"All that pain and suffering just to give birth to a girl," Rachel complained after they brought her daughter to her.

They named the baby 'Martha' after Ben's mother, and he tried his best not to show his disappointment that the child had not been a boy. Eventually, he grew fond of his daughter, but his discontent mounted as his longing for a son went unfulfilled. And worse, Rachel often turned away from him. "Benjamin, you know that I am not well and it is painful when you try to enter me."

Rachel herself suggested a solution that was a dream come true for Benjamin. "I know how much you long to have a son. Since I cannot give you one, why don't you lay with Heli? She has two sons and will probably give birth to another if you plant the seed in her. I don't mind her being the mother of your child, but there is one condition: no one, especially the child, is ever to know the truth as long as either of us is alive."

Benjamin knew that Rachel was up to something. She never offered anything that didn't have a silver lining in it for herself. But he couldn't find a flaw in the plan, not an immediate one at any rate. He began to seriously consider her offer. And part of him was consumed with the idea.

He and Rachel talked to me together. Rachel said, "Heli, Benjamin needs an heir to carry on the House of Benjamin name, and I am unable to have another child. We have decided that you would be the perfect mother to that heir if you are willing to go along with our wishes—one being never to reveal to anyone that you are the child's actual mother."

They needn't have worried about my being willing, but it was not like I had a choice. I was proud (and secretly thrilled, though I tried not to show it) to bear an heir for the House of Benjamin. And I thought that it would mean more security for my children and me.

I was wrong.

Chapter Forty-Five

Awake, O north wind; and come, thou south; blow upon my garden, that the spices thereof may flow out. Let my beloved come into his garden, and eat his pleasant fruits.

Song of Sol. 4:16

I WAS NOT SURE WHEN Benjamin was going to come to my bed. Apparently, he was a little hesitant as well since he took his time about it. He was probably as diffident as I about how to begin such an illicit but sanctioned affair. Although I was like a virgin bride when I awoke and felt him reaching for me, one touch and I was completely lost.

I had always wondered what other women meant when they talked about making love with their husbands and said 'the earth moved.' I found out that first night with Benjamin.

He was consumed with his need, and once he began, he quickly finished. But he was just getting started. There were many beginnings that first night.

I had loved my husband, but my lust was a timid emotion trapped in a young girl's body. Now I was a woman. I had suffered through much in life and had become selfish enough to take what was offered and to ask for what wasn't.

Benjamin said that I was the lover men fantasize about. I was quiet and reserved as I went about my duties for the family, but at night when I opened my arms and my body to him, I was a volcano of passion. After all, I had always been in love with him, and I had years of pent-up emotion I had carried around for him. I was tender in my caresses but wanton in my lust for him. We both knew we would never get enough of each other. Unfortunately, Rachel knew it as well.

Magda, I'll pause here to comment on what I have just shared with you. I hope by the time you read this, you will have experienced the same love for a man that I had for Benjamin and will understand why I have included such an intimate revelation in my memoirs. I fear your childhood may have robbed you of the ability to open your heart and soul to another person. That takes a child-like trust. Find a way to rid yourself of those demons—ima called them happiness leeches. They were a gift from the evil Rachel. Give them back. You carry them at a tremendous cost to your happiness. There is no greater happiness than being joined body and soul with another human being.

Chapter Forty-Six

"Dearly beloved, avenge not yourselves, but rather give place unto wrath: for it is written, 'Vengeance is mine; I will repay,' saith the Lord."

Romans 12:19

RACHEL'S PLAN WAS WORKING. BENJAMIN had stopped bothering her for what had become repugnant to her. The shallow excitement that had carried them through their first few years had turned to indifference on her part, and later to revulsion. She could not bear for him to touch her.

A few weeks after I lay with Benjamin, my monthly blood did not appear. Nor did it happen the following month. I was sure I was with child—Benjamin's child.

When I told Benjamin, his happiness filled the house with renewed laughter. And now that he knew I was carrying his child, his passion for me was layered with a tenderness that surprised both of us. At last he would have what he had longed for: he was going to father a child, surely a son, with a woman he was deeply in love with.

But it was not to be. On a beautiful spring day, I gave birth to a daughter with flaming red hair, the very image of Maria. As I held my daughter for the first time, offering my breast to this tiny creature whose suck was unbelievably strong, first I laughed and then I cried, worried about Benjamin's reaction.

But Benjamin took one look at his beautiful daughter and whispered to me, "Our daughter will be named Mary after Maria, but we will call her Magda."

Unfortunately, when Rachel saw you in my arms, she said contemptuously, "I will abide by our agreement to this extent: the child may call me 'mother,' although she is not to call me by the familiar 'ima.' She will be included as part of the family in all outward respects, but you will be in charge of her in every other way. And of course she will have no dowry or inheritance."

I hung my head but held my tongue. What was I to do? I was defenseless, and Benjamin couldn't, or wouldn't help. I had expected Rachel to be disappointed, but I never imagined she was capable of such malevolence. What would become of me and my children? We were at the mercy of this malicious woman.

As Rachel talked, she looked around my room, eyeing the small touches that made it mine. What it lacked in expensive appointments it made up for in charm. For an instant she looked envious. But she remembered herself and continued her rant. "Although it is not your fault that you did not give birth to a son, you have failed to fulfill your part of the bargain. However, I expect you to honor your promise to tell no one, especially your daughter, that you are her real mother. I have a daughter, Martha, and did not want another . . . especially a redheaded one! Benjamin and I wanted a son.

"I am not a fool; I realize that, although your services as my husband's concubine are no longer needed, he will continue to visit your bed. Feel free to welcome him with open arms and your other bedtime talents that have so bewitched him. But if you conceive again, you are to get rid of it. If you refuse to do that, you will find somewhere else to live."

I sat for a moment trying to digest all I had heard. I was sick about the nightmare I had created for myself, my sons and my baby daughter. I was caught between Rachel and Benjamin in a lopsided triangle that I had helped to construct . . . one that I was on the short side of. My guilt was such that it wouldn't allow me to see that I hadn't really had a choice. The master had ordered and the servant had obeyed. The consolation was that at the end of the day I had my daughter, Magda.

Then the years of madness began as the woman you called 'mother' made such a difference between you, who could do nothing right, and Martha, who could do no wrong. But rather than letting the situation defeat you, you reacted by resorting to bad-girl behavior to gain Rachel's attention, even if it was attention in the form of a tongue-lashing or an occasional blow.

Can you imagine how many times I wanted to kill Rachel for striking my child? I worried that Rachel was creating two monsters—Heli and Magda.

Your way of coping was to play the court jester and by indulging in crazy antics. You became the butt of the household gossip. "What's that crazy Magda done now?"

I wonder how different you would have been had Rachel loved you. Oh well, I wouldn't change a thing about you. Who am I to argue with perfection? (Little joke, Magda. As you would say, throw in something amusing from time to time.)

But still . . . do you remember the time when Martha was sitting in Rachel's lap and you tried to climb up beside her? Rachel jumped up like she had been bitten by a snake. "All right, story time's over. Magda, go find Heli and tell her you need a bath."

You came running to me, crying, "Heli, am I dirty?"

"No, child, why would you ask such a thing?"

"Mother told me that I needed a bath. Heli, am I bad? Does mother love me?"

My heart broke for you, Magda. You knew at just three years old that something was wrong with the way your 'mother' treated you.

Magda had to pause for a moment. She was crying so hard she couldn't see through her tears. Although she had no memory of Rachel shunning her and telling her she needed a bath—it had happened when she was only three years old—she wept now for the child it had happened to.

Heli had been right—most of her story would be hurtful and bring up painful memories. All of it would test her mettle as the invincible Magda others thought her to be. "Oh God, if they only knew," she sobbed.

Moments later she began to read again.

Looking back, it seems that I was destined to have only intermittent happiness, little oases of good times surrounded by mostly bad times in a tumultuous life. But I made the best of it and found peace with my existence. I had two healthy sons and a beautiful daughter—I was blessed.

By the time you were six years old, your formative years had turned you into a little demon. *'Heli,'* I thought, *'be careful what you wish for.'* I had wanted a little Ben for Benjamin, but what I got was a little Hellion for Heli. But I loved you, Hellion or not; you were my beautiful Magda.

As the years went by, you became famous in Magdala; rather, infamous. With your unforgettable face and red hair, you were known to everyone. You had a great curiosity about all people, regardless of who or what they were. Even Magdala's prostitutes would invite you in to give you a talking-to about 'being a good girl.'

Your constant presence around Magdala's docks, talking with fisherman, boat builders, shop vendors, beggars and the occasional leper was fodder for Magdala's gossip mill. By the time you were ten years old, there was already talk about where you were headed.

I don't know how much that kind of talk bothered you, or even if you were aware of it—certainly, not much got by you—but it certainly hurt Benjamin and me.

However, I think it gave Rachel a sick kind of satisfaction, even though she complained incessantly that you were ruining the family's good name.

But everyone's disapproval of you only made you more outrageous in your behavior. The more people talked about you, the more you gave them to talk about. You refused to dress like a young lady, and the veil was nothing more than a prop in your wardrobe . . . to be worn only when you needed a disguise. You found nothing wrong with your best friends being prostitutes or young men from the working class. You were always in the wrong place at the wrong time. But you always landed on your feet . . . often because Benjamin's money bought you out of trouble.

Rachel's cruel treatment of you grieved Benjamin as much as it did me as he witnessed your quest to win her love achieve just the opposite result. It seemed the harder you tried to please her the more you annoyed her.

In every sense of the word, except the official one, I was your mother. When you fell and skinned your knee, you ran to me. When you woke up from a bad dream, you crawled into my bed—you slept in my bed more often than in your own. I must have rocked you for hundreds of hours in the old rocking chair Abe built when I was a child. When you were in trouble with Rachel, a daily occurrence, you sought refuge in my arms.

Meanwhile, Rachel's hatred of me and jealousy of the relationship I had with Benjamin took on a life of its own. She became a carping tyrant who treated all but Martha with contempt. What Martha wanted, Martha got.

As you know, Martha was born with a talent for homemaking and being a mother—thus far, a wasted talent. By the time she was ten years old, she was helping to run the house, displaying an efficiency and organization that even I lacked. The women in the Arbela community started coming to Martha for her recipes and household tips.

But Martha longed for a baby brother to dote on. Nearly every day I would hear her say to Rachel, "Ima, why can't you have a son like my friends' mothers do? All my friends have adorable little brothers, but I have only Magda. Yech!"

She certainly didn't want a sister who might turn out to be another *you*. Even when you were a baby, you cried if Martha came near you. Forgive me, Magda, but you were about as cuddly as a sack of snakes; and you kept the whole house upset all the time with your crazy schemes and outrageous behavior. Martha wanted a nice, lovable, normal little brother.

And that is why Rachel decided to become a wife again to Benjamin: to give Martha a little brother and to avenge the wrong she imagined I had dealt her. It would be quite a coup for her to give birth to Benjamin's son. What a blow that would be to her rival, Heli. She felt sure that the dangers of giving birth were long since passed, and she had no doubt that she would have a son this time. She had gained weight and felt better than she had in years. Overnight she changed into the sweet and loving Rachel she had been when Benjamin first married her.

Benjamin was surprised that I had come into his bed. That was a first. It was always he who crept into my bed late at night, several times a week. That I had dared to come to him inflamed him with desire. He felt my warmth against his back and my hands fondling him as he turned to me, ready. But it was not Heli, it was Rachel.

But no matter, a man is a man is a man and he was—ready. So he went into Rachel for the first time in years. And when she didn't leave his bed, he took her again; and again the next night. And night after night Rachel endured the pain of their lovemaking. Nothing was going to deter her from her plan to give Benjamin a son.

But something was wrong. After several months, Rachel had failed to conceive. Incredibly, she came to me for advice. She wanted me to supply her with the herbs and ointments that would make her more responsive and make her more fertile. I hadn't the nerve to tell her that what she needed didn't grow on trees. I longed to tell her that she needed to be like a tree—like a willow . . . to bend down to mother earth and gather her fecundity. She would not have understood if I had told her that she didn't need herbs, she needed to be more of a woman. She needed to nurture others with loving care and bathe them with her tears when they hurt.

But I said only, "As you wish."

So once again I was part of a triangle with Rachel and Benjamin. I supplied my rival with the magic potions that would deliver my beloved into the enemy's arms.

She had come to the right place. I had a vast knowledge of perfumes, herbs, ointments and their infusions, thanks to a lifetime apprenticeship to Maria. I bought frankincense, myrrh and nard from a perfumer. I gathered herbs and plants by the basketful from my garden: horny goat weed—yes! ashwaghanda, aloe vera, mandrake, ginkgo biloba, gentian, sarsaparilla, ginseng, soy and chili peppers. And from the sea, oysters for the zinc they contained. And finally, rhino horn from a dealer of special aphrodisiacs who sold them from the back of a stall in the market place.

I became my own worst enemy as I prescribed the magic that would aid in Rachel's conception. I blended perfumes to make her body more enticing; ointments and creams to smooth her skin and make it supple inside and out; I even massaged her to help her relax. I had betrayed Rachel's worst enemy—and that was I.

When Rachel missed her monthly blood, she took pleasure in telling me before anyone else. She began to dream of a new life, a life that didn't include Heli and Magda. After she gave birth to Benjamin's son, she planned to send us away. She would not subject the scion of the House of Benjamin to the poison of living with mad Magda and her concubine mother.

As Rachel's belly grew, she glowed with a new sweetness, the sweetness of revenge.

And when the time came, at last she had a son. She had won, but she had paid the ultimate price for her victory.

Vengeance is mine saith the Lord, I will repay.

As Magda came to the end of the diary, she let it fall from her lap, not at all relieved by Heli's explanation of the events that had robbed her of a happy childhood. She lay back in the sand and pondered what Heli had written about the troubled child she had been.

She looked toward the horizon that rested in the high cliffs beyond the sea and prayed that God was somewhere out there listening. "Lord, do you love me? Am I bad? I don't want to be, please help me."

Magda lay at the edge of the water and wept, not caring that the incoming tide was soaking the bottom of her tunic. Had she really been that much of a problem to everyone?

Chapter Forty-Seven

To every thing there is a season, and a time to every purpose under the heaven . . .

Eccl. 3:1

THE TIDE WAS GOING OUT when Jesus crossed the shore road and jogged through the sand, knowing he would find Magda near the headland. He climbed to the top of the huge rocks and looked down. And there she was, curled up in the sand. He clambered down beside her and gathered her into his arms.

"My Magda." Nothing bothered Jesus more than knowing Magda was hurting.

She rested her head on his shoulder, but he felt her shaking in a silence that preceded a violent storm. She began to cry, gut-wrenching sobs that racked both of them.

"Heli was my mother," she finally said. "I think my inner child always realized that."

Jesus held her, not speaking. He wanted her to talk.

So she talked. She talked about all the horrors of her life, feeling the hurt now more than ever after learning the truth—that the people she had trusted most with her heart and life had deceived her, failed her, and robbed her of one of the most important human qualities—the ability to trust.

A full moon was shining on the sea when at last she sat up, back straighter, and started to comb her fingers through her matted hair.

"When I ran out here to these rocks where I hid so many times as a child, Rachel's face swam before me like Leviathan, the monster that stole my childhood. At least that's one less demon, but a few more to go before I rest."

Her voice had become lighter, her joy returning. Nothing ever got Magda down for long, even learning that her childhood had been a lie.

After a while Jesus asked, "Magda, where is the diary?"

Magda jumped up, realizing she had forgotten that she had put it down beside her when she had finished reading it. She began to look all around, digging through the sand, looking around the rocks, even wading into the water, hoping it was floating in the shallows. The diary was gone.

"Jesus, while I was lying here oblivious to everything, the diary must have floated away with the tide."

Then they turned and looked at each other. The diary was gone, but maybe that was not such a bad thing. Maybe it belonged in the same watery grave with the strands of Rachel's hair.

"So be it," Magda said. "I'm not going to look back and turn into a pillar of salt like Lot's wife, Edith. I'm going to forget about the past and just look ahead. I'm ready to start down a new road. It's my turn to ask, are you coming with me, Jesus?"

Not wanting to answer Magda's question—she couldn't handle the truth just now—Jesus silently gathered her into his arms. And in spite of her distress, she felt that familiar pull, heard those tinkling bells playing on her skin and singing deep in her loins. *I wonder if Jesus feels the same?* He did but . . .

Jesus pulled away and closed his eyes, clearly grappling with that familiar longing. In that moment he realized more clearly than ever the temptations mortal man must face every day of his life. There were so many do's and don'ts, shalts and shalt nots, eat this, not that—conflicting rules doing battle—it was understandable how ordinary man was constantly overpowered by sin.

So many times Magda had asked Jesus why God had created man with powerful urges and desires only to shackle him with rules that forbade his giving into them. His response was always the same, "The way is narrow. Sin is the wide, easy way. God's first rule is that man act out of self-love. If your right hand offends you, cut it off. The spirit is willing but the flesh is weak."

Magda's response was always the same, "Well, that clears that up."

Taking hold of her hand, Jesus said, "Magda, do you remember when John baptized me and you weren't ready or much disposed to a 'public dunking,' as you referred to it? And then on the way to Jerusalem to meet with Joseph of Arimathea, you mentioned that you felt the time was approaching, but I knew it wasn't a good time? Well, I believe the time has come."

Magda hesitated for a moment, knowing that the woman who was about to walk back the way she had come so many hours before was hugely changed. She had learned a very hurtful truth. But it had set her free, and nothing would ever again be the same in her life. Even her love for Jesus had changed into something stronger: stronger but less demanding . . . only wanting what he could give, not what she could wheedle out of him.

But that didn't mean she wouldn't try a little gentle persuasion.

She nodded her head slowly. "Yes, it is time. I am ready."

Hand in hand they climbed back over the rocks, crossed the road, hiked up the footpath, and walked through the gate at the back of Benjamin's property.

Magda sat down on the garden bench and bowed her head. Jesus took her hands in his and knelt before her.

"God has kneaded you and shaped you like a potter making a perfect vessel. He has brought you to your knees with pain and tempered you with fire, and now you are ready to emerge, free of your imperfections.

'To every thing there is a season, and a time to every purpose under the heaven: A time to be born and a time to die;

> A time to plant and a time to uproot;
> A time to kill and a time to heal;
> A time to wear down and a time to build;
> A time to weep and a time to laugh;
> A time to mourn and a time to dance;
> A time to scatter stones and a time to gather them;
> A time to embrace and a time to refrain from embracing;
> A time to search and a time to give up;
> A time to keep and a time to throw away;
> A time to tear and a time to mend;
> A time to be silent and a time to speak;
> A time to love and a time to hate;
> A time for war and a time for peace.'

"Magda, the time has come for you to embark on a new journey—one that you will have to make without me. You will need to take on the whole armor of God. That means it is time to throw off that false front you have been hiding behind, a guise that is filled with demons that are your enemies. It is time for you to strip off your masquerade, to borrow a line from one of your poems. Are you ready?"

"Yes, Jesus, I am ready," Magda said quietly. "You are right, I know it is time."

One by one Jesus commanded her to let go of all those vain things that charmed her so—her talismans, her obsessions, her false prophets:

"Pride, be gone." Magda had excessive vanity.

"Envy, leave her." Magda had always envied any woman who was close to her mother, especially Martha.

"Gluttony, she is no longer hungry. She thirsts no longer." Magda loved rich food and wine.

She had sat still and had been quiet for as long as she could. She looked up and stared at him. "Jesus, if I give up rich food can I still have my wine? I'll cut back, will that make you happy?"

"We are not making me happy, My Magda. This is about you. We are removing the demons that destroy your own happiness. Only you will know when enough is enough and enough is too much; when you should cut off that which offends you."

She bowed her head again and he continued, "Lust, depart from her and leave your better half, compassion." It was no secret that Magda indulged the physical pleasures of her body.

"Anger, you are dissolved. My Magda, your wrath will be turned into power for good." Magda too often wounded others with her sharp tongue.

"Greed, be gone. Greed is wanting more after your hunger is satisfied. Magda, you are wealthy beyond counting. You have great spirituality. You are loving and warm and giving and there are many who love you. You lack for nothing. The quest is over." But he suspected that was not quite true.

Magda had lost count—was that six or seven? Was the exorcism complete?

To lighten the moment, she said, "You know, Jesus, you just might have relieved me of a weight that I have carried around as long as I can remember. I do feel different, as though I have lost a great burden. And you finally get your wish. I know you have been itching from the day you first met me—let's see, you were about two months old—to perform that exorcism on me. Thank you for waiting for the right time to rid me of those old buddies of mine—my nemesis. Or is the plural, nemesissies?"

Jesus smiled and said, "It was nothing. I'm surprised there were only six. I was prepared to work a lot harder. However, I think there might be one stubborn demon evading me, but it isn't *sloth*. No one would ever accuse you of being lazy."

Magda sat quietly, savoring the moment and wondering if, when she rose from the bench, she would feel any different. After all, Jesus had exorcised the demons that she had carried around for as long as she could remember.

She stood up, a little shaky, and immediately fell to her knees. She bowed her head and clasped her hands on the stone bench that gleamed before her like an altar. Jesus knelt beside her and they wept—for things past and things that were to come.

After a while, Jesus took her hand, pulled her to her feet and embraced her. Magda couldn't resist asking, "Jesus, is this a time for embracing?"

"Yes, but for a moment only, then I have another request, My Magda."

"Jesus, you are never satisfied."

"What I am about to suggest is as much a gift for you as it is for your father. Now is the time *to heal, to mend* the rift with your father. Go to him and say the words that will be utterly healing to both of you. Tell him that you forgive him."

"Well, Jesus, I was thinking about doing that when I was lying in the sand letting the water lap over me. I know that no one would have needed to tell me that Heli was my mother if I hadn't been so self-absorbed. It's nearly impossible for anyone to trick me and yet I walked around for all these years, hearing but not understanding, seeing but not perceiving. Now I understand what you meant when you said that to your disciples."

Magda was almost afraid to walk into her father's bedroom. Was he still alive? The room was dark and the smell of death clung to the drapes, the boards, the bedcovers, to Benjamin. He lay in the dark, struggling to breathe. When Magda walked in and leaned down over his bed to kiss him, he reached out for her like a drowning man reaching for a lifeline.

He opened his eyes and said, "I prayed you would come back, Magda."

Magda felt a surge of love for her father filling the spot in her heart that had been closed all of her life.

"Abba, I forgive you. I forgive Heli. I love both of you. I love you even more now that I know the truth. I thank you for the love you gave me.

"I know that you did the best you could. As I have matured, I see how hard it is to always do the right thing, especially when life gives you a problem like Magda."

Benjamin let the tears roll down his cheeks without trying to wipe them away. He had Magda's hand in his own and her forgiveness in his heart. He didn't want anything to interfere with the moment.

And those words of forgiveness filled the room with peace . . . and *joy.*

Sometime during the early hours of the morning, Benjamin died. They found him with a wonderful look of peace on his face.

Magda, Martha, and Lazarus stood at the foot of his bed holding hands while Jesus prayed. But it was a prayer for the living. The three siblings were at peace with each other. No parents' miserly love to compete for.

Chapter Forty-Eight

I opened to my beloved, but my beloved had withdrawn himself and was gone; my soul failed when he spake: I sought him, but I could not find him; I called him, but he gave no answer.

Song of Sol 5:6

FORTY DAYS AFTER JESUS ROSE from the dead, he and a more peaceful Magda were finally going home to Bethany. They were walking down the road that led into the highlands. One final journey to Judea.

Magda held Jesus' hand tightly as they walked and talked; rather, as Magda talked, searching for the right words, using her newfound, subtle persuasiveness. "Jesus, it is time." No more words were needed. He knew what time it was.

Jesus looked straight ahead, smiling, saying only, "My Magda."

Magda was relentless. She was in the fight of her life . . . *for* her life, for a new life. And she continued her gentle entreaty all the way to Bethany.

Jesus' only response was to squeeze her hand, smile his mysterious smile, and murmur, "My Magda."

The stone wall that encircled Malama came into view. Magda turned to face Jesus, took his face in her hands and silently asked him one more time. He could feel her heart beating; her female fragrance filled his nostrils. It perfumed the air like a flower in bloom, its petals opening and whispering the longing of the ages:

> *"The fig tree has ripened its figs,*
> *And the vines in blossom have given forth their fragrance.*
> *Arise my darling, my beautiful one,*
> *And come along."*

Jesus pulled her close and said, "Magda, my Magda."

Epilogue

"A BUNDLE OF MYRRH IS my beloved unto me; he shall lie all night betwixt my breasts. I am the rose of Sharon and the lily of the valley. He brought me to the banqueting house, and his banner over me was love. His left hand is under my head and his right hand embrace me. I charge you, O ye daughters of Jerusalem, that you stir not up nor awaken my love til he please. The voice of my beloved! Behold, he cometh leaping upon the mountains, skipping upon the hills. My beloved is like a roe or a young hart: behold, he standeth behind our wall, he looketh forth at the windows, shewing himself through the lattice. My beloved spake, and said unto me. 'Rise up, my love, my fair one, and come away. For, lo, the winter is past, the rain is over and gone. The flowers appear on the earth; the time of the singing of the birds is come, and the voice of the turtle is heard in our land. My beloved is mine and I am his; he feedeth among the lilies until the day break and the shadows flee away, turn my beloved.

By night on my bed I sought him whom my soul loveth; I sought him, but I found him not. I sleep, but my heart waketh: it is the voice of my beloved that knocketh, saying, 'Open to me, my sister, my spouse, my love, my dove, my undefiled; for my head is filled with dew, and my locks with the drops of the night. I have put off my coat; how shall I put it on? I have washed my feet; how shall I defile them?

My beloved put his hand by the hole of the door, and my bowels were moved for him. I rose up to open to my beloved; and my hands dropped with myrrh, and my fingers with sweet smelling myrrh, upon the handles of the lock.

I opened to my beloved, but my beloved had withdrawn himself and was gone; my soul failed when he spake. I sought him, but I could not find him. I called him, but he gave no answer."

Early the next morning Jesus found Magda weeping in the garden. "My Magda, we'll be together again. I promise I will come back and take you with me."

As he walked away to the summit of the Mount of Olives, he called out, "And, lo, I am with you always, even unto the end of the world."

And he ascended into Heaven.

I guess I was meant to make my journey in flight, like those drifting, ephemeral clouds—ever moving, seemingly transparent, yet defying inspection by disappearing at the probing touch of one who would try to know me, thus trap me, making me lie down in the dearth of the earth, and no more—The Moon and I.

AMEN.